About the Author

George Fairbrother held a variety of jobs before turning his hand to writing. His interest in politics and history was inspired, from afar, by the works of Alan Bleasdale, Peter Flannery, Ken Loach and many others.

When not working at the computer, he enjoys spending time outdoors, organic gardening, cooking, walking, listening to Status Quo, and reading Patrick O'Brian.

The Banqueting Club

George Fairbrother

The Banqueting Club

Olympia Publishers

London

www.olympiapublishers.com
OLYMPIA PAPERBACK EDITION

First Published in 2019
Olympia Publishers
60 Cannon Street
London
EC4N 6NP

Printed in Great Britain

Dedication

To *our friends in the north*, with thanks.

Prologue
KNIGHTSBRIDGE, WEST LONDON
Autumn 1992

"Are you ready?"

"No more so than usual, but, as you constantly remind me, an agreement is an agreement is an agreement. Carry on with the inquisition."

"Sorry, what I should have asked is, are you ready, My Lord?"

"Enough of that. Just get on with it."

"Right, bonny lad. Give me a minute, this old cassette recorder sometimes has a little trouble getting going."

"I know how it feels."

"You have to press play and record at exactly the same time otherwise it… Is the tape going round, can you see? There should be a little red light, is it on? I think it is. Right. Now, just for one last time, I'd like to start by going over the weeks leading up to the '83 Party Conference."

"Again? Well, if we must."

"As Chief Whip, you were widely praised for your part in the massive landslide election win that summer. Everyone expected you to be appointed Party Chairman, but, in a chain of events that caught everyone by surprise, you were suddenly announced as the new Home Secretary instead, and old Dickie Billings, despite being long past retirement age, was shunted out of Environment to become the new Chief Whip and Party Chairman."

"How many times have we been over this? Sir Dick Billings was an inspired choice for both of those key roles. As you know, he was one of the best tactical campaigners in the country, our longest serving and most experienced MP, and someone who was not afraid to assert his authority as and when required. Don't forget, I'd been Home Secretary under Douglas-Home, so I hardly think I was the least likely candidate once that position fell vacant. And, for that matter, I don't see what Dick's age had to do with anything. On that logic, both of us should've been pensioned off years ago."

"The Police Commissioner also resigned around the same time, not to mention the Northern Ireland Secretary. An awful lot of *ill health* about, wouldn't you say?"

"Yes, well, all part of the rich tapestry of political life."

"All too convenient if you ask me. I have a theory."

"Really? You do surprise me!"

"As we now know, extensive planning was underway, in secret, during the autumn and winter of '83, for the showdown with the miners. Remember, we discussed it at the time? I'd been tipped off about coal stockpiling and planned pit closures."

"I remember. Leaks were an ongoing frustration. Mr Scargill wasn't the only enemy within."

"It was common knowledge at that time that your Home Office predecessor was on the way out. The Prime Minister needed someone in that critical role capable of rising to the occasion. Someone like-minded and loyal, who would have the courage to stay the course during what was clearly going to be a politically difficult and even potentially dangerous time. Someone with a strong enough majority in his own constituency not to have to give a fig about personal popularity. Sound familiar?"

"I have no idea what you're talking about."

"The whole sequence of events was a fix from the start. A once in a generation opportunity for dramatic, all-encompassing reform was staring you in the face, but for it to succeed all the right people had to be in place. The majority was massive, over a hundred and forty seats..."

"One hundred and forty-four."

"One hundred and forty-four, right. By then, your work as Chief Whip was done. The Awkward Squad had been battered into submission. Stanley Smee was safely out of the way in Northern Ireland — what a baptism of fire that turned out to be — and the Parliamentary Party was finally united, or at least gave every appearance of being so. Dickie Billings had to be quietly shuffled out of Environment because of his cosy, some might even suggest corrupt, relationship with Sir Eddie Donoghue. So, his becoming Chief Whip and Party Chair was the perfect solution all round. The decks were now clear for the next looming battle, the big one, an all-out attack on Arthur Scargill and the National Union of Mineworkers."

"These movements and appointments were all part of the normal cut and thrust of day-to-day government. If filling positions on merit is some sort of crime in your Trotskyite world, then I plead guilty as charged."

"With the Police Commissioner conveniently gone, the way was clear to appoint your man, Ron Coburn. With Coburn in place as the nation's most senior police commander, your good self as Home Secretary, Dickie Billings marshalling the troops from the whips' office and Sir Peregrine Walsingham as Cabinet Secretary, well, let's face it, it was a formidable council of war for a Prime Minister on a crusade."

"Crusade? Council of war? You really are getting carried away."

"I'd like to get to some specifics. Will you now, finally, on the record, admit that, as Home Secretary, you initiated surveillance, phone taps and the like, on Arthur Scargill, Austin Wells, and other senior union officials?"

"You've asked me this before, and I'll give you the same answer. Cabinet matters are subject to the Thirty-Year Rule, and then there's the Official Secrets Act to consider. You, of all people, should understand that. These are matters upon which I can make no comment, even now."

"You oversaw the mobilisation of a multi-force police flying squad: specially selected and trained officers who were deployed to picket-lines around the country. Was this because there were concerns in government that local officers might be too sympathetic to the miners, being members of the same communities, and might not go in hard enough?"

"I don't know what you mean by not going in hard enough. Regional constabularies were, in a number of cases, not equipped to deal with civil unrest on that scale. If a local Chief Constable asked for our assistance, we were ready and willing to provide it, purely in the interests of the rule of law. You've always deliberately misrepresented the background of the Miners' Strike. It was a dispute between the Coal Board and the National Union of Mineworkers. The government was not involved, other than as trying to keep the peace in the face of violent and disruptive actions by criminal thugs."

"If you ask me, a number of those thugs were wearing your uniforms, but I'll come to that. Right, bonny lad, cards on the table. I know you'll dismiss this as another one of my conspiracy theories, but hear me out. Everything was connected. Your violent suppression of the pickets was just the opening salvo in a much wider social strategy, of which your department was the chosen flag-bearer. The tactics refined against the miners became part of a plan for more aggressive policing generally. The Police and Criminal Evidence Act may have theoretically created a greater sense of accountability, but my assessment of your general attitude as Home Secretary was that, as long as the paperwork was clean, your boys could do as they liked. You also hardened the regime against the IRA soldiers in the H Blocks…"

"Now I really do have to stop your little sermon. I will not have them referred to as soldiers. They were terrorists, murderers. As the Prime Minister said, 'crime is crime is crime.' The steps I took were essential in keeping our nation safe. And besides, I wasn't going to allow a repeat of that Maze Prison fiasco."

"You were front page news around the country, pictured at the vanguard of major police operations — Orgreave Coke Works, Greenham Common, as well as a number of inner city disturbances — actually dressed in police riot gear, apparently instructing senior officers. It makes it very difficult for you to convincingly distance yourself from some of the more controversial police actions. In fact, you made quite an art form out of defending the indefensible. Do you accept that this led to the perception that policing had become dangerously politicised during your tenure?"

"I do not, and I have no wish to distance myself. I was merely demonstrating that the police had my full support, a fact which, I was later told, was very much appreciated by rank and file officers. Look here, you have to remember the nature of the times. A matter of weeks after I took office, Harrods was bombed. Ninety people were injured and six were killed, including three police officers. A few months later, a young WPC was gunned down —in cold blood — right in the centre of London. Armies of rogue miners were disrupting the operation of pits, and there were fifty thousand women blockading the Greenham Common RAF base, threatening national security. Three and a half million people were out of work, the inner cities were cesspools of broken families, unwed mothers, drugs, wanton vandalism, violent crime and organised civil unrest. Communities were breaking down before our eyes, the established order was in grave danger, as we paid a heavy price for years of failed social policies and weak leadership. What was I supposed to do? Just sit back and watch, while everything we had spent a lifetime fighting for descended into chaos?"

"Now who's sermonising? It's all very well bemoaning the end of civilisation, man, but your government wasn't just an innocent bystander as all this trouble unfolded. With respect, you need to acknowledge your mistakes, accept your fair share of the blame. Anyway, community is a funny word for a Thatcherite. Don't tell me that you're conceding that there might be such a thing as 'society' after all?"

"Spare me your outdated Marxist waffle, I've been putting up with it for over forty years, God help me. Let's not get bogged down in those arguments again or we'll be here until one of us drops dead. Mind you, the way this ordeal is dragging on, death is losing its sting."

"Whose idea was it to lay riot charges against a number of miners identified, rightly or wrongly, as strike ringleaders? Why pursue charges that carried a potential life sentence for working people who had otherwise no criminal record? There must have been other options."

"You would have to ask the Crown Prosecution Service. They took their decisions based on the evidence provided."

"I'm glad you raised the issue of evidence. Let's consider the behaviour of your own police flying squad. A number of picketers sustained injuries that were never adequately explained. Then there was the falsifying of statements, and the bullying of other officers to do likewise, in support of serious criminal charges that would otherwise never have stuck. From my reading of court transcripts, a number of your lads were very lucky not to be facing serious assault and perjury charges. Not even the judges you tried to fix could overlook the gaping holes in the police evidence."

"Look here, they were not *my lads*. I would also remind you that Commissioner Coburn, with my wholehearted support, initiated a full independent enquiry into the behaviour of some officers, a small number, that may have overstepped the mark. Disciplinary action was taken in several instances. Ron Coburn had an unsurpassed record of fighting corruption and championing police reform — he was always known as Honest Ron. Do you really think he would have knowingly stood for any misconduct of that nature within the nation's police?"

"For the record, *I* was the first one to refer to him as 'Honest Ron' when I reported on his efforts to clean up West End Central. Be that as it may, it wasn't long before things started to unravel, legally and politically. Protests were directed at you personally, friendly newspapers turned against you, and even members of your own government ran for cover. The wet-dry divide re-emerged, and there were increasing demands for your resignation."

"Granted, one or two of the weak-willed wet brigade started flapping about — true to form — but the vast majority, including the Prime Minister, remained steadfast in their support."

"One little hidden tragedy in all of this is, what happened to your Parliamentary Private Secretary who was a member of your government with a genuine social conscience. A rare phenomenon at that time, even you'd have to admit. Had things turned out differently, she could have gone all the way. She had the strength and the talent. The first black female Prime Minister, on the Conservative side. The ultimate validation for the Windrush generation, and the redemption of Tory politics. But her association with your Home Office, particularly after the Brixton riots of '85, made her unelectable two years later. She became a pariah in her own community despite her years of hard work on their behalf, and even her own family disowned her."

"I genuinely regret what happened to Janice. She didn't deserve that."

"Would it be fair to say that your own position finally became untenable after the controversy surrounding the poll tax riots, leaving you no alternative but to resign?"

"It certainly would not. I resigned as Home Secretary following the change of leadership. I'd been closely associated with Margaret for so many years, championed her ascendancy in '75 and then fought for her leadership in 1990. I want to make this very clear. My resignation as Home Secretary was purely based on the leadership change, not arising from any decisions I had taken."

"Would you concede that the more conciliatory approach embraced by your successor, reaching out to communities and bringing rogue officers to account, has turned out to be more effective than your more, shall we say, resolute approach?"

"Charles Seymour is a fine Home Secretary, but it's a different time. I would suggest that the reason he is able to take such an approach is largely due to the hard decisions I took during my tenure. He might even tell you that himself if you ask him."

"Actually I did, and he has."

"That bears out my entire argument, then."

"I guess your career prospects under the new PM weren't helped by that rather infamous indiscreet comment."

"No, that's true. I never saw that tabloid hack skulking behind me. It was a private conversation."

"Mind you, it made a lovely headline, didn't it? I have it framed on the wall of my study as a matter of fact. "FROM IRON LADY TO LIMP DICK, HOME SECRETARY LAMENTS.""

"Thank you for reminding me."

"Funnily enough, in all the years we've known each other, I'd never heard you use that expression. I'd never known you to be indiscreet under any circumstances."

"No, it was a favourite line of old Dickie Billings, God rest him. I was still fuming over the ballot, it just slipped out. An unforgivable lapse. I dread to think what my father would have made of it."

"How do you see the future of the Conservative Party: now that Mr Major has defied expectations by managing to secure a small, but at least workable, majority earlier this year?"

"The work we did over the last twelve or thirteen years has laid the foundation for us to be in power until the next century. I also predict Charles Seymour will be a future Prime Minister."

"There'll be at least one more election before then, and I'd suggest that, the way the majority is shrinking, this could be your last term in government. Anything can happen."

"Don't be ridiculous. The only way Labour could even get close to power again would be to take a dramatic lurch toward common sense, free themselves from the trade union yoke and reinvent themselves in the image of the Tories. Can you see that happening?' No, of course not. What do you think your revered heroes Nye Bevan and Ellen Wilkinson would have to say about that? They'd be doing somersaults in their graves. No, you mark my words, the Conservatives will see the country through to the next century and beyond, with Charles Seymour as Prime Minister."

"Well, we'll see, but I'd remind you that Mr Kinnock got *reasonably* close to power this time. By the way, how does it feel to see your constituency held by someone outside of your own family for the first time in... well, for the first time ever in fact?"

"*Sed fugit interea, fugit irreparabile tempus.*"

"Very profound, bonny lad. I must have dozed off during Latin lessons at my ragged school. What does it mean?"

"Something like, 'the time is lost, which will never renew'."

"I think we can both relate to that. Finally, before we finish, is there anything else you'd like to say on the record?"

"No, thank you. I've said way too much as it is."

"Nothing at all? Look, old marra, this is the last opportunity, we're about to go to print. Here's a chance for you to put your side of the story, to redeem your reputation. For the sake of history if nothing else. You like to portray this rock solid, tough public image, but I know you're not the proper bastard you pretend to be. Give me something I can use, man. Please."

"I'm perfectly comfortable with my reputation. It's too late in the day to be coming over all sentimental. The past is the past — we can't change it. I did what I had to do. In any case, as time was marching on, I was wondering if we'd ever see this great tome of yours in print. We're not getting any younger."

"Speak for yourself. As it happens, the first volume will be out before Christmas. It'll be called *Economic Warfare – Thatcher and the End of Consensus*. What do you think?

"Godawful title. Imagine waking up on Christmas morning to find that in your stocking! The best thing you could do with it would be to burn it in the fireplace to keep warm."

"Let me turn off the recorder. I can't quite see which one is the stop button, my eyes are a bit... I think that's it. No, it's this one, ee, flippin' 'eck, that was rewind. Wait a minute..."

"Here let me, you really are a doddery old fool. There."

"Right, now that we are definitely off the record, between old marras, is there anything you regret? Anything you'd do differently?"

"Between old friends, and off the record. Well, it goes without saying that I regret that Eileen was with us at Brighton in '84. As you know she never felt comfortable in our political world, she really only came that year because it had been such a difficult time and she wanted to support me, and because it was our fortieth wedding anniversary. I regret that she went upstairs to bed while we were all working late in the hotel dining room. I think Rick always blamed me, he was always much closer to his mother."

"I'm sure that's not true. He's been such a success. You must be very proud of him."

"Well, yes, I am. We certainly get on much better these days, which is some consolation for an old man. And my young grandson, James, can debate with me on politics for hours, and usually has the better of the argument. But enough of this. What about you, the great self-appointed champion of the working class? You must have some regrets."

"Of course, where do I start? I should've listened to Arthur Scargill when he predicted just how far your programme of pit closures would go, but I never took him seriously. Then, when I knew for sure, or at least had reliable inside information, I was so intent on the deal we did for my exclusive access to Number Ten that I lost sight of my responsibilities as a reporter, and, I think, as a decent human being. I know how Robert Johnson must have felt."

"Who was Robert Johnson? I don't remember him."

"The legend is that he sold his soul to the devil in return for becoming the best blues guitarist ever."

"I don't see the connection."

"No, you wouldn't."

"I think you're being a little hard on yourself. You've made your mark: bestselling author and historian, television and radio personality, the official chronicler of the Thatcher government. Not a bad achievement for a boy from Jarrow who can't even work a cassette recorder."

"Perhaps. We're both hostages to the past, in so many ways. I regret some of the things I wrote about you during the turmoil of '84, and then afterwards."

"You had a job to do, as did I. I always knew it wasn't personal."

"Referring to that other little adventure around that time, the one we don't talk about, how close did I get to who was really behind it?"

"Nowhere near."

"I thought not. Anyway, I do want to thank you. None of this would have been possible without your support. The former Prime Minister has been very generous with her time, as have a number of your senior colleagues. Even Sir Peregrine was remarkably candid, for a civil servant. Archie Prentice wouldn't have a bar of it of course, despite your best efforts on my behalf, but I didn't expect otherwise. Pity, because I would have loved to have asked him about Harold Wilson's resignation... Yes, yes, I know, you don't have to say it. Another conspiracy theory. Now, one last question, still off the record."

"Oh God, better make it quick. I'm dying for a pee."

"Tell me about the Banqueting Club."

"...So, with broad celebration of Britain's newly rediscovered strength at home and abroad, under a strong and suddenly popular Prime Minister, a "Bargain Basement Boadicea", according to Labour's Denis Healey, inevitably, speculation began to grow about the timing of the next general election..."

"...The latest a general election could be called was May 1984, but there were compelling reasons for the Prime Minister to consider going to the country early. By 1983, inflation was trending downwards and the economy was showing early signs of recovery. Unemployment remained devastatingly high, however, with well over three million out of work: the highest sustained unemployment since the Great Depression. Despite these mixed signals, the government was riding a wave of popularity, thanks to the Falklands victory, and senior colleagues, led by key strategist and Chief Whip Norman Armstrong, were urging the Prime Minister to seek a renewed mandate to continue their wide-ranging programme of social and economic reform..."

From *Economic Warfare – Thatcher and the End of Consensus* (Volume 1)
  By Alf Burton
  © 1992 Donoghue Publishing and Broadcasting.

CHAPTER ONE
AUTUMN 1983

As Chief Whip, Norman Armstrong was one of the few politicians in Westminster content to ply his trade out of the public eye, deftly scheming and manoeuvring in the shadows beneath the sensitive radar of the lobby correspondents. His portfolio was party discipline, instilling, by force or inducement, a sense of common purpose amongst a large and disparate collection of government MPs. Norman often joked that his role was the political equivalent of making the trains run on time, a more charitable observation than offered by his old friend Enoch Powell, who once opined that the Commons without whips was like a city without sewers.

Both Norman Armstrong and his deputy, Charles Seymour, were consummate practitioners of the dark arts that informed the whips' day to day operations, their ongoing mission to secure the smooth enactment of their government's legislative agenda. They were the armaments of the ship of state, aimed inwardly toward their own wavering backbenchers. Their ammunition, fired with uncanny accuracy, ranged from rubber bullets of charm and strategically offered incentives to missiles of robust aggression, intimidation, and even blackmail. An extensive network of carefully nurtured informants kept the whips fully informed about even the most intimate details of their MPs' public and private lives, to the extent that the senior whips knew more about most of the government members than did their own families, which, as Norman often reflected when updating the secret dirt book, was not necessarily a bad thing, for the sake of Honourable Members' domestic bliss.

As the euphoria of the summer's election triumph receded in the face of the cooler winds of autumn, the Chief Whip and his staff were much occupied in overseeing the passage of what was known within the government as the Donoghue Amendment, although for public consumption it was dressed up as the Local Government Planning Efficiency Initiative. It was a contentious change to existing planning laws, and one that would particularly favour billionaire media and property mogul Sir Eddie Donoghue, the Conservative Party's largest individual donor: personal friend to a number of senior Tories, including Norman Armstrong himself, and a fervent admirer of the Prime Minister.

The practical consequences of this amendment made it much easier for Donoghue's construction companies, which specialised in tower blocks, shopping centres and office complexes, to expedite approval for major developments. The Chief Whip knew that not everyone in government was happy, and had become aware that a small group of dissident backbenchers, known in the whips' office as the Awkward Squad, were actually going to side with the opposition and vote against it. This wasn't a major issue in itself, the government's crushing majority and the reassuring dominance of the Dry faction, who were lockstep in support, would see the bill pass convincingly. For the Chief Whip, it came down to a matter of pure principle. Once you let backbenchers go their own way, he believed, it was a short trip to complete and suicidal anarchy within the Party, a nerve-wracking state of affairs against which Norman, Charles, and their assistant whips had waged a relentless battle during their government's fraught and divided first term.

The ringleader of the Awkward Squad was Stanley Smee, Parliamentary Private Secretary to the Secretary of State for Environment: an egregious example of treason in the Chief Whip's eyes, and one that was not going to go unpunished.

Norman had just got off the phone with Number Ten — a special surprise was being planned for Mr Smee — when he looked up to see Charles Seymour standing in his office doorway, lightly tapping the doorframe. The Chief Whip always worked with his door ajar, frequently gratified at how indiscreet unsuspecting visitors could be when chatting away in the outer office. Information, after all, was the most potent weapon in the whips' armoury.

Norman regarded his deputy over his half-moon bifocals. "Yes, Charles?"

"Alf Burton is on the line, Chief Whip."

Charles Seymour was not surprised when Norman asked him to put the call straight through. As a general rule, the whips' office avoided contact with lobby correspondents, but Alf Burton was a special case. The veteran reporter and Chief Whip had been friends for over thirty years, a mutually beneficial alliance, professionally speaking, but one that both men acknowledged was highly unlikely.

Norman Armstrong was pure, unashamed upper middle-class Conservative Establishment, a decorated RAF veteran from a long family line of Tory MPs. His outer suburban constituency, Stonebridge Southeast, was the safest Conservative stronghold in the country, and had been represented by his family since its days as a pre-reform pocket borough, returned each election by a small number of voters under the direct control of the Armstrongs themselves. Alf Burton once observed that if a medal was struck for fanatical Thatcherism, Norman would have proudly displayed his, right next to his Distinguished Flying Cross.

By contrast, Alf had been born in Jarrow to a family of shipyard workers. By his teenage years, having watched his home and community decimated by the heartbreaking ravages of chronic unemployment, poverty, starvation and consumptive disease, he was already strongly glued to the political views that would come to shape his entire life and career. He arrived in Westminster in 1947, by then a veteran of the Jarrow March, Spanish Civil War, and Merchant Navy. A crusading reporter, he vociferously supported the Labour Manifesto, creating an outcry of Tory indignation when he used his glowing obituary for Jarrow MP and Education Minister, Ellen Wilkinson, to call for the abolition of the House of Lords, and cheered on his idol, Aneurin Bevan, when he likened Tories to vermin and called for their complete annihilation, paving the way for generations of socialist government.

In rare moments of sentimentality, both Alf and Norman might have acknowledged that they were so much the better, professionally and personally, from their association with each other. Norman had, early in their friendship, encouraged the firebrand young reporter to moderate the partisan tone of his writing and to consider opposing views with more of an open mind. Alf, for his part, had reminded Norman that his own safe constituency was not representative of much of Britain, and had helped to open his eyes to some harsh social realities, particularly in the North. Alf conceded that, even after more than thirty years in the parliament, Norman still had a long way to go towards displaying any degree of social conscience, but he was sufficiently encouraged to describe the Chief Whip in a recent column as 'the *almost* acceptable face of Thatcherism'.

"Alf!" Norman cried with genuine affection. "How goes the revolution, comrade?"

"Why-aye, Brother Norman! Can we meet? The usual place?"

The Chief Whip felt the first faint stirrings of apprehension. Alf Burton was the best informed, most widely read, political reporter in the business, and if he was asking for a secret meeting, it didn't always mean good news. Sensing the implied urgency, Norman agreed to meet Alf within the hour.

Before leaving his office, Norman placed a call to the Secretary of State for Environment, Sir Dick Billings, whose long political service afforded him the additional honour of being named Father of the House. Sir Dick was notorious for his short temper, outrageously indiscreet public statements and generally irascible nature. As a result, many of his colleagues found his demeanour far from paternal.

"Norman, you old rogue. What are you up to then?" The Chief Whip was one of the few people with whom the Environment Secretary was happy to engage in friendly banter.

"Bad news, I'm afraid, Dick. Your chap, Smee, is going dark on the Donoghue Bill."

"The little prick," Sir Dick sighed. "Mind you, I can't say I'm surprised. I know there were sound political reasons for his appointment at the time, Norman, but that limp-dick gets right on my wick, always banging on about democracy in local authorities, imagining corruption all over the place, being holier than thou. A sanctimonious, self-righteous shit! I wish I had your chap, Seymour. Now, there's a man I could work with. Fucking hell, on this of all bills!" There was a brief moment of silence before he continued, his gravelly voice now subdued. "I can't afford this to go tits up. I'd value your advice, Norman."

The Chief Whip understood. Beneath the bluster, the loud vulgarity and the aggression, Sir Dick Billings could be as insecure and fearful of his position as the most junior backbencher. "We're a long way from disaster," Norman reassured him. "I've already spoken to Number Ten. Smee's replacement is being arranged as we speak." Norman felt an uncomfortable degree of personal responsibility, having engineered Smee's appointment to this relatively senior departmental role in the post-election reshuffle, as a tactical move to placate the Awkward Squad. He wouldn't be making that mistake again. "He'll be one of us this time," Norman promised. "No more appeasement of the wet brigade. It's time to let them know once and for all who's in charge. The country voted overwhelmingly for Thatcherism this time, not for Smee's brand of snivelling have-it-both-ways political faintheartedness."

"Couldn't agree more," Sir Dick Billings concurred. "Fuck 'em!"

"In the meantime, if it's all right with you, I'll have Smee over to Number Twelve for a little chat. I'd quite like to smoke out his den of traitors, although we already have a good idea who they are. I'll also let him know that his career, such as it was, has hit an unexpected roadblock."

The relief was evident in the Environment Secretary's voice. "Thank you, Norman. It's not easy for me at the moment, as you know. I'm on thin ice. Margaret has only just forgiven me for that Toxteth business in '79. I never thought I'd get back in the Cabinet this late in the day. You spoke up for me, as you've always done, and I appreciate it. They're all watching me closely, just waiting for me to cock it all up. This reform might be the last significant thing I can do in support of the cause. You've stuck by me for years and I won't let you down while I've still any breath in my body. Burton's already been poking his nose in, by the way, sniffing around asking stupid questions. Gave him short shrift, of course, the fat bastard."

"Don't worry, Dick," Norman soothed. "Everything will be fine. And leave Alf Burton to me."

As the Chief Whip prepared to leave his office, he reflected upon how 'that Toxteth business' Dick alluded to, had nearly sunk the elderly MP's career for the last time. Alf Burton had written about the controversy in his regular syndicated column, Westminster Watch, the previous year when Sir Dick, to almost universal surprise, had made it back into the Cabinet.

…With our collective attention focused on the Falklands, only the keenest of Westminster Watchers may have noticed the quiet ministerial reshuffle that last week returned Tory warrior Sir Dick Billings, from backbench obscurity to the Cabinet post of Secretary of State for Environment.

In a long and turbulent career, Sir Dick has served no less than eight Conservative Prime Ministers in varying roles and, it must be said, with varying degrees of success. His profile has been lower in recent years, particularly so following a 1979 Toxteth campaign speech, during which he responded to a black heckler by effecting a mock Caribbean accent and exclaiming, "Who dat! Smile so dat I can see you!" The resulting fracas led to a riot that destroyed a community centre and caused major damage to a number of shops, left several policemen injured, and ended any hopes that Sir Dick might have harboured for a key position in a new Thatcher government.

Loathed by the Labour Party — Aneurin Bevan once referred to him as 'the dirtiest rat amongst the Tory vermin' — and not even universally popular within his own side, he is favoured by strong support from the Tory Dry faction and, in particular, influential Chief Whip Norman Armstrong. Sir Dick has been a vocal critic of local authority inefficiencies, and may prove an inspired choice for a Prime Minister intent on reform across the entire government sector. Sir Dick clearly has the ability to undertake such a major responsibility, but will the accident-prone Westminster veteran be worth the risk? Only time will tell…

It was a troubled sky and cool breeze that greeted Norman as he emerged into Downing Street from the whips' office at Number Twelve. He stopped briefly to chat with the police constable on duty outside Number Ten, then walked out into Whitehall, from where he hailed a black cab for a trip to South London.

Norman gave directions, and then settled into the back seat. Within a few moments he noticed that the driver, in typical fashion, could deftly negotiate the heavy London traffic while spending much of the time peering into the rear view mirror with only the occasional cursory glance forward.

"Beggin' your pardon, Guv'nor," the cabbie said as they crossed the Westminster Bridge, "but aren't you Mr Norman Armstrong, the Chief Whip?"

Norman was somewhat taken aback. Chief Whip was not a position widely known outside of parliamentary circles. "That's right," he replied.

"You'd know Mrs Thatcher, then?" the driver observed, briefly glancing at the road ahead before returning his gaze to the mirror.

"I do," Norman replied, a little tentatively. Despite the popularity of the government, he recognised that the country was deeply divided. When meeting the Great British Public, he was never quite sure if he was going to be offered a handshake or a punch in the face.

"What's she really like then, if you don't mind me asking?"

Norman relaxed. In spite of his privileged background he was no elitist, and always enjoyed escaping the echo-chamber of government and stifling tea-and-sandwiches constituency functions to hear fresh, unfiltered perspectives.

"Well," Norman replied, "she's very much as you see on the television. Strong and resolute." Conscious that he was sounding too much like a trite and patronising election slogan, he added, "On a personal level, she's exceedingly generous and very kind."

The cabbie smiled. "Just as I thought," he said. "My lad was in the Falklands, by the way. Copped a nasty one at Goose Green, bullet nearly took off the old crown jewels — just missed, went straight through his thigh, the lucky little beggar. He's doing great now, though. I've got him on the Knowledge, he's going to join the family business, so to speak."

Norman found himself warming to the middle-aged cabbie. "I'm so glad your son is recovering. We owe all those boys a great debt."

"I was in the service myself, Royal Marines — Suez, Tanganyika and a few places in between— Never a scratch, me. You know, Mr Armstrong, my lad told me that those poor Argentine squaddies were just kids, had virtually no kit. Freezing cold, no shoes. Unbelievable, in this day and age. We certainly gave Galtieri a right seeing-to. Good on Mrs Thatcher, I say!"

The two men chatted amiably throughout the journey until the cab pulled up outside a corner pub, the best days of which were evidently long past. The faded lettering above the door was just legible: The Kings Head. Est. 1650.

"Are you sure this is the place?" the driver asked doubtfully, eyeing the dirty windows and peeling green and white paint with distaste.

"This is it," Norman confirmed as he opened the cab door. "Do you mind waiting? I won't be any longer than half an hour."

"No problem. I'll see what their shepherd's pie is like, although, looking at the place, I don't hold out too much hope. I'll just nip round the corner and park."

Norman entered the crowded public bar, and was at once confronted by eye-watering clouds of smoke from countless cigars, pipes and cigarettes, and the pungent smell of sweat, beer and steamy damp. This wasn't his kind of place at all, and each time he came he promised himself it would be his last. He saw that Alf Burton had already arrived, and had, as usual, chosen a quiet corner booth away from the windows. Two pints stood on the scratched table, one full, one half empty. Froth hung from Alf's untidy moustache like melting snow from a window ledge as he fought to open a stubborn packet of pork scratchings.

Norman had to duck, weave and sidestep through the press of bodies to reach the table. He felt very much out of place in his sober Savile Row suit, with gold cufflinks and precision-folded handkerchief visible above his breast pocket. A number of patrons eyed him with a curiosity bordering on suspicion as he pushed past. Norman slid his legs under the table, fretting about the effect of the cracked and pitted leather bench seat on his neatly pressed trousers. He shook hands warmly with his old friend, observing with amusement his usual attire, faded beige mac, frayed collar and loosened tie. Norman smiled. It was all an act, an image carefully cultivated, as a number of Norman's colleagues had discovered to their cost. Alf's dishevelled, absent-minded amiability had, over his long career, charmed any number of devastating admissions, indiscreet comments and breaches of confidence from generations of unsuspecting MPs, falsely secure and confident in their own superiority over the scruffy, shambling man in the old mac who looked like he needed help to tell the time.

Both men were busy, so enquiries about respective families were heartfelt, but brief. Norman was about to launch into his carefully-constructed argument in favour of the Donoghue Amendment, but was momentarily blindsided by Alf's opening question.

"How much do you really know about Charlotte Morris?"

"What? Charlotte… who? What's this got to do with...?"

"What's this got to do with what?" Alf questioned, looking puzzled. "What did you think I was going to ask?"

"Nothing, nothing. Forget it, go on."

"Charlotte Morris," Alf repeated.

Norman recovered quickly. "Ah yes, tea lady at Number Ten, if I recall correctly. What's she been up to then?"

"Very droll, Chief Whip," Alf replied in a very creditable impression of Sir Humphrey Appleby.

"Wait a minute," Norman corrected himself. "My mistake, she was a tea lady at the Foreign Office."

"You know fine well who I'm talking about," Alf went on, suppressing a smile. "Charlotte Morris, the war correspondent, novelist, historian and alleged spy. A courtier to old Bertie, Edward the Seventh himself. Wrote a controversial book about Kitchener, so incendiary that it wasn't published until after they both were dead. Accused him of war crimes from Omdurman to the Transvaal and of being a closet shirt-lifter, amongst other things."

"I might have heard of her." Norman sounded noncommittal, but Alf recognised the keen interest reflected in the intensity of his old friend's gaze. "I hope you haven't dragged me half way across London just to discuss a long dead second-rate gossipmonger," Norman went on. "Some of us have to run the country, you know."

"I think the lost manuscript might have turned up," Alf said, matter-of-factly.

Norman felt a sudden and unanticipated surge of anxiety. He leant forward. "Are you telling me you actually have it?"

"No, but I have a strong lead. I'll know for certain by the end of the week. I think it's the real thing this time."

Norman thought carefully, resisting the urge to fidget. He did his best to portray an air of aloof nonchalance, but he knew Alf wouldn't be fooled. They were both well aware of the significance. Norman noted that Alf's own self-possession was beginning to fail. He was nervously drumming his fingers on the table, and, having finally defeated the foil packet, was shoving pork scratchings into his mouth one after the other.

"What do you intend to do with it?" Norman asked.

"If it is, in fact, the genuine article, I'll hand it directly to you. Not to the government, mind, to you personally. To do with as you see fit. I won't even read it, you have my word."

"In return for what?" Norman asked.

"Full and unhindered access to the Prime Minister and the inner workings of government. In depth interviews, full and frank disclosure, spread over your remaining term, or terms, in power. No meddling minders in the way, keep Ingham's press office well out of it. The hunger strikes, Falklands, Iranian Embassy siege, Foreign Office shenanigans, Civil Service cockups, nothing out of bounds. I, in turn, promise to embargo my reports until either the Prime Minister has retired or the government is out of power."

"You might be waiting a long time," Norman remarked. "Our majority could easily see us through to the next century."

"God help us all if that turns out to be the case," Alf replied with a smile. "You know me, I've always played the long game, so I'll take that chance. But think of the benefits for the government. There aren't too many people capable of enshrining your legacy and presenting it to as wide an audience as what I could. This will be the definitive, day-by-day history of the Thatcher years. I may always be a pinko by your standards, but my reporting has always been fair." Norman's eyebrows shot up, prompting Alf toward a minor qualification. "All right, in recent years, at least, but I'm still the best person to write in detail and with objectivity about this government. You know it makes sense."

Norman nodded, acknowledging the merits of Alf's pitch. As well as his work in newspapers and on radio, the Fleet Street veteran, whose inside knowledge of Westminster was without peer, had written some of the highest selling political books in history, widely praised biographies of Labour and Conservative luminaries and accounts of landmark political events. His most recent publication was the unlikely number one bestseller, *Decade of Discontent*, a warts and all account of the battles between the trade unions and the governments of Heath, Wilson and Callaghan. He was probably the most widely read and influential political writer in the country. The Prime Minister herself was a fan, at least in private.

"Who else knows about this manuscript business?" Norman asked.

"No one, apart from us and my source. I haven't told anyone in my office, not even my gaffer. So do we have a deal?"

"I'll make a couple of calls," Norman told him. "There'll be no problem. I'll call you at your flat tonight so we can discuss terms."

"Champion. Now then, what are you up to with the miners?"

"You've lost me."

"Coal is being stockpiled all over the shop. I've been reliably informed that the Coal Board, with the full support of your government, is planning to close a massive number of pits, ones they consider to be not profitable enough. Possibly as many as eighty or one hundred are in the frame. The union won't stand for it of course, Scargill will come out all guns blazing, but that's exactly what you want. This time it will be a fight to the bitter end, like nothing we've ever seen before. You'll finish the job that Heath couldn't, fettle the unions once and for all. I can't see your illustrious Prime Minister going wobbly at the first sight of blood, either. There'll be no backing down. This will be long, violent and divisive, worse than anything we can possibly imagine. Lives will be destroyed, some will be lost. The country will be very different when this is over. And so will we." Alf spoke with the resigned sadness of someone who had already conceded final defeat and was confronting a dark, frightening and uncertain new world.

Norman looked around, worried that they were being overheard, but the general din of layers of conflicting conversations made it unlikely. The proposed coal industry restructure was known to only a select few senior Cabinet members and some trusted executives of the Coal Board. There was no point denying it, Norman thought, Alf wouldn't have brought it up if he hadn't been one hundred per cent confident in his source.

"Who leaked this?" Norman hissed. "I'll have his head on a spike on London Bridge."

"You know better than that, bonny lad. This is part of my deal for access. I want to be inside the tent when things kick off in the New Year."

"You're not going to use it, then?"

"Not today. Let's just say I'll be looking forward to your telephone call tonight."

The two men rose and shook hands. Alf's pint was empty while Norman's remained untouched. The cab driver, seated on a stool at the bar, scoffed the last few bites of an unexpectedly enjoyable shepherd's pie and followed Norman, jostling his way through the scrum of patrons, toward the street. As Norman pushed through the swinging front door, he heard Alf yelling, "Tirra, bonny lad! And don't think I'll be letting you off the hook over the Donoghue Amendment!"

Both Norman and the cab driver were less inclined toward small talk on the trip back. Norman's mind was fully occupied by the metaphorical hand grenades that Alf had lobbed in his path, while the cabbie was feeling some ominous internal rumblings, and was wondering whether the shepherd's pie had been such a good idea after all.

A short time later, the cab pulled up not far from Downing Street. As Norman paid the driver, tipping generously, he handed him a wallet-sized card. "These are my numbers," he said. "If ever you hear anything in your travels that you think I should know, give me a call. I'd consider it a personal favour, and the Prime Minister will appreciate it too."

"Righto, Chief," the driver said. "Here's mine. You'll know who to call next time you need a quick trip to Heathrow, or anywhere else for that matter."

As the black cab disappeared into the traffic, Norman looked at the card. Eric Baker. He made a mental note to organise a personal letter of thanks from the Prime Minister in recognition of his family's service. The Chief Whip's long experience had taught him that even the most unlikely relationships, if carefully cultivated, had a habit of bearing golden fruit.

Within a few moments of Norman's arrival back in his office, Charles Seymour made an appearance at his doorway. "Sir Eddie Donoghue phoned for you, Chief Whip," he said. "No less than three times, as a matter of fact. To say that he was sounding worried would be something of an understatement."

"Thank you, Charles." Norman knew that the billionaire had his own network of spies throughout the government, in fact, a number of his former senior legal executives now worked for Sir Dick Billings at the Department of Environment, and had been instrumental in drafting the Donoghue Amendment. There were researchers and informants planted in other government departments, as well as in the offices of key MPs from all the major parties. Sir Eddie had obviously been informed about the Awkward Squad's activities and was keen to be reassured that all was well. Norman understood Donoghue's distress. The Chief Whip's own connections in the City had informed him that the Donoghue Group was borrowing heavily in support of a massive expansion of their building, transport and media interests. The amounts, Norman had been told, were in the hundreds of millions of pounds, possibly into the billions. Sir Eddie was precariously highly geared, and was relying on a series of legislative changes cutting government oversight and red tape in order to expedite a number of major projects right across the country. Any uncertainty or unwarranted delays could very easily unsettle his bankers, some of whom were apparently already having misgivings over his ability to service the mounting debt. With three and a half million out of work, a massive employer like the Donoghue Group's going belly-up was not something any responsible government could ever countenance, and Norman was very aware that a disaster on that scale could very easily bring HM government crashing down in its wake. Their need was reciprocal — a desperate, fearful and insecure marriage with mutually assured destruction if things went wrong.

"I'll call Eddie this afternoon," Norman replied. "Anything else?"

"Stanley Smee will be here in a few minutes."

"Right, let's get him out of the way so we can get on to more important things." Knowing how much his deputy enjoyed roughing up troublesome MPs, Norman invited Charles to sit in.

In due course, Stanley Smee arrived at Twelve Downing Street and was invited straight in to Norman's private office. Charles Seymour sat on a chair in the corner, legs crossed, pen and paper in hand to make notes. Smee was nervous, but buoyed by his contention that the moral ground was his, and he was determined to put his case assertively. As soon as he sat down, the Chief Whip let fly.

"You little shit!"

Smee could not have looked more surprised had Norman slapped his face and challenged him to a duel. "Now, steady on," he managed.

"What are you thinking, you ungrateful little rat, going your own way on the Local Government Efficiency Bill?"

"You mean the Donoghue Amendment," Smee replied, with just a hint of suicidal defiance. Charles Seymour smiled inwardly. This was going to be even more enjoyable than he had anticipated; the poor hapless Smee was about to be chewed up and spat out.

"You're hardly in a position to be flippant," Norman responded. His voice was low and controlled, his stare intense and icy. The remnants of Smee's courage seemed to slip though his sweating hands like grains of sand.

Smee had a number of concerns over the bill in question, and he wasn't the only one. He felt that allowing Donoghue Constructions a virtual free hand to knock down houses and community assets, often bypassing the local approval process, and to replace them with tower blocks, offices and shopping centres was a slippery slope that ran roughshod over democracy at its fundamental level. It hadn't escaped Smee's attention that a number of crumbling, unsafe council flats which were now earmarked for demolition and rebuilding, had also been built by Donoghue Constructions a generation earlier. It was, as Smee had told a secret meeting of the Awkward Squad, like providing a set of keys to the man who'd once burgled your house and inviting him to do it again. Smee's boss, Sir Dick Billings, had predictably expressed an opposing view, not very politely as it happened, informing Smee that if the nation's ungrateful layabouts weren't happy with their Donoghue council flats they were perfectly entitled to go and live in a cardboard box on a garbage strewn waste-ground under a flyover somewhere. And, not only that, any moves toward keeping the meddling, amateurish extravagant busybodies in the local authorities out of serious decision making had to be good for the country. And furthermore, if a patriotic creator of wealth, jobs and housing like

Sir Eddie Donoghue benefitted along the way, so much the better: a just reward for his long and proven commitment to Britain. So, if Smee had a problem with any of it, Sir Dick concluded, he should seriously consider fucking off and joining either the Labour Party or the SDP, where he could sit and wring his hands with the rest of the pinko do-gooders while the Tories set the country to rights once and for all.

Stanley Smee had weathered the tirade, as he had many others, in stoic silence, quietly suspecting that Sir Dick's own personal wealth might be heading in an upward direction as a result of his championing of the Donoghue Amendment. He had no proof, of course, but the number of former Donoghue employees now working within his department were a constant reminder of the intrigue at play. He also suspected that Sir Dick's constant public lambasting of the Greater London Council was more about their opposition to a number of major Donoghue projects than their alleged financial profligacy.

Smee had prepared and rehearsed all of his arguments like an actor memorising a long and difficult speech for a West End opening night, but now that he was actually face to face with the Chief Whip, whose lethal verbal arsenal and personal power were feared throughout the Party, he couldn't remember a thing. Unconsciously, he slipped lower in his chair.

Charles Seymour watched with a discreet smile, and understood perfectly. Norman's reputation was such that most MPs who found themselves in Smee's position had subconsciously conceded defeat before they had even sat down.

"In case you hadn't noticed," the Chief Whip continued, "we're dealing with an unemployment *crisis* in this country, and it's only getting worse. The closure of the Chatham Dockyards alone will cost seven thousand jobs in the New Year. Do you

41

have any idea just how many new jobs this amendment will lead to? Many will be in depressed areas. Liverpool, the industrial North, all over Britain in fact. It's time to turn the so-called managed decline of Merseyside, and the North generally, on its head, and bring home our army of skilled workers who are currently forced to earn their living in Europe and the Middle East. Good, well-paying jobs for decent working people — no doubt you might even find some of those in your own constituency, if you look hard enough. So, what do I find? You and your little band of weak-kneed bed-wetters are not only planning to vote against the bill, thereby damaging the government and the country, but also to stab your Secretary of State in the back and, if that wasn't enough, betray your Prime Minister at the same time."

"But, the democratic process…" Smee offered weakly

"Bugger the democratic process to hell!" Norman spat. "The government has placed great importance on the passage of this piece of legislation, hence it will be a three-line whip. Do you have any idea of the consequences of defying a three-line whip? What's your majority?"

"Um, three thou…just under four thousand…"

"Three thousand nine hundred and seventy-six, to be precise," Norman stated, glancing briefly at some notes on his desk. "A big improvement on your performance in '79. How do you account for that?"

Smee sensed a lifeline to safer ground. "Well," he said, "I focused on local issues during my first term, and my campaign last summer went awfully well…"

"Bollocks!" the Chief Whip interrupted loudly. "You owe everything to your Prime Minister, whose courage and integrity were the bedrock of our election victory, not your amateurish campaigning in your godforsaken constituency. The PM herself endorsed your promotion to PPS this term, and this is how you repay her? Do you even understand the role of a PPS? You have no personal opinion, you are there to support your Secretary of State and the policies of this government, not go off on some ill-judged, windy moral crusade. What do you think, Mr Seymour?"

Charles Seymour grimaced and sucked air through his teeth. "Let's face it, it doesn't look too good, Chief Whip. Still, the Prime Minister can be merciful, and that junior Ministry at the Northern Ireland Office is still vacant. Perhaps Mr Smee's talents might be better suited there."

Smee felt his innards churn like a washing machine, his heart was beating heavily in his chest and he was suddenly short of breath. He wondered for a split second if he was about to keel over from a heart attack, right there in the Chief Whip's office. Wanting to kill your career was one thing — par for the course in politics, he thought — but wanting you actually dead was in another league altogether.

"Oh my God!" Smee uttered, rubbing his chest as his panic-stricken eyes darted between the Chief Whip and his smirking deputy.

"But," added Charles Seymour, thoroughly enjoying his role in their own little piece of theatre, "Now that Sir Dick knows that Mr Smee has been plotting behind his back, I'd suggest that Belfast might be the safer option."

"Good point," agreed the Chief Whip.

The ordeal was then brought to a brisk conclusion. Crushed and shamed, and calmer in defeat, Smee agreed to support the bill, and readily gave up the names of the other members of the Awkward Squad. He pledged his loyalty to the Prime Minister, and Norman placed an avuncular arm around the shattered MP as he walked him out of the office, offering a few unexpected words of conciliatory kindness.

Charles Seymour sat back, reflecting on the genius of the Chief Whip, while Stanley Smee sloped off to the Department of Environment to clear his desk.

"Poor chap," Norman Armstrong commented as he returned to his desk. "Right, Charles, who else do we have, as if we didn't already know?"

"Let's see," Charles consulted his notes, "Stuart Farquhar, no surprise there. Perkin Warbeck, Lambert Simnel, Janice Best, and a couple of no-hopers no one is likely to listen to anyway. No mention of one former Prime Minister though: perhaps he's decided to sit this one out."

"Ah well, no more rebellion from that quarter." Norman rubbed his hands together. "Right, go and have some fun then, Charles. Remind them which side they're on. Be tactful with Janice Best, though, we don't want our only black female MP running off to Alf and telling him we're a bunch of patronising, racist bullies. Well, not all of us, at least."

"What are your plans for the afternoon?" Charles asked as he stood up. "Don't forget to put Sir Eddie out of his misery."

"I'll phone him right now. Then I'm off to the Cabinet Office. No rest for the wicked, eh?"

"Anything I should be aware of?"

"No, just a social visit with Sir Peregrine. It's time to start thinking about our annual Battle of Britain reunion. Nothing for you to be concerned about."

***

Later that afternoon, Stuart Farquhar MP walked the shortish distance from the House of Commons to his spacious and rather comfortable office, and discovered his desk hidden under a rickety wall of cardboard boxes. Two men in dustcoats were gathering up his books and personal mementoes, and Charles Seymour was perched on the edge of his desk reading Farquhar's copy of The Guardian.

"What's all this?" Farquhar asked, although he had a good idea.

"A reallocation of members' accommodations, Chief Whip's instructions. Sorry about the inconvenience." Farquhar noted that Charles Seymour sounded more triumphant than apologetic. "We've chosen a nice quiet location for you, one where you'll have plenty of time to reflect on the value of loyalty."

Seymour then led the MP on a long walk through a maze of corridors until they finally arrived at what must have been the furthest corner of the parliamentary buildings. The Deputy Chief Whip opened a door at the end of a corridor and gestured Farquhar to enter.

The first thing Stuart Farquhar noticed was the damp and musty smell, and the fact that there was no window. A pile of buckets and a mop rested against a desk which seemed to take up most of the floor space. Seymour turned on his heel without a word and strode off down the corridor, the sharp echoes of his footsteps sounding to the desolate MP like gunshots from an executioner.

"Excuse me, Mr Seymour," he called. "Was this a cleaners' room? What am I supposed to do with the mops and buckets?"

"You'll find out next time it rains," Charles Seymour called without turning around. Farquhar also thought he heard the words 'treacherous twat', but he couldn't be sure.

CHAPTER TWO

"Nice to see you, Norman, how are things?" Sir Peregrine Walsingham, Cabinet Secretary, gestured Norman to a comfortable chair in the corner of his sprawling, handsomely appointed office. "Sherry? I know it's a bit early, but I think we've probably earnt it. I'm damned sure I have!"

Both men sat down and raised their glasses. Sir Peregrine said, "My secretary mentioned something about the Battle of Britain reunion. It can't be that time already! I still haven't recovered from the last one."

"Actually, no," Norman replied. "I didn't want to say on the phone."

Sir Peregrine nodded with satisfaction as Norman explained his manoeuvrings around the Donoghue Amendment, was appalled to hear that whispers about the coal restructure were already in circulation, and was momentarily stunned when Norman explained that Alf Burton might have uncovered the long lost Charlotte Morris manuscript.

"Now of all times, for that damned thing to surface," Sir Peregrine muttered.

"I have a plan," Norman said.

Sir Peregrine smiled. "I had a feeling you would. Tell me."

Norman referred to some brief handwritten notes, a draft terms of reference for the government's proposed agreement with Alf Burton. Sir Peregrine nodded his approval.

"I'm sure Margaret will agree. He's not such a bad chap, for a red. But we can't let things take their own course. We have to step in now. I know he's a friend of yours, but..."

"I understand," Norman said. "There's too much at stake."

"Right then, I'll phone Archie straight away."

Poor Alf, Norman thought, once Sir Archibald Prentice's shadowy department was let out of its box, there was no telling how things might end up.

***

The following afternoon, Alf was walking to his bus stop for the short ride from Westminster to his flat in Pimlico. He was feeling unusually pleased with himself: the previous night, Norman Armstrong's promised phone call had confirmed acceptance of his proposal for exclusive access in return for giving up the Morris manuscript and his continuing silence about coal stockpiling and proposed pit closures. All that remained now was to meet with his source and take delivery of the papers, to which end he was booked on a west-bound train out of London the following night.

He was thus contentedly preoccupied as he strode along Whitehall, his familiar mac acting like a billowing sail in the strong late afternoon breeze. He became aware of a Leyland Marina idling on a double yellow line just a few steps ahead of him, its kerbside rear door open.

"Oh, aye?" Alf uttered, stopping abruptly as a tall man stepped into his path.

"Good afternoon, Sir," the man said, "would you be requirin' a minicab at all?"

Alf noted the Ulster accent, the open denim jacket over a white T-shirt and long red hair, tied back but splaying in the wind like a horse's tail. "Nae thanks, bonny lad, now if you'll excuse me…"

At that moment, Alf felt strong hands grab both his arms from behind and something cold and hard pressed into the small of his back.

"Nice and easy now, Mr Burton," another Ulster voice whispered. "Into the car, there's a good lad."

Before he could resist, Alf was propelled through the open door into the back seat and within a split second two large, unsmiling men slipped in on either side of him, pinning him like a well-worn and shabby paperback between two heavy bookends. The man with the long red hair slid in behind the wheel. Alf noted that it took him two attempts to close the driver's door and the selection of first gear was accompanied by a harsh grinding noise and a muttered curse. The car lurched into the traffic and was gone.

***

Norman Armstrong looked up from his desk to see Charles Seymour in the doorway.

"There's a chap on the phone for you, Chief Whip, says his name is L Baker. Claims he's a friend of yours, and needs to speak to you urgently. He's most insistent. He doesn't sound like one of our sort of chaps at all. Shall I take a message or just tell him to bugger off?"

Norman thought for a moment, something rang a bell. Wait a minute, not L Baker, El Baker, Eric the cabbie. "No, put him straight through, please Charles."

"Really?" Charles remained sceptical, hesitated for a moment, then returned to the outer office to have the call transferred.

"Eric, my dear chap," Norman exclaimed. "What a pleasant surprise. How are you?"

"Fine thanks, Mr Armstrong. Listen, you know how you asked me to call you if there was something I thought you should know?" The loud traffic noise in the background told Norman that Eric was calling from a phone box near a busy road

"Yes, of course."

"I'll move the fucking cab in a minute!" Eric yelled, his attempt to cover the mouthpiece barely muffling his sergeant-major's yell. "I'm on important government business. Fuck off!" Eric uncovered the mouthpiece. "Sorry about that, Mr Armstrong, traffic warden poking his nose in, now, I just saw something a bit funny. The geezer you met at that iffy pub yesterday, I just saw some rough-looking lads bundle him into a Leyland Marina and take off. It's a bit odd I know, but it looked to me like he was being kidnapped."

"What?" Norman dropped his pen, his amusement over Eric's row with the traffic warden evaporating in an instant. "Are you sure it was the same man?"

"Yeah, I know him anyway. He's been in the cab a few times, he signed my copy of *Decade of Discontent*. Wrote a nice dedication, as a matter of fact. But you can't mistake that old mac he wears."

Bloody Archie Prentice and his gang of pirates, Norman thought. In the middle of rush hour, in front of God knows how many witnesses. A classic ill-thought out… "How long ago did this happen?"

"About twenty minutes ago. It took me a little while to find a phone box and then I had to put up with that tosser that didn't want to put me through…"

"Yes, yes, sorry about that. Is there anything else you can tell me?"

"Sorry Mr Armstrong, I was stuck in traffic quite a distance away, not far from the old Banqueting House on Whitehall it was. The car was a Marina, sort of a mustardy colour, I think one of the lads had long red hair, that's about all I can tell you. The car blew a bit of smoke from the exhaust. I was too far away to get the number. Sorry."

"No, no, you've done very well. Have you told anyone else, the police?"

"No, I thought it best to talk to you first."

"Good man, good man. Thank you, Eric, now I must ask you not to mention this to anyone. I can't say any more, suffice to say it may be a national security matter. Can I rely on you?"

"Of course, Mr Armstrong, schtum."

Norman hung up, his mind racing. "Fuck!" He exclaimed loudly. The outburst was so unfamiliar and out of character that Charles Seymour, the new junior whip, Janice Best, along with their office typist, Mrs Bliss, all converged on his doorway at a run to see if he was all right.

***

The elegant Victorian terraced townhouse to which Norman Armstrong returned each weeknight had been acquired by his grandfather, Colonel Fforbes Armstrong, nearly a century earlier.

In the heart of exclusive Knightsbridge, it had been purchased as a convenient home for when the Colonel was in London, a rare occurrence during a long and eventful career that had been spent largely in the colonies of southern Africa. The pied-a-terre had also been put to good use by the Colonel's brother Piers Armstrong, one-time First Lord of the Admiralty, and that generation's custodian of the family constituency.

Norman spent most of his evenings alone, escaping from the intense and unrelenting pressures that shaped his working days in the upstairs library, of which little had changed since it had been furnished in the late Victorian style by his grandfather and great uncle. The walls were papered in a dark red, almost maroon, behind an intricate filigree pattern. There was a large, ornately carved desk facing inward from near the front window, a corral of three armchairs in front of a large fireplace, and a floor-to-ceiling bookshelf extending the entire length of one wall displaying a number of rare, leather-bound first editions, political works and military histories. Opposite the shelves and next to the doorway, a large portrait surveyed the room: the old Colonel himself, resplendent in the white helmet and red coat of his regiment, the Queens Own Natal Rifles. Beneath the portrait there was a large sea chest, containing the living, breathing histories of over three centuries of warfare through the eyes of generations of Armstrong warriors. Diaries, memoirs and service records, many stained with the mud, dust and even blood of battle, provided immediate, firsthand accounts of battles and skirmishes from Marston Moor, Waterloo, Crimea and Southern Africa to the modern, mechanised wars of the twentieth century.

The chest itself, although around two centuries old, had been a late addition to the library, and had been presented to Norman just the previous year. The Chief Whip had been approached by a small group of senior naval officers, deeply concerned about proposed reductions to the surface fleet, and unhappy that their strategic objections were being ignored at the Ministry of Defence. The officers made their case to the Chief Whip, who in turn used his influence with the Prime Minister, urging her to suspend the cuts pending a more detailed feasibility study. In the meantime, the Falklands emergency erupted, vindicating the need for a large and flexible fleet. The officers were so grateful that they presented him with a sea chest once owned by one of Nelson's legendary Band of Brothers and hero of Trafalgar, Post Captain Sir Charles Speers. As well as the engraved plaque expressing their appreciation, they proudly pointed out the roughly carved inscription on the lid:

Chas. R Speers. Lieutenant

HMS Formidable 1791

In moments of reflection, Norman sometimes wondered whether that single act, his part in preserving a fleet that had the capability to respond quickly to the South Atlantic, would turn out to be his greatest contribution to the nation, other than his pivotal role in the election of Margaret Thatcher as Conservative leader in 1975.

Norman had been widely credited by his colleagues, and indeed the Prime Minister, for the effectiveness of the campaign that had led to their crushing election victory in the summer just gone. Norman and Sir Dick Billings, a crafty campaigner behind the scenes despite his tendency toward embarrassing public gaffes, had drafted a strategy that focused almost entirely on trumpeting the government's record, their professed resolution, rather than on making unsustainable election promises. It had proven to be a largely successful tactic. However, Alf Burton had written of his suspicions that beneath the scripted self-congratulations there must have been lurking a secret Tory manifesto detailing even more devastating cuts and austerity measures, an unwelcome post-election surprise for unsuspecting voters still dazzled by the reflected glory of the Falklands. Alf's speculation — Norman and Sir Dick's tight control of the campaign meant that for once he had no inside information one way or the other — was then given a good run in other media. But the Prime Minister went on to give a characteristically strong performance during a pre-election interview on BBC Television, refusing to be drawn on specifics and convincingly rebutting fears of any hidden agenda.

In public, Norman refused to concede that the government's popularity was so closely tied to the victory in the Falklands, but behind closed doors he was much more of a realist. He accepted the rather inconvenient truth that it was, in fact, the mass-transportation capabilities of the Royal Navy's intact surface fleet that not only made possible the timely liberation the Falklands, but, by that ability, also liberated an increasingly unpopular government from a slow and agonising march to inevitable electoral defeat. The Chancellor's first budget, delivered just weeks into their first term, had set out plans for an all-out attack on inflation by squeezing the money supply through a raft of punitive measures including severe cuts to government spending, interest rate hikes and a dramatic increase in the rate of VAT. It was an economic blueprint that Norman could enthusiastically champion from the refuge of the safest Tory seat in the country. However, the wider electorate took a very different view. Unemployment went on to exceed even the most pessimistic predictions. As the months went by, the government's popularity plummeted and a number of long-serving, loyal, MPs found themselves in real danger of losing their seats. The whips' office, meanwhile, was fully occupied with quelling the panic and division that was driving a wedge through the first-term Parliamentary Party. If it had not been for the overblown and evil ambitions of an Argentine dictator, Norman often reflected, well, it didn't bear thinking about...And, thank God for a Prime Minister who was not for turning!

Norman was approaching retirement age, and while Dick Billings had proven that retiring in one's sixties was far from a forgone conclusion, Norman had no intention of being a Billings-esque Father of the House in his dotage. He revelled in his role as Chief Whip, remained a devoted Thatcherite, and accepted that he had reached the pinnacle of his achievable goals. See this term through, he thought, the work would be done, the country reshaped, strong and confident. Then it would be time for him to bow quietly out, avoid the Lords as his father had done, and quietly fade into placid domestic mediocrity, contemplating what might have been.

Norman, it now appeared, would be the last in the long family line of warrior-statesmen, his son Rick having expressed absolutely no interest in either the military or the political life, despite Norman's strongly communicated admonition that their only offspring had a sacred responsibility to carry on the family tradition. Rick's mother had been firmly on their son's side and had silenced Norman on the matter once and for all some years before.

"It's not Rick's fault that he's an only child in a family where the typical male," she scolded her husband, "spends half his life stabbing people in the front on the battlefield, then the other half stabbing them in the back in Westminster. Rick has made the decision that he doesn't want to do either. That's fine by me and it should be fine by you. That's all there is to say on the matter."

Norman threw up his hands, and Rick gratefully went his own way. He now ran a public relations firm, a very successful and lucrative one by all accounts, although Norman had little, if any, understanding of what they actually did. All that the perplexed father could see was that Rick seemed to spend most of his time with a lot of effeminate musicians, artistic eccentrics and odd bohemian types, a pointless waste of his family talent in Norman's view but, recognising this battle as well and truly lost, he gave every impression of his ongoing blessing.

Eileen Armstrong, for her part, had been a reluctant, albeit supportive, participant in her husband's career, choosing to stay away from London in their comfortable family home in the constituency. On the site of the mediaeval village of Stonebridge, the Armstrongs' immediate neighbourhood, like much of the wider constituency itself, was the suburban embodiment of manicured middle-class aspiration: higher income families living in large houses amongst fanatically maintained lawns and gardens, where social problems had the decency to remain quietly hidden behind closed doors. It was an environment in which Norman and Eileen found contented sanctuary, a fortress of undisturbed serenity in a turbulent country, but one which Rick found stifling, false, and often deeply offensive to his liberal sensibilities, and from which he had escaped at his earliest opportunity.

Norman therefore led a lonely and somewhat monastic existence during the weeks of parliamentary activity, spending most evenings alone, reading, writing and keeping up with the news on television when not working late at his office. Once or twice a month he would dine with Alf and Dolly Burton at their flat, Dolly feeling that it must be bleak and lonely spending solitary evenings in what she regarded as a dark and depressing

Victorian museum. Alf was far less sympathetic toward Norman's domestic arrangements, but genuinely enjoyed his company and valued his friendship, and always took the opportunity to at least try to broaden Norman's interest in music, which extended no further than Vera Lynn and Val Doonican. Alf's own tastes — and extensive record collection — tended more toward Status Quo, Elvis, the Animals, Geordie, The Who and the Rolling Stones but he had now accepted that Norman's musical appreciation, like his emerging social conscience, was a work in progress and still had a long, long way to go.

No matter how late Norman arrived home, he would always phone Eileen, a routine they had clung to as long as Norman had been in the parliament.

"Hello darling, how was your day?" she would always ask, her voice soft and with a loneliness-masking façade of brightness.

"The usual shambles of course," was his standard reply, before the conversation meandered pleasurably between local matters — Eileen provided invaluable support in Norman's constituency office — and the latest family news. Despite the crippling demands of the parliamentary life, and the fact that both husband and wife were strong-willed to the point of stubbornness, the marriage had been happy and enduring. They had first met in the latter half of the war: both had been pilots. Following the Battle of Britain, Norman transferred to Bomber Command under Wing Commander Archie Prentice, now Sir Archie, and the head of a government intelligence department that everyone knew about, but the existence of which was universally denied. Eileen flew for the Air Transport Auxiliary, delivering planes from the factories to airfields across the country and ferrying aircraft between locations in response to operational demand. On one very warm midsummer's day in 1943, Eileen had just delivered a spanking new Spitfire to the aerodrome that was also home to Norman's Lancaster squadron. Norman, along with his navigator Perry Walsingham and bomb aimer Ronnie Coburn, were slouched in deck chairs, taking in the smell of the freshly cut grass, smoking and enjoying the sunshine and cloudless blue sky.

"You know, chaps," Norman commented as Eileen strode past, her hair sculpted into a decidedly unusual arrangement, having been moulded in the sweaty confines of her flying helmet, "It's a rum do, letting these women fly. They should be in the mess, serving drinks and making sandwiches for real pilots." She halted, then turned and walked over to the reclining airmen, stopping right in front of Flight Lieutenant Armstrong and meeting his smug gaze with a defiant stare of her own. She was close enough for Norman to observe how nicely she filled out her flying suit, and he could smell an unexpectedly arousing combination of aviation fuel and American perfume.

"I'd be perfectly happy to make sandwiches for a real pilot," she said, standing over Norman and taking note of his purple and white Distinguished Flying Cross ribbon. "Perhaps you could show me where I might find one!" With a lightning quick motion, she kicked the leg from under Norman's deckchair sending him sprawling backwards, arms flailing, on to the grass. Perry Walsingham burst into laughter, while Ronnie Coburn simply stared in open mouthed wonder. To Norman's acute embarrassment, a small group of mechanics and a refuelling crew had also been watching, and they applauded, cheered and whistled enthusiastically.

The following evening, Norman returned to his quarters to find a small parcel, neatly wrapped in brown paper and tied with string. Inside was a Spam sandwich, inedible as he soon discovered, but the perfumed note with a telephone number he also found inside the package held far more promise. They were married a little over a year later, a small affair attended by their families and with Archie Prentice, Peregrine Walsingham, Ronnie Coburn and a small gathering of ATA pilots forming a guard of honour.

Their son, Richard Fforbes Piers Armstrong, named after Norman's father, grandfather and great uncle, was born exactly nine months after VE Day. Medical advice resulted in the Armstrong family line being restricted to one heir and no spare for the second generation in a row. As a result, Eileen understood what it cost her husband to graciously concede the looming end of an influential military and political dynasty that could be traced in a direct line back to the Parliamentarian armies of the Civil War and subsequent judicious change of allegiance just prior to the Restoration.

Norman was, if nothing else, a rigid creature of habit, so the change in his evening routine was a sure sign that he was feeling deeply unsettled over the apparent kidnapping of Alf Burton. He had tried unsuccessfully that afternoon to contact Sir Archie Prentice and Peregrine Walsingham, but neither had been available, only serving to heighten Norman's feelings of agitation. Norman enjoyed privileged and immediate access to the nation's most powerful politicians and civil servants, and to be politely fobbed off by underlings was highly unusual and deeply concerning. For the first time in living memory, the first call he made on his arrival home was not to Eileen, but to an old friend from the RAF, Ron Coburn, who was now an Assistant Commissioner in the Metropolitan Police.

"Ron," he said after keeping small talk and pleasantries to the bare minimum that politeness required. "Sorry to bother you at home, but I need to ask you something, in the strictest confidence."

"Of course, Norman. How can I help?"

"Do you know if there were any incidents recorded this afternoon on Whitehall? Any disturbance, maybe a possible kidnapping even? Dangerous driving. Anything at all?"

"I'll see what I can find out and get right back to you."

Norman was thankful that Ron hadn't asked for more details. He paced the length and breadth of the library while he waited for the return call. Within five minutes, the old black telephone on Norman's desk jangled, he pounced and picked up the handpiece at the end of the first ring.

"The duty officer at the Yard made a few calls for me," the Assistant Commissioner informed him. "Nothing at all. What's this about, Norman, if I can ask? Wait a minute, my beeper's going off. That might be something."

"Ron, if what I think has happened, has happened, that will be the Commissioner. He'd have just been contacted by the Home Secretary, with instructions to find out what you're up to."

"The Home Secretary? Jesus, Norman, what's going on?"

"Relax, I'll take full responsibility. Tell the Commissioner that you were acting on a request from me. There'll be no further consequences."

"That doesn't sit well, Norman, I don't want to drop you in it. Is everything all right? Is there anything I can do?"

Norman was touched by the genuine concern in his old friend's voice. Even after forty years, the old camaraderie was still there, unshakeable. "Honestly, Ron, its fine. Alf Burton's got himself into a bit of a pickle. I think our old friend and CO Archie

Prentice might be up to his old tricks again. I best not say any more at this point."

"Prentice? Tread carefully then, Norman, he's a tricky customer. You know, he still refers to me as Young Ronnie, like he did when I first joined the squadron in '43. It got up my nose then, as well."

Having completed the phone call with Coburn, Norman relaxed somewhat, taking some comfort from the feeling that he had regained at least a degree of control over unfolding events. He poured a single measure of Scotch from his grandfather's decanter and sat behind his desk. He estimated that the phone would be ringing within the next five minutes. It was, in fact, seven minutes and forty three seconds.

"Good evening, Archie," Norman said as soon as he picked up the phone. "You took your time."

"Never mind that," Sir Archibald Prentice's palpable irritation gave Norman a high degree of satisfaction. "I've just had to put the wind up the Home Secretary — young Ronnie Coburn's been poking his nose into matters that don't concern him — apparently at your behest. What do you think you're playing at?"

"Archie, the man is an Assistant Commissioner of the Metropolitan Police. If a crime is committed on his patch, I'd have thought that it would be perfectly reasonable for him to make enquiries."

"Let's not waste each other's time. How much do you know about what happened with Burton, and how did you find out?"

"You're not the only one with informants around the place," Norman countered. "All I know is that your keystone cops snatched him this afternoon, no doubt to get to the bottom of this manuscript business. I'm just trying to find out what's happening, and to make sure he's okay. And, can I say, to grab him in broad daylight in front of God knows how many witnesses, virtually in sight of the Houses of Parliament, even by the standards of your department is reckless and foolhardy in the extreme. You can't just seize someone of Alf Burton's stature and expect it to go unnoticed."

"I agree," Prentice said, "very amateurish."

"And another thing...What?" The intelligence chief's admission caught Norman off guard.

"It wasn't us, Norman, for God's sake. You were always prone to going off half-cocked. How you survived the war, I'll never know. If you get off your high horse for long enough, I'll tell you what happened. It appears that he's been taken by an IRA splinter, calling themselves the Irish Revolutionary Brotherhood. This is the first time we've been aware of them, operationally speaking."

"How do you know?" Norman asked. "Why would they want Alf? Anyway, it doesn't make any sense. Wait, my doorbell is ringing, I'll have to..."

"That'll be one of my chaps, he'll drive you to Number Ten. I'll be briefing the Prime Minister and Cabinet Secretary in thirty minutes. We'll discuss it then."

***

Sir Peregrine Walsingham, Sir Archibald Prentice, Norman Armstrong and the Prime Minister met in a briefing room adjacent to the Prime Minister's private office. The lighting was soft from a number of shaded standard lamps while coffee and sandwiches were laid out on a low table between some comfortable armchairs.

"Will the Home Secretary be joining us?" Sir Archibald asked, after the initial pleasantries had been exchanged and coffee poured.

"Not tonight," replied the Prime Minister. "I want to keep the details between ourselves, at least for the moment. Now Archie, perhaps you would be kind enough to tell us everything you know."

"Thank you, Prime Minister. This afternoon, Alf Burton, senior lobby correspondent and national political editor for the Donoghue Media chain, was kidnapped on Whitehall. Our sources have told us that a group identifying themselves as the Irish Revolutionary Brotherhood is behind it, although at this stage there's been no formal claim of responsibility, and no demands have been made. There's no reason to believe that Mr Burton has been harmed at this stage, we expect to receive some communication from the kidnappers in due course. In terms of motive, we're examining a number of options, but we can't rule out the fact that the Irish might also have become aware that he was chasing the Morris manuscript. After all, we don't have any details about who he was dealing with as part of his own investigations, or who his own source is. They might have been hawking it all over the place, for all we know. It's not unreasonable to think that Irish republicans were aware, either by accident or design. They might see a golden opportunity to destabilise the monarchy and government, assuming the manuscript's contents are as inflammatory as generations of rumours have implied."

"Norman," Sir Peregrine said, "You know Alf better than any of us. Can you think of any other reason that he might be on the radar of Irish terrorists?"

"Nothing that immediately comes to mind," Norman replied. "He's always been very even-handed in his reporting of the Troubles, he condemns violence on both sides. He's only really written spasmodically on the Northern Ireland situation, and then only from the political perspective. I think he quietly supports a united Ireland. I can't think of anything he's written or said that might put a target on his back."

"Right then," Sir Archibald said. "My department will take it from here. We'll coordinate with Special Branch, RUC and the other usual agencies. Norman, Perhaps I can ask you a few questions, general background that might be helpful?"

"Of course, anything I can do to help," Norman replied.

At that point the Prime Minister made to retire upstairs to the residence; a mountain of briefing papers awaited her attention, and would keep her up until the early hours. She expressed her appreciation for the update, requested to be kept informed of developments, then passed on her love to Eileen and promised Norman a weekend invitation to Chequers in the not too distant future.

"What's happening about Alf's wife, Dolly?" Norman asked after they had said their goodnights to the Prime Minister.

"Sir Eddie Donoghue is with her as we speak," The Cabinet Secretary replied. "I phoned him earlier this evening. He's also agreed to have a team comb through Alf's recent articles and tapes of his radio programme to see if there are any clues."

"What are we doing publicly?" Norman asked next.

"The Northern Ireland Office will be making a full statement tomorrow."

"We shouldn't underestimate the public reaction," Norman commented. "Alf is quite a celebrity. His articles, books and radio programmes reach millions. He's very popular. This is going to be a big thing."

"Agreed," said the Cabinet Secretary.

"What I'd like to know," Sir Archibald interjected, "is how a red radical like Burton comes to work for a man like Eddie Donoghue. I mean, Sir Eddie's never been backward in expressing his personal support for a strong Tory agenda. And he puts his money where his mouth is. Am I right in thinking he's the largest individual donor for the Conservatives?

"Yes that's true, but Sir Eddie has always held his media interests at arm's length," Norman explained. "Alf told me that when he was first headhunted back in '77, Eddie promised him complete editorial independence, and has, I gather, been mostly true to his word. In any case, Alf is no longer the socialist crusader that he was during the forties and fifties. In those days he might just as well have been Nye Bevan's press secretary. These days his work is generally pretty well balanced, in my estimation, and he's built Donoghue's political reporting unit up to be the best in country, feeding his newspapers, radio networks and regional ITV franchises. They also sell-on a good deal of their coverage to other networks, both at home and abroad. He's worth a lot of money to Eddie's media division, particularly now that Donoghue Publishing handles his books as well. He was a good catch, and it was a very smart move on Eddie's part. In fact, Rupert's been after him for years — offered a massive contract, apparently — but to no avail."

"Do you think," Sir Archibald asked, "just playing devil's advocate, that Burton could have set this all up himself? A big publicity stunt over the Morris manuscript?"

"Alf may have a few funny ideas, but he's no traitor, and he's no militant republican, in the Irish sense or constitutionally,"

Norman responded emphatically. "He understood, understands I should say, that the surrender of the manuscript to us is in the national interest. Besides, I believe he never intended to use the manuscript for anything other than as leverage towards his deal for Number Ten access."

The intelligence chief clearly wasn't convinced. "Can a leopard really change his spots that dramatically? He's written and said some highly questionable things over the years. We have quite a file on him. Don't forget, he once said that Nye Bevan was being kind when he referred to Tories as vermin and called for our, sorry I mean your, extinction." Norman smiled at Prentice's self-correction. As a top intelligence officer, Prentice was supposed to be apolitical, like the Cabinet Secretary.

"Look, Archie," Norman argued, "You don't have to tell me. Friends or not, I've been on the wrong end of his commentary on more than one occasion. He once called me the Stonebridge Skinhead over some comments I made about antisocial behaviour in the black communities."

"Following the death of King George the Sixth," Sir Archie continued, putting on his heavy-rimmed glasses and consulting some notes in his lap, "he called on the Labour Party to look back to their 1923 conference, when they had discussed the abolition of the monarchy, now that it was clear that George Lansbury's anticipated peaceful social revolution wasn't going to materialise. He also wrote that he believed that a fair society could only be achieved under a socialist republic free of, and I quote, 'the anachronistic shackles of an evil class system intent on crushing the ambitions of the working class'. And that's just the tip of the iceberg. At one point, he as good as accused the Conservative side of politics of, and I quote once again: 'a concerted campaign of genocide against the northern working class', based on the death rate in depressed areas."

"For God's sake, Archie," Norman huffed with exasperation. "That was over thirty years ago, I'd hate to have some of the things I've said thrown back in my face after all this time. His background is very different from ours: he grew up in a very different world. Have you read his book on the Jarrow Crusade? The conditions in some areas of the North during the Depression made even the worst aspects of Dickensian London look like a picnic. Growing up surrounded by death, disease, and chronic unemployment — around seventy percent, I think, from memory, in Jarrow itself — has to affect your general outlook. Having said all this, though, if you think that Alf might be harbouring a secret republican agenda and sees this manuscript as a way to further that cause, you're way off the mark. He might have been right behind a President Attlee, Bevan, Cripps or even Churchill, believe it or not. But times have changed, and, as far as I understand his current position on that issue, he thinks that the constitutional arrangements as they stand might be imperfect, but are as good as we can hope for."

"Big of him, I'm sure," Sir Archie muttered.

"He's a patriot, in his own way," Norman continued. "I'll also remind you that he risked as much as any of us during the war. We could at least shoot back when we were under fire, he was a sitting duck in those old tubs criss-crossing the Atlantic."

Sir Archie frowned. "Well, you may be right, and I respect your judgement, of course, but my job is to be suspicious, so I'll keep an open mind. The most important thing is to secure this damned manuscript."

"And to bring Alf home safely," Norman reminded him.

"Yes, that too," Sir Archie added, with no great enthusiasm.

"Well then, let's hope this Irish Revolutionary Brotherhood make contact soon," Sir Peregrine said, signalling the end of the meeting by standing up. "By the way," he went on, "how is the Northern Ireland Secretary? I hear he's been taken ill."

"Not too good apparently," Norman replied. "Charles Seymour is at the hospital as we speak, finding out how he is. An ambulance carted him off from the House this afternoon. Heart attack apparently."

"Oh dear me," lamented Sir Peregrine. "That leaves his department rather depleted. Thank God for their Permanent Secretary."

"And for Stanley Smee," Norman added, eliciting a dark chuckle from Sir Peregrine.

***

Stanley Smee took his seat on the front bench in the packed House of Commons, three Ministers away from the Prime Minister. In his hand was a statement that the Permanent Secretary at the Northern Ireland Office had written for him. His palms were damp with perspiration, and his insides were being compressed under the weight of a bowel-loosening sense of panic. To be a junior minister at the Northern Ireland Office was one thing, but the sudden, unexpected absence of the Secretary of State had elevated the former unofficial leader of the Awkward Squad to astonishing heights of responsibility.

"Bunch up, damn you!" Smee looked up to see Sir Dick Billings urging the MP on his right to make room, allowing Sir Dick to squeeze roughly between the two, forcing his space with his elbows. "Thought I'd come and offer you some support, old cock," Sir Dick said, while Smee reflected that the so-called support of his old boss was something he could quite happily have done without.

"Your security detail in place?" Sir Dick asked. Stanley Smee nodded, then Dick went on gleefully, "You're now a bigger assassination target than the Prime Minister herself. Better keep your head down, eh? Those Irish bogtrotters don't miss very often!" Before Smee could offer anything in reply, the Speaker broke in above the hum of conversation in the Chamber.

"Order! Order! A statement from the Minister representing the Secretary of State for Northern Ireland. Mr Stanley Smee!"

Smee stood up and accidentally knocked his glass, spilling water on his trousers. Dick Billings snorted with amusement while the Acting Northern Ireland Secretary concentrated hard on stopping his hands from shaking and his knees from buckling.

"Mr Speaker," was supposed to emerge confidently from his dry mouth, but all that was audible was something of a strangled squeak. Surprisingly, Dick Billings placed a steadying hand on his arm and muttered, "You'll be fine, lad, just let 'em have it."

"Mr Speaker." Smee took some comfort from the sudden steadiness in his voice. "I inform the House that yesterday, the national political editor for Donoghue Media, Mr Alf Burton, was kidnapped by an Irish Nationalist group identifying themselves as the Irish Revolutionary Brotherhood." The House erupted into gasps, but quickly fell silent under the Speaker's admonition for order. "I trust the House will understand that security considerations prevent me from offering too much detail at this time. However, I assure the House, Mr Burton's loved ones and the nation, that this government is doing everything in its power to bring him safely home." Cries of 'hear, hear' burst from both sides of the aisle, in a rare moment of bipartisan harmony. "Mr Burton is a valued member of our Westminster family," Smee continued, enjoying and rising to his sudden and unexpected control of the chamber. "We've all learned from his best-selling books, his newspaper columns and weekly radio programme. Mr Burton is a war hero, having been a wireless telegraphist in the merchant navy, sailing the dangerous waters of the Atlantic, the Mediterranean and the convoy routes to Murmansk during the last war, before which he fought fascism with the International Brigade in Spain. He has been a lobby correspondent since 1947: a champion of democracy and I assure the House, and indeed the nation, that nothing will undermine this government's resolute approach in our fight against terror at home or abroad." Smee sat down, amid emphatic cries of "hear, hear" and MPs waving their order papers, their outstretched arms like a forest disturbed by a strong wind.

Stanley Smee looked to his left, and met the Prime Minister's eyes. She smiled and nodded in appreciation. Even Dick Billings, eyebrows raised in surprise, muttered: "Not bad, I suppose," which, for Stanley Smee, was the highest praise imaginable.

At that moment, assassination target or not, Stanley Smee felt more formidable than Winston Churchill.

CHAPTER THREE

"Sir Eddie Donoghue is on the line, Chief Whip."

"Thank you, Mrs Bliss, I'll take it right away. And close the door, please."

In the days since Alf Burton's kidnapping, it hadn't gone unnoticed in the whips' office that, for the first time in anyone's memory, the Chief Whip's door was shut a good deal of the time.

"Strange and unsettling times," Charles Seymour remarked, eyeing the closed door to Norman's office, as Mrs Bliss returned to her typewriter.

"I'm sure he's just worried about Mr Burton," she replied.

"Perhaps," Charles speculated, before returning to his own office.

***

"Any news, Norman?" Sir Eddie asked almost straight away.

"None at all, I'm afraid."

Eddie was not surprised, and had been working up a theory of his own. "There's something very strange going on here, Norman. Do you want to know what I think? Well, I'll tell you. This has nothing to do with Irish republicans. This is a government job. Alf has upset someone and the security services are teaching him a lesson. This old shite about the Irish republicans is a cover, we both know it's been done before. They asked me to have my senior editors trawl through Alf's articles and tapes of his radio programme, I'm sure that's just to shut me up and keep me occupied. And listen to this, Norman, none of my sources in Northern Ireland, the Republic, even Boston or New York, have ever even heard of the Irish Revolutionary Brotherhood. The government line is full of holes. As you know, I've offered a reward of one million pounds for information leading to Alf's safe return, blanket coverage in my newspapers, City Radio network and on my TV stations. Not a word. What does that tell you?"

"I've had the same suspicion, Eddie," Norman confessed. "And between ourselves, I've received an assurance from the highest level that the security services are not involved."

"Can I ask who from?"

"I can't tell you that, I'm sorry. But Eddie, this is a big thing, you can tell by the press coverage across the board. The government is doing everything it can to get to the bottom of this, multiple agencies are involved. I was at the initial briefing, it was held at Number Ten with the Prime Minister. That shows you that it is being handled at the top level. The Prime Minister herself is monitoring the investigation. As soon as I know something, I promise you, Eddie, you'll be the first to know, after Dolly of course."

"Well, I can't ask more than that, Norman, and I take you at your word. I know that you're about the best-informed member of the government — if you don't know, then no one does. All I ask, Norman, is that you remind anyone who'll listen what a valuable friend I am to this government, and that I will be very grateful to get my best reporter back."

"I'm doing that already," Norman assured him.

"I had no doubt, had no doubt," Sir Eddie replied. "You know he actually has a fan club? The Westminster Watchers, named after his newspaper column. They've camped out in reception at my Fleet Street offices, some sort of vigil. They look like escapees from the Darby and Joan Club."

"Yes, they've been to Westminster as well. I had my new junior whip Janice Best give them a tour of the Houses of Parliament and a cup of tea. They went away happy enough."

"Well, life goes on. I did want to thank you for your part in seeing the Local Government Efficiency Bill through, it was a relief to see that pass. Sending that gobshite Smee off to Northern Ireland was a master stroke: even he can't make that mess any worse than it is already. The Donoghue Constructions' share price is heading up to record levels. I have a whole raft of projects ready to kick off. I wish you'd taken up my offer of a few shares. That would have been your pension taken care of."

"Quite enough of that kind of talk, Eddie, you know that's not how I operate. The bill is in the national interest, that's good enough for me."

"In my case, a happy confluence of national and self-interest, you might say. Anyway, our old friend Dickie Billings has a big smile on his face."

"For God's sake, Eddie, not on the phone."

"Relax, Norman, all I meant was that Dickie was happy to see the bill pass, nothing sinister. You do worry too much."

"Right, then." Norman consciously steered the conversation in a safer direction. "The Prime Minister would welcome a big announcement on jobs some time in the spring. Think you might be able to accommodate?"

"By the spring? That shouldn't be a problem, my people are working on the figures now. I don't think you'll be disappointed. By the way, do you think there might be a photo opportunity with Margaret in the offing? It looks good for the shareholders, and keeps those City leeches at bay."

"Eddie, if the figures are that good, I'll get you a bank holiday weekend at Chequers."

"That'll do me! Now, turning to our cable television roll-out. I've been giving some thought to your suggestion of a channel devoted entirely to news and politics. I think I can make it work. We can feed off our news coverage from our ITV regions, newspapers and radio, and fill in the rest with a good dose of commentary and opinion. And, Norman, I'm talking about our kind of opinion. A strong editorial line, for the Conservative side."

"Not before time, Eddie." Norman had long been a strong critic of the BBC and had been particularly incensed by their coverage of the Falklands, which he considered way too even-handed, leading him to break with the Chief Whips' practice of staying out of the public eye, and publicly to question whose side the national broadcaster was actually on. A genuinely conservative news channel was just what the country needed, in Norman's view, to bring some common sense to the national discourse.

"I think you've always been too reticent about using your own media, Eddie," Norman said. "Rupert has never been shy about expressing a political opinion, and it hasn't done his bank balance any harm. There are other papers that take an opposing view, it all balances out. Between your papers, radio and television, you reach millions every day. It's a waste of a unique resource. We could have used a bit more support from that quarter during the last term."

"We've argued about this before." Sir Eddie's tone took on an air of impatient frustration. "Look at where my ITV franchises are. It's not exactly blue-ribbon Conservative heartland. If I start waving the Tory flag, people will be switching off in droves, and who could blame them? My television stations are invited guests in people's homes, Norman, that's why I insist that all of my presenters are impeccably groomed and dressed, speak well and politely, and respect the audience by keeping their opinions to themselves. The figures speak for themselves. My television stations, radio and newspapers reach across all demographics meaning that I can sell advertising to anyone. Objectivity is the key to reaching the widest audience, regardless of what that colonial carpetbagger Murdoch might have to say. Alf Burton's political unit was, that is to say is, the bedrock of my news division, which brings in the cash hand over fist. Why? Because it sticks it to both sides equally — the punters love that. But leaving that aside, Norman, I think I do more than my fair share for the cause, wouldn't you say? I could buy the Houses of Parliament for the amount of money I've donated over the years."

"Of course, Eddie, no one is questioning your loyalty, or your commitment."

"I should fucking well hope not!" There was a moment of awkward silence, before Eddie continued, his tone softer. "I apologise, Norman. That was out of order. This Burton situation has got me rattled…no excuse. I'm sorry for speaking to you like that."

"We're all feeling the strain, Eddie," Norman replied. "Think no more about it."

"But," Eddie went on, brightening up. "This cable channel will be a different animal. A paying audience, a paying London audience, will subscribe on the basis of our editorial platform, so we won't be shy about our real alliances there. Now, one last thing, Norman. The way things are going, I'll need someone to handle public relations for me. The days when you can just muddle through by getting reporters pissed at your expense and hoping they say nice things about you are gone. There are an awful lot of misunderstandings circulating about the recent planning amendments, and, no doubt, when this cable TV deal goes public, the usual suspects will be running around causing trouble, whipping up outrage, although, thanks to you, most of them are now out of the way. Nevertheless, it's getting more and more important to keep public opinion on my side. You understand all this, Norman, you're the masters of a cleverly constructed campaign. A real professional outfit is what I need, to get me good coverage right across the board. Any suggestions? I hear there's a young fellow named Armstrong who's doing very well in that caper."

Norman smiled. "So I hear. By all means, call him, but leave me well out of it. If he thought that his old dad had any part in this he'd run a mile. He's obsessed with making his own way, on his own merits or not at all."

"Sharper than a serpent's choppers, eh Norman? Don't worry. I understand, I'll set the wheels in motion. My daughter Erin will handle it. The next generation barking at our heels already, eh?"

**

As several more days passed with no word from the kidnappers, Norman became increasingly preoccupied. He was starting to feel like he had been played for a fool, and that the briefing with the Prime Minister had been all part of a charade to shut him up and keep him out of the way. He had no doubt that the Prime Minister was being kept equally at arm's length, protected from the uncomfortable reality by her top civil servants. In normal circumstances Norman was the ultimate government insider, trusted and admired for his judgement and discretion, privy to secrets and plans well beyond his remit as Chief Whip. But now, for the first time since the Tory election losses almost a decade earlier, he was feeling very much on the outside, and was finding it all quite difficult to comprehend.

He was now firmly of the opinion that Sir Eddie, blissful in his complete ignorance of the chain of events leading to Alf's kidnapping, had actually stumbled upon the truth, albeit from a completely incorrect premise, in line with Norman's initial theory that Sir Archie Prentice had been behind it all along. This posed a real, deadly problem. Irish Republicans were one thing, they could at least be talked into something resembling reason if the circumstances were right. Archie Prentice's department, on the other hand...

With the normal channels of information closed off and increasingly desperate for news, Norman had, on the advice of Eileen, swallowed his pride and made an appointment with the Acting Secretary of State for Northern Ireland, Stanley Smee. Having to go cap in hand to the very man Norman had ritually humiliated just days before was one of the more uncomfortable experiences he had endured in recent times. Smee had been gracious, Norman privately conceded that he might not have been quite so magnanimous had the positions been reversed, but it soon became apparent that Smee knew even less than Norman did, and was merely reading from a script provided by his Permanent Secretary: in effect, the script originally written by Sir Archie Prentice and communicated via the Cabinet Secretary.

A tearful and desperate phone call from Dolly Burton had done nothing to settle Norman's unusually frazzled nerves, during which Dolly had begged him to do something, anything at all. "He always says that you're the smartest, toughest man in parliament," she sobbed, and after blowing her nose loudly into the telephone, continued. "Please, Norman, help us. My poor wee Alf, what are they doing to him? Please, Norman!"

His confidence and sense of purpose faltering, Norman realised with alarm that he was losing touch with the complicated raft of legislation that the government was working on. Luckily Charles Seymour had stepped up, and Janice Best, a happy accident in terms of her appointment, which had been a tactical move to separate her from the Awkward Squad, was proving competent and extremely hard-working. Her eloquent and charming approach was in stark contrast to Charles Seymour's sneering aggression and the unlikely pairing was proving to be a highly effective combination in marshalling the backbenchers.

Norman came to a decision, and buzzed Mrs Bliss. "Is Mr Seymour in his office?" he asked.

"Yes, Chief Whip," she replied, "He's just got back from the Commons with Miss Best."

"Ask him to come into my office, please, right away."

"Yes, Chief Whip."

Charles was seated opposite Norman within one minute, the office door closed behind him.

"Charles, I need you to take over," Norman said, without any introduction.

"What? I, er…take over? What do you mean exactly?" It was rare for Charles Seymour to be lost for words.

"Just for a little while. I'm too preoccupied with this Burton business to be much use. Between ourselves, I intend to discreetly look into things myself."

"I'm glad," Charles replied straight away. "If anyone can get to the bottom of this, you can. We all like Mr Burton, he needs someone like you in his corner. Good luck, but go carefully. These Irish are mad bastards, I don't have to tell you. Look at what happened to poor Airey Neave, right in the midst of Westminster for God's sake! You can rely on me, Norman, I won't let you down."

Norman felt a strong urge to confide his suspicions. There was no one he trusted more than his deputy, but almost immediately, he changed his mind. The fewer people caught up in this dark and increasingly dangerous mess, the better. "I have complete faith in you, Charles, I hope you know that," he reassured his deputy. "There are a couple of things I need you to do."

"Yes, of course. Anything."

"I want you to take another look at advisors, researchers and general staffers. We have a good idea who Donoghue's people are, but we need to keep an eye on who his enemies might be. Look at anyone who's not part of the permanent civil service establishment, even the drivers, cleaners and tea ladies. Every department. Let's bring the dirt book completely up to date."

"I'll get on to that straight away."

"Also, we can't afford any unfortunate rumours or public disquiet about our closeness with Donoghue. Some people are still agitating over the Local Government Efficiency Bill, not to mention the fact that Donoghue Publishing and Broadcasting has just been granted prime franchises for the new cable television network, ahead of the legislation. We can't afford anything to come out that might look like a conflict of interest. Keep a close eye on Dickie Billings, there are times when he needs to be protected from himself. Smee's replacement as Dick's PPS is a good chap, one of ours. He'll keep you informed."

"Do you think there's something funny going on between Sir Dick and Eddie Donoghue?"

"If there is," Norman said, "they'd be smart enough to make it untraceable, but I don't want to take any chances. If things are going to blow up in our faces, we need to have a contingency plan in place to deal with it."

"I understand. What do I tell people if they ask where you are?"

"Say that I'm working on plans for the party conference."

***

That night, Norman sat at his grandfather's desk in the upstairs library and considered the current position. In the normal course of events his life was built on discipline and routine. The nightly phone call to Eileen, one measure of Scotch, working at his desk under the watchful eyes of generations of Armstrongs, the hopeful anticipation of a repeat of *Dad's Army*, the *Nine O'clock News* on the BBC and then to bed. The routine that had underpinned his life, and his success, was now in an uncommon state of disarray.

He lifted a silver framed photograph from the corner of the desk and held it. It was his favourite: Richard and Norman Armstrong, proud father and elated son, on the day that Norman had been elected to the family constituency vacated by his retiring father. He would need every last shred of his inherited wisdom and judgement to steer his way through this current situation, he thought.

Norman knew that he owed much of his political talent to his father, a popular and hard-working local MP and a senior member of Churchill's War Cabinet, his most celebrated accomplishment in a long and distinguished career. Norman replaced the photo and eyed the one of his great uncle, Piers Armstrong, one time First Lord of the Admiralty and brother of Norman's grandfather, the famous colonial solder Colonel Fforbes Armstrong. It was a constant battle to live up to the towering legacy of generations of Armstrongs who had been at the centre of politics and Empire for centuries. Even now, approaching his mid-sixties and with more than three decades in the parliament behind him, Norman struggled under the suffocating shadow of their collective achievements. There were times when he privately acknowledged that Rick was well out of it.

Norman had selected a book from the shelves, it was open on the desk in front of him. It was Alf Burton's exhaustive study of post-war transatlantic politics. He smiled. Trust Alf to call it *Working Class Heroes*, in honour of its principal protagonists, Ernie Bevin, Harry Truman, and Aneurin Bevan. Norman had opened the seven hundred page opus to the page on which Alf had written his personal dedication.

To the living proof that *not* all Tories are no-good, brain dead gobshites after all,

    Your old marra,

    Alf

The note referred back to the very first time they had met. Norman had just been elected to the Commons in the general election of 1950, while Alf had already cemented his reputation as a strident Welfare State advocate and sworn enemy of the Tories. Alf always made it a point to speak to newly-minted MPs, he found their enthusiasm and idealism a tonic against his increasing cynicism and slow descent into disillusioned acceptance that his optimism following the 1945 election was dying a slow death.

Alf first confronted the young MP by forcefully asserting that it was a disgrace that one family could control a constituency for generations, and that now, thank God, this sense of entitlement was being shattered by a new generation who were achieving power through merit rather than because of who their father was or what public school they went to.

Norman retorted that Alf shouldn't get too comfortable in his failing socialist paradise. The government's hold on power was tenuous at best, and it wouldn't be long before the Conservatives were back in their rightful place, running the country. He then added that he had been democratically elected by a large margin, and that he had previously fought for his country in the RAF, unlike the reporter who, in Norman's assessment, was probably a conscientious objector, or even a traitor, and had undoubtedly spent the entire war crouching in a communist funk hole writing adoring letters to Stalin. In fact, Norman went on to suggest, if Mr Burton was so keen on the way the reds did things, he would be perfectly welcome to jump on the next plane and bugger off to Russia, where he would unquestionably feel more at home. And besides, Norman concluded, it was a bit rich for a Welfare State devotee to be bemoaning others' perceived sense of entitlement.

At that point, Norman felt that he had won the argument convincingly and turned to walk away, however, Alf had no intention of yielding, having taken a good deal of offence at having had his patriotism and courage called into question. Alf blocked Norman's path, and asserted that while the young Norman Armstrong had been sitting on his privileged, well-fed arse in idyllic teenaged upper middle-class comfort, Alf had been out at the front of the Jarrow Crusade, had fought fascism in Spain, and had then joined the Merchant Navy after the outbreak of war, in the service of which he had been torpedoed no less than four times.

The debate continued, and they soon found themselves in Annie's Bar, a frequent haunt of Alf's but one to where Norman had never been. The discussion was unrelenting, fuelled by Alf's willingness to keep refilling Norman's glass. A sizeable audience had assembled as the two men debated depression-era economic policy, refought the war, extolled the relative merits of Clement Attlee and Winston Churchill, and presented their opposing views on the Beveridge Report, the nationalisation of major industries, and the future of the country, as it struggled to emerge from its war-induced financial woes, which, Norman asserted with an unfortunate degree of smugness, had only been worsened by the Labour government's obsession with spending money it didn't have.

Had Alf been writing an account of the discussion for his editor, he would have described it as a frank exchange of views. He might have also described their demeanour as increasingly tired and emotional. Both men struggled to maintain their composure, but things began to get out of hand when Norman could no longer stand looking at Alf's frayed collar, stained tie and ill-fitting jacket and sneeringly offered to introduce him to the Armstrong family tailor on Savile Row. The reporter got unsteadily to his feet, stared at Norman with as much intensity as his bleary, exhausted eyes would allow, loudly called him 'a nae good ignorant brain-dead gobshite,' then swung a clumsy round-house punch that missed the young MP by a large margin. The tottering reporter then overbalanced and fell heavily to the floor, shattering a chair on the way down and eliciting a synchronous gasp from the enthralled spectators. Norman looked down at the prone, groaning figure with a combination of admiration and amusement. A firm friendship was born.

Norman shook his head and smiled at the memory. Alf had nurtured a long interest in the missing Charlotte Morris manuscript. How had he first heard of it? Of course, Norman recalled, it was Dick Billings being his usual loud and indiscreet self.

There had been a celebration drinks party at Number Ten following the Tory success at the 1951 election. Norman recalled walking toward the familiar black door on the way to the party, when he had been accosted by Alf Burton.

"Why-aye, Norm!" Burton cried, appearing out of nowhere beside him. "Not bad going, only in the parliament since last year and already a junior minister at the Exchequer. A meteoric rise, wouldn't you say? Nothing to do with the fact that you old da' is a friend of Winston's, I suppose?"

"Bugger off, there's a good chap." Norman quickened his pace, his long stride meaning that Alf had to half-jog like a heeling puppy to keep up.

"Any chance you can get me an interview with the Prime Minister?"

"Certainly not!"

Alf was left standing in Downing Street as Norman was admitted into Number Ten, then shown to the reception room. Norman remembered having noticed Dick Billings, separate from the throng of dinner jacketed guests, looking intently at a framed photograph on the wall. He was already quite under the weather, and was projecting an air of resentful aggression.

"I say, Winston," Dick was saying, "who's that old trout in the picture with Lloyd George?"

The Prime Minister shuffled toward the picture, whiskey in one hand and cigar in the other. "That's Charlotte Morris," the Prime Minister explained. "She was being honoured for opening her family estate as a hospital for shell-shocked officers during the Great War. They had some remarkable results with those poor chaps, using experimental treatments pioneered by Doctor Rivers. She wrote a book called *The Talking Cure*, which, I understand, is considered the standard work on the subject. I knew her during the South African war, Young Norman! My dear boy, how are you?"

The Prime Minister noticed Norman hovering nervously around the fringes of the gathering of senior politicians, and beckoned him over. "How is your father enjoying his retirement?"

"Very much, thank you, Prime Minister," Norman replied.

"Shame he declined his peerage, we could have used a man of his wisdom and ability in the Lords."

Dick Billings was visibly very unhappy at suddenly not being at the centre of the Prime Minister's attention. He moved suddenly sideways and wedged himself between the Prime Minister and the young MP, accidentally knocking the Prime Minister's hand and spilling a small amount of his drink onto the carpet. "The notorious Charlotte Morris, eh?" Dick said, a little too loudly. "Wasn't she one of old Bertie's harem?"

"She was His Majesty's advisor on colonial affairs," the Prime Minister explained.

"Not just *colonial* affairs, from what I hear, eh?" Dick snorted. "Now wasn't there some sort of scandal over an unpublished manuscript? Something about a secret order of mad monarchists…"

"Just gossip, Dick, that's all, now if you'll excuse me," The Prime Minister moved away, calling behind him, "Do give my best regards to your father, Norman, and I look forward to seeing great work from you at the Exchequer."

Dick eyed the young man coolly. "Junior man at the Exchequer, eh?" he grunted. "Only been in the parliament for five minutes. It took me nearly seven fucking years and a war to get any sort of decent job. What've you got that I haven't?"

Norman was unsure how to deal with the notoriously ill-tempered MP — this was very awkward. Dick might have had the reputation as something of a drunken, ill-mannered buffoon, but he was very influential, particularly within the hard-right faction of the Party. Norman's father had advised him to make every effort to be cordial with the older MP, commenting that he would make a much better friend than enemy, and to be warned, he wasn't anywhere near as stupid as he appeared to be. Norman shuffled uncomfortably, starting to feel a sense of quiet panic, but to his relief Dick made the next move.

"I'm bored with all this," he huffed. "I need a proper drink. There's a little pub I know, not far from here. Would you like to join me?" Norman felt it was more a command than an invitation.

Several minutes later, after a brisk and silent walk through some narrow lanes that Norman had never known existed, they arrived at small but elegant public house. "Two large brandies, and be quick about it, my good man!" Billings bellowed, as soon as he was through the front doors.

The two settled at the bar. Dick demolished his brandy in one gulp, then brought the glass down heavily on the bar to attract the landlord's attention.

"Just gossip, bollocks!" Dick spat, by means of kicking off the conversation.

"I beg your pardon?" Norman replied, gingerly sipping his brandy.

"That manuscript, the one that our great leader described as just gossip. Let me tell you, we're all for the high jump if it ever comes to light, we'll be out of power for a generation, never trusted again."

"I'm afraid you've lost me."

"That missing manuscript! Old Charlotte Morris was right at the heart of things, scandals in the Lords and the monarchy, our lot. Knew where all the bodies were buried, and I'm not just speaking metaphora-metaphoralora — sod it! There was this secret society of, well, they were dangerous bastards, thought they were so clever, had their fingers in..."

"What's this about Tory scandals? Tell me more!"

Dick looked around to see Alf Burton sidling up behind him like a creeping pantomime villain. "Fuck off, Burton, this is private conversation." After the reporter had waved a cheery farewell and disappeared out into the street, Dick warned, "watch out for that fucker, red bastard. Look here Armstrong, do you mind if I give you some advice?"

"I'd welcome it," Norman replied, suppressing an unedifying belch. He was finding the brandy almost impossible to stomach, but felt duty bound to persist out of politeness.

"Winston is yesterday's man," Dick told him. "I'd be surprised if he lives through this term, to be frank, you only have to look at him. Make sure you have friends that are going to be around long enough to see you right, career wise.

"Like you, you mean?"

"Me? Lord, no. You'll give me a wide berth if you know what's good for you. I'm the most unpopular man in the Party, that is, until someone needs some dirty work done, then I'm suddenly everybody's best friend for five minutes." Dick noticed Norman's rather perplexed expression. "I see you're wondering why an embittered old bastard like me is taking the trouble to talk to you like this. Well, I'll tell you why. A few years ago your father saved my career, probably my life in fact. There was a cock-up in my department. It was during the war, and the stakes were high. The Cabinet were baying for my blood, but your father stepped in and got me off the hook. He's been a good friend to me over the years, better than I've deserved, if I'm honest. I owe it to your father to give you what help I can."

Norman's mind snapped back to the present. The rumours surrounding the Morris manuscript had been a nagging anxiety bubbling beneath the surface of conservative politics, from the Commons to the Lords and within the aristocracy, for as long as he could remember. The contents were thought to be extremely damaging, although no one seemed to know, or at least wouldn't say, what those contents were. We're all for the high jump, Dick Billings had said all those years ago. How much did he know?

Norman surveyed the wall of books, there was an entire shelf dedicated to the works of Charlotte Morris, many were first editions acquired in Norman's grandfather's time, and were now extremely rare and valuable. Norman selected a leather-bound volume entitled *QONR – The Honour and The Glory*, and returned with it to the desk. It was the history of Norman's grandfather's regiment, the Queen's Own Natal Rifles. He considered the handwritten dedication inside.

To Dear Colonel Armstrong,

To whom I owe so much, and can never repay

CM 1903

Over a period of fifteen years, Charlotte Morris had written a spectacularly successful series of detective novels, featuring a dashing red-coated colonial officer, Captain Richard Fforbes. The hero, it was common knowledge, had been inspired by the old Colonel himself, and the collection of novels, all of which were represented in the shelves of Norman's library, had made Charlotte Morris, in her mature years, a worldwide literary sensation, running a close second to Conan Doyle and Sherlock Holmes. Was that what the author was grateful for, Norman wondered, providing the inspiration for her most lucrative literary creation? Did the Colonel know about her contentious manuscript? Unlikely, in Norman's estimation. Colonel Armstrong was by all accounts, a loyal, long serving and courageous soldier of Empire, there was no way that he would knowingly have brooked anything that might have put the stability of the government or the Crown at risk, no matter how close he might have been to its author.

Norman stepped over to the old sea chest beneath the Colonel's portrait, opened the lid and carefully rummaged amongst the diaries and letters inside. First, he set aside his father's unpublished memoir of life in the Royal Flying Corps, which was a somewhat atypical contribution to the voluminous family histories. Unlike the majority of personal accounts which, as a rule, extolled the virtues of courage, honour and the overriding glories of war as the ultimate test of manhood,

Lieutenant Richard Armstrong had compiled a bitter, melancholy obituary for all of the young airmen lost during the Great War. Emboldened by Lieutenant Siegfried Sassoon's 1917 Soldier's Declaration, he had then gone on to question, angrily and at length, the validity and morality of the war as a whole.

Norman was particularly gentle with a volume that was barely holding together, *In Defence of La Haie Sainte*, Major James Armstrong's personal account of Waterloo as an Aide-de-Camp to Wellington. Then he found what he was after, a collection of dust-stained black covered diaries tied together with a faded red ribbon, Colonel Fforbes Armstrong's private journals. Norman returned to the desk and carefully untied the ribbon, aware that these formed only a small part of the Colonel's personal papers, most of which had been lost following his death in South Africa in 1924.

That was a story in itself, Norman reflected. The old boy had spent his final years on his farm not far from Pietermaritzburg, fighting a private war against the Union of South Africa by referring to his property as the Armstrong Free State of Natal and employing a number of his old comrades as farm hands, his retired Sergeant Major drilling them daily as a nostalgic, red-coated private militia.

The bundle of journals on the desk in front of Norman accounted for a period between 1875 and 1902, with a number of gaps left by the lost volumes. Norman chose to begin at 1902, the closest to the date of Charlotte Morris's dedication in *QONR* — *The Honour and the Glory*. It seemed as good a place as any to begin. He examined the scrawly handwriting, it took some time for him to become accustomed to his grandfather's abbreviations and lack of punctuation. The Colonel had been a very active and busy man, his daily diary entries were compiled in haste and only insofar as his onerous duties would allow. Norman soon found himself engrossed in first-hand accounts of privileged colonial life in Natal, at war and during times of relative peace.

A series of entries from the southern hemisphere spring of 1901, focused Norman's concentration.

CM in trouble — Letters seized. Too vocal for own good about those infernal camps. Her position has merit but damned silly way to go about things — won't listen to reason

CM. Charlotte Morris, obviously. Norman was aware that she had been one of the most vocal critics of the British concentration camps on the veld, the full horrors of which were finally revealed in her controversial biography of Kitchener, which had been published posthumously. He read on.

Out of hand, CM arrested on spying charges. Trumped-up rubbish! Doing what we can. Tried to warn her! HK on the warpath.

HK must have referred to Lord Kitchener. The Colonel's anger and frustration leapt from the page and Norman suddenly felt a strong connection to the grandfather he had never met but whose presence lay heavy in his old library, and indeed upon Norman's life.

A number of references to the progress of the war followed, before another significant entry just caught Norman's attention as he skimmed the pages.

Poor Fruity Simmonds died today. Dysentery. Not many old boys left — More of my chaps dying from disease than Boer bullets. Understand father's frustration about Crimea — lessons of history soon forgotten.

HK told me today QONR to be broken up. Giving me a new show — Natal Rangers — Success! with CM. Asked WC to intervene with HM, charges dropped CM and DK to embark from Durban Friday thank God — RMS Lady Georgiana. Close Thing all round!

Norman had no idea who DK could be, but his knowledge of Armstrong family lore helped him to make sense of the rest. Charlotte Morris was making trouble over the concentration camps, and had developed an obsessive hatred of Kitchener. The implication in the diary seemed to be that the military command had concocted spying charges against her to shut her up, perhaps permanently. Norman's grandfather had asked Winston Churchill, earlier in the war a correspondent for the Daily Mail on loose attachment to the QONR, and, by now, Conservative MP for Oldham, and a man with solid connections to the Palace, to intervene on her behalf. Whatever machinations followed secured her release and she returned to England, with DK, whoever that was, to become a special adviser to the King.

That at least explains why she was grateful to the Colonel, who had helped to get her out of a very tricky and dangerous situation. But it must have been a big risk for Colonel Armstrong to take, defying the senior military establishment, of which he was such an enthusiastic, and very senior, member. And after all that, Norman realised, he was still no closer to understanding where the so-called lost manuscript fitted in.

Norman scanned the shelf dedicated to the works of Charlotte Morris, fiction and non-fiction, novels, biographies and collected essays, fruits of a prolific literary career spanning five decades. He lost count of the number of volumes. Where in God's name to start?

It was time for the news. Norman walked over to the old black and white television set, pulled the on/off knob, then after waiting for the tube to warm up, made some adjustments to the aerial and tweaked the vertical hold as the picture came into focus. The television was one of the few concessions toward relative modernity in the library, along with the electric light and an art-deco style radiogram purchased by his father half a century earlier.

The screen clock ticked through the last few seconds of eight fifty-nine, the news theme played, and then the familiar, precise voice of Michael Buerk summarised headlines that included the opening of the new Isle of Dogs Enterprise Zone, part of a major East End redevelopment by Donoghue Constructions, news that nineteen of the thirty-eight escapees from Maze Prison remained at large, and the growing calls for a crackdown on football hooliganism. He then moved on to the news in detail. "Good Evening. The Acting Secretary of State for Northern Ireland, Mr Stanley Smee, said today that the authorities were following a number of leads in their efforts to solve the mystery surrounding the kidnapping of prominent political correspondent, author and radio host, Alf Burton. Although investigations have pointed toward an IRA splinter group, Mr Smee confirmed that no contact has yet been made with the kidnappers, but that encouraging progress is being made. Mr Smee said that the kidnapping of Mr Burton appeared to be unrelated to the Maze prison escape."

Norman watched as Stanley Smee spoke earnestly into a BBC microphone. Having addressed efforts to recover the remaining Maze escapees, referring in a general way to their investigations in South Armagh, he turned to the matter of Alf Burton. "Our agencies are working around the clock, and we are

following up a number of very promising lines of enquiry..."
Norman had to acknowledge that Smee was growing into his new
job, and was surprisingly good in front of a camera. Aside from
the fact, of course, that he knew buggering sod-all about what
was going on!

"Just like me," Norman groaned, slouching back in his chair.

CHAPTER FOUR

When Norman opened his eyes, the television was emitting an irritating hissing noise, and the screen was an avalanche of electronic snow. His head ached and his neck hurt from the awkward angle it had assumed after he fell asleep in his chair. He couldn't actually remember much after Stanley Smee, other than the fact that Sir Dick Billings had, according to the newsreader, been the keynote speaker at a function celebrating the opening of the Donoghue Isle of Dogs development, during which he'd launched another blistering and typically colourful attack on the Greater London Council and was now calling for its immediate abolition.

Norman stood up, stretched, moved his head slowly from side to side and rubbed his neck. It was very unusual for him to fall asleep in front of the television, he cursed his faltering self-discipline. He concluded, with all the sound reasoning that his sleepy brain could muster, that he needed to rethink his strategy. He would come at it again, fresh, first thing in the morning. Yawning, he stepped out of the library, and reached back inside to switch off the light.

Suddenly he was a sixteen-year-old, in pyjamas and dressing gown, standing in exactly the same spot looking back through the half-opened doorway. In the flickering firelight he could see three men in the easy chairs around the fire. The room swam in brandy fumes and cigar smoke. His father was there, Winston Churchill, also Padraig Donoghue, a wealthy and politically active owner of a chain of newspapers. Wait, there was a fourth man, he was seated on a less comfortable chair slightly apart from the other three. Good God, Norman realised, it was a young Dick Billings!

After raising their glasses in honour of the birth of Padraig Donoghue's son, Eddie, they turned to the subject of the meeting. "Baldwin is being bloody-minded in the extreme," Norman recalled his father saying. They were discussing the abdication crisis, and everyone present was desperately trying to save the King.

"Even the Christmas trade is off," Padraig Donoghue grumbled. "Advertising revenue is down across all of my papers."

"Not to mention the small matter of a constitutional crisis," Winston Churchill observed wryly.

"What I can't understand," Dick Billings chipped in, "is why certain people have let things get so far. The country in turmoil, civil war in the Royal Family, government paralysed. The monarchy is at more risk now than at any time since Cromwell's day, and yet, no sign of them! And yet they intervened when..."

"Enough said, I think," Churchill cautioned.

"Who are you talking about exactly?" Padraig Donoghue asked, leaning back to consciously include Dick Billings in the conversation for the first time.

"The Banqueting Club, of course," Dick Billings replied.

"I really think we should return to the matter at hand," Richard Armstrong cautioned. "Now about the morganatic marriage suggestion. I know this has been rejected, but can we revisit..."

"Wait a minute, Richard," Padraig Donoghue held up his hand, his journalist's curiosity aroused. "Who are the Banqueting Club?"

"We really shouldn't be discussing..." Churchill began.

"Oh don't be such an old woman, Winston," Dick Billings interrupted. "They think they're all so clever and secretive, but they're not as smart as they think they are. Their full name, Paddy, is the Most Worshipful Order of Liege Knights of Charles the First. What a mouthful, eh? They're monarchist fanatics, obsessed loonies, supposedly secret, but my mother used to work for..."

"Enough!" Norman's father's tone was sufficient to stop Dick Billings in mid-sentence. "We don't want to be here all night. In normal circumstances we'd all thinking about packing up and going home for Christmas, but this crisis is dragging on. Winston, back to the option of the morganatic marriage, is there anything more we can do to play for time?"

The older Norman burst back into the library. Dick Billings was the man he should have been talking to all along, he realised. Suddenly wide awake and energised, he sat behind his desk, lifted the telephone receiver and dialled a number he knew by heart.

***

"Fuck me, Norman!" Sir Dick Billings said, having answered the phone almost straight away. "What time is it?"

"I don't know, after midnight. Are you sober?"

"More or less. Why?"

"I need to ask you about something. Do you remember...?" Norman stopped, he could hear some crackling and static on the line. Surely not!

"Do I remember what?" Dick prompted.

"Never mind, can I come round?"

"What, now? What's this about?"

"A boring administrative matter, that's all, Dick. But I'd like to deal with it before tomorrow. It's my fault, I'd forgotten all about it."

"You're always welcome, Norman, you know that. Anyway, I'm doing fuck-all else, more's the pity!"

After hanging up, Norman reached for his wallet and selected a business card. He dialled the number, and a surprisingly alert voice answered on the third ring. Within fifteen minutes a black cab pulled up out the front of Norman's house.

"Eric, my dear chap, thank you so much," Norman said as he climbed into the back seat. "I'm very sorry to drag you out at this time."

"No problems at all, Mr Armstrong. I've been working late anyway, I'd just got home."

Norman gave Eric Baker directions, then said, "I know this sounds a little strange, Eric, but would you mind keeping an eye out to see if we're being followed."

"Righto, Guv'nor." If Eric was surprised by the Chief Whip's request, he gave no indication. In just a few minutes, the cab stopped out front of the Victorian red-brick façade of Romford Mansions, behind which Sir Dick Billings lived alone in a first floor flat.

"All clear," Eric reported matter-of-factly. "There was no one behind us the whole way."

Dick greeted Norman in pyjamas and a frayed dressing gown, pocked with burns from decades of falling cigarette ash. Norman noted that he was possibly not quite as sober as he had indicated, and that, in the time between their phone call and Norman's arrival, he had worked himself up into a frantic level of red-faced agitation.

"Fucking hell, Norman," he cried straight away. "If this is about my private arrangements with Eddie, it was all done through third parties, nothing traceable. You know I'd never do anything to embarrass..."

"For God's sake, Dick, stop talking! This is about something completely different."

"Oh, right then. Forget I spoke." Dick's distress melted away, he handed Norman a glass of brandy and gestured him toward a faded armchair opposite Dick's own. Norman glanced around the room, noting the faded art-deco chic, a sad, threadbare relic of jazz age elegance.

"So, what's so important that causes you to knock on my door at this time of night?"

Norman stood up and walked to the front window. He pulled back the curtain and observed that the street was deserted, save for Eric Baker, arms folded, leaning back on the bonnet of his cab, diligently keeping watch.

"One night," Norman began, returning to his chair, "it must have been leading up to Christmas, 1936. You were at our home in Knightsbridge. My father was there, as was Winston Churchill and Padraig Donoghue."

"1936? Are you quite well, Norman? It's a funny time of night to come over all nostalgic."

"You were discussing the situation involving the King and Wallis Simpson."

"There were crisis meetings almost every night around that time, I don't doubt that there was one at your house," Sir Dick recalled. "Your father was one of the King's strongest supporters, along with Winston. Paddy Donoghue's papers were behind us as well, like Beaverbrook's. How do you know about all this anyway? You would've been barely out of your cradle."

"I was sixteen, as a matter of fact. I was listening outside the door."

Dick chuckled. "You were obviously born to be Chief Whip!"

"If my memory is right, you made mention of something about a group called, was it, the *Banqueting Club*? I got the impression that my father and Winston were keen to change the subject."

Dick emptied his glass and poured another. He gestured toward Norman with the bottle, Norman shook his head. "What's this really all about, Norman?" he asked quietly.

"In strict confidence, Dick."

"Of course."

"I met with Alf Burton, just before he was kidnapped. He told me he had a strong lead to the lost Charlotte Morris manuscript. He agreed to hand it over, in return for a deal that gave him preferred access to Number Ten, exclusive interviews and so forth, for a future book about the government. I reported the meeting to Peregrine Walsingham, who then, with my blessing, notified Archie Prentice."

"A perfectly sensible course of action," Dick affirmed. "That fat communist twat has a habit of poking his nose in where it doesn't belong. Got more than he bargained for this time, eh?" Dick thought for a moment, then continued, "Ah, I see where you're going with this, you obviously think that all this bumfluffery on the news about the Irish is a cover. You're probably right, it seemed a bit funny to me from the off. It's more than likely that Alf is in some dark basement getting the living shit kicked out of him by Prentice's goons, until he gives up his source, at which time he'll just disappear without trace. Well, we won't see him again. Sorry Norman, I know that he was a friend of yours."

Norman gloomily agreed with Sir Dick's assessment. He also felt the suffocating burden of guilt. If only he hadn't run straight to the Cabinet Secretary, like an eager prefect reporting a rebellious house-member. If only he'd had the judgement to allow things to take their natural course! Alf would have turned up, handed over the manuscript just as he'd promised, and this mess would be behind them all.

"Look here, Norman," Dick soothed, sensing his friend's distress. "You did the right thing. That damned manuscript is like a Polaris Missile with Red Alf's fat finger on the button. It had to be deactivated, you had no choice but to go to the Cabinet Secretary. You did your duty, the national interest trumps everything, even friendship."

"I'm sure you're right, but it doesn't make me feel any better."

"I'm going to give you some advice, Norman old cock, even though I know that, for all the good it's going to do, I might as well be talking to my chair, but hear me out. Leave this well alone. The fact that you're in my flat in the middle of the night asking dangerous questions tells me that you're planning some sort of harebrained intervention. I advise you against this in the strongest possible terms."

"I can't help feeling that I'm well past the point of safe return," Norman said. "It would really help me if you could tell me everything you know about the manuscript and this Banqueting Club."

"Right then," Sir Dick said resignedly. "As there's no chance of your seeing sense, you'd better have another drink."

Having refreshed the glasses, Sir Dick settled back in his chair. "Why are you so interested in the Banqueting Club, anyway?"

"I don't really know," Norman confessed. "I'm wondering if there is some connection, I'm clutching at straws really. Who were they, and why were they called the Banqueting Club?"

"Named themselves after the old Banqueting Hall, you know, where Charles the First was executed. They formed to further the cause of the Restoration; once that little job was done, they became royal protection vigilantes. Any time the crown, the protestant crown I should add, might be at any sort of risk, they stepped in. And they would go to lengths way beyond what any legitimate government or monarchy would, even in the bad old days."

"How do you know all this?"

"Did you know that I grew up on the Sandringham Estate?"

"No."

"Bollocks you didn't, you've probably got an entire chapter on me in your little book. Anyway, my father was a doctor — he went to Gallipoli with the Sandringham Company under Captain Beck. You know how that ended up."

"Yes, I'm sorry."

"My dad mainly looked after the estate workers, but his senior partner attended the royal household, personal physician to old Queen Alexandra herself. My mother went to work for him, some general cleaning and typing, but really it was just an excuse for him to take care of us after my father was killed. He was very keen for me to continue my education rather than going to work on the Estate. He took me under his wing, to a degree."

"Dick, this is all fascinating, and I'd be very happy to discuss your family history one day, but what has got to do with...?"

"After school, if my mother was working at the doctor's house, I would stop there on my way home. One day she was doing some repairs on a ceremonial uniform. The doctor was there as well, he told me it was for his Mason's Lodge. He was very proud of it, he even showed me a large, expensive-looking medallion. It was on the end of a chain, like a mayoral badge of office. It was the Stuart Coat of Arms. The full regalia was like the uniform of the old Cavaliers, you know, big hat with a feather, ridiculous trousers, wig, the whole shooting match. On another occasion, he was having some kind of meeting, three or four old men sitting around: well, everybody seems old when you're a lad of thirteen or fourteen. I remember they were discussing whether or not to grant asylum to the Tsar and his family. That was a real dilemma for them I suppose, a Royal household closely related to ours ousted by revolution and in fear of their lives. But there were concerns over the spread of revolutionary sentiment, of course, and I remember they didn't seem to think much of the Tsar himself. I remember thinking it was a bit strange calling someone who looked just like our own King, I think the words the doctor used were common murderer. That particular problem rather conveniently disappeared without them having to lift a finger, as it turned out. Funny how some things stick in your mind, like your recollections of that meeting at your house, earwigging at the door, all those years ago."

"So the doctor was part of it, then?"

"Yes, he had to be. It didn't register at the time, of course, but looking back it makes sense. He always seemed way too nice to be mixed up in that kind of caper. Look Norman, they were dangerous fuckers, monarchist fanatics — High Tory catholic-hating nutcases. But if you think they might have a hand in Burton's situation, you'd be wrong. If this was forty years ago, they would've been my number one suspect. If there was even a hint of any risk to the monarchy or the so called *establishment...*" Dick mouthed the word establishment with lip-curling distaste... "this would have been just the sort of job they would have got their teeth into. When it suited the government to not be directly involved in some sensitive operations, like knocking someone off for instance, they knew who to call on. Dirty work done at arm's length — something we've become very good at over the years."

"So," Norman ventured, "it stands to reason then, if they, the current generation of members, became aware that Alf had uncovered the manuscript, conceivably through Archie's department or even the Cabinet Office, they could actually be the ones responsible for the kidnapping. It's also conceivable that they know a good deal more than us about the manuscript's contents, and see a risk to the stability of the monarchy or the government or both. Archie, as a result, has complete deniability — he was technically telling the truth when he told me he had nothing to do with it — and he can now make a big show of going after the non-existent Irish Revolutionaries to his heart's content."

"A great theory, Norman, but impossible. The Banqueting Club has been out of business since the war."

"How can you be sure?"

"Because they overstepped the mark once too often, and the word came down from the very top, possibly even HM himself. Not the way we should be doing things in this country any more, makes us no better than the Nazis, that sort of reaction."

"What did they do, exactly?"

"They killed Padraig Donoghue."

"What? No! He was killed during an air raid."

"His body was pulled out of the debris of a bombed East End knocking shop. Trouble was, he was dead before his poor broken corpse was dumped under the rubble."

"That sounds a little far-fetched to me," Norman scoffed.

"You can either believe me or not, makes no difference to me," Dick replied with a hint of anger. "You asked me and I'm telling you what I know, against my better judgement. If you think I'm just a senile, blustering old fool, you can fuck off home and let us all get some sleep. No skin off my nose either way."

"Sorry, Dick. Please go on."

"It goes back to a situation that happened when I was at the Ministry of Information during the war. I recruited Padraig Donoghue and a couple of his top reporters to work for us. As you know, a lot of large houses and estates were used as military installations, but at the same time a number of titled families had close family ties with Germany, some of whom, you might recall, had been quite complimentary about Hitler right up until the time the jackboots marched into Poland. Remember that the former King himself appeared quite sympathetic to the Nazis for a while, much to your father's disappointment, I might add. Anyway, the wider security implications were obvious. Paddy and his scribblers were sent off to interview a number of earls, dukes, lords and ladies and an assortment of minor royals, whose estates were being used by the military, to talk about their contribution to the war effort for propaganda purposes. You know the sort of thing, all classes pulling together to poke Adolf in the eye. The real purpose was to dig around and find out about how tangible these links to Germany were, if they existed at all, and whether or not any of these nobs had divided loyalties and were playing both sides, so to speak. Notes of their interviews were then passed on to Intelligence for analysis."

"Was Donoghue aware of the real purpose of what they were doing?"

"It was never spoken about, but he was no fool."

"It all sounds like a sensible precaution to take," Norman said. "A good plan, cleverly conceived and discreetly executed. I take my hat off to you. So what went wrong?"

"It turned out that someone was, in fact, passing information to the Jerries. A fifth columnist was caught and under interrogation, gave up his informant. Guess who?"

"How would I know? It could've been anybody."

"Paddy Donoghue himself."

Norman stared. "He was a traitor?"

"I'm afraid so."

The fact that the father of the largest Tory donor, Sir Eddie Donoghue, a personal friend of Norman, Dick Billings, and many other senior party members had actually been a traitor during wartime, took a little while for Norman to process. "Does Eddie know?" he asked.

"No!" Dick replied emphatically, sitting up straight and pointing his finger at Norman. "And I intend to keep it that way. Nobody knows. You must give me your word of honour on this, Norman, I insist."

"Yes, you have my word." The implications of this rather stunning revelation, Norman thought, would have to be considered more carefully at a later time. "What does all this have to do with the Banqueting Club?"

"To save his own skin, Paddy laid a very clever trail back to an obscure relation of the Royal Family, some sort of distant cousin several times removed, on the Saxe-Coburg-Gotha side. This poor chap had been born in England and had fought with distinction in the trenches, but had unwisely let slip to one of Paddy's boys during their interview that he had relatives in the senior ranks of the Luftwaffe and the SS. The old boy was completely innocent, had more than proved his loyalty to Britain, but Paddy still managed to stitch him up. It looked like Paddy was going to get away with it. Now, I know you'll remember the nature of the times, Norman: morale at home was a critical factor, with the invasion threat hanging over us. There was intense paranoia. If this had got out, even a rumour, all the misgivings about the Royals' German background would have resurfaced, and, don't forget, the shadow of the Abdication Crisis still lingered. They weren't going to take chances on any loss of faith in the government or the monarchy. Let's just say a favour was done at the behest of someone close to the top of the aristocratic pile. Enter our friends from the Club, and the next thing we know Paddy was being pulled out of the rubble of an East End house of ill-repute. Problem solved. It was all hushed up of course."

"Are you one hundred percent sure that the spy was Donoghue?"

"It was Donoghue, all right. Anyway, as you would imagine, harbouring a Kraut infiltrator within the Ministry of Information was a cock-up of massive proportions in itself. If that ever got out, once again, the damage to morale would have been devastating, can you imagine what Lord Haw Haw would've made of it? Germany Calling! Germany Calling! Your Ministry of Information is actually working for us you ignorant, doomed British fuckers! I was the one that recruited Paddy, he was my best friend, and the entire initiative had been my idea, so I was also under strong suspicion. It didn't help that I wasn't one of them, of course."

"One of them?"

"You know, one of the old school tie brigade, the come and dine at my club old boy, types. Your lot, in fact. No, Winston only ever gave me the time of day when he needed me for some godawful job no one else would touch with the proverbial bargepole. I'd love to see their faces now that it's *Sir* Dick, eh? Fuck 'em! Your father was different, though, a real gentleman. Anyway, it was your father who was brought in to sort out the mess, under orders from the old man himself. He managed to contain the damage, saved my bacon at the same time, and then we all got on with the war. Except for the old Worshipful Liege Maniacs of Charles the First, who went off and quietly hung up their hatchets in disgrace."

Norman was still struggling with the fact that the father of one of the Conservative Party's most generous supporters had been feeding sensitive information to the Nazis. How many British lives had that cost? "Why did Paddy do it?" he asked. "He was wealthy, a great success in this country in business, very influential politically. What was his game?"

"It was all about Ireland." Dick replied. His eyelids were beginning to close, but he fought to stay alert. "Paddy got it into his mind that Hitler would've reunited Ireland and ended British occupation in Ulster."

"He couldn't have been that naïve, surely," Norman scoffed. "Did he think it was going to be some sort of golden paradise under Nazi occupation? How could he have been so stupid?"

"Well, he had a bee in his bonnet over the Easter Rising, the executions, and then the behaviour of the Black and Tans after the First World War..." Dick's head nodded forward and he emitted a snort, a deep breath, then his head snapped upwards. He tried to refocus his eyes upon Norman.

"What was the alternative?" Norman asked.

"Alternative to what?" Dick slurred

"You said that the Banqueting Club had effectively been shut down over what they did. What was the alternative? Donoghue was a spy, undermining the war effort. He would've been executed anyway. Why were people so squeamish? It seems to me that whoever was mixed up with the Banqueting Club at that time should've been given medals, not sent to Coventry. Why was that little operation any different to the countless other covert killings that would've been going on left, right and centre? I would've happily killed him myself, twice!"

"You were fighting a very different war, you at least could see who your enemy was. Anyway, they got sloppy, a young Scotland Yard detective began asking some very uncomfortable questions, something about the fact that Paddy's injuries didn't quite match your typical bomb victim. He was getting close, right on their trail, then suddenly, as I recall, his reserved occupation status was conveniently amended so he could join up. He was invited to join one of the cloak and dagger shows and, being a patriotic young man, jumped at the chance. He handed over his files and no one ever heard from him again. Slippery slope."

"When you say, no one ever heard from him again, you're not suggesting that...?"

"Not directly. He was killed on his first mission. Make of that what you will."

There was so much more Norman wanted to ask. Could all this be true, or had a mundane if tragic reality been embellished in the late night, drunken ramblings of an old man, a perpetual embittered outsider, whose memory was not what it was?

German spies conniving to incriminate innocent royals? Killing policemen?

"I always felt a responsibility toward young Eddie," Dick continued. "Guilt, I suppose."

"I don't see what you had to feel guilty about," Norman observed. "Regardless of how it came about, old Donoghue senior got what was coming to him."

"Perhaps," Dick said, "but it wasn't the poor little chap's fault, was it? You were blessed, Norman, you had your father for a good part of your adult life. For my generation it was different, as almost all of our fathers never came home, and the ones who did weren't the same. I guess that's why I always tried to look out for young Eddie, even after he came of age and took over the family business. It'd been run by a council of accountants until then, they did a reasonable job. But I always tipped Eddie off if there was a major privatisation coming up. That's how he got hold of the failing remnants of Speers Shipping, by the way..." Dick's head had lolled forwarded again, but this time didn't move. Norman stood up and rescued Dick's glass before it fell from his fingers.

"Dick, wake up," Norman shook him gently, there was no response. There was nothing else for it. Norman bent down, placed his arms around the unconscious figure and lifted him in an awkward combination of an intimate waltz and a fireman's carry. The two men half staggered to Dick's bedroom, where Norman laid him gently onto the double bed. Scanning the room, with the help of rays of the residual light from the living room, Norman suddenly felt uncomfortable, an intruder into a private, secret world. On the bedside table was a photograph, a face from the past, a film star of the thirties, perhaps? No, it was Dick's wife, killed in one of the first air-raids of the war. There was a ladies' dressing table against the far wall, still laid out with hairbrushes, cosmetics, and a gold cigarette case. Another photograph stood in front of the mirror, a young and handsome couple dressed for a fashionable night out in pre-war London — the Ritz or the Savoy perhaps — followed by dancing at the Café de Paris, or at an exclusive Belgrave Square house party. Norman tried to reconcile the old man in the threadbare dressing gown, snoring away and with a bubble of dribble visible on the corner of his mouth, with the man in the photograph, upright and proud in white tie, his black hair smoothed down either side of a meticulous centre parting. Even then there was something behind his smile, a hint of angry defiance. The lady, the same face that shone from the portrait beside the bed, radiated pure sunshine.

"You know, I so much hoped to be killed during the war," Dick murmured as Norman removed his slippers and straightened the bed covers as best he could. "I was genuinely disappointed to still be here on VE Day. I tried to get into one of the secret shows, after that Donoghue cock-up there was no hope of that of course. I went through a series of pointless jobs. Department of Economic Warfare was the worst, my God! I envy you, Norman, decorated pilot, Battle of Britain, and then Bomber Command. Never before has so much been owed, no wait, never before has so much been owed by so few, to so few, I'll get it in a minute, Never before in the human field of..." Dick's voice trailed into silence as he began to snore, loudly and rhythmically.

"Relax, old friend," Norman whispered. "We all did our bit, in our own way. Get some sleep, we'll talk again tomorrow."

"Norman." Dick's voice caught Norman just as he was tip-toeing out of the bedroom.

"Everything's fine, Dick, just go to sleep."

"Beware of Prentice," Sir Dick warned sleepily without opening his eyes. "We should pretend this conversation never happened, I've forgotten all about it already..."

By the time Norman let himself out of the flat, descended the stairs and emerged onto the street, the faintest hint of the dawn was perceptible above the glow of the streetlamps. Eric Baker was sitting in his driver's seat, still wide awake. Norman was profuse in his apologies.

"Not to worry, Chief, you're paying for it after all. I've been on sentry in worse places."

Norman spent the short trip back to his home in contemplative silence. There was so much more he wanted to know, he felt that he had only scraped the surface. Dick seemed remarkably well informed about a society that was supposed to be clandestine, and the old doctor was particularly cavalier — no pun intended — about the secrecy of the organisation. Rubbing his eyes against exhaustion, Norman questioned just how much of Dick's rambling nocturnal account would still seem even remotely plausible once his thoughts had been refreshed after a good sleep.

One aspect that Norman didn't believe for one moment, was that the Banqueting Club had just faded quietly away into peaceable retirement, as Dick had described. Fanatics who were suddenly abandoned by the very people they were fighting to protect, in Norman's experience, just went deeper underground, felt unappreciated, became murderously resentful and even more dangerous. Beware of Prentice? Even Ron Coburn had observed that Prentice could be tricky, a fact that Norman knew well, but was Dick Billings hinting at something more sinister?

But the matter at hand was the fate of Alf Burton, had he really drawn any closer to the truth on that particular issue? Was there a link between the manuscript and the Banqueting Club? Even if there was, what could be done about it? Probably nothing.

Norman had been at the heart of government for decades, and, thanks to his family, he had been a natural, comfortable part of the so-called establishment that Dick Billings so reviled. His apprenticeship at the loving hands of his father had been lifelong, and yet he'd never heard so much as a whisper about the Liege Knights of Charles the First. How much had his father known about them? Norman had always believed that there had been no secrets between father and son, but since Alf Burton's kidnapping, all of the reassuring and hitherto rock-solid foundations of his life seemed to be shifting in an earthquake of uncertainty.

The cab arrived at Norman's Knightsbridge home, Eric having made easy work of the light early morning traffic. Before Norman could reach for his wallet, he heard an abrupt screech of tyres and a large black Ford Consul sedan appeared as if from nowhere, stopping very close to the back of the cab.

"Behind us, Mr Armstrong," Eric said calmly, studying the rear-view mirror. "Any orders?"

Two heavyset men alighted from the black sedan, overcoat collars turned up against the cold of the morning. One approached Eric's door while the other opened the kerbside passenger door and leant in. Observing the pistol partially concealed by the man's long sleeve, Norman fleetingly wondered if he was about to be arrested, kidnapped or assassinated.

"I must ask you to come with us, please, Mr Armstrong."

"Look, I just have to pay—"

"We'll take care of that. Please Sir, right away."

With some not-too-gentle encouragement, and with no time to protest, Norman found himself being bundled out of the cab

— he noted with some relief that the pistol remained pointed at the ground and not at him — and then into the backseat of the black sedan. The armed man scanned the street then ran around the car, holstered his gun and slid in behind the wheel. This must be how Alf had felt, Norman mused, as the car reversed abruptly, pulled out from behind the cab, stopped for a split second to pick up the other man, then, with engine revving loudly and a longer squeal of tyres that echoed in the silence of the empty street, sped away.

Eric Baker, clutching a fistful of five, and ten pound notes, coolly watched the car disappear out of sight. "That's not something you see every day," he said out loud, and wondered just what he'd got himself into.

***

"Jesus, Norman, you gave us all quite a scare. Where in God's name have you been?"

Norman looked to his right to see Assistant Commissioner Ron Coburn sitting next to him, the collar of his striped pyjamas just visible above his coat.

"Ron!" Norman's surprise was evident. "What the hell is going on? Good God, steady on!" Norman gripped the front seat as the Ford swerved violently from behind a slow moving bus and onto the wrong side of the road, the driver having managed to judge the gap between the front of the bus and an oncoming van with incredible precision. Or incredible luck. The black sedan then veered abruptly back onto the correct side of the road, leaving the bus well behind. Dennis Waterman and John Thaw had a lot to answer for, Norman thought, through gritted teeth. Since *The Sweeney*, perfectly sensible policemen had taken to wearing brown suede jackets, calling each other *Guv'nor* and *my son*, referring to their police stations as 'the factory' and driving like maniacs.

"Relax, Norman," Ron Coburn said. "These are my lads, the best in the business. Anyway, where were you?"

"A man is entitled to a private life, you know," Norman retorted, his uncertainty giving way to annoyance at being manhandled — at gunpoint no less — into an unmarked police car and then driven at suicidal speed through early morning London.

"Oh, I see, sorry. Mum's the word, of course," Ron replied, embarrassed.

"I didn't mean I was... oh never mind. What the hell's this all about, Ron? There'd better be a very good explanation."

"There's been a death threat against you. Orders for your protection have come down from the top. Armed officers were assigned to you straight away. When you couldn't be reached at your house, the duty officer phoned me at home. With all this Irish activity about, it was thought best not to take any chances. You had a quite a few people worried."

"Where are we going now, then?"

"An old friend of ours is going to put you in the picture. Archie Prentice is going to brief you personally."

CHAPTER FIVE
Trafalgar Hall, Cornwall
1919

For just over a century, the main upstairs bedchamber at Trafalgar Hall had been known as the Great Cabin, in honour of its first famous occupant, Captain Sir Charles Rochester Speers. On a clear day the panoramic view, visible through a large expanse of paned glass predictably referred to as the stern-windows, encompassed fields of fertile pasture divided into a number of tenant farms, a market-village and several miles of jagged coastline which extended to a headland, from which an ancient ruined castle keep protruded like a broken, blackened tooth.

Just two months after the Armistice, and with the tired, drooping remnants of the Christmas decorations looking more mournful than merry, the winter rains beat against the stern windows, and the mist restricted the view to not much farther than the home lawns and topiary garden. Dorothy Keppel stood facing outwards, gazing vacantly at the water coursing in streams down the glass panels.

"Not long now, I'm afraid." Doctor Sir Cedric Knollys placed a gentle, supporting hand on Dorothy's arm.

"Thank you, Doctor," she replied, keeping her tearful eyes firmly toward the windows and the hidden world beyond. "I cannot tell you how much I appreciate your being here. It was so kind of Her Majesty to spare you from your duties at Sandringham."

"As soon as Her Majesty found out that poor Mrs Morris was failing, she insisted I attend straight away. Of course, I would have willingly come to your side in any circumstances: after all, we've all been friends for a long time. I look back at our days at Court with the late King as some of the happiest of my life."

The centrepiece of the Great Cabin was a roughly hewn four-poster bed, incongruous in the otherwise Georgian splendour of the cavernous room. The bed had been constructed by Captain Speers's ships' carpenter following the Battle of Trafalgar, from timbers salvaged during the refit of the badly damaged HMS Warrior, and was decorated with engravings and the initials of generations of long-dead mariners. It was family legend that the spirits of the sailors lived within the warm embrace of the bed, the Captain's own coxswain and boat's crew ever ready to ferry departing souls to the next world.

Charlotte Morris, granddaughter of the legendary fighting captain, was slipping in and out of consciousness, but appeared comfortable at least, her breathing had settled, and was now much easier. She was lying almost at the edge of the large, soft mattress, the vast majority of room taken by two elderly and rather ill-smelling wiry haired lurchers, Gladstone and Bertie. Any attempts to encourage the dogs to abandon their forlorn vigil, or at least to take up less room on the bed, were met with cold stares and a flat refusal to budge.

Now back at the bedside, Dorothy and Doctor Knollys eyed the barely perceptible rise and fall of Charlotte's chest, the time between movements was growing longer and longer, and then with a rattly, extended exhalation of breath, there was finally no movement at all. Doctor Knollys placed his fingers on the thin, almost skeletal wrist, and nodded his confirmation that there was no pulse.

Dorothy moved away while the Doctor completed his examination. Within a few moments, he joined her at the stern windows.

"So what is to be done?" He asked quietly.

"I suppose nothing, at least, not until the will is read."

"I don't have to remind you..."

"No, you do not!" Dorothy's voice was harsher than she had intended. She softened her tone. "We both remain, do we not, Dr Knollys, in sickness and in health, and for better or worse, loyal servants of the Crown?"

"A lifetime's work, Miss Keppel. A lifetime's work."

***

"Good morning Ladies and Gentlemen, my name is Arthur Twilley, and my family has had the inestimable honour of serving the Speers family for over one hundred years in matters of law." The solicitor's sonorous voice addressed a gathering that included Dorothy Keppel, Doctor Knollys, as well as the Chairman of the Board and a number of senior executives from the Speers business conglomerate. "I think we're all here. Are we? No? Just one more to come, so we'll wait a few more minutes."

The reading of Charlotte Morris's will was being held in the room adjacent to the Great Cabin, once the bedchamber and dressing room of Lady Georgiana, the formidable wife of Captain

Charles Speers, and more recently the office and sitting room shared by Charlotte and her devoted companion and secretary, Dorothy Keppel. Mr Twilley sat behind the desk at which Charlotte, with Dorothy's help, had worked on some of her most memorable novels, curated a lifetime of essays and articles, and had researched and written her widely praised account of shellshock treatment, *The Talking Cure*. A stenographer sat in poised silence next to the solicitor while Gladstone and Bertie lay in their usual places, next to Charlotte's chair and half under the desk. Every so often, an intensely foul smell permeated the air, causing those present to wrinkle their noses and peer suspiciously at their neighbour, until it became apparent that the culprit, or culprits, were lying on the carpet by the desk. Twilley coped with admirable restraint, although at one point the stenographer muttered, "oh my god," and brought a handkerchief up to her nose and dabbed at her watering eyes.

As Mr Twilley shuffled his papers and the gathering made stilted, hushed conversation, Dorothy reflected upon the final hours of Charlotte Morris's life, and the several weeks since. At one point during her gradual fall into irrevocable unconsciousness, Charlotte had suddenly jerked awake, reached for Dorothy's hand and grasped it with surprising power.

"Dorothy, my dear," she rasped. "There is something I must tell you."

Doctor Knollys, half dozing in an armchair opposite the bed, eased himself up and made to leave the room, but Charlotte called, "No, no, Doctor. Please stay. Dorothy must not face this alone. You are a dear and trusted friend, I'll feel so much more at peace knowing that you'll be by her side."

"Of course, Mrs Morris." The Doctor walked to the bedside and placed his hand on Dorothy's shoulder.

"Listen carefully," Charlotte said, waving away a proffered glass of water. "In Africa, just before we were, just before we left, I wrote something..."

"That's right, my dear," Dorothy soothed, "you finished the first of your Richard Fforbes stories, *The Colonel's Dilemma*. What a wonderful success it was, and the fourteen books that followed. You are famous, loved all over the..."

"I'm not talking about that!" Charlotte barked, and tried to raise herself off her mountain of pillows, but fell back almost immediately. Gladstone and Bertie, suddenly alert, regarded her with concern, then, satisfied that she was comfortable again, laid their heads back down. She continued breathlessly, each word an effort in itself. "I wrote something else, things that should never have been put to paper. I was so angry, oh that wicked buggering Kitchener, evil man, probably poisoned all the fish in the seas off Orkney when his vile corpse went into it, God rot his black soul!" Doctor Knollys coughed uncomfortably, having been a friend of the Kitchener family for most of his life. He was trying to craft a polite protest, but Charlotte continued breathlessly. "Forgive me, Doctor, but I'm well beyond good graces. I wrote in anger, what I knew, things I learned about... secrets... It would do so much damage to friends, people we love. Poor Georgie, it could ruin everything, and for young David... But they must be stopped! Mr Twilley has sealed instructions, the will..."

"Who must be stopped, dearest?" Dorothy enclosed Charlotte's bony hand in her own. "Please don't distress yourself. You must rest."

"There'll be all the time in the world for that," Charlotte uttered, and then fell silent, fading into sleep for the last time.

Sitting opposite Mr Twilley in front of the desk where they had worked together since their return to England almost two decades before, Dorothy's eyes began to well with tears. Doctor Knollys took her hand and gave it a reassuring squeeze. At that moment the awaited arrival burst into the room amid a flurry of apologies, and took the last spare seat at the rear of the assembly.

Dorothy leaned over and whispered to Dr Knollys, "Who's that?"

Knollys turned and nodded at the new arrival, who smiled and offered a discreet wave in return. "Piers Armstrong. Tory MP, would have been Prime Minister before the war — was seen as the natural successor to Arthur Balfour — had his side not been routed by Campbell-Bannerman's Liberals, of course. He's done very well in the coalition. Charming fellow, very influential, even now."

"Armstrong?" Dorothy thought there was something quite familiar about the military bearing and sharp features.

"And I'll tell you something else," Knollys whispered. "He wouldn't have put up with all that nonsense of the so called People's Budget and the tomfoolery around those Liberal Peers. Drove our late King to an early grave, that philandering Asquith and his gang of..."

"Right, perhaps we may now begin," Arthur Twilley announced, tapping his finger on the desk to stem the quiet murmur of discussion like a presiding judge. "Thank you all for joining us here at Trafalgar Hall this morning, as we formally read the last will and testament of the late Charlotte Georgiana Victoria Morris, nee Speers, of course. It has been a great honour for me to serve the late Mrs Morris, as well as her late brother, as my father and grandfather did for her father and grandfather, that is to say, their fathers and, their father and grandfather..." Dr Knollys huffed and stole a discreet glance at his pocket watch. It was going to be a long morning, if this old fool was going to keep blithering around the peripheries, he thought. "...Now, Miss Keppel, before we come to the terms of the will in detail, there are a number of brief matters to be discussed. First, I have a sealed envelope to be handed to you, in accordance with my instructions. Perhaps you would be kind enough to confirm aloud, for the benefit of our stenographer, that the seal is intact to your satisfaction."

Dorothy accepted the envelope, carefully examined the seal then showed it to Dr Knollys who nodded his own approval. "Thank you Mr Twilley, that appears to be in order." She placed the envelope in her lap, oblivious to the keen interest shown by Piers Armstrong, MP.

"Now, Miss Keppel," Twilley continued, "As you are aware, you have been appointed literary executor and sole beneficiary of any and all royalties attendant to the late Mrs Morris's publishing, past, present and future. You have also been bequeathed a significant shareholding in Speers Shipping, Speers Tyneside Shipyard, and also Speers Colonial Holdings; as a result, you will take Mrs Morris's seat on the board of directors. There was a murmur of "hear, hear" from the assembled Speers officials and one "jolly good show."

"There are also a number of personal and charitable bequests that are already being attended to. We must now turn our attention to the matter of Trafalgar Hall and its surrounding estates. As Mrs Morris leaves no descendants, and since the death of her brother in the West Indies twenty years ago — himself childless I should add — it regrettably comes to pass that Mrs Morris was the last direct descendant of Charles Speers, the great fighting captain, one of Nelson's own Band of Brothers, and the founder of the global leviathan that is Speers Colonial Holdings. We must, therefore, now revert to instructions, left for this very eventuality, by the great man himself, whom my own grandfather, Augustus Twilley, had the honour of serving for over forty years, and who personally took these instructions not long before the Captain's own death, nearly seventy years ago."

"Oh, Lord, do get on!" All eyes turned to Dr Knollys, who realised with alarm that he had actually spoken aloud, causing Dorothy to stifle a chuckle as she regarded Arthur Twilley's expression of wounded indignation.

"I beg your pardon, Doctor?" Twilley said.

"A great man, Mr Twilley, as you say," Dr Knollys blurted loudly. "The old Captain, planning for every contingency. A great, great man!"

"Well, quite," Twilley agreed. "Now, getting on, referring to the relevant clause in the original Speers' will, Trafalgar Hall, its furnishings and artworks — with the exception of those items specifically bequeathed to Miss Keppel — and its estates, are to be gifted to the Admiralty, with the following conditions." Mr Twilley carefully fitted a monocle between his left eyebrow and cheek, squinted to hold it in place and looked down at the papers spread out on the desk. "That the building, known as Trafalgar Hall, be utilised as a nursing and rest home for ill, retired and impoverished seafarers and that the funding of same will be jointly underwritten by the Lady Georgiana Trust, the Speers companies' pension and sickness funds, with additional support from the Admiralty Sick and Hurt Board, or whatever equivalent entity is in place if and when this clause is enacted. It is further anticipated that income from the estate's farms and gardens will support the operation of the hospital, and provide meaningful employment to those sufficiently able-bodied patients and residents. These instructions also afford a degree of discretion to His Majesty's government, through the Admiralty, enabling the use of areas of the building and the surrounding grounds for any military purposes, as seen fit, provided the primary function of the buildings — the infirmary and nursing home — are not impeded in any way."

Mr Twilley then outlined, at considerable length, details of a number of additional specific philanthropic bequests to be granted in the various overseas territories throughout which the Speers companies had a presence, encompassing Malayan rubber, East African agriculture, West Indian sugar and rum, cattle ranching in the Argentine, railway construction and operation throughout the colonies as well as general commerce, shipping and trading in the Far East.

A number of these altruistic projects — including schools and medical missions — had been established under the stewardship Charlotte's brother, Nelson, who had suffered terribly under the burden of family guilt owing to the company's enthusiastic acquisition of slaves under Charles Speers himself, and an ambivalent attitude to the welfare of native retainers more generally under the next generation. It had been, in Nelson Speers's estimation, a deep stain on his grandfather's reputation for courage, business acumen, general amiability and kindness, particularly to the foremast jacks at sea, and tenant farmers and jobbing employees on land. It was a philosophy fully supported by Charlotte, who, in direct actions and in her writing, had frequently championed the cause of the disadvantaged and oppressed throughout the Empire, many of whom, her critics frequently observed, had suffered inordinately as a direct result of the rapacity of her own family's business operations, and from which, they also pointed out, she happily continued to draw a colossal annual dividend.

"This brings me to a further special clause," Twilley continued, "the details of which I am forbidden from disclosing in this room. However, following certain enquiries, which I am likewise unable to expand upon, and following instructions once again found in the original will, which I am also unable to disclose publicly..." Twilley stopped, having noted Dr Knollys's loud exhalation of breath and impatient fidgeting. "I am sorry, Dr Knollys," he said, "are we keeping you from something more important?"

"No, of course not, Mr Twilley." Knollys replied, reddening once again with embarrassment. "It's just a little stuffy, that's all. Please do go on."

Twilley allowed a few seconds of silence, daring the doctor to say anything further. Dorothy had a lace handkerchief pressed against her eyes and her body shuddered almost imperceptibly as she tried to stop herself laughing out loud. The Doctor's comical antics were a welcome distraction from her general, almost chronic depression, borne out of grief, the mental exhaustion from two years working around the clock with sufferers of shellshock, and, despite having been generously provided for in Charlotte's will, a deep uncertainly about what the future might hold.

"I'm very sorry, Miss Keppel," Twilley said, misinterpreting Dorothy's wavering self-control and glaring at the Doctor. "I know this must be very distressing for you. Now, as I was saying, the rooms known as the Great Cabin and its adjoining suites, the Lady Georgiana boudoir and dressing rooms, including the room in which we are now sitting, are to be set aside for, and I quote," Twilley paused for dramatic effect, then said, "special use." He looked around the gathering and then, with a sense of self-importance that made Doctor Knollys roll his eyes, concluded with "On that matter, I can say no more." Twilley then looked in the direction of Piers Armstrong, who merely nodded. The subtle exchange was noticed by Dorothy who had averted her eyes from Arthur Twilley to try to conquer her giggling once and for all. She leant over to the Doctor and whispered.

"Did you see that? What do you think that's all about?"

"See what, my dear?" Knollys looked blankly at her.

"Nothing, never mind," she replied, but studied Armstrong with greater interest.

"Miss Keppel, perhaps, if you are feeling well enough, you could update us on the closure of the officers' hospital and your own plans to vacate, which I understand are well underway."

"Thank you, Mr Twilley, I am fine," Dorothy replied, her composure regained. "The last of the patients will be departing in the coming days. It will then be just a matter of the beds, some of the equipment and medical records to be relocated. The remaining medical and administrative staff are seeing to it. I anticipate that the building will be empty and available within the month, if that is acceptable."

"More than acceptable, thank you, Miss Keppel. Now, moving on, or, for Doctor Knollys's benefit, *getting on*, we turn our attention to some interim financing arrangements for…"

***

"I thought that dithering old fool would talk forever," Doctor Knollys said between mouthfuls. "And that monocle, I ask you! Ridiculous affectation!"

Dorothy smiled. "He's been a loyal friend to the Speers family for a long time."

"Yes, and his father before him, and grandfather before, as he never tired of telling us." Doctor Knollys gestured to the waiter for more wine. They were dining in the great hall, given over for a staff and patients' dining room as part of the hospital for shell-shocked officers that had taken up Trafalgar Hall, with the exception of the private Great Cabin and Lady Georgiana apartments, for the previous two years. With most of the patients either discharged or transferred to other hospitals, there were only a small number of diners scattered throughout the manor's feature reception room. Several doctors and one or two of the patients well on the way to recovery.

Charlotte Morris had funded the dining room personally. With à-la-carte food prepared by the Trafalgar Hall chef, and fresh meat and produce from the estate farms and gardens, it was much more like an upscale London restaurant, complete with potted palms and crisp and elegant table settings benefiting from the family silverware and wine cellar, an oasis of familiarity and hospitable normality for young men barely able to function under the crushing burden of their war psychoses.

"You did remarkable things here," Doctor Knollys commented, looking around the room. A number of trestle tables and chairs had been stacked against the wall, awaiting removal, and out of place against the grandeur of their surroundings. It was easy to imagine a scene from a Jane Austen novel, with country gentlemen, Nelsonian naval officers and local militia captains with their ladies, laughing and dancing, Mr Darcy looking stern and discontented in a corner with a beaming Mr Bingley.

"It'll be strange to see the house empty again," Dorothy replied. "But it is nice to think that it will be put to good use." She took a sip of wine. "What do you think all that whispering and winking was about over the Great Cabin and the Lady Georgiana Rooms?"

"Lord knows, perhaps something to do with Room Forty, Naval Intell…Oh blast! I shouldn't have said…Have you managed to secure other accommodations, by the way, Miss Keppel? If you find yourself temporarily embarrassed, our home on the Sandringham Estate has a spare room, and Lady Knollys would love the company."

"You are too kind, Doctor, but with the help of Mr Twilley I have acquired a lovely home in Mayfair. There will be much to do with Charlotte's publisher, and I feel I really need to be in London to fulfil my duties on the Speers board. The domestic staff from Trafalgar Hall will be coming with me, Charlotte would be pleased to know that we'll all still be together. I hope the Navy will be kind to the tenants and estate workers, but I suppose that is no longer within our control. But back to the subject of the so called 'special use' of the Great Cabin and Lady Georgiana suite: your friend seemed to be very much in on the secret."

"My friend?"

"Piers Armstrong, the MP. You pointed him out to me."

"Oh, him," Knollys waved his hand dismissively. "He's no friend, as such, just a passing acquaintance."

***

After dinner, Dorothy and Doctor Knollys retired to the Lady Georgiana Suite where, seated in front of an enormous fire that warmed the room and bathed their faces in a comforting glow, Dorothy carefully unsealed the envelope and, with a deep breath, began to read aloud.

My Dearest Dorothy,

That you are reading this letter means I have departed this life and that my last will and testament has been formally read. It also means that a certain matter, the importance of which cannot be overstated, is yet unresolved.

Just prior to our rather hurried departure from Durban in 1901, I left some documents in the safekeeping of our dear old friend and protector, Colonel Fforbes Armstrong. As I have left you with this heavy burden, my love, I owe you as detailed an explanation as I can give you.

Dorothy allowed her hand holding the papers to fall to her lap. "Of course!" she exclaimed. "I know why that MP looked so familiar. I should have thought of it at the time. He's Colonel Armstrong's brother. There's quite a family resemblance."

"You might be right," Doctor Knollys said noncommittally and Dorothy continued reading.

Given the nature of our departure from Natal, it would have been far too dangerous to have those documents in our possession. We were being watched, and our baggage was being searched. Although I kept much of this from you at the time, my dearest, for your own protection...

Doctor Knollys coughed and shifted uncomfortably in his chair. "Perhaps you would prefer to read the remainder in private, just in case there are intimate, that is, personal, ah, oh dear me..."

"We have no secrets, Sir Cedric," Dorothy said with a tone of resigned acceptance. "And besides, Charlotte and I spent much of the last two decades hiding our true feelings for each other. It was agonising at times, I'm well beyond any such sensibilities, between friends at least. It's a relief to finally be honest. Charlotte trusted your discretion, as do I. In fact, Doctor, the entire Royal Family have entrusted you with their very lives for decades, so I'm sure I can trust you with my own now rather obsolete secret. And don't forget, it was Charlotte's dying wish that you be fully informed, for my sake."

"I understand. I too have felt the burden, over many years, of keeping secrets. My profession, you understand. It weighs heavily. I am honoured to be able to be of service, my dear Miss Keppel."

Dorothy continued reading aloud

I can tell you now that our lives were in grave danger. If it had not been for the good Colonel, Mr Churchill, and the kind intervention of His Majesty, we might never have left Durban alive.

I urge you to personally call upon Colonel Armstrong, (I will ensure up to date information regarding his address is enclosed herewith) show him this letter as a means of proof of my wishes, retrieve those documents, and destroy them. Unread! I urge you, in the strongest possible terms, to carry out my wishes. There is so much at stake: so much damage could be done to people whom we have loved and served for years. I so deeply regret writing what I did, but I can only conclude, with hindsight, that my mind was driven to irrational action by anger, by the horrors of the camps, those false accusations, and the fear of our lives.

"Good Lord," Doctor Cedric Knollys exclaimed. "This is all very dramatic. 'In fear of your lives,' Mrs Morris wrote. Was it really so? Do you have any idea what the documents are about?"

"I knew Charlotte was in trouble, that we were in trouble, but I had no idea just how dangerous things had become, until this moment. She put on such a brave face, for my sake. As for the documents, the only unpublished manuscript that I was ever aware of, was the biographical study of Kitchener, which we first tried to publish in the spring of 1914. But, of course, when he was appointed Secretary of State for War in the summer, well, something as critical as Charlotte's book was never going to be allowed into circulation. As to what Charlotte is alluding to here in her instructions, I cannot say."

"What did she have against Herbert, against Earl Kitchener?" Knollys asked. "I always found him to be a thoroughly decent chap. A genuine hero, and a terrible loss to our Empire, and to our war effort."

"Charlotte became quite obsessed with the so called 'camps of refuge' during the war with the Boers. Around twenty six thousand died in those tents on the veld, Doctor. It was heartbreaking to see death on such a scale, women and mostly little children. Starvation and disease on a scale you couldn't possibly imagine, in conditions which resembled an oven in summer and an icebox in winter. Houses and farms razed to the ground and the occupants, women and little children mostly, and old people, rounded up like cattle. All at the hands of our own beloved Empire. All totally unnecessary."

"I remember," Dr Knollys said. "There were questions tabled in parliament, as a result of Mrs Morris's protestations."

"Yes, Mr Lloyd George spoke up for us, and one or two others from amongst our Radical friends. Then of course there was the wonderful work of Emily, that is, Miss Hobhouse. But by the time even Salisbury, Chamberlain and Brodrick grudgingly conceded that reform was necessary, the damage —

and the killing — had already been done. Charlotte laid the blame squarely with Kitchener, although I think one could argue that Lord Roberts was the principal culprit, at least initially. But there's no doubt that Kitchener embraced the camps with enthusiasm. On one famous occasion, Charlotte actually called him a 'murdering swine' to his face, in the presence of his usual coterie of young officers. It didn't go down too well, as you would imagine."

"I dare say," the Doctor replied.

"She was writing letters to Members of Parliament, Lords, and even to Buckingham Palace, thinking that the new King, whom she already knew personally, might be sympathetic. But I had no idea that they — I mean the military hierarchy — would resort to what they did, false accusations of providing information to the Kaiser, in order to discredit her. Fortunately for us, Colonel Armstrong and Mr Churchill intervened, and we were able to return to England. But Charlotte stayed so very angry. She took a hatefully critical point of view over Kitchener's entire career and worked on the book, just a few chapters, each year. Even she conceded that it was far from objective, although I think factually accurate. By the time it was ready for submission, the publishers ran a mile. After all, it was 1914, and Kitchener had just become Secretary of War. Another hastily written Richard Fforbes adventure placated them, but Charlotte felt that it was almost a sacred duty to expose the full horrors of the camps and the behaviour of our own, shall we say, heroes, however long it took."

"I didn't mean to pry." Doctor Knollys could see that Dorothy was becoming increasingly melancholic as she reflected on some of the unhappier, and even fearful times. "Let's not dwell on past causes for sadness," he said. "There's so much to look back on, so many good memories. Charlotte's series of Richard Fforbes adventures, how many books? Fifteen was it? Sold all over the world, millions of copies. A wonderful legacy."

"Yes our publisher tells me they've received sacks and sacks of mail since Charlotte's death."

"And didn't the final novel cause a sensation! Siegfried Sassoon was very complimentary in The Times. But people were very unhappy that the gallant hero met his demise on the Western Front. Even Lady Knollys was quite bereft."

"The funny thing about that, Doctor, is that *An Heroic Departure* was the most critically lauded, but the least successful, of all the Fforbes books. Charlotte's loyal readers seemed to prefer a world of red-coated chivalry where the hero conquered his enemies, solved a murder or two, then made it to the club in time for an afternoon gin and lemon with body and limbs intact. The realities of the Western Front, which Charlotte wrote about in such vivid detail thanks to the personal accounts of many of our patients, were just too confronting for people whose loved ones were facing that very reality each day. The idealised 'world of old' was much more palatable. It was all a myth, of course. I experienced those so-called glorious days at first hand. But Lady Knollys might be happy to know that Captain Fforbes is going to fight again. There's an unfinished draft of a new story, I am going to complete it, based on Charlotte's notes. The publisher is very excited."

"Is that not going to be a little awkward, given that the good Captain was killed off? The public reaction was quite extraordinary."

"The death of our hero was a mistake. Charlotte realised that. But she had written fourteen previous books and she felt that the series had run out of steam. She hated *Iceberg Right Ahead*, the story she had to write quickly to fulfil her contract obligations after the Kitchener book was rejected. Setting the story on a Speers Liner, aboard which he solved a murder and took command just in time to avoid a Titanic-like disaster was quite nonsensical — I'm embarrassed to be even talking about it — but it sold very well, believe it or not, and the Speers' board were so pleased with the publicity that they're sponsoring a reprint this year, as they return to their peacetime passenger schedule. It wasn't poor Charlotte's finest literary moment; I think she was hoping that the book would sink without trace — oh dear, an unfortunate analogy. But, as a result, she was determined that what she thought would be the final story be the best in the series, and the most realistic. That's how *An Heroic Departure* came about, a straight story about a colonial soldier, steeped in the old traditions, facing the horrors of the Western Front. But the reaction stunned everyone, so, under intense pressure from her publisher, Charlotte came up with a scenario in which the Captain's death was falsely reported — mistaken identity — and in which he was lying anonymously in a military hospital, shell-shocked and with memory loss. He eventually recovers his wits, and there are one or two outlines for a murder mystery that Charlotte was working on when she fell ill, and that I am planning to develop further. The setting may well be Versailles, or even Russia."

"Fascinating. I'll enjoy reading that myself." The Doctor's calculated distraction had cheered Dorothy somewhat, but there were still some difficult truths to be dealt with.

"What are you going to do about these documents?" he asked. "And how can I help?"

Dorothy shuffled the papers in her lap, while Knollys reached for the poker and disturbed the burning timbers in the fireplace, releasing a shower of sparks.

"Here is Charlotte's last update, from 1916."

29th May 1916

I have just met with Colonel Armstrong at his home in Knightsbridge. He is looking so well. I was humbled to see an entire shelf in his library devoted to our books, Dorothy my dear. His brother, the MP, lives there now.

The Colonel is in London with the first and second battalions of the Natal Rangers, with whom he will soon be embarking for the trenches. Rumours abound about a "Big Push" to break through the German lines. He informed me that the documents in his charge have been lodged with the Royal Bank of Natal, Pietermaritzburg, in his personal safe deposit box. In the event of his death in France, his own will provides instructions for the documents to remain sealed, and be released only to either myself or my nominee, personally. He assures me that his solicitor, a Mr Warbeck, is unfailingly discreet and trustworthy. I do not foresee any difficulties for you. In any case, I have just approved the purchase of the bank by Speers Colonial Holdings.

"The Colonel was wounded at the Somme," Dorothy informed the Doctor. "He was one of the few survivors: the Natal Rangers were virtually all gone in a matter of hours, perhaps a matter of minutes. He was deeply upset, a number of his regulars had been with him since the days of the QONR. The reserve battalion ended up in East Africa, so I believe. The Colonel actually had dinner with us here at Trafalgar Hall when he had recovered sufficiently to travel, just after Christmas 1917 it was. He told us he was returning to South Africa and was going to finally retire to a farm in the uplands not far from Pietermaritzburg. It was the first time I'd seen him since we left Durban. I had no idea that Charlotte had spoken to him before he went to France."

"If I speak to my old chum Piers Armstrong," Doctor Knollys suggested, "I could find out exactly where his brother is now. Then, I take it, an adventure to the end of the Dark Continent might be in the offing."

Dorothy hesitated. '*My old chum?*' Earlier that day the Doctor had tried to pass him off as a passing acquaintance, while rattling off his career details with easy familiarity. Something wasn't quite right. "No thank you, Doctor," she said firmly. "I am familiar with Warbeck and Warbeck Solicitors. I will write to them and then call on them personally in Pietermaritzburg, if necessary, but I'm sure the Colonel won't be too difficult to find."

Dorothy reflected on Piers Armstrong's attendance at the reading earlier that day. As soon as the formalities had been completed, he had departed, citing urgent business in London, and had not stayed for the luncheon laid on in the great hall. The Armstrong family resemblance was distinctive, she thought, but in the Colonel's countenance was a soldier's strength, yet an underlying warmth and obvious kindness, traits he had demonstrated time and time again. In his brother, on the other hand, Dorothy sensed a deep malevolence. Any warmth in his smile was diminished by his cold, almost emotionless eyes. "I must remind you, Doctor, everything we have talked about must remain between us, everything relating to these secret instructions from Charlotte must not be discussed outside of this room. I ask for your word of honour on this matter."

Dorothy's apparent change in tone unsettled the doctor, who replied, "Of course, my dear, of course. Everything that has passed between us today is in the strictest confidence."

"Your word of honour, Doctor, if you please."

"You have my word of honour."

Dorothy relaxed a little. "Thank you. I must apologise for my insistence. I must be a little overwrought, what with everything that is happening.

"Think nothing of it, my dear," the doctor replied, with absolutely no hint of having taken any offence. "It's been a long day for all of us. Now, my dear lady, if I leave now I will just catch the last train. Thank you for your marvellous hospitality. No wonder you had such wonderful results with your patients, eating that food every day, being looked after so well. Lovely."

"Are you sure you won't stay, Doctor? There's a comfortable room made up especially, and you would be most, most welcome."

"I thank you, but Her Majesty — I refer to Queen Alexandra — is not currently in the most robust of health. Another little secret, strictly between us, of course. I don't like to be away from Sandringham for long. Perhaps you would be kind enough to ring for your chauffeur to take me to the station."

"I'll do much better than that, Doctor. I'll drive you myself."

Doctor Knollys looked suddenly anxious. "Are you sure?"

Suitably rugged and muffled against the cold, Dorothy and Doctor Knollys descended the grand staircase. They politely greeted the lamp-wielding, starched night-sister who was in the middle of her rounds, checking on the few remaining patients, then walked out into the foggy night. Dorothy directed the Doctor to a military motor-ambulance, the size of a small omnibus, parked on the sweeping curve of the circular driveway.

"Good God!" Knollys exclaimed. "You're not going to drive that? Are you sure you won't ask your chauffeur?"

"Please don't be alarmed, Doctor. Driving this ambulance has been my job for the last two years and more. Mind the step."

The Doctor soon relaxed as he realised that Dorothy was a practiced driver, hauling the heavy steering wheel smoothly around with singular effort and changing gears as second nature. She drove along the tree-lined driveway, then through the gateway to the estate, a stone structure reminiscent of a scaled-down Admiralty Arch. The Doctor ducked, involuntarily, as they passed beneath the archway, which appeared to offer little clearance on either side, or above. He rubbed his gloved hands together and raised his overcoat collar against the cold air that blew in through the open sides of the cab as the ambulance picked up speed. "If you don't mind my asking, Miss Keppel, what did happen to Mrs Morris's husband?"

"Charlotte never spoke much about him," Dorothy said, almost shouting against the noise of the engine, the rattling of the vehicle itself, the wind and the road noise. It was proving to be a rough ride, and Doctor Knollys almost bounced out of his seat as Dorothy drove directly over an unseen pothole. "God help the poor patients," he muttered, gripped the outer windscreen pillar with one hand and the edge of his seat with the other, and gritted his teeth.

"Charlotte was twenty-two years older than me," Dorothy explained. "I was actually born the year she was married. By the time I first went to work for her when I was twenty-five, her marriage was in the distant past. It wasn't something she felt comfortable talking about, and I never pressed the issue. I know that her husband's name was Reginald Morris, and that he was a lieutenant in the QONR. That's how she first met Colonel Armstrong, I think he was a Captain in those days. It proved to be an unhappy marriage. Lieutenant Morris gambled and drank, and worse. He died in, I think, 1876 or '77. The circumstances were a bit unusual, it was either a duel or a fight with another soldier. It was all kept very quiet, no breath of scandal. Have you read the first of the Richard Fforbes adventures, *The Colonel's Dilemma?*"

"Yes, a long time ago. We still have the first edition copy at home that Mrs Morris signed for us."

"Charlotte once told me that aspects of that story bore, shall we say, quite a resemblance to parts of her own life as a young military wife. Whoops-a-daisy! Hang on tight!" The ambulance bumped and rattled violently over a rutted stretch of road, and the Doctor was tremendously relieved when they pulled up at the railway station, several minutes later.

CHAPTER SIX

Norman Armstrong sat facing Sir Archie Prentice in the depths of the intelligence chief's secure headquarters, understanding for the first time what it must feel like to be a backbencher seated nervously opposite the Chief Whip and bracing for the onslaught. He also called to mind an experience half a century earlier, in front of his school headmaster following some student shenanigans, noting that the feeling of impending doom rendering him unusually nervous now was not dissimilar to how he had felt as a short-trousered mischief-maker all those years ago. The Cabinet Secretary was also present, seated to one side, a fact that Norman found at least a little reassuring. "So who is it that wants me dead, then Archie?" he asked with forced levity. "One of the Maze escapees? Militant Tendency? A disgruntled backbencher? Stanley Smee perhaps?"

"No one, you prized pillock," Sir Archie spat. "That is, if you don't count me! I had to have a pretence to stop you making a fool of yourself over this Burton business."

"Oh, I see," the Chief Whip replied with a combination of simmering annoyance and relief. "Actually, I don't understand at all."

"Well now, Norman, you're nothing if not predictable," Sir Archie continued. "I knew that you wouldn't be able to leave this alone, running around in the middle of the night asking damned silly questions about murderous monarchist vigilantes, I ask you! I remember having to discipline you about your recklessness forty years ago. You haven't changed. That DFC didn't make you invincible then, or mean that you were right all the damned time. If I'd let you follow your risky impulses then, neither you, Peregrine here, nor Young Ronnie would have survived the war. Your names would be on a war memorial somewhere, an eternal monument to your reckless disregard for danger. I've now saved your bacon for a second time. At that time I probably saved your life, this time I've definitely saved your career."

"Archie, I have no idea what you're talking about, wait a minute… Asking questions about monarchist… How do you…?"

"Oh, use your brains, Norman, just for once."

"You're bugging Dick Billings's flat!"

"We are, and that's probably the first correct deduction you've made in recent days."

"But why?"

"Nothing to do with this kerfuffle. He's way too close to Donoghue, and I'm not just talking about corrupt under-the-counter share acquisitions. Donoghue keeps some strange company, on the wrong side of the Irish Question, if you understand what I mean. I know he's a big supporter of the government, and there's no indication that he's actively involved in any republican activities, but forewarned is forearmed."

"Are you tapping my phone as well?"

"Yes, well, we were. But only since the beginning of this Burton business."

"Oh, that makes it perfectly in order then," Norman responded sarcastically.

"Oh, get off your high horse, Norman. You would've done the same thing in my place."

Norman calmed down. "Well, you might be right. Sorry, did you say 'were'? When did you stop?"

"About an hour ago."

"You see, Norman," Sir Peregrine interrupted, "we couldn't let you embarrass yourself. You're too valuable. You were letting personal feelings affect your judgement, going off on this crusade. You've looked after us for so long, on just this one occasion you needed a little looking after yourself."

Norman's feelings of agitation had by now subsided into a vaguely discomforting blend of contrition, embarrassment and gratitude. He directed his question at Sir Archie. "What was this charade with Ron Coburn and his lunatic flying squad all about then? They grabbed me at gunpoint, for God's sake!"

"I couldn't let on that I knew where you were, for obvious reasons, and I needed you brought in right away. I didn't think you'd respond to a polite invitation, so I concocted the ruse about this death threat and then let Young Ronnie's finest take it from there. From what I gather, it was a thoroughly professional piece of work." When Norman did not reply, Sir Archie continued, his tone much softer and more conciliatory. "Perhaps the best way to proceed from here, Norman, is for you to ask me some questions to put your mind at ease. You have my word, I'll answer as truthfully as I can."

"Do you have Alf Burton?"

"Yes and no. Indirectly, I would have to say yes."

"Has he been harmed?"

"Of course he hasn't," Sir Archie retorted indignantly. "What kind of people do you think we are? I don't employ goons to beat the living shit out of people, despite what our friend Billings seems to think."

Norman found himself momentarily unable to speak, overwhelmed with relief that Alf was still very much alive and, assuming Archie was really telling the whole truth, in one piece. Sir Peregrine stood up and placed a reassuring hand on Norman's shoulder while Sir Archie, equally mindful of their old RAF comrade's intense mental exhaustion, buzzed for coffee and bacon butties all round. He assured Norman, with uncharacteristic kindness, that there was nothing like a hot sandwich of fatty bacon dripping butter for breakfast, to steel the mind for the rigours of the day ahead.

"I have some more questions, Archie, if I may." Norman said after a few moments, having recovered his composure. Sir Peregrine sat down again.

"Go on," Sir Archie said.

"What about the Liege Men of Charles the First, the Banqueting Club?"

"It did exist, before the war."

"So Dick was right about that, at least."

"And that's where Dick Billings's grasp on reality ends. It's true that it was an old society dating back to the seventeenth century, and that they were known as the Banqueting Club. In more recent times, they met every so often, dressed up in ludicrous costumes, drank copious amounts of wine and imagined what it might have been like to lead armies of cavaliers against Cromwell's New Model Army. But that's where it ended, Norman. Granted, they may have had some political influence around the time of the Restoration and the Glorious Revolution, but in recent years they were nothing more than a bunch of harmless barking mad old men escaping from their wives, dressing up, and wishing they'd been born three hundred years earlier. The society just faded away because the members grew old and died off, and there was no one to take their place. Who would? Grown men dressing like cavaliers and pledging allegiance to Charles the First, I ask you! Everything Billings told you about murder and political manipulation, all pure fantasy — the product of years of resentment about his never really being accepted by his colleagues. He could never be one of us, no matter how hard he tried, and no doubt felt some guilt for bringing a German spy into the heart of the Ministry of Information during the war. And too much, you know," Sir Archie mimed raising a glass. "You shouldn't set too much store by the words of an embittered, drunken, lonely, failed old man, Norman. Dick was just desperate to be relevant."

"He was sensible enough to warn me off," Norman observed.

"True," Sir Archie acknowledged. "But for completely the wrong reasons. Rampant paranoia."

"What about Paddy Donoghue?"

"Exactly as you thought all along. Killed during the blitz."

"Was he in a knocking shop?"

"Yes."

"What was he doing there?"

"What do you want, Norman, diagrams?"

"You mean he was just..."

"He had something of a taste for the proverbial bit of rough. He was notorious for it, actually. Don't look so surprised, Norman, how many married backbenchers' chestnuts have you pulled out of the fire, quite literally?" Both Sir Archie and Sir Peregrine chuckled, although Norman was too preoccupied to see any mirth.

"Was he really a traitor?"

"Oh yes, no doubt about it. My predecessor had an extensive file on old Paddy Donoghue."

"What about Dick's assertion that the Banqueting Club knocked him off to protect a royal relative from Paddy's efforts to incriminate him?"

"Norman, does that sound even remotely plausible? It's the plot you might find in a cheap novel written by a talentless hack — no Jeffrey Archer by any means — something you might read on a long flight to God-knows-where, as an absolute last resort."

"So what happened?"

"Donoghue was given up, as Dick said, by a fifth columnist under interrogation. He was placed under surveillance, to see who else might have been involved. It's conceivable to think that he might have also been using the knocking shop to meet contacts, I suppose, as well as his other, er, activities, but you were right when you told Dick that he got what was coming to him. He was about to be arrested when fate laid its icy fingers. He would've been shot in due course, in any case."

"And the investigating policeman who was rather conveniently shipped off to some secret show, and was never seen again?"

"It's all here," Sir Archie tapped a file on the desk in front of him. "A perfectly routine report for the Coroner relating to the demise of Padraig Seamus Donoghue and several others at 27 Old Cleveland Lane, Whitechapel. The verdict, death by enemy action. The young DC who prepared the report, a hardworking fellow of ambition and talent, was recruited into SOE soon afterwards, due to his superlative abilities, it wasn't uncommon. There was no conspiracy, there were no inconsistencies in the report. You can read it yourself if you like. He, like many other brave young men, Lord knows we knew enough of them, died in the service of his country. The only cover-up, if you could call it that, was from Dick's own department, who didn't want any hint of scandal about harbouring a Jerry spy, for understandable reasons, and who wanted to present Donoghue as a patriotic press baron, killed, like many other civilians, in the blitz. It was all rather cleverly engineered by your father, as Dick said. Nothing ever came out."

"All right," Norman said, "I can see that it all seems to make sense. What's in this Charlotte Morris manuscript, then, and why have we been tying ourselves in knots about it for generations?"

"I don't know," Sir Archie replied, "and that's the honest truth. My word on it."

"Then why all this cloak-and-dagger carrying on, staged kidnappings — Smee on the television every night telling us they're making progress — all this disruption for something we don't even know is damaging? We've been paralysed with fear for generations, and for what? The damned thing could be a recipe for old Tum Tum's favourite dessert, for all we know!"

"You were sufficiently concerned to run straight to Peregrine here when you first found out that Burton might have it." Sir Archie pointed out, "and to immediately notify me. You're as much a part of this as we are."

"Who is Tum Tum?" Sir Peregrine asked.

"It was a nickname for Edward the Seventh," Norman explained. "Charlotte Morris was his special advisor on colonial matters during his reign, but I think also quite well connected there when he was still Prince of Wales and getting up to all sorts of shenanigans. It's conceivable therefore that she was very well informed about the goings on at Court and in the government."

"Oh yes, that's right," said Sir Peregrine. "She was caught up in a spy scandal, wasn't she? Something about passing information to Boer sympathisers in Europe?"

"Allegedly," Norman replied, choosing to remain silent about his own family's deep involvement in that rather awkward matter. He was grateful when Sir Archie moved the conversation forward.

"Thank you for the history lesson, Norman," said the Chief of Intelligence. "To the matter at hand. My job is like yours in many ways: it's about not taking any chances. If, as Chief Whip, you see political danger, one of your backbenchers causing trouble for instance, you act pre-emptively. There's no one better than you at putting out political fires before they're even lit. Margaret has a lot to be grateful for, as does the entire Conservative side of politics. Let me tell you something, Norman, I do the same thing when it comes to the security of our country, of the monarchy, of the Lords, of everything that we've spent our entire lives defending. I respect your judgement when it comes to party politics, I only ask that you respect mine when it comes to national security."

"Fair enough, Archie," Norman agreed. "Fair enough. I take it then, that Alf hasn't given up his source?"

"No. That's where you come in."

"What can I do?"

"First, let me ask you something," Sir Peregrine interjected. "How do you think Dick Billings would go as Chief Whip and Party Chairman?"

Norman felt his stomach muscles contract and he was overcome by a tidal wave of distress to the point of nausea, which then morphed into an intense, smouldering anger, and shame. His face turned a deep shade of red. I'm being sacked, he thought, after all these years of service. They no longer trust me, I'm finished. Skulking about like some amateur detective, listening to drunken old fools in the middle of the night, Oh God, the humiliation! He forlornly reflected on what his father might have made of his complete and utter failure, and how in the space of little less than a fortnight, he had not only destroyed his own career but irreparably disgraced a distinguished family name, generations in the making.

There was a distraction: the coffee and bacon butties arrived. Then Sir Peregrine, who could read Norman's mind like an open book with very large print, immediately put his mind at rest. "Relax, Norman. The Prime Minister has asked you to serve as Home Secretary. This is a formal offer, on her behalf."

"What? But I thought... Home Secretary, you said?"

"We need you, Norman. Next year is going to be one hell of a fight."

Norman's paralysing terror ebbed away, and his breathing slowly returned to normal. Almost. "I accept, of course, with gratitude," he said eventually. "But what about the current one? He's only been in the job for five minutes."

"He'll be resigning this morning, on health grounds," Sir Peregrine stated. "We all know he hasn't really been up to it. We need someone to build on the work of Mr, sorry, *Viscount* Whitelaw, I should say, not run away from it. The Prime Minister has the perfect pretext: his department's supervision of the police has been a farce, the wrong people being shot by trigger-happy plods, while football hooligans, protestors and terrorists are running riot."

"What if he won't resign?" Norman asked. "He can be stubborn."

"Resignation or sacking, it makes no difference," the Cabinet Secretary stated firmly. "But I think he'll see sense on this occasion. Either way his desk will be cleared by nine fifteen this morning. Now, is Billings up to being Chief Whip and Party Chair? We've got to move him out of Environment quietly. The Donoghue connection is too risky for us to ignore. He's done the job he was required to do, everyone who matters is happy with the outcome. It's time to pull up the drawbridge."

"He'd be a fine Chief Whip and Party Chairman," Norman replied with sincerity. "He's one of the best campaigners in the business, and he knows how to keep order. He looked across the desk to the Intelligence Chief. "I dispute your assessment of him, Archie, with great respect, he's no failed old man."

"Not that it's any concern of mine," Sir Archie observed, "but he drinks too much for my liking. And he says stupid things. I can't imagine Margaret being too happy if another smile-so-dat I-can-see-you fracas occurs during a future campaign."

"In all fairness, Archie," Norman countered, "organised agitators were heckling Dick throughout the entirety of what was a very good speech about job creation and social order on Merseyside. You can only be called a fascist honky cunt so many times before you hit back. It wasn't a clever thing to say on Dick's part, but I can understand it. I might have said something just as bad had it been me."

"What about the drinking?" Archie persisted.

"If drinking too much was a barrier to high office, we'd lose almost all of the Cabinet and probably half the civil service."

"Even so," Sir Peregrine offered, "It's generally known that the only person that can control Billings is you, Norman. We'd be relying on you, to a degree, to protect us, and indeed him, from himself."

"No one can control Sir Dick," Norman acknowledged. "But everyone comes at a price. His talents, in my opinion, make him worth the risk. I'll do what I can."

"Right, that's settled then," said Sir Archie, rubbing his hands. "Now, how do you think our Young Ronnie would like to be Police Commissioner?"

"Ah, I think he'd like it very much," Norman said, puzzled.

"Good, and do you think he's up to it?"

"Well, yes, of course, there would be no one better. But as I understand it there are other Assistant Commissioners senior to him, not to mention the fact that the Commissioner himself is younger than Ron is and it doesn't look like he's going anywhere for a while. But as a purely academic question, I think young…" Norman checked himself, knowing how much his friend hated being referred to as Young Ronnie. "I think Ron would be the best Commissioner we've had in a very long time, possibly ever."

"That'll be your first job as Home Secretary, then," Sir Peregrine said. "Appointing a new Commissioner of the Metropolitan Police."

Norman hesitated. "I'm all for that, of course," he said, "but what grounds do we have to remove the existing one? Is that not going to be politically difficult? There'll be some tough questions to answer."

"As it happens," Sir Archie said, "he's got himself into a spot of bother. Remember Cyril McCann?"

"Can't say I do."

"Come on, Norman. You must remember the old Sultan of Soho, from when you were Home Secretary under Douglas-Home. These days, he's what our friends in the press might call a *West London Character*. Known as Y-Fronts McCann on account of the fact that he apparently once strangled some poor chap with his own underpants."

"*Allegedly!*" Sir Peregrine ventured, smiling.

"Quite so," Sir Archie continued. "In any case, old Y-Fronts used to get up to all kinds of dubious activities in the good old days. Pornographer, pimp, standover merchant, a thoroughly unpleasant piece of work. Young Ronnie finally sorted him out good and properly in the mid-seventies, sent him down for quite a few years. Our soon-to-be former commissioner was involved as well, although I don't think his hands were entirely clean."

"Oh yes, I remember now," Norman said. "It ultimately led to the corruption enquiries at West End Central. Ron was promoted to Commander on the back of it all."

"Mr McCann is back in business, in a minor way, having not long been released from Pentonville. Anyway, our esteemed commissioner recently renewed his acquaintance with Mr McCann, and has since been seeing a lot of a young dancer from one of his establishments. Not just any dancer, apparently, one of McCann's favourites, if you get my meaning. I think the current police vernacular is going OTS."

"OTS?"

"Over the side."

"Oh, I see. He's been shagging McCann's girlfriend, in other words," Norman commented, thinking of how his son Rick would have phrased it.

"In a nutshell, although rather unattractively put, if I might say so. Anyway, my chaps have some rather interesting photographs, I'd imagine that they'll be showing the Commissioner," Sir Archie glanced at his watch, "right about now. He'll see the sense of a quiet resignation. No doubt he'll develop a medical condition all of a sudden that necessitates a quick, discreet exit. Probably the pox, eh?" Sir Archie snorted with laughter at his own joke.

"It's a bad season for the general health of some of our colleagues," Norman observed wryly. "I wonder if, years from now, someone will look back and see more than a coincidence."

"Actually, it's a very good season," Sir Peregrine commented. "Dead wood being cleared out at a great rate."

"Right, now that you're Home Secretary-designate," Sir Archie said, "I can put you fully in the picture about Burton, and how I think you might be able to help. I would remind you that everything we discuss here this morning is subject to the Official Secrets Act. But first, let's take a few minutes to eat breakfast."

"Archie," Norman said through a mouthful of bread and fatty bacon, "You told me about Alf before I'd accepted the role of Home Secretary. What if I'd said no?"

"What was it that Don Corleone said?" Sir Archie remarked. Then, in a convincing, totally unexpected and croakily theatrical imitation of Marlon Brando, rasped, "I'll make him an offer he can't refuse!" All three men, leaning forward and dabbing paper napkins as they tried preserve their expensive suits from dripping melted butter and runny egg, erupted into comradely laughter.

"Who is this Donald Corleone, and where does he come into all of this?" Norman asked.

***

The meeting concluded after the new Home Secretary presented a hastily conceived plan to end the impasse with Alf Burton and Sir Archie granted a small favour in return. Then both Norman and Sir Peregrine were driven back to Norman's house in Knightsbridge by Sir Archie's driver. While Norman was changing suits and freshening up in preparation for a morning meeting with the Prime Minister, Sir Peregrine phoned his own driver and instructed him to pick them both up from Knightsbridge. They sat in the downstairs kitchen, sipping coffee while they waited.

"Sorry that you were dragged into this," Norman said. "Have you been up all night as well?"

"Oh no," Sir Peregrine replied. "Only most of it."

"Tell me, Perry, why did Archie use Special Branch officers to snatch Alf? Why didn't he keep it in-house, as it were?

"It's the way his department works. His people are not much use for anything beyond listening to other people's phone calls and opening their letters."

"And passing information to the Russians."

"Quite, although not quite so much recently: that we know of. But back to your question: for jobs that require more practical skills, he brings in either members of the Special Branch or sometimes the SAS. It also means that if it all goes wrong, then Archie can say he had nothing to do with it, and lives to fight another day with reputation, and budget, intact."

"Is Ron Coburn mixed up in all this?"

"No. Your little adventure was a different thing altogether. That was all done through normal police channels, the more people that knew about an apparent death threat towards you the better. All fitted nicely into Archie's carefully constructed illusion. And besides, Ron is far too honest for Archie's brand of plotting and conniving."

Norman's shoulders slumped and he stared vacantly into his coffee cup. The adrenaline of death threats, furious drives through early morning London, sparring with the nation's Chief of Intelligence, the dread of being sacked, immediately followed by an unexpected promotion, had receded like the outgoing tide in the face of a rampaging surge of exhaustion.

"Buck up, old chap," Peregrine encouraged.

"Perry, did you ever feel that I was reckless, when we were flying missions? Did you ever feel I took dangerous risks?"

"What? No, of course not. It got a bit hairy at times, but we made it through, unlike most of our friends. There was no one else I would've wanted to fly with. I'm sure if you ask Ron, or other chaps from our crew, they'd say the same thing."

"Really?" For once in his life, Norman felt the need for reassurance.

"Don't pay any attention to Archie's carrying on. Its only jealousy."

"Jealousy?"

"Of course. You flew Spitfires and Lancasters, with great success. One of the Few, a DFC thoroughly deserved, married a beautiful, glamourous pilotess from the ATA — is pilotess even a word? I don't know — anyway, not to mention God knows how many missions flown over Germany, back home safe each time. Poor Archie flew a desk for most of the war. Let's face it, Norman, he may have outranked you, but you represented everything he could never be, or have."

"Funny, I never thought about it that way."

"He's also probably feeling very embarrassed about the pig's ear he's made of the Burton kidnapping. All this expense, conniving, subterfuge, manpower, publicity and aggravation, all for nothing. You were on to them straight away, and I wouldn't be surprised if others had their own suspicions as well." Norman thought immediately of Sir Eddie Donoghue. *This is a government job. Alf has upset someone, and the security services are teaching him a lesson. This old shite about the Irish republicans is a cover, we both know it's been done before.* Sir Peregrine continued, "I don't think Archie really thought this one through, do you? And when all was said and done, the special branch rozzers that he lined up for the job couldn't even get Burton to reveal his source. The only thing left for Archie to do was to swallow his pride and ask you sort out his mess. That can't have been easy for him. I have a feeling some heads are going to roll. Not his, of course." Sir Peregrine started to chuckle.

"What's so funny?" Norman asked.

"I was just thinking of the time you first met Eileen. What did you say to her? Something about how women should be making sandwiches for real pilots, was it? Your face when she kicked you fair and square on your smug backside. A priceless moment." They both laughed. It was a nice moment that recalled their friendship of old. Both were now so busy, and their respective roles so defined, that they rarely had the chance to just relax and chat. Peregrine went on, "Old Dickie Billings, eh? What an enigma he is. All that about secret societies, conspiracies, knocking people off."

"You've heard the recording then?"

"Yes, sorry old boy. It was clear you weren't convinced by Dick's ramblings, there's nothing for you to feel embarrassed about. Completely implausible. As Archie said, the rantings of an embittered old man. And yet…"

"And yet what?"

"Remember I took early demob? Went straight into the Civil Service leading up to the 1945 election."

"I remember," Norman replied. "You were going to work in what was going to be my father's department, had the election gone the other way."

"That's right. I was so much looking forward to working for him, too. He would have been a fine Secretary of State for Reconstruction."

"That's politics," Norman lamented. "You fell on your feet nicely, though."

"Well, I guess we've both done all right, ups and downs notwithstanding. I remember there was a planning meeting with your father, not long before the election. It was business as usual. No one in government thought for a minute that they were going to lose. He was going to offer Dick Billings the position of his PPS."

"I didn't know that," Norman said.

"I remember questioning him about it at the time. I must have been mad, young and stupid, it wasn't my place at all to poke my nose into political appointments, but your dad took it with very good grace. I only knew Dick by reputation. Even then he was not universally liked, or even trusted. His demeanour tended to put people off, as you know. He hasn't changed. Anyway, I suggested to your father that Dick was probably the last person we would want in our department. I remember your father telling me not to underestimate him and that he wasn't anywhere near as ignorant as he seemed, not to be put off by his unfortunate manner and that he would be a worthy addition to our new department."

"I remember my father said pretty much the same thing to me. Better friend than enemy, he said. But I still don't quite see where you're going with this."

"Me neither," Sir Peregrine acknowledged, shrugged, and drained the last of his coffee as the doorbell rang signalling the arrival of his driver. "I have no idea what I'm talking about. But one thing I do know," he said, as they made their way along the passage to the front door, their footsteps echoing starkly on the polished timber beneath the gaze of generations of uniformed Armstrongs, framed in portraits on the walls, a silent guard of honour. "You're going to be as fine a Home Secretary as you were Chief Whip. The country is in good hands."

Once in the back seat of Sir Peregrine's black sedan, he pressed a button and a dividing glass screen rose and separated them from the driver.

"I'll tell you another thing," Sir Peregrine said. "Archie Prentice is a survivor. You don't get to where he is, and stay there decade after decade while your colleagues around you all fall by the wayside, without knowing a few dirty tricks. He'll be desperately worried that this debacle might have dented his reputation, even though only a very small number of people are ever going to know about it. He's lost face in front of us, at least in his own estimation."

"I still don't see what you're driving at," Norman said

"I'm just saying that we should keep our wits about us, that's all. You know what they say about how dangerous a wounded predator can be. And, by the way, who'd have thought old Archie was a movie buff?"

"Movie buff?"

"Yes, his quote from *The Godfather*."

"Whose Godfather?" Norman asked, still confused over the identity of this Mr Donald Corleone, whom Archie had quoted so melodramatically.

"You really should try and get out more," Sir Peregrine said kindly.

"My son tells me the same thing," Norman conceded, none the wiser.

As the car turned into Downing Street, the conversation returned to business. "Tell me, now that I'm about to be Home

Secretary," Norman asked, "does Archie actually work for me, or for you?"

"That, my dear fellow," Sir Peregrine replied. "Is a fascinating topic for debate."

***

Rick Armstrong looked up from his desk to see his business partner standing in the doorway, lightly tapping the frame. Rick always worked with his office door open, for reasons he never could quite explain.

"What's up, Terry?" he asked, glancing up from some concept album covers on the desk in front of him.

"Not much," Terry answered, entering the office and taking a seat on the opposite side of Rick's desk. "What are you working on?"

"Ever heard of the Forgotten North?"

"A few decaying cities, lots of smog, rains all the time, no one has a job and people walk around saying eh-oop and why-aye, man."

"I think you might have missed a stereotype there."

"They all wear flat caps. I'll work on a few more."

"You do that. The Forgotten North is a punk band, quite successful a few years ago, had a minor hit with *Fuck You, You Fascist Cunt*."

"Charming. What was the B Side?"

"*Die, Tory Scum*."

"Your father would've appreciated that one, I'm sure."

"They've cut a new album, much more mainstream. Think Status Quo with a social conscience. We've been asked to do some promotion for them, a big album launch leading up to a national tour. I'm looking over some sample album covers."

"Well, I suppose you know what you're doing, doesn't sound too promising to me."

"And you're the expert, of course. Who was it that lost us the Culture Club account? Never amount to anything, you said. And what did you call Boy George?"

"Don't remind me. What are you doing next Tuesday week for lunch?"

"I feel that you're about to tell me."

"We are having lunch in the executive dining room of Padraig Donoghue House, Fleet Street, as guests of Erin Donoghue herself."

"Really?"

"You don't sound too excited. We could be in the running for the PR account for the entire Donoghue Group. Media, construction, transport, the whole thing! This could be huge!"

"Maybe, but Sir Eddie Donoghue is an old friend of my dad's, and any time one of his cronies is involved, I have an uncontrollable urge to run very fast the other way."

***

"It's nice to have you back, Norman," Charles Seymour said, feeling so pleased to see the Chief Whip that he used his first name. He was hoping that things were getting back to normal, but his heart sank when Norman Armstrong instructed him to sit down, and close the door behind him. As soon as he sat down, he noted with alarm that Norman appeared to be in the throes of clearing his desk.

"What's going on?" Charles asked quietly.

"First of all, Alf Burton is safe. His release is being negotiated as we speak, and we expect him to be home by the end of the week."

"That's very good news, congratulations." The two men shook hands over the desk. "I'm sure you played a big part in it."

"Well, perhaps one day I'll be able to tell you all about it. But to more immediate matters: I am moving to the Home Office as of now. Sir Dick Billings will be taking my place here as Chief Whip. I also expect Dick to be our next Party Chairman. I've withdrawn my candidacy."

If Charles Seymour was hurt or disappointed that someone else was being brought in to the whips' office over his head, he didn't show it. After a brief moment, he said, "Congratulations again, Norman, or should I say Home Secretary. It's thoroughly deserved, and I know that getting back to the Home Office has been an ambition of yours for a long time."

"I need you to stay here for a little while, just to make sure Dick is on the right track."

"Of course."

"As soon as the time is right, I'm going to bring you over to the Home Office as my Special Minister of State, that's if you accept, of course."

For the first time, Charles Seymour allowed his relief to show and he smiled widely. "I'd be honoured to work for you at the Home Office, Norman."

"Right, I'm glad. Now, to our little books. I'll leave the one with the green cover here, for Dick's reference. I'll take the other one with me."

"That's probably sensible," Charles acknowledged. "Considering the number of pages devoted to Sir Dick himself."

"I'm going to offer Miss Best PPS. What do you think?"

"She's a clever operator, hardworking and trustworthy. Apart from that, it's a superlative move politically. It'll help relations with minority communities, and with Smee in Northern Ireland, and Stuart Farquhar so desperate to get his old office back that he'll do anything we tell him, it fucks the Awkward Squad once and for all, if I might put it like that."

"What about Warbeck and Simnel?"

"Very quiet. By the time Dick takes over, there won't be much for him to do."

"That's certainly the idea."

***

By lunchtime, Norman was seated behind his desk at the Home Office, attended by his Permanent Secretary, Sir Godfrey Powell, and Principal Private Secretary Roger Davenport. He was due back at Number Ten later that afternoon for more extensive briefings, but had one or two pressing matters to set in motion.

"First things first, Roger. Can you phone Assistant Commissioner Coburn at New Scotland Yard, send him my compliments, and ask him to attend the Home Office at his earliest convenience?"

"Er, excuse me, Home Secretary," Sir Godfrey interjected. "But the chain of command. We always go through the commissioner's office: it's highly unusual for us to speak directly to extraneous personnel."

"Ron Coburn will be the commissioner, by the time he leaves this office," Norman explained. "Now, I intend to bring someone in from the outside to be my driver. If all goes to plan, he'll do a couple of days advanced driving with the Met instructors, then he'll report to me first thing Friday."

160

This time Roger Davenport turned a shade of pale and Sir Godfrey held up a restraining hand. "As you wish, of course, Home Secretary, but there are procedures. The Home Secretary's driver is a senior post, the unions won't stand for an outsider. There'll be terrible trouble."

"Roger, go and phone Mr Coburn as I asked. Godfrey, I have fond memories of working with you twenty years ago, when you were an undersecretary, and I had an all-too-brief stint here in the Douglas-Home government. I hope we're going to have the same fruitful working relationship this time." The new Home Secretary's tone was genial, but the meaning was clear. Sir Godfrey got the message, but knew his own responsibilities as well. He marked out his own territory. "Of course, Home Secretary. Although I will never hesitate to offer my advice, if I think it appropriate."

"I'd expect nothing less, Godfrey. Perhaps we can lay on a few drinks in the next few days, so I can get to know the senior staff."

"Of course, Roger will make the arrangements. But I must caution you about this driver. I'm sure we can accommodate, but it will take a little time. There are security checks, for a start, and we'll need to at least consult with the union. It's highly irregular."

"I have no intention of consulting with anyone." Norman tapped a folder on his desk. "This is the security clearance. Approved by Sir Archie Prentice himself. Satisfied?"

"Abundantly, Home Secretary." Sir Godfrey Powell came to the realisation that he would now be working in a very different Home Office.

As soon as he was alone, Norman took a business card from his wallet, smiled, and began dialling.

***

"Congratulations, Norman," Ron Coburn said, as soon as he took a seat in Norman's office. "Sorry, congratulations, Home Secretary."

"Norman is fine, Ron, just like always. Thanks for coming over at such short notice. It's been a long day, and night, for both us. I'm afraid we have to be brief, I'm due at Number Ten."

"All right for some," Ron replied, smiling.

"I'm offering you the post of Commissioner of the Metropolitan Police."

Ron laughed, then suddenly fell silent in the face of Norman's serious expression. "Now hang on, Norman, Home Secretary. It's not that easy. Besides, even if the position was vacant, I'm not the most senior Assistant, and then there's the Deputy..."

"Ron, the Prime Minister herself is asking you to serve. Are you really going to let a bunch of mediocre timeservers stand in your way?"

"Since you put it like that," Ron replied, "Of course, I accept. It's an offer I can't refuse."

"It certainly is," the Home Secretary affirmed. "Now, next time you're in Soho I suggest you pay a visit to Y-Fronts McCann and thank him."

"Thank McCann? Why, for God's sake?"

"This is twice now that he's boosted your career."

***

"About time you got off your enormous socialist backside and got back to work!"

Alf Burton was watching television from a cheap, vinyl-covered armchair. The room was upstairs, large, with high ceilings, but nondescript. Much of the original decor had either been painted over or removed. There was a large, roughly crafted four-poster bed in the middle of the room. Norman noted that Alf wouldn't have been too uncomfortable during his captivity. The front windows had been boarded up, and a number of newspapers and writing pads, filled with Alf's handwritten notes, were strewn on the floor around his chair.

Alf looked around in surprise on hearing the voice of the new Home Secretary. Norman noted that he appeared in good fettle, apparently none the worse for wear, and was sporting a Glasgow Celtic tracksuit.

"Why-aye!" Alf replied, rising to his feet. "A republican stronghold is a funny place for a Home Secretary to turn up bold as brass. Congratulations, by the way, I've been keeping up with all developments on the news. I've already written all about it for my next Westminster Watch column. Just in case I made it out of here alive, like."

At that moment the man with the long red ponytail entered the room and, following a nod of approval from the Home Secretary, approached Alf with his arm extended. "I'm from Special Branch. Sorry I can't introduce myself properly. No hard feelings over all this I hope, Mr Burton."

Alf readily took his hand. "None at all, bonny lad," he assured him. "I've been in need of a little holiday for a while. This has been quite a rest-cure."

"I'll be downstairs, Home Secretary," the Special Branch officer said, then withdrew.

Norman looked at his old friend, feeling a strong urge to embrace him. Instead, he gave nothing away, but did allow his handshake to linger. "Are you all right, Alf? Really? They didn't harm you at all?"

"No, I'm canny, thanks marra. These were good lads. To tell you the truth, I rumbled them as polis almost straight away, their accents slipped every so often, then they just gave up. I think they were at a loss once it became apparent that I wasn't going to tell them anything. So what happens now?"

"I need to get you home. You'll have enough time to give Dolly a big kiss, then the two of you can have a nice second honeymoon in Blackpool at Sir Eddie's expense."

"The party conference? Dolly will just love that!"

"But first there are some very important matters to settle. Tomorrow morning, the Donoghue media group will be exclusively reporting that top level negotiations with the Irish Revolutionary Brotherhood, involving the Secretary of State for Northern Ireland and the Home Office, have secured your release."

"That's nice, bonny lad. Stanley Smee deserves a bit' credit for all the effort he's been putting in. Looks very good on the news, don't you think?"

"You're unharmed, and extremely grateful to Her Majesty's government for working tirelessly on your behalf and you'll be making a full public statement to that effect in due course. On the way back to London, you're going to tell me absolutely everything about this blasted manuscript, including identifying your source to me. You're also going to sign Official Secrets Act documents to the effect that the truth of this little adventure will never be revealed to anyone. In return, our deal over preferred access to Number Ten, on the terms we discussed, stands."

"What if I say no?" Alf said with half a smile, although, being a realist and very much wanting to go home, he had already decided that he would agree to any and all of the Home Secretary's terms.

"This is an offer you can't refuse, to quote a mutual friend of ours."

Alf laughed, then fell silent as he noticed Norman Armstrong's unsmiling countenance. "Where do I sign?" he asked hastily.

***

There were more handshakes and backslaps all round, as Alf bid farewell to his captors. His freshly laundered clothes were returned to him in a large paper bag, and he was relieved to see his old mac neatly folded within. He readily signed a copy of *Decade of Discontent* for one of the officers, thanked them all for their rough and ready kindness and said, "Well lads, I'll be glad to be home. I do miss my Dolly."

"You miss your *dolly*?" One of the officers queried with eyebrows raised in disbelief.

"My wife, Dolly."

"Oh, right. Sorry."

Alf and Norman walked out into the night and approached the Home Secretary's ministerial car.

"I think you two have met before," Norman commented, as Eric Baker touched the peak of his chauffeur's cap, before opening the rear doors in turn. "I think you should buy Eric a drink," Norman told Alf, "He was the one who spotted you being snatched on Whitehall. Without him, I'd still be running around after non-existent Irish splinter groups." Eric smiled at the recognition, but was still at a loss to comprehend the events of the previous few days. At the beginning of the week, he'd been happily driving his cab, by week's end he was personal driver to the Home Secretary. The Home Secretary! The general attitude of the other ministerial drivers had been frosty, to say the least, when he'd first reported to the parliamentary garage, but that didn't worry him one bit. His son Jamie was almost through the Knowledge, so the cab wouldn't be off the road for long. Cushtie, as Del-Boy would say. The biggest challenge so far had been remembering to say, "very good, Home Secretary," instead of "Righto Guv'nor."

The gravel driveway crackled under the tyres, and Alf looked out the back window as a large stately home, grey in the moonlight, receded behind them as the car picked up speed towards the main road. A second black sedan appeared behind them and kept pace. The car passed under a stone archway just before it turned left out of the estate, and accelerated smoothly.

"So, this is where I've been the whole time," Alf commented. "That's one mystery solved. If I'm not mistaken, this is what used to be known as Trafalgar Hall. I couldn't see it when I got here, I was blindfolded, you see. A lot of fun that was! This used to be a kind of hospital and nursing home for impoverished, aged and infirm seafarers, I remember visiting someone here years ago, not long after the war."

"I have no idea," Norman replied. "But whatever it is or was called, and wherever it is, you're going to forget you were ever here."

"Forgotten already, bonny lad."

"I phoned Dolly, by the way. She knows you're safe."

"Thanks, Norman. I appreciate that. She must have had a rough time of it."

"Eileen tried to get her to come and stay at our home in the constituency, walk in the garden, play with the dogs, lunch at the tennis club, keep her mind off things. She was adamant she was not going to move from your flat, just in case you walked in the door."

"She's a good old stick, our Dolly."

"Now, I have some coffee in this thermos, and something a little stronger tucked away if you need it. It's a long drive to London. Start talking."

CHAPTER SEVEN

The RMS Lady Georgiana was making heavy work of an angry, conflicted sea as she turned laboriously northwards, having emerged from the Strait of Gibraltar for the final leg of her voyage home. It had been a hot trip through Suez and the Mediterranean, during which chronic boiler malfunctions had caused her twin stacks to belch clouds of black smoke which then hung over the decks like a suffocating blanket, seeping through vents and portholes, and leaving a coating of black soot on beds, carpets, and surfaces — driving the maids to distraction, and making the already stifling cabins intolerable.

In spite of the rough seas, which made the bones of the old ship creak and groan constantly, and had everyone perpetually off-balance, it was a relief to be in fresh air. Dorothy Keppel, content in the satisfaction of a mission well accomplished, was looking forward to getting home, where the happy task of decorating her new house awaited: a distraction from the past, a new beginning.

The one and only Stateroom in the Lady Georgiana was, in Dorothy's estimation, much like the ship herself, reminiscent of a dowager duchess fallen on hard times but stubbornly refusing to admit it. The timberwork needed a good polishing, and the carpet was faded and worn, yet Dorothy felt a strong sense of connection with the ship, named after Charlotte's spirited grandmother. The ship was the last survivor of a trio of elegant luxury liners affectionately known as the Speers Ladies, built on Tyneside by Speers' own shipyard, and launched in the early 1890s. All three soon set the benchmark for luxury and prestige on the high seas, as they plied the oceans of Empire during the dying years of the nineteenth century and the long Edwardian summer.

Only the Lady Georgiana had survived the Great War. Her sister ships, the Lady Emily — named for Charlotte's mother — struck a mine in Suvla Bay, while the Lady Charlotte, a troop transport, had been engaged by a German U-boat within sight of Alexandria, and the resulting terrible loss of life was worsened by the fact that an escorting destroyer, which had come to the stricken ship's rescue, was, herself, torpedoed.

But as the end of the twentieth century's second decade loomed, the Lady Georgiana was showing clear signs of having outlived her time. On her return home, she was to be paid off with great ceremony, and then quietly sent off to an ignominious death at the breakers' yard. Despite the discomforts, the lingering smoke, and the two days they had spent drifting without power off the sweltering Horn of Africa while the engines underwent running repairs, Dorothy had fallen in love with the ship's faded elegance. And there was an additional sentimental link, she had brought Dorothy and Charlotte home from Durban when they had narrowly escaped with their lives nearly two decades earlier.

Despite the sense of urgency conveyed in Charlotte's instructions, and the gentle but firm encouragement from Doctor Knollys, coupled with Dorothy's own desire to see Charlotte's wishes honoured, several months had elapsed between the reading of Charlotte's will and Dorothy's embarkation for Durban.

As it turned out, her assertion to Mr Twilley that any trace of the officers' hospital would be gone within the month had proven to be overly optimistic, and the solicitor was forced to seek a delay in the handover of the estate to the Admiralty. All directors of the Speers companies were required to be available for frequently convened board meetings in London, with a number of major decisions called for as the company transitioned from its war footing to peacetime operations. Charlotte's publisher had been very keen to capitalise on the worldwide attention that the author's passing had brought them, and with a resurgence in sales of the Richard Fforbes series, they had called on Dorothy to consult regarding the re-issue of a number of other works that had been out of print for several years. Amongst factual volumes and little known novels Dorothy recommended, the publisher agreed that the time might now favour the publication of the previously rejected Kitchener biography, predicting that in the jaded cynicism, even anger, of the new post-war world in which all gods were dead, previously revered icons of Empire were fair game. The volume they were most interested in, of course, was the new Fforbes mystery, which Dorothy promised would be edited and ready for submission on her return from South Africa.

Having been tugged and pushed in several directions at once since Charlotte's death, an exhausting process mentally and physically, Dorothy had been looking forward to some weeks of peace and quiet at sea. She was adamant that her senior position in the company should not warrant any special treatment, but this had inevitably fallen upon deaf ears. She had also decided to sail without any attendant staff, delegating them to focus wholly on the move from Trafalgar Hall to her new Mayfair home. Gladstone and Bertie, keenly aware that they too were being left behind, had stared with disapproval as she packed, then had withdrawn to sulk and didn't even surface to say goodbye.

From the moment she entered the Speers Line office in London, her presence had been managed in the fashion of a royal visit, and she found herself having to console the devastated, almost tearful shipping agent when he informed her, with wringing hands, that the new, fashionable and fast Calcutta Queen had been withdrawn from service at the last moment, to be replaced by the old Lady Georgiana.

The fact that Dorothy was travelling without a companion was the cause of much concern — although not, Dorothy noted, from Doctor Knollys — so the Lady Georgiana's senior first class maid was assigned exclusively to Dorothy for her voyage as well as her stay in South Africa, and the Lady Georgiana's young Third Officer was entrusted by the Captain to ensure that her every need was attended to while on board.

Third Officer James O'Malley, rising rapidly through the ranks, was as close to Speers Line royalty as could be, directly descended as was from Sean O'Malley, Captain Speers's own sailing master at Trafalgar and then the first Captain, and then Commodore of the Speers Line in its exciting, formative years.

Early in the outbound voyage, O'Malley had taken Dorothy on an extensive tour of the ship, during which he proudly informed her of his own seafaring heritage, and that an O'Malley had been working on Speers ships, sail and steam, since the formation of the line in 1806, and even before then, with the famous Captain Speers himself at a number of notable engagements, culminating in the great victory at Trafalgar.

O'Malley had been so enthralled by his own storytelling, and captivated by his willing audience, that he was about to relate the famous command that precipitated one of the most notable naval engagements of Trafalgar, in which Speers's fifty gun fourth-rate, HMS Warrior, had engaged two French ships of the line by sailing between them. "And then, Miss Keppel," O'Malley explained as they toured the first class promenade, "On observing that the two French men o'war were setting a course for Nelson's HMS Victory, and despite being outgunned by a large margin, Captain Speers issued that famous command to my great-great-great-, er, that is to Sailing Master O'Malley, which was, of course, 'Lay us between them two big b…'.'" James O'Malley stopped mid-sentence, mortified that he had nearly let slip a terrible vulgarity in the presence of a lady, and a director of the Speers Line no less.

Dorothy smiled. "I think the command was, *lay us between them two big buggers, Mr O'Malley*, if my grasp of the history is correct." James O'Malley turned a bright shade of red, partly relieved and quite stunned. Dorothy put him out of his misery. "I edited Charlotte's book about her grandfather," she said. "I remember that quotation very well. And I remember thinking, what a fine seaman Commodore O'Malley must have been. Captain Speers held him in very high regard as his sailing master. I have no doubt you'll live up to his fine legacy."

The tour continued, but even a natural enthusiast like James O'Malley couldn't hide the fact that the ship was old, slow, and at the end of her life. The Chief Engineer, another third or fourth generation Speers' mariner, had been courteous and welcoming as they observed, from the catwalk, the hellish below-decks world of the stokers and engineers, but despite his best efforts his countenance displayed an overriding, perpetual anxiety, and he had to excuse himself constantly to attend to an endless stream of problems and crises.

Dorothy dined at the Captain's table each night, and enjoyed chatting with the first class passengers, some of whom were deeply impressed by the fact that she was a notable shipping and business magnate while others were avid readers of Charlotte Morris, lamented her passing and were somewhat star-struck in the presence of the great author's own secretary and editor. They produced, for Dorothy to sign, seemingly endless copies of Charlotte's work, mainly her popular *Postcards from Empire* series and Richard Fforbes volumes, including, much to her good-natured, smiling disapproval, the new edition of *Iceberg Right Ahead!* It proved easy to get to know the passengers well. The first class accommodations were only one third full, as many had changed their travel arrangements when it had been announced that the modern, faster and more luxurious Calcutta Queen was being withdrawn in favour of the famously superannuated, slow, and now, sadly, unfashionable, Lady Georgiana.

Following a not altogether comfortable, but at least convivial, voyage, Dorothy's first call on her arrival in Durban was to the Speers' offices. They had been warned of her pending arrival and had a welcoming party of Speers' managers and other local luminaries waiting on the quayside as the weary old ship, attended by a small flotilla of steam-tugs, manoeuvred into her assigned berth.

As the Speers Line had a significant interest in the local railways, a special train was scheduled to take Dorothy and her maid-in-waiting, Agnes Kelly, to Pietermaritzburg, where she would be staying in the Grand Hotel which, a generation earlier, had provided a fitting degree of luxury for the officers — and their ladies — of the colonial armies.

On the second night of her stay, she was guest of honour at a dinner with old friends from the QONR. Dorothy had thus far not revealed her intentions to locate Colonel Armstrong, the pretence that she was on an inspection tour of Speers' interests had been totally convincing, if the frantic efforts of the Speers staff to please had been any indication. But she felt sufficiently comfortable amongst the old soldiers, most of whom Dorothy knew from the Boer War, and whom Charlotte had known since before the first Boer War and the Zulu conflicts, to reveal at least part of her plans. She was seated next to a former Captain of the Natal Rangers, now a Major of the South African Mounted Rifles.

"When do you intend to call on Colonel Armstrong, if I might ask, Miss Keppel?" Major Powell enquired.

"Of course, Major. I hope to make the journey to his farm tomorrow. I have some business here relating to my role as a director of the Speers Line and Speers Colonial Holdings, and I am also doing some work on a sequel to *QONR – The Honour and the Glory*, detailing the birth of the Natal Rangers and the first and second battalions' experiences on the Western Front. I'm looking forward to interviewing the Colonel."

One of the QONR old boys, heavily whiskered and red faced, refilled his glass and passed the port to his left-hand neighbour. "Ridiculous, volunteering for active service at his time of life," he grumbled. "No wonder he got himself all shot to pieces. Modern soldiering is a young man's game, no place for us old relics, what? Did things differently in our day, no good standing up in plain sight in your regimental finery when some

174

damn Boer's pointing a machine gun at you, what? We learned that the hard way, twenty years ago. What do you say, Major?"

"What I can say, Sir, is that we were very pleased to have Colonel Armstrong with us at the front. He was a fine commanding officer, the men admired him very much."

"Is it true that Colonel Armstrong went over the top in his old regimental uniform, red coat and white helmet?" asked Dorothy.

"Perfectly true, Miss Keppel."

"There you are!" cried the old soldier. "Past it! Proves my point entirely."

"That *Honour and Glory* book was a dashed fine piece of work, if you ask me," another old soldier remarked. "Who would have thought that a woman could write about the army in that way? I take my hat off to her."

"She was a fine woman, Mrs Morris," Old Whiskers interjected. "Too good for that rogue of a husband of hers, thoroughly bad egg if you ask me. Fforbes Armstrong had his measure, what? Called Morris out, right in the officers' mess, remember? Told him to name his seconds, and threw scotch right into his..."

"Steady on, old boy," another QONR veteran murmured. "Ladies present, eh?"

"Good God, my dear Miss Keppel." Old Whiskers backtracked suddenly. "Forgive the ramblings of an old soldier."

"We don't see too much of the old Colonel these days." The quietly spoken retired officer, who had cautioned Old Whiskers, hastily steered the conversation away from any cause for discomfort. "He has a farm not far from here: has named it the Armstrong Free State of Natal, and has appointed himself governor. Won't have a bar of the Union. Keeps a few of his old comrades as a private militia. Completely harmless, but barking mad."

"Perhaps, Miss Keppel," Major Powell offered, "You will permit me to drive you to see the Colonel? I can lay my hands on an old boneshaker, it should only take us an hour or so to get to his farm. I'd like to see him again myself."

"That would be exceedingly kind, Major, I'm sure," Dorothy replied. "I accept your offer with gratitude."

***

'Boneshaker' was something of an understatement, Dorothy thought, as the roadster, top down, rattled and bumped over the rutted track that meandered up the long and gentle slope leading to the Armstrong Free State farm. During the journey, Major Powell cautioned Dorothy that Governor Armstrong was a stickler for protocol, so certain courtesies that might on the face of it seem quite ludicrous to the detached observer, were required to ensure access to the Governor's private world.

"Why is he so opposed to the Union?" Dorothy asked as they jolted and bumped along.

"Doesn't trust the Boers, essentially," Major Powell replied. "Thinks they're too cosy with the Bosch. The rebellion of 1914 was the last straw in his eyes. Colonel, that is, Governor Armstrong, is not even convinced that the European war is really over. He thinks the Germans are just biding their time, secretly preparing for another offensive while pretending to accept the terms of the peace conference. If the Germans re-mobilise, the Governor feels that another set-to with the Boers will be inevitable. He's still very suspicious of the term 'armistice'."

Dorothy was pleased to finally arrive at the Armstrong farm, the main gate of which consisted of an immaculate white panel fence, a flag pole flying the Union Flag — of Great Britain — and wooden hut serving as a sentry box. As soon as the car pulled up, a man in robust late middle age appeared, approached the driver's door of the car and stood to attention, his immaculately polished Martini-Henry rifle shouldered. He was wearing a patched and faded red coat of the British Army from a lifetime before, khaki trousers, long boots that shone like mirrors, and a yellowing pith helmet.

"Major Albert Powell, South African Mounted Rifles, and Miss Dorothy Keppel, of the Speers Colonial Company," the Major announced. "Our compliments to Governor Armstrong, and we respectfully seek permission to cross the border and beg an audience with His Excellency."

Dorothy stood up, stretching her aching legs and back, steadied herself by holding onto the top of the windshield, and regarded the sentry. "Good heavens!" she cried. "Corporal Benson. Can it really be?"

"Beggin' your pardon Miss Keppel, Corporal as was. Now Colour Sergeant Benson of Governor Armstrong's own militia."

"It's wonderful to see you, Colour Benson." With a wide smile, she jumped down, ran around the car and embraced Benson, as Major Powell looked on, with eyebrows raised in dismay.

"I take it you two know each other then," the Major commented.

Dorothy released the sentry from her arms and he immediately stood back to attention, his rifle ordered. "Corporal Benson, as he then was, was incredibly kind to us, Mrs Morris and myself, in our troubles twenty years ago," she explained.

Benson was visibly deeply saddened to hear of Charlotte Morris's death, expressed his condolences, but then snapped immediately back to duty. "Turn out the guard!" he shouted, and, after a few moments, an older, white-haired sentry appeared, using his rifle as a substitute walking stick.

"Take over here, Private Willis," Colour Sergeant Benson ordered. "I'll be escorting our guests to the see the Governor."

Benson climbed on to the running board, and the car proceeded along the roadway that cut a path through the expansive veld of high, swaying grass: a scattering of trees and distant, dark kopjes dotted the uneven horizon. Beef cattle grazed contentedly and silently watched the car as it drove into the compound of the main homestead, a whitewashed bungalow facing a courtyard surrounded by barrack room accommodation for the farm hands, a kitchen and grass parade ground. The union flag was flying proudly here as well.

Colour Benson jumped from the running board as the car came to a stop, ran up to the doorway of the house with a youthful agility, and banged loudly on the door.

Within a few moments the door was answered by a Zulu butler, wearing the crisp whites of a mess waiter. His face was young, but there were flecks of grey in his hair.

"Ah, Corporal Black, there you are," Benson yelled in his parade-ground voice. "Major Powell's compliments to the Governor. Major Powell of the South African Mounted Rifles, and Miss Keppel, to see the Governor!"

"Turn it in, Sid," the butler said, in the broadest East London accent Dorothy had ever heard. "I'm not bleedin' deaf, and you can stop trying to impress your friends. Major, Miss Keppel, please come through to the study and I'll call the Guv'nor." Dorothy entered just ahead of Major Powell, then Corporal Black made a point of closing the door emphatically behind them, before Colour Sergeant Benson could enter.

They were escorted into a spacious study and library, light and airy thanks to full length windows that opened on to the lawns and parade ground on one side and on to a private garden and conservatory on the other. They were immediately offered refreshments.

"Forgive me, Corporal Black," Dorothy said, "but if you don't mind me saying so, you have rather an unusual accent, and is Corporal Black really your name?"

"God bless you, Miss," Corporal Black explained, as he opened the drinks cabinet. "I've been with the regiment man and boy. I was adopted, like, by the lads, when I was no more 'n a nipper. They named me Black, never could see why. The Colonel was good enough to keep a few of the lads with him when he set up this farm, when he came back from Blighty."

"Good Lord above!" At that moment the Governor himself entered the room from the conservatory. "I thought I heard voices. Major Powell and, is it Miss Keppel? It can't be. It is! What a wonderful surprise!" The Colonel embraced Dorothy, and grasped the Major's hand in both of his. His eyes glistened with emotion as he ushered them both to sit down as Corporal Black served drinks, and ordered luncheon to be laid on at the double. The warmth in his eyes was just as Dorothy had remembered, but his military bearing had withered somewhat. He limped as a result of wounds at the Somme, and his back was beginning to stoop with age. He was philosophical on the matter of Charlotte's death.

"It happens when you get to my time of life," he told them. "One by one, everyone you know and love passes on. I won't be far behind, I dare say."

"Not for years," Major Powell said, raising his glass.

"Ah well, I've had a good run. Professional soldier for more than fifty years. By rights I should have been left on a battlefield years ago. I'm sure there was a Zulu spear or Boer bullet with my name on it somewhere. We should have been ordered to Isandlwana, but somehow the message never reached us in time. We were able to redeem ourselves a few months later at the relief of Eshowe, that's when our lads really showed what we could do. A couple of scrapes fighting the Boers, then nearly bought it at the Somme, eh, Major? That was a close thing all right."

Major Powell and Fforbes Armstrong began to reminisce about the Natal Rangers and the Western Front, until Major Powell hesitated over Dorothy's presence.

"My dear chap, don't be shy in front of Miss Keppel," Governor Armstrong said. "She's seen and heard it all. Don't forget she worked with Mrs Morris at their hospital, and edited that marvellous work, *The Talking Cure*. Nothing we can say here can shock her, I'm sure."

The talk continued throughout luncheon and beyond. Dorothy was shaken to hear Major Powell's account of coming upon a German machine-gunner who had died shackled to his gun by handcuffs. She wondered if the world could ever recover from such brutality. Could things ever be the same?

She recalled the village not far from Trafalgar Hall, once a thriving, well fed and palpably happy community supporting the surrounding agriculture. A pals battalion had been raised in 1915, comprising the villagers and some estate workers. One by one the telegrams came, a black veil of collective mourning descended, and now the village seemed empty, devoid of any optimism toward the future, sad and disturbing. Doors that had been habitually flung open in welcome now remained firmly closed.

Dorothy had found, on her last visit, the very air itself stuffy with irrevocable desolation. She had been at a meeting of the parish council, and had offered to fund a memorial to be built on the village green, and tearfully considered the long, long list of the fallen, most of the surnames appearing multiple times. Such scenes, she lamented, were no doubt being played out all over Britain and her Empire. Even the Royal Household itself was not immune, the company of Sandringham estate workers virtually all gone, including Doctor Knollys's own junior partner, Robert Billings, whom Dorothy had met years ago, and had found to be a polite, although rather withdrawn, individual.

"So how are things on the home front?" asked the Governor.

"In my experience, disturbingly quiet," Dorothy told him. "Empty streets, curtains drawn. So much sadness. It's not only the war deaths, of course — we then had the influenza."

"I met a chap before I left England," Governor Armstrong said, "Sassoon was his name. Siegfried, can you believe that? Funny name for one of ours, makes you wonder if he was on the wrong side, eh? Brave chap, Royal Welch if I'm not mistaken. Poet, apparently, but I wouldn't know anything about all that. Won the MC. Very affable. Have you met him?"

"Yes," Dorothy replied. "He visited a friend who was a patient at Trafalgar Hall. He wrote a very kind review of Charlotte's last Richard Fforbes book."

"Did he, by God? He was very critical of the general attitude of those at home, had a lot to say on the subject. All too flippant for his liking."

"I haven't found that at all. In my experience the sense of mourning is all-encompassing."

"Won't last," the Governor sighed. "Everyone will want to hear the war stories for a while, stand pints in the public house, look after the widows and orphans, even give the time of day to chaps with arms and legs missing. And broken faces. Give it three or four years, a poor chap will mention something that happened in France and he'll be shouted down with 'oh, not that bloody war again.' You mark my words, it will happen. I'm glad I won't be around to see it. Couldn't blame a chap for wondering what it was all about, eh, Major?"

"I think we must try to believe that it was all for a purpose, Governor, there's nothing else we can do."

"Best not to dwell, best not to dwell. Well, here's a bit of good news for a change. My son Richard has finally done something about the family line. I've just learned this week that his charming wife is expecting. Bound to be a boy, the Armstrongs' first born always are and I'm sure Richard and Fiona won't let us down. The poor little chap will have quite a burden to shoulder, my brother Piers has been terribly remiss about ensuring the succession. I left things a bit late myself, the soldier's life. Took a terrible toll on his mother. I miss her to this day. I'm glad she wasn't here to see me after the Somme. Young Richard had been back in England of course, stayed with my brother. Damned good education. He went into the Royal Flying Corps. I used to look up from our trench at those flimsy kites and wonder if it was Richard at the controls. A good son, he visited me at every opportunity when I was convalescing. They had the life, eh, those flying chaps? Back to a warm and dry bed each night. Mind you, they earnt it. I convinced Piers to retire, he's an MP, you know. He was First Lord of the Admiralty at one stage, did quite well in the coalition. Thank God I didn't have to go into politics, I haven't got the gift of it. Young Richard will take over the family seat, set up for life he'll be."

It was clear that the Governor was delighting in the conversation and was rambling happily away, and neither Major Powell nor Dorothy were inclined to interrupt. Could this charming, decent and fine old gentleman really have killed Charlotte's husband in a duel? Dorothy contemplated. And why?

During a brief lull in the conversation, Fforbes Armstrong excused himself for a few moments. On his return, he presented Dorothy with a leather despatch pouch bearing the initials of his old regiment, QONR. "I believe this is why you're here," he said.

Dorothy was stunned, and glanced furtively in the direction of Major Powell.

"I would trust Major Powell with my life, in fact, I did. This is not something you should have to deal with alone, Miss Keppel. Even now your visit here is probably being noted."

Noted? Dorothy silently thought. Noted by whom? "I have a letter from Charlotte," she said. "It was with her will. It authorises me to…"

"I don't need to see any proof," the Governor said, raising his hand. "I know what you meant to Charlotte, Mrs Morris. I know that she trusted you as if you were her…Yes, I know that she trusted you and that's good enough for me. Here's a funny coincidence. Did you know that my Grandfather and Charlotte's grandfather actually met? At Waterloo of all places!"

"You mean Captain Speers?" Dorothy was incredulous, as well as being quite relieved that the conversation had briskly moved away from the subject of the QONR pouch. "What was he doing at Waterloo?"

"Captain Speers wasn't going to miss out on that kind of adventure if he could help it. He managed to call in a favour from Uxbridge, Wellington's brother-in-law, well, not his brother-in-law exactly, but he'd run off with… no, perhaps the less said about that the better, not one for idle gossip, what? In any case, Speers and Uxbridge were old friends, and that's how Charlotte's grandfather ended up as part of the Duke's entourage. My own grandfather, James Armstrong, was an aide to Wellington, and acted as a battlefield guide for Captain Speers. My grandfather talks about it in his memoir, I gather they got on rather well. The Captain was fascinated by watching the soldiers form square and line in response to charges by cavalry and infantry. I wonder what they would have made of the Western Front, eh? Mind you, Waterloo was no picnic either, from what old James Armstrong wrote. And of course, Miss Keppel, you would remember that it was at the Duchess of Richmond's ball the night before the Battle of Quatre Bras, that the old captain first laid eyes on the Honourable Georgiana Wellesley, a cousin of the Duke himself. And that turned out rather well, despite the age difference."

At sunset, with the white painted bungalow and surrounding barrack buildings and stables bathed in a beautiful glow of deep African orange, the Armstrong Free State of Natal Militia paraded. They numbered about the size of a small company. The bugle sounded, and the flag was lowered with the appropriate solemnity. Armstrong's Army, Dorothy thought, noting that a number of the men had empty sleeves pinned to their shoulders and some had deep facial scarring — one poor man appeared to have virtually no bottom jaw at all — while others stood to attention as best they could, leaning on makeshift crutches, with their trouser legs pinned neatly up over the stumps of their knees and hips.

"Carry on, Colour Sergeant," The Governor commanded.

"Sah!" Benson saluted, turned one hundred and eighty degrees as if on a pivot, and then dismissed the parade to their evening leisure. After more than two years amongst shell shock,

Dorothy could recognise the signs, as could Major Powell from an even closer perspective, and they gloomily watched some of the men shuffle away, shoulders slumped and heads bowed, as if in a bewildered torpor.

"This all reminds me of Trafalgar Hall," Dorothy commented. "It appears you have your own convalescent home here, Governor."

"All of these boys do their part. They all have their little jobs on the farm. Native workers do the heavy lifting, as it were. After what they went through for me, how could I see them cast aside? If they ever want to talk, as long as I have breath in my body, they'll never hear the words 'not that bloody war again!'"

After dinner, and an emotional goodbye, Dorothy and Major Powell set off for Pietermaritzburg. It was a much slower trip back, with the hood now up against the cool of the deepening night. The headlamps barely penetrated the darkness and the Major, leaning forward and gripping the wheel with white knuckles, struggled to find the path of the track. They were both preoccupied; even thousands of miles away, the horrific legacy of war intruded like an unwelcome guest who had turned up unannounced, ruined the party, and then refused to leave. As they drew nearer to Pietermaritzburg, the road improved, and conversation became easier.

"It's easy to forget that the war extended well beyond France, the Dardanelles and the deserts of Mesopotamia," Major Powell commented. "A number of my boys fought not too far north of here, in fact, the third battalion of the Natal Rangers were there as well. Hard to imagine, isn't it? Thousands upon thousands of soldiers, our side and the Bosch, native soldiers and carriers on both sides, chasing each other like madmen all around East Africa, dying like flies from disease and exhaustion. To what purpose, in the end?"

***

As Dorothy sat at her desk in the Stateroom of the Lady Georgiana, she remembered fondly her time with Governor Armstrong, and the kindness of Major Powell, who did not ask once about the leather despatch pouch that Dorothy held tightly in her lap all the way back to Pietermaritzburg. For the remainder of her stay, either Major Powell himself or another officer of the Mounted Rifles remained close by, and even provided an escort to the port of Durban, seeing her safely aboard the Lady Georgiana.

Dorothy's initial intention had been to oversee the destruction of the manuscript in the presence of Governor Armstrong, and she had confided her plans to Doctor Knollys when they shared afternoon tea the day before she sailed. Doctor Knollys had been adamant that the documents should be retrieved and then examined by those whose sacred vocation was the on-going protection of the Royal Family. The Doctor did not specify who those people were — no doubt he considered himself one of those trustees — not without justification. Dorothy acknowledged this, and, in the end, she found it hard to argue with someone who was not only an old friend, but someone who was as closely connected to the Royals as one could be while not being of the blood.

But Dorothy still had reservations. Charlotte's instructions had been very clear. It made her deeply uncomfortable to be so blatantly ignoring them, and the cold, calculating demeanour of Piers Armstrong, obviously a close confidante of Doctor Knollys, but someone whom the Doctor had clumsily tried to portray as a casual acquaintance, niggled at her like a stone in her shoe.

Dorothy regarded the leather despatch pouch on her desk in front of her. Inside remained the sealed envelope, undisturbed for almost twenty years. Also on the desk was a second large envelope: the completed manuscript for the new Richard Fforbes story. Dorothy had made the most of the slow trip out, her free nights in Natal and the unexpected additional days, as the ship drifted in the Gulf of Aden on the voyage home while undergoing repairs. Having edited Charlotte's work for over two decades, and referring to Charlotte's own handwritten notes, Dorothy was able easily to replicate the author's distinctive narrative style: the fast pacing, sharp dialogue and concise descriptive paragraphs. She also felt very close to Charlotte, felt a spiritual connection, even, while reading her words, expanding her ideas and then writing on her behalf, and wondered, not for the first time, how she would endure the rest of her life alone.

Nevertheless, she was reasonably happy with her efforts. The style gave every impression of being a genuine Charlotte Morris manuscript, and Dorothy was looking forward to presenting the fruits of her labours to the publishers when she returned to London. She had entitled the story *A New Beginning*. It seemed appropriate on a number of levels. She smiled to herself. Imagine accidentally handing over the wrong manuscript?

Her attention returned to the envelope inside the pouch, wondering once again what was concealed inside the battered old piece of QONR memorabilia that could be so damaging, so devastating. She recalled Charlotte's written plea, 'destroy the manuscript unread', the word 'unread' underlined so heavily that the paper itself had been scored.

"Well, I am sorry, Doctor," Dorothy spoke aloud, "but Charlotte's instructions must prevail. I should never have entertained any other course. Tonight, that envelope is going over the side. And as for you, Mr Piers Armstrong MP, whoever you *really* are..."

"Beggin' your pardon, Miss Dorothy," Agnes Kelly appeared in the doorway. "It's time to be dressing for dinner."

CHAPTER EIGHT

"Do you want the long version or the shorter version?" Alf asked, the arched gateway to the Trafalgar Hall estate having now disappeared well into the darkness behind them.

"Everything you know. And I mean everything," Norman replied firmly.

"Right. As you know, I've been interested in the mystery of the lost manuscript for thirty years, ever since Dickie Billings let it slip in that pub. Remember?"

"I certainly do. Dick told me I should have nothing to do with you, on account of the fact that you were, I think his words might have been, a red fueker, or similar. I'm starting to think I should've taken his advice."

"Ha'way bonny lad. At least I make things interesting for you. Now, one thing I've discovered over the years, is that everything is connected to everything else, in ways that you could never possibly imagine."

"I'm listening."

"Charlotte Morris died in 1919, at Trafalgar Hall. There's our first funny coincidence. Her grandfather was Charles Speers, hero of Trafalgar, one of Nelson's Band of Brothers, and founding father of the Speers international conglomerate. Now this is where it gets even more interesting. Who did I work for when I was in the Merchant Navy? Speers shipping. Who did most of my family work for? The Speers shipyard on Tyneside. Where did I end up, having been kidnapped by HM government? The very same room in which old Speers lived, and died, and where his granddaughter Charlotte Morris took her last breath. And why was I kidnapped by HM government? Because of something Charlotte Morris wrote! You couldn't make this up. And who owns the shipyard now? There's a clue in its name, Speers-Donoghue. As I said, everything is connected to everything else."

"Well, you've always loved a good conspiracy to get your teeth into."

"Makes the world go round, marra. Anyroad, here's my theory, for what it's worth. I think the existence of the manuscript was revealed at the reading of Charlotte Morris's will. She might have even made some kind of deathbed confession, we'll never know. It's my contention that Dorothy Keppel travelled to South Africa…"

"Sorry, wait. Who did you say?"

"Dorothy Keppel. She was Charlotte Morris's secretary and long term companion. Why do you ask?"

"No reason, go on." That was at least one mystery solved, Norman thought. The 'DK' to whom the Colonel had referred in his diaries.

"Where was I? Dorothy Keppel, that's right. I think she travelled to South Africa to retrieve the manuscript from someone to whom it had been entrusted, based on instructions, or information that had been revealed during the reading of the will."

"Do you know who that might have been?" Norman asked.

"Can you guess?" Alf replied.

"This is your story. You tell me."

"Now, you've always dismissed Charlotte Morris as little more than a courtier and gossip monger, at least that's the impression you've always given me. Perhaps one day you'll tell me what you really think. But, let's look at the facts. It's not just anyone who gets an ocean liner named after them, even if their own family owns the shipping line."

"I think that particular ship was either torpedoed or she hit a mine, during the Great War. Either way, she sank like a stone. There's a lesson there, about the consequences of sailing into dangerous waters."

"Too late for me, bonny lad. But to continue, her family was wealthy beyond anything we can imagine, they make Sir Eddie Donoghue look like a market street trader. Their interests spread throughout the world. Shipyards, plantations, factories, shipping lines, ranches, their fingers were in everything. But the Speers corporate history is dark and dirty. Slaves, mistreatment of native workers and residents, arbitrary land acquisitions running roughshod over native rights, corrupting colonial administrations and tribal kings, even allegations of piracy at sea. It was the third generation, in the form of Charlotte's brother Nelson, which started to at least try to make amends. When Nelson Speers died just before the turn of the century, leaving no heir, everything went to Charlotte herself. The management was delegated of course, but Charlotte continued to try to redeem the family name. A number of company assets were actually returned to the communities from which they'd been acquired, and a global humanitarian programme was initiated. Charlotte had to fight the cigar-smoking moustaches of the board of directors tooth and nail, but she prevailed. A formidable woman! I would have liked to have met her."

"It might be quite a long drive to London, but at some stage you're going to have to get to the point." Norman was anxious to know just how much of his own family's involvement Alf had uncovered.

"When she was reporting on the Boer War, Charlotte was granted access to a concentration camp, I think near Bloemfontein. She then investigated conditions in the camps throughout the Transvaal and Orange River Colony, and began to campaign strongly for reform. She came into conflict with Kitchener and the military command, and they were so anxious to get rid of her that I believe they concocted evidence that she was feeding information to the Germans who, as we know, were sympathetic to the Boers. She was actually arrested, along with her secretary, but they were then suddenly released without explanation and she returned to England to take up a position at Court."

"Do you know how her release was secured?"

"No, but this is what I mean about influence. Not even Kitchener, the military command, or the colonial administration could fettle her. Now, we jump forward to 1919. Within a few months of Charlotte Morris's death, Dorothy Keppel travelled alone to Durban. She spent a week there, or at least in the province, and then embarked for home. On the Lady Georgiana, a Speers ship. Remember what happened?"

"The Lady Georgiana," Norman repeated thoughtfully. "That was the one that foundered off the coast of Spain, wasn't it? Largest peacetime loss of life since Titanic."

"That's right. Poor Dorothy was never seen again. The official line was that she struck a mine that had come loose from the North Sea Barrage and had been drifting for two or three years. Now, the Lady Georgiana was never meant to make that voyage in the first place. The line's flagship, Calcutta Queen, was pulled from service at the last minute and the old Georgiana was substituted. She was about to be paid off, and was in very poor shape. She was a modern day coffin ship, in actual fact."

"Are you suggesting that this disaster somehow ties in with the manuscript?"

"No, even I think that's one conspiracy too far. But it's not beyond the realms of possibility that it was an insurance swindle. I'm still working on that one. But back to the reading of Charlotte's will, I have a copy of the minutes taken by a stenographer. The minutes record a sealed envelope being handed to Dorothy Keppel, with no further explanation, other than Dorothy's confirming that the seal was intact. And, the minutes list those present at the reading. There were a number of Speers executives, the Chairman unsurprisingly, as well as a chap named Cedric Knollys. Who do you think he was?"

"How would I know?"

"Physician in Ordinary to the Royal Family at Sandringham. Served Victoria, then Edward, and by that time was taking care of old Queen Alexandra. He'd been friends with, or had least had personally known, Charlotte Morris for twenty years or more."

"What does he have to do with anything?"

"I don't know for certain, but he's the royal connection. This must be how the existence of the manuscript became known in certain circles." Norman considered Dick Billings's rambling account of the goodhearted, yet apparently sinister, Sandringham doctor. Could it all have been true after all? But then, now that Alf was safe, what did it even matter?

"There was someone else at the reading that might interest you?"

"Oh?"

"One Piers Armstrong, MP."

This surprised Norman, though his expression remained impassive. One way or the other, his family was in it right up to their necks.

"So, several months after Charlotte's death, Dorothy Keppel sails to South Africa, and she's there for a week while they patch up the poor old Georgiana for the trip home. In the meantime, she retrieves the manuscript from her contact."

"Yes, yes, so you've already said. Who was the contact?" Norman's pretence of indifference was just beginning to crumble.

"I'm not certain. But I think it might have been your grandfather."

Finally, getting to the point, Norman thought. "And why would you think that?"

"I'll explain..."

"Wait a minute, if the manuscript is at the bottom of the Bay of Biscay, how is it that you were going to get hold of it? Have you invested in a diving bell, and are you going to explore the wreck?"

"Nothing so exciting, bonny lad. There was a stateroom maid on the Lady Georgiana, by the name of Agnes Kelly. As a director of the company, it's beyond doubt that Dorothy would have been granted that prime suite of cabins, so Agnes was probably assigned exclusively to Dorothy for the voyage. She, Agnes I mean, apparently made it to a lifeboat, but died before they were picked up, either from injuries or exposure, we don't know. Some personal effects were returned to her family, where they remained forgotten in a loft for the past sixty odd years. Amongst other things, there was an old leather despatch pouch, a little water-damaged and mouldy, but bearing the initials, are you ready?"

"Oh just bloody well get on with it, you north country cretin!" Although trying hard to appear oblivious to the conversation, Eric Baker stifled a chuckle at the Home Secretary's outburst.

"Keep your shirt on, bonny lad. You told me that you wanted to know everything. The initials on the pouch were QONR. Ring a bell?"

"Queen's Own Natal Rifles," Norman acknowledged.

"Correct. Inside the pouch was an envelope, sealed."

"Good Lord," was all Norman could manage.

"Now, a few weeks ago, the current occupiers of the old Kelly family home were having a bit of a clear out, and guess what they found? And being honest and upright citizens — as rare as a caring conservative — they considered it their civic duty not to disturb the seal on the envelope, and to donate the artefacts, which included Agnes's pay book and some other old Speers Line gems, to our museum on Tyneside, where we have a permanent exhibition commemorating the sinking of the Georgiana. So, they let their fingers do the walking, and discovered that the secretary of the Lady Georgiana Trust — which administers the museum — is none other than, guess who?"

"Surprise me," Norman sighed.

"That would be me! And, it turns out that those fine upright citizens are not only honest and discreet, but are big fans. As a result, in return for surrendering some interesting but valueless items, at least in a monetary sense, they spend an evening with me, receive a free autographed copy of *Decade of Discontent* as well as a grand tour of Padraig Donoghue House, and then watch me do my radio programme, assuming I still have one, the next time they're in London."

"A bargain," Norman muttered.

"So, I was planning to pay them a visit when Special Branch..."

"Tell me why you think my grandfather was involved."

"Your grandfather had been a friend and protector to Charlotte for almost half a century. She had married into the regiment, an officer named Morris. Well, obviously. The marriage had been championed by Lady Georgiana Speers, Charlotte's grandmother. Don't forget, Charlotte's own mother had died in childbirth, so the redoubtable Lady Georgiana took it upon herself to raise Charlotte and her brother Nelson in the Speers fashion, along with their father Horatio, who, by then, was running the empire, and absent most of the time. If the timeline seems a little off, remember that Georgiana was thirty odd years younger than the old Captain, who had died a year or two before Nelson — Nelson Speers I mean, not the other Nelson — was born. So, the marriage to Morris was one of Georgiana's rare misjudgements. He proved to be a coward, a drunkard and a gambler, and gave poor Charlotte a bad time, much to the disgust of his fellow officers, and one Captain Fforbes Armstrong, as he then was. Lieutenant Morris was rather conveniently killed: apparently his fighting skills weren't quite so effective when matched against another soldier, rather than his young wife."

"How did he die?"

"I don't know exactly. Probably a duel, but that's just a guess. But from then on, Charlotte Morris was effectively under your grandfather's protection. I mean in the literal, honourable sense, I'm not implying anything untoward. Charlotte herself obviously held him in high regard. You only have to read *QONR – The Honour and the Glory* to realise that. That book should by rights have been called 'The Honour and the Glory of the Great Colonel Armstrong, with a bit of occasional help from a few chaps in the Regiment'. And you have to admit, the Richard Fforbes series, leaving the murder mystery aspect aside, is nothing if not a warm and loving tribute to a fine, colonial soldier. So, it stands to reason, who would Charlotte trust more than anyone on earth with something as sensitive as a contentious manuscript? Given the spying allegations that surrounded her departure from Durban, she wouldn't have wanted to have any papers of that nature in her possession."

Norman decided to offer some limited insight of his own. "My grandfather helped her, and her secretary, this Keppel woman, return to England. He asked Winston Churchill to appeal to the King."

"Thank you for confiding that," Alf replied. "I had put it down to her own family influence, but your grandfather's involvement makes perfect sense. It also points to the trust between them. I'm even more convinced now that the old Colonel held the documents."

"What about his brother, Piers? Where do you think he came into it, then?" Norman realised that he actually knew very little about his secretive, unmarried great uncle, whose political career had been as long and important as his military service had been short and undistinguished. Even though Piers had lived in the Armstrong's Knightsbridge home for around two decades, there was virtually nothing to mark his presence, no portrait, no diaries, just one small, framed photograph. Even Norman's father, who had stayed with his uncle during term breaks from school, had spoken little about him.

"Ah, now, bonny lad, here's where we come to the really interesting part." Alf stated, "The old Colonel was, by all accounts, a thoroughly decent, honest and honourable man. Piers Armstrong MP, on the other hand, was a totally different kettle of..."

"Excuse me, Home Secretary, Mr Burton," Eric interrupted. "The news is on the radio, we've just missed the start."

"Turn it up, please, Eric."

"In what is being described as the literary event of the decade, a manuscript by the Edwardian author Charlotte Morris, thought lost for more than six decades, has been discovered, and is due to be published before Christmas..."

Norman and Alf sat in stunned, open-mouthed silence, staring straight ahead. Eric whistled softly. There's going to be trouble now, he thought. They listened as the newsreader continued her explanation, including some details of the manuscript's contents, and the proposed publishing date, before moving on to other news.

"Turn it off, please Eric," Norman said with ominous control. There were a few moments of silence — the air sliceable with any sort of sharp object — while Norman collected his thoughts, and Alf sat looking out of the window, decidedly queasy.

"Right, shall we recap?" The Home Secretary said finally. "But first, to coin a phrase, you are without doubt, hang about, I'll even do the accent, *a nae-good brain-dead, ignorant gobshite...*"

"That's a bit harsh," Alf protested weakly. "And you've actually misquoted..."

"Tell me, oh great investigative reporter and the nation's principal political commentator. What was in this bollocking manuscript? Enough dirt to bring down the monarchy, the Lords and the entire Conservative establishment? End civilisation as we know it? No? Just remind me, according to the news, what has paralysed half the government, the security services, the police, as well as causing chaos at Donoghue House thanks to a blockade by your cardigan-and-woolly-hat-wearing fan club. Well?"

"Okay, bonny lad. Fair cop." Alf spoke in a desolate monotone. "It's a Richard Fforbes story. Previously undiscovered, apparently. Charlotte Morris fans are ecstatic."

"That's right. A fucking detective novel!"

"It was an easy mistake to make!" Alf cried. "I jumped to the wrong conclusion, that's all!"

"And so much for your fine upright citizens, your *big fans*. Looks like they got sick of waiting and took matters into their own hands." Norman turned and looked out of his own window. It was starting to rain. Rivulets of water ran along the glass making intricate patterns and reflected the overhead motorway lights and the headlamps of other cars. After a few moments, he turned back and looked at Alf. "Well," he said with a faint smile. "You have to laugh, I suppose."

***

General amiability had been restored by the time they reached the outskirts of London. As good a time as any to start leaking, Norman thought.

"Here's a couple of things for you, so you can hit the ground running. Dick Billings is Chief Whip, probably common knowledge by now. But he's going to be Party Chairman as well. That won't be confirmed until the conference, but you're welcome to use that any time and attribute it to sources close to

Central Office. And on the subject of Dick Billings, I'm asking you, as a personal favour, to leave him alone."

"What do you mean?"

"Whatever you have, don't use it."

"Whatever I have on what, like?"

"Don't make this any more awkward for me than it already is. You know what I'm referring to."

"Don't use it? Alf exclaimed, once again the tenacious, crusading investigative journalist. "You're crackers, man! You know I have nothing against him personally, I actually quite like him in a strange, baffled kind of way, but his behaviour as Environment Secretary has been outrageous. Outrageous! He and Sir Eddie set up this nominee company to do *apparently* secret share deals, Eddie's way of saying thank you for tailoring government policy to suit his own ends. Again. If I know about it, then others are sure to as well. The gifts in appreciation of the Donoghue Amendment are probably the most blatant example of quid pro quo policy I've ever encountered. Blatant corruption, Norman, and it's not just Dickie Billings with his fingers in the till. And don't get me started on this cable television franchise..."

"I know Eddie gives you a free rein, but dropping him in the middle of an alleged corruption scandal might be one step too far in the cause of editorial freedom."

"This will be the ultimate test case. Remember the series we did a few years ago on the corrupting of local council housing committees, and the substandard housing that resulted? Donoghue Constructions was at the heart of all that, they were paying bribes all over the place and then skimping on building materials. Eddie wasn't very happy, things were a bit frosty between us for a while, but he didn't spike the story, or even try too hard to get us to drop it. And besides, any hint of corruption in this case won't even get close to Eddie himself, he knows how to insulate himself."

"Do you have proof at this stage? Documents, paperwork?"

"Not quite, but I'm getting close."

"The so-called Donoghue Bill is a good bill. It's going to create jobs, and actually do away with the potential for corruption at a local level. It's in the national interest, you're wrong to suggest it was purely there to appease Sir Eddie. A favour to me. Leave him alone."

Alf squirmed uncomfortably. "All right, but only out of respect for our friendship. But, if Dick's general conniving gets so flagrant, so publicly known that it can't be ignored, and let me tell you it's not far away from that, I'll have to run with it."

"Fair enough, I can't ask any more."

"I forgive you for ratting me out to the security services, by the way. There's no need to apologise."

"I have no intention of apologising."

"Well, you should, actually. You as good as tried to have me quietly done in."

"Rubbish, you were never in any danger."

"It didn't feel like that when I had gun stuck in my back and was bundled into a car and driven off, bonny lad! Do you have any idea how that feels?"

"I do, as a matter of fact."

"No you don't, how could you?"

"Suffice to say, I can empathise."

"Bollocks!"

The back and forth continued, prompting Eric to quietly question whether they reminded him more of an old comedy duo, or a long-married couple.

As they neared Alf's flat, things became a little more reflective. "Let me tell you something a bit funny," said Alf. "Did you see that old four poster bed in the room I was held in?"

"I didn't take any notice."

"Fascinating piece of furniture. I'd read about it in Charlotte Morris's biography of her grandfather. I wondered about it when I first got there, but the significance didn't really sink in at the time. It was only as we were driving out this evening when I realised I had actually been in Trafalgar Hall all along, that it all fell into place. Apparently the woodwork was salvaged from the HMS Warrior, the ship that Speers famously took between two French ships of the line during the Battle of Trafalgar."

"What happened?" Norman asked.

"What do you think? The Frogs knocked the living shite out of the Warrior and killed two thirds of Speers's crew, but it was seen as one of the decisive moments that tipped the balance of the battle. Anyway, there was something a bit odd about the bed, not in a bad way, but it just felt comfortable, reassuring. And here's something else, I kept wanting to sing 'Farewell, Spanish Ladies', we used to sing it for a laugh as we passed the Rock into the Med during the war. I hadn't thought about it for years, it suddenly came back to me. Now, bonny lad, guess what were the last recorded words of old Speers himself, who expired in that very room, in that very bed apparently?"

"Surprise me."

Alf began to sing, prompting Norman to groan and Eric to look into the rear vision mirror in surprise. "Farewell and adieu, to you fine Spanish ladies, Farewell and adieu to you ladies of Spain. For we've received orders to sail home to England, um, then, ee I've forgotten the bastard words… something about… we'll see you again? Ah Bollocks!"

"And you had the nerve to call me crackers earlier," Norman muttered, as Alf's croaky, uncertain rendition faded into an embarrassed silence.

Upon their arrival at Alf's flat, he invited both Norman and Eric inside for a thank you drink, but Norman declined. "I think Dolly deserves your undivided attention for a while. You're going to be quite a celebrity when the story breaks first thing tomorrow."

"What do you mean, *going to be* quite a celebrity?"

"Sorry, it must have slipped my mind that you're already more famous than Vera Lynn."

"Well, thanks, Norman. For everything." He bade goodnight to Norman and Eric, then disappeared through the front door of the unprepossessing block of flats, walking a little stiffly after the long, long drive, and clutching his bag of clothes as if it was his most treasured possession.

CHAPTER NINE

Dorothy instinctively knew that the poor Lady Georgiana was going to founder. The ship had been groaning and crying with each plunge into the deep troughs between towering waves, but after one deafening crash — Dorothy thought it could have been an explosion but wasn't sure — the ship suddenly lost steerage way, and her bows settled lower into the oncoming sea. Dorothy watched a pencil roll across her desk and fall to the deck, a sure indication that the list was noticeably worsening.

Agnes was frantically stuffing clothes into steamer trunks as Dorothy became aware that the cries of the passengers making their way along the passageway outside her stateroom were becoming more and more panicked, fearful, and less assured that the safety of a lifeboat was within reach. Dorothy grabbed the QONR pouch and double checked that the envelope was safely inside. There was another grinding sound, metal against metal under extreme duress, and the ship lurched to port before settling again. The Georgiana was starting to break up, battered to death by the angry sea, wall after wall of grey-green water rampaging mercilessly against the hull. Dorothy realised, with a sense of calm acceptance that even she found surprising, that survival was now highly unlikely.

"Agnes, leave that and come here," she commanded. She thrust the despatch pouch into Agnes's hand. "Find a lifeboat. Take this with you. If we don't meet again, take it to the address I've written inside. It will provide for the rest of your life, you'll want for nothing."

Tearfully compliant, Agnes took the pouch. "I, I don't understand. What about you?"

"Don't worry about me, my dear. I'm a director of the company, they won't let me come to any harm. You go and find your friends, there's not much time. Good luck, and God bless. Remember what I said. And thank you for taking care of me." Dorothy embraced Agnes, then propelled her toward the stateroom door.

Once alone, Dorothy returned to her desk but found she was unable to remain upright without reaching out for support. One hand for you and one for the ship, she thought. She reached for the remaining envelope, then sat on her bed, gripping the edge of the mattress with one hand and holding the envelope in the other. She absently noted that the seal remained firmly intact. The human noise from the outside the cabin was becoming louder still, and the sense of frenzied pushing and shoving was becoming even more chillingly intrusive. If there was one thing she could not abide, it was being jostled in an unruly throng.

The stateroom door burst open, and in lurched Third Officer O'Malley. "Miss Keppel, thank God! The Captain sent me to find you. We still have time, if we hurry." The young officer was trying very hard to appear calm and seamanlike against the prevailing chaos.

Dorothy stood up, envelope in hand, and walked unsteadily toward James O'Malley, who clutched the bulkhead with one hand and extended the other.

"Clap on to my hand, quickly," he cried. As she reached out for him, there was one final, apocalyptic sound of tearing, gouging metal, the slope of the deck increased to the point where the ship must surely capsize, then, as the cabin twisted into a grotesque shape, timberwork splintered and rivets popped, a crater opened up and the deck gave way beneath her feet. Dorothy Keppel plummeted silently into the abyss, and O'Malley roared "No!" as he realised that the only thing that remained clasped in his outstretched, desperate hand was a sealed envelope.

CHAPTER TEN

"Congratulations on your speech at the Party Conference, Home Secretary," Godfrey Powell said. The Permanent Secretary, along with Norman Armstrong, Charles Seymour, Janice Best and Roger Davenport were meeting to plan the week's diary.

"Thank you, Godfrey," Norman replied. "All in all, it was quite eventful."

"Who was that funny little chap who got up and told us we should be bombing Russia and kicking away Michael Foot's walking stick?" asked the Permanent Secretary.

"Kenny Everett," Charles Seymour replied. "He's a comedian. The Young Conservatives organised him, I think."

"Extraordinary," Godfrey Powell commented then noticed both Charles Seymour and Janice Best trying very hard not to laugh out loud. "What's so funny?" he asked.

"Oh for God's sake," Norman threw down his pen. "Just tell him and get it over with, then we can get some work done,"

"Well," Charles continued. "In the bar on Saturday night, Dick Billings walked over to where Stanley Smee and his wife were having a quiet drink together. Dick was well and truly under the weather by this time."

"He'd been drinking something he called an Admiral's Flip," Janice added, "half Brandy and half champagne. Glass after glass for most of the evening."

"So he was quite, well, you might say, tired and emotional," Charles went on "and he said something like, 'Still alive then? Those bogtrotters must be slipping.' I think that was the gist of it." Janice nodded her confirmation, then Charles added, "Not surprisingly, Mrs Smee didn't see the funny side, stood up and thumped Dickie fair and square in the face. He hit the floor faster than the Labour Party's approval ratings."

"No!" Godfrey and Roger cried in unison.

"Fortunately the Home Secretary's driver, Eric, as well as our detective, were in the bar with us, they carried Dick up to his room and revived him, I gather, with a jug of iced water over his head and several black coffees down the hatch."

"As they were carrying him out," Janice added, stifling a giggle, "He half woke up, noticed the detective's long red ponytail and yelled, 'Unhand me, Madam! Don't you know who I am?'"

"Good Lord!" Sir Godfrey spluttered, dabbing his eyes that were now teary with laughter. "How did you manage to keep that quiet?"

"Fortunately, it was quite late,' Charles replied. "Alf had gone up to bed long ago. The only reporter left was Roland Moreland."

"Oh God, not him!" Godfrey groaned. "Wasn't he that BBC interviewer who gave the Prime Minister such a roasting over the Belgrano affair last year?"

"The very same," Norman confirmed. "Eric got him plastered, then I had to bribe him with exclusive interviews with just about every Cabinet Minister at the conference. Convincing the Prime Minister to sit down with Moreland again wasn't easy, but I understand that, this time, he was a perfect gentleman. Such is the dignity of politics at the highest level, people. Now, if we can all compose ourselves, would it be too much to ask to get on with our work?"

***

The Home Office drinks party proved to be an outstanding success. The initial plans for a small, intimate and quite informal function had gone the way of all good intentions, and, in the days leading up to the event itself, the guest list took on a life of its own, and just grew and grew. In addition to the senior Home Office staff, guests included the Police Commissioner and Mrs Coburn, a number of cabinet ministers, along with a couple of older friends and mentors, including Enoch Powell, now the Ulster Unionist MP for South Down, and Lord Home of the Hirsel, in whose brief administration Norman had first served as Home Secretary twenty years earlier. Denis Thatcher was representing Number Ten, and was in animated conversation with Sir Dick Billings and although Norman was ever vigilant, and to that end had entrusted Charles Seymour to ensure that the Chief Whip behaved himself, Sir Dick was proving to be the very model of good manners and conviviality, his black eye now barely noticeable. Sir Eddie Donoghue had cornered Patrick Jenkin, Sir Dick's successor at the Department of Environment, and was offering a number of suggestions as to how the Local Government Efficiency Initiative could be enhanced even further, purely to the nation's economic advantage of course, and how, in a couple of years, maybe three, a stunning development of luxury flats overlooking the Tyne River in Jarrow could be the shining beacon of the resurgence of the Northeast. Meanwhile, Alf and Dolly Burton, who had arrived to a warm ovation, were chatting away happily with Janice Best, Archie Prentice and Eileen Armstrong, who had travelled up to London especially. Even Stanley Smee, now grudgingly respected by even the driest of MPs, owing to his surprising success as Northern Ireland Secretary, appeared to be enjoying himself, and was in amiable conversation with Norman Tebbit and Roland Moreland, a late addition to the guest list as part of his incentive to remain silent over the Party Conference fracas. Roger Davenport had assumed the duties of host with enthusiasm and panache, hovering constantly, and ensuring no glass was empty for long, and platters of finger food remained within easy reach at all times.

Norman surveyed his new empire with satisfaction, the only disappointing note being that Rick had declined his invitation, citing a previous engagement. He was chatting with Sirs Godfrey Powell and Peregrine Walsingham.

"I rather let the side down, too young for the last war, you see," Sir Godfrey was saying. "I joined the Home Guard, though. In fact, I was in the same platoon as Jimmy Perry, who went on to write *Dad's Army*. Nice chap. Jimmy and I were the real-life Private Pikes."

"I do love *Dad's Army*," Norman said. "And *Steptoe*. They don't make 'em like that these days, more's the pity. My grandson says that something called *The Young Ones* is the funniest thing on the box now. I can't make head nor tail of it."

"Let me tell you something," Godfrey added. "Jimmy always said he based the character of Pike on himself, but Mrs Pike was actually based, I think, on my mother. She used to turn up to our parades, steam in like the Mallard, and berate our CO for keeping me out at all night in the cold, worried I'd catch my death."

"What do you think of *Yes, Minister*?" Sir Peregrine asked.

"Very good, most of the time," Sir Godfrey replied. "I must say their writers are very well informed."

"The government's leaked like a sieve since day one," Norman muttered.

Sir Peregrine moved away to mingle, and Godfrey continued. "It's nice to see Mr Burton home safely. Would I be correct in thinking your intervention was the critical factor in the negotiations?"

"Well, you're kind to mention it in that way, but it was really a joint effort involving Archie's people and Mr Smee. I really only became involved in the final stages." How much did Sir Godfrey know? Norman wondered. They both looked in Alf's direction, noting that he now appeared to be in deep discussion with Roland Moreland.

Sir Godfrey smiled. "Do you think that Mr Burton is looking more and more like Rumpole, or is it the other way round?"

Norman chuckled. "I think Leo McKern is better looking," he joked. "The funny thing is, Alf is so successful, with his book sales and his Donoghue contract, that he could buy and sell the both of us several times over, and yet he still lives in the same flat in Pimlico that he and Dolly moved into when they first came south just after war, and he insists on wearing those old suits and that ghastly mac. I'm sure he does it just to annoy me."

"All part of the image, I suppose," Sir Godfrey observed. "It's certainly served him well over the years. Am I right in thinking he was in the merchant navy during the war? I think Mr Smee alluded to that in his statement to the House?"

"That's right. He was torpedoed four times, apparently. They were brave as lions, those merchant service chaps. Before that he was fighting with the International Brigade against Franco in Spain."

"Do you ever wonder what the world would be like if all the people we lost during the wars, were still here to make their contribution?"

"A damned sight better than it is, I shouldn't wonder." Norman replied.

"I often think about that in the context of my brother. Here we are, celebrating your very welcome arrival as our new Home Secretary and Mr Coburn's rather surprising elevation to Commissioner. I wonder what my brother could have done had he survived the war: perhaps he might have been commissioner, or at least a deputy or assistant."

"Was your brother a policeman?"

"Oh yes. One of the youngest detectives in Scotland Yard in the first couple of years of the war. He had a very promising career ahead of him. He was recruited by SOE and was killed on his first mission, sadly."

Norman felt a chill. Way too much of a coincidence for comfort. He recalled Dick Billings's words:

"Anyway, they got sloppy. A young Scotland Yard detective began asking some very uncomfortable questions, something about the fact that Paddy's injuries didn't quite match your typical bomb victim. He was getting close, right on their trail, then, suddenly, as I recall, his reserved occupation status was conveniently amended so he could join up. He was invited to join one of the cloak and dagger shows and, being a patriotic young man, jumped at the chance. He handed over his files, and no one ever heard from him again. He was killed on his first mission. Make of that what you will..."

"What happened, exactly?" Norman asked, with a mild sense of dread. "Sorry, I hope you don't mind me asking?"

"No, not at all, not at all. We don't know what went wrong, he was sent into occupied Holland, so we were told, something to do with supporting the resistance, I suppose. He was captured, and we never heard from him again. He's dead, of course, we know what those Nazis did to spies. Are you all right, Norman? To coin an old cliché, you look like you've just seen a ghost."

"Thanks, Godfrey, I'm fine. It just brings you up short when you think of some of the people we lost."

"I hope my brother would be proud of me, Permanent Secretary at the Home Office, and a 'K' to go with it. I think he would be. I've done it for him, in many ways, worked hard all my life to get on. One thing I know, he'd approve of our Mr Coburn."

Norman wasn't quite sure what to ask next, actually he was sure that he probably shouldn't ask anything else at all, but morbid curiosity trumped his feelings of caution. "Do you know why your brother was recruited into SOE? Had he been particularly successful, um, I mean was he working on anything in particular that might have attracted their attention?"

"Not that I'm aware of," Sir Godfrey replied. "As far as I knew he was just doing the day to day work of your typical lower rank detective. Chasing spivs and black marketeers, forged ration cards and petrol coupons, that kind of thing. I suppose there must have been paperwork and procedures relating to deaths during bombing raids. Nothing remarkable, but they obviously saw something in him that they wanted. I know he was chuffed at having been asked, and didn't hesitate to say yes. Do you mind if I ask you something, Home Secretary?"

"Be my guest."

"My father was a regular, a colonial in fact. He was a Captain in the Natal Rangers, and then went to the Somme. He was damned lucky to make it through: almost all of those chaps were killed on the first morning. He went back to South Africa, was made up to Major, and did a stint with the Mounted Rifles before moving back to Blighty just in time for me to be born. My brother was actually born in Durban, by the way, quite a few years older than me he was, I always looked up to him. But what I did want to ask you, is that the Colonel of that regiment, the Natal Rangers I mean, was a chap named Armstrong. Ford Armstrong was it? Could that be any relation?"

Norman smiled. "Fforbes Armstrong. He was my grandfather."

Sir Godfrey beamed. "My goodness me! My father always spoke so very highly of him. He told me that Colonel Armstrong went over the top at the Somme in his old regimental uniform of the Queen's Natal Rifles. White helmet, red coat, the lot. Is that true?"

"I'm afraid it is. He was getting a little eccentric by then. It didn't do him any good, they shot him full of holes as soon as he stuck his head above the parapet, which is hardly surprising. He survived though, went back to South Africa, and died in the mid-twenties. I never met him, sadly."

Sir Godfrey shook his head. "My father is still alive, you know. He's ninety-one. I'll be seeing him at his care home at the weekend. He'll be thrilled to know that I'm now working with Colonel Armstrong's grandson. Isn't it a small world?"

***

Both Rick Armstrong and Terry Cox were captivated by Erin Donoghue, although both found her a little intimidating. Her effortless authority belied her youth, and neither could take their eyes off her spectacular cascade of red hair. They had enjoyed a tour of Padraig Donoghue House, the editorial floors, offices, and especially the City Radio Studios on the top level. There was also a small television studio, from where London news reports were linked to their regional television stations, and a new studio area under construction to house their new cable television operation. They were then invited to the executive dining room, where Sir Eddie's own chef prepared a memorable three-course meal, with wine, that seemed to take up most of the afternoon. From the wall beyond the head of the dining table, an imposing portrait of Padraig Donoghue dominated the room.

"An impressive-looking fellow," Terry commented, feeling the portrait's disapproving eyes boring into him. It was as if the patriarch was reading Terry's mildly wine-addled mind as his daydream involved Erin Donoghue lying on the table, moaning, panting into his ear, long fingernails scoring his back and her legs wrapped around his...

"That's my grandfather," Erin said, forcing Terry to guiltily refocus on the meeting. "He inherited a couple of small newspapers from his own father, and by World War Two he'd become as influential as Beaverbrook and Rothermere. He was killed in the blitz. Uncle Dickie was a great support to my grandmother, and then to my dad too, when he took over at just twenty-one. What a responsibility for such a young man! It was my dad that expanded into shipping and shipbuilding, transport, and then, of course, independent television and commercial radio."

"Uncle Dickie?" Terry queried.

"Oh, sorry. I'm referring to Dick Billings, actually Sir Dick. He's just been made Chief Whip and Tory Party Chairman. He helped us out quite a lot when he was Secretary of State for Environment."

I'll bet he did, Rick said inwardly, as Erin continued. "I know he's been a bit of a controversial figure in the past, but my dad thinks the world of him."

"Will Sir Eddie be joining us?" Terry asked

"No, he's at a function at the Home Office," Erin replied. "Alf is there as well, what a relief to have him back with us. Imagine Irish republicans kidnapping Alf, of all people! It's too ridiculous for words. I know my dad is very grateful to your dad, Rick, and his role in negotiating Alf's release. Actually, come to think of it, I'm surprised that you're not there with them."

"I had a previous engagement," Rick replied, smiling.

"Well, I'm honoured that you're here instead. Now, let's talk some business. We have a lot of big projects coming up. In construction, media and transport. We need to bring a much more professional approach to the way in which we engage the media, and the public. We've copped a bit of a pasting over the Local Government Efficiency legislation, despite the fact that it's going to create thousands of jobs. The Labour Party and the unions seem to hate us, I don't know why. These are relationships we can improve upon, but we need some help. We're also looking forward to the launch of our cable television service."

"You have your own radio, television and newspapers," Rick said. "A professional media operation already. I don't see why you need to bring in outsiders."

If Terry could have reached Rick's ankles, he would have kicked them under the table until they were black and blue. He was as good as talking Erin out of hiring them, for fuck's sake! Terry could see a yacht and even a private jet on the back of this deal, and was determined to pursue it at all costs. He was about to intervene, but Erin continued.

"My dad insists on complete editorial independence for our media operations, he won't plant stories or use them to the obvious benefit of the rest of the business. He believes that's how we keep our licences, our high viewing figures and circulation, and make profits. Alf is one of our biggest assets. He wouldn't work for us if he felt that he was under any sort of obligation to our corporate interests. And besides, we need positive coverage nationally, and in Europe. Our own media, on its own, is not enough."

"Why us?" Rick asked.

"Nothing to do with you, if that's what you're implying," Erin told him, with a flash of anger that Terry found unspeakably alluring. "My dad has enough political connections, I even have a few of my own. We don't need you just because your name is Armstrong. This is my project, I want you to work with us because of your professional reputation. Does that satisfy your conscience, or your pride, or whatever it is that's making you uncomfortable?"

"Well, uh, yes," Rick replied.

"What do you think of this?" Erin produced a black and white photograph and slid it across the table.

Terry leant over to look closely. "Looks like a jumbo, 747 is it? I can't quite see whose it is."

"It belonged to the government of Burkina-Faso."

"Is that a real place?"

"We've just bought it. The jet, I mean, not the country."

Now that's a private jet, Terry thought.

"We're buying up a few more," Erin told them.

"A brand new international airline?" Rick sat up straight.

"I thought that might attract your attention," Erin said. "So, are you in?"

"Definitely!" Terry and Rick cried in unison.

"Wonderful. My dad will be so pleased."

"Just one thing," Rick added, ignoring his business partner's expression of pure venom as he produced a bulky envelope from his jacket pocket. "It's a cassette and a note. Can I leave it here for Alf, please?"

"Of course. Anything else?"

"No!" Terry exclaimed loudly.

"Good," said Erin. "Now, let's talk money."

CHAPTER ELEVEN

"Trouble, Norman!" Sir Archie had phoned the Home Secretary on their secure line, meaning that the call would not be minuted by Roger Davenport.

"What's amiss?" Norman asked.

"I've been a bit concerned about all this coverage of the Burton kidnapping. You warned us at the start that the reaction was going to be big. I admit I'd underestimated just how well known he is. It's been everywhere: newspapers, radio, TV, and not just Donoghue's either. And now, to top things off, a meddling amateur reporter is being very awkward, actually questioning our version of events. Damn cheek! He's suggesting that the Irish connection was a cover, all about discrediting the republican cause. He's actually accusing us of engineering the whole thing. I ask you! He's not one of Rupert's or Eddie's of course, a freelancer in Dublin. Some local rag over there has picked it up, no one else seems to be showing much interest, at least not yet, but it's only a matter of time. We need a distraction. Fast."

"Leave it with me, Archie," Norman replied, then buzzed his private secretary. "Roger, can you please get me the Cabinet Secretary, the Chief Whip, and then Alf Burton. In that order."

***

"You're listening to a midweek City Roundup special, on the City Radio network right across the nation, with me, Alf Burton. First off, I need to say a big thank you to everybody who has sent cards, letters, phoned the station or come up to me in the street. Your good wishes and kindness have meant so much to me, and to my beautiful wife who has suffered through this ordeal much more than me. I'd also like to thank my gaffer, Sir Eddie Donoghue, and members of the government who have worked so hard for my release, even though I'm sure there were one or two that privately hoped I might just quietly disappear never to be seen again. No, but seriously, Mr Stanley Smee, the new Secretary of State for Northern Ireland never gave up, and Norman Armstrong, our new Home Secretary, also played a key role. I'd also like to express my appreciation to all of the people behind the scenes, the police, security services, senior civil servants, all of whom played their part in securing my safety. For security reasons, I can't say too much about the kidnapping, I'm helping the authorities as much as I can. Suffice to say I was not harmed in any way, actually I was treated rather well. I'd also like to thank my old marra Mike Parkinson, who filled in for me for the last couple of shows. Now, to my track of the day. I'm going to break with tradition and actually play a new song, it's a band called The Forgotten North, and this is the first single off the new album, *Winter of Discontent*. If you love good rock and roll with a strong message, this is for you. Go out and buy it, you won't be disappointed. A very good friend of mine is managing the group. Rick, you're on a winner, bonny lad, and if you're listening, call me to set up a time to bring the boys in for an interview. Anyway, here it is, the title track and first single, *Winter of Discontent*, by the Forgotten North. Tory Chief Whip and Party Chairman Sir Dick Billings joins me next, don't gan' away!"

Alf stood up, double checked that his microphone was off, and welcomed Dick Billings as he entered the studio, red-faced, having just been enjoying Sir Eddie's hospitality in the executive suite. The two men faced each other across the studio bench, on which Alf had his papers scattered in an untidy arrangement. Alf's panel operator sat, just visible, behind the mixing desk.

"Sir Dick," Alf said as they shook hands, "what a treat to have you in the studio, it's very rare to be able to talk to the Chief Whip."

"Nice to be here Alf, old cock. When are you going to buy a new suit? No wonder Eddie doesn't let you do much television." Sir Dick settled into the seat opposite Alf, adjusted his microphone into position and then put on his headphones, as *Winter of Discontent* played out to its conclusion.

In this winter, of our discontent
No jobs to work at, no more rooms to rent
In this winter garbage piled high in the street
Huddle 'round the gas fire, but no copper for the heat
In this winter, in this winter, in this winterrrrr…

These were obviously lyrics that appealed to Alf's sensibilities, he also enjoyed the driving rhythm guitar and throaty vocals. Sir Dick wasn't so sure and as soon as his headphones were on, grumbled, "What's that godawful fucking noise?"

Alf's panel operator turned on both microphones and the red ON AIR sign illuminated above the door. "It's ten past four," Alf announced. "You're listening to a City Roundup midweek special. My guest is the new Tory Chief Whip, Sir Dick Billings. A very warm welcome to the programme."

"Nice to be with you, Alf, although it must be a relief for you to be back with us. A close thing from what I hear, it was nearly a case of *Auf Wiedersehen, Pet,* eh?" Dick snorted with laughter at his own witticism, causing the audio levels to spike into the red and jolting Alf's panel operator into some hasty knob twiddling.

"I'd like to ask you about the local government efficiency amendment, legislation you championed while Secretary of State for Environment. Quite a number of people have raised concerns over the fact that the bill appears to favour major property developers, of which our proprietor here at City Radio is one, at the expense of due process at a local level. Is Britain's architectural heritage at risk, as your critics assert, and how can the government justify this blatant appeasement of billionaire Tory cronies?"

"That question just serves to demonstrate your general ignorance of reality, Alf, if I might say so. The removal of legal obstacles allows for progress, for businesses to become even more successful, and thereby to employ more people. I know how concerned you are about unemployment, so the initiatives taken by this government should be music to your ears. Certainly a more attractive tune than the one we just heard. Who are these critics, by the way? If you give me their names I'll be happy to personally guide them toward common sense, one idiot at a time."

"Congratulations on your election as Conservative Party Chairman. We've just seen a change of leadership in the Labour Party. How do you see the Labour Party under Mr Kinnock, and how will this affect your political strategy in the future?"

"The Labour Party will be just as pointless under this new chap as it was under, er, his name escapes me..."

"Michael Foot."

"Was that who it was? Either way, we won't be changing anything. We are not for turning, Alf, remember that."

"How much blame should be laid at the government's door for the many social and economic problems confronting Britain today? The country is divided, the rich getting richer, the poor even more desperate. Millions out of work. Inner city poverty, crime, and racial tensions are worse than ever. This can't be the Britain you envisaged when you were elected for the first time in '79. I'll remind you of the Prime Minister's words at that time. Where there is discord, may we bring harmony. Where there is error, may we bring truth. Where there is doubt, may we bring faith. And where there is despair, may we bring hope. I put it to you that those words ring hollow in the face of the reality you've created."

Norman was seated at his desk, listening to the radio. He smiled with a deep sense of satisfaction. "Hook, line and sinker bonny lad," he murmured, and leant forward to listen.

"This behaviour is part of the general moral decline we're fighting against," Dick observed. "As Mr Tebbit said recently, when his father was unemployed during the depression he didn't riot, he jumped on his bicycle, went looking for work and didn't stop until he found it. You know all about this, Alf, I read your first-hand account of the Jarrow March. I'll bet that surprises you! You didn't rampage through villages smashing windows and burning down houses, you put your case in an orderly, and might I say, British fashion."

"That may be true, but, after walking three hundred miles, we couldn't even get recognition from Westminster. The only member of the government that gave us the time of day was Richard Armstrong, the father of our current Home Secretary by the way, and he had to defy Cabinet collective responsibility to do it. His career didn't recover until the war when his friend Winston Churchill became Prime Minister. Perhaps the current generation has learnt from the fact that polite and peaceful activism falls on deaf ears, and that Conservative governments have a generally ambivalent attitude to the plight of the poor and unemployed?"

"I reject that entirely. Typical socialist propaganda. Do I need to remind you that the Baldwin government, in power at the time of your Jarrow March was, in fact, a National Coalition?"

"A Conservative government by any other name."

"A Government of One Nation Conservatism perhaps. Mr Baldwin, who I remember well and under whom I served, was a champion of Mr Disraeli's desire to unite the two nations of Britain, the rich and poor, as one. I'd remind you what Mr Baldwin said at the 1929 election, that the prosperity of trade and industry should not be as an end in itself, but as a means to improve the condition of the people."

"Unfortunately, Sir Dick, Mr Baldwin's new *Compassionate Conservativism*, or whatever you might like to call it, passed us by in the Northeast then, and is well and truly dead and buried under Thatcherism now."

"Well, we've wandered away from my main point, which was. Which was — um — oh yes! One Nation! What you have these days is your inferior foreign culture infiltrating communities and encouraging lawlessness. My message to them is, if you don't like our British way of life, go back to whatever godforsaken part of the world you came from."

Alf looked through the glass partition at his producer, whose panicked face showed a combination of excitement and dread. The lights on her telephone switchboard lit up one after the other.

Alf's young panel operator was also suddenly paying close attention. He gestured to Alf, drawing his finger across his throat by way of asking whether or not he should pull the plug, but Alf shook his head, anticipating that the best was yet to come.

"So, just to clarify what you're saying, Sir Dick, is that..."

"What I'm saying, Alf, to your listeners, and indeed the country, is this. Listen carefully. Either be British, or bugger off!"

"Bingo," Norman Armstrong said to himself, and turned off the radio.

***

As usual, Roger Davenport was first to arrive at work the next morning, where his first task each day was to lay out the morning papers for the Home Secretary's perusal. When Norman arrived, he noted the array of headlines with amused interest

DICK WHIPS MINORITIES
CHIEF WHIP, CHIEF RACIST
RACIST RADIO RANT EXPOSES PM'S DICK
DICK GOES HARD ON IMMIGRANTS
DICK DOES IT AGAIN

"I've also saved a column by Mr Burton in this morning's *Daily Focus* for you to read, Home Secretary," Roger said, handing him a copy of the Donoghue broadsheet. "I thought you might find his opening paragraph amusing."

Norman read the highlighted passage.

"Mrs Thatcher once paid tribute to the highly effective William Whitelaw, by assuring us that every Prime Minister needs a

Willie! The fact that Viscount Whitelaw is now in the Lords, and considering this latest case of foot-in-mouth displayed by the accident prone Conservative Party Chairman and Chief Whip, Sir Dick Billings, Mrs Thatcher might well be asking herself if, in fact, any Prime Minister needs a Dick."

"Dear, oh dear," Norman sighed. "Alf missed his calling, he should have been writing scripts for Carry On movies."

"And," Roger added, "Miss Best is quite anxious to see you."

***

In the ensuing days, coverage of Alf Burton's kidnapping vanished from the pages of the nation's press, the Forgotten North was feted as the next big thing in music, with Rick's slogan 'The Thinking Fan's Status Quo' being widely repeated, and the pointy end of the Billings interview itself was replayed at every opportunity throughout the nation, in parts of Europe and as far away as the United States, Canada and Australia. Isolated pockets of unrest and protest inevitably erupted, but the response by the Metropolitan Police was swift, even forceful in places, and with Commissioner Coburn, Honest Ron himself, skilfully handling negotiations with community leaders, incidences of violence were kept to a minimum. The majority of protestors, many of whom were sporting "Bugger off Dick" T-shirts, remained loud and raucous, but fundamentally peaceful. Even the more militant factions of the Opposition, no fans of Norman Armstrong, nor of the police generally, had to concede that the response by the authorities had been measured and reasonable.

Former members of the Awkward Squad, led by Stuart Farquhar, offered a restrained condemnation, although they were painfully aware of the power Sir Dick wielded as Chief Whip and Party Chairman, and Farquhar still harboured hopes of returning to his old office. The dampness of his current accommodation, he was convinced, was contributing to his chronic cough, and was surely shortening his life.

In consideration of the difficulties faced by Janice Best, whose South London constituency, Streatham and Vauxhall, incorporated the district of Brixton, Norman Armstrong allowed his PPS to become the public face of the Home Office response, which was that, in general terms, they unreservedly condemned any form of racism, but would not hesitate to enforce the rule of law.

Then, amongst the almost unanimous condemnation and outrage from the nation's media and political elites, a groundswell of support began to appear, quietly, on the streets. 'Be British or Bugger Off' posters and graffiti appeared on abandoned buildings and fences, next to, and over, peeling bills advertising upcoming gigs and shows. But in the end, sparsely attended street meetings of far-right nationalists never gained much traction in the face of a strong and highly visible police response. The Home Secretary himself weighed in, publicly endorsing the conciliatory statements made by Janice Best, while also making it very clear that lawbreakers would not be tolerated on either side of the argument. Newspapers divided down predictable lines, and began arguing amongst themselves through their daily editorials, while the state of Britain was discussed endlessly on the radio, television news programmes and chat shows.

As the national debate entered its second week, Norman assessed that the job was done and it was time to move on. Having first consulted with the Cabinet Secretary, he phoned Sir Dick Billings and instructed him to initiate phase two.

"Sorry, Dick," Norman said. "Once again you've been called on to do the dirty work."

"I don't mind," Sir Dick replied. "I'm more popular than ever. I've even been invited to break away from the Tories and form my own party. This is turning out to be bigger than Enoch and his *Rivers of Blood*. Remember how Burton foamed at the mouth over that one? We certainly gave him more than he bargained for this time eh? But you're right, my fifteen minutes of fame is up, it's time to quieten everyone down and get back to business. I'll call Central Office and get the statement out."

"Thanks, Dick. You're a loyal servant of the cause. Don't think it doesn't go unappreciated."

"Well, I'm grateful for that, Norman. I've sometimes felt in the past... No let's not dwell, water under the bridge. Mind you, being knocked out by the wife of a Cabinet Minister was a new experience, even for me. I deserved it of course, said something stupid to Smee. My own fault."

"I was there," Norman reminded him

"Oh yes, of course. One more little moment in a career full of embarrassments. I'm thinking it might be time to slow the old alcohol intake, it's been a habit for over forty years, since my wife..."

"You're not doing yourself any good," Norman said.

"I know. But Norman, I'm feeling better than I have in years. Energised, excited. I'm a new man. And you and I, what a team we are, some of the capers we've been involved in. Remember that no confidence motion against Callaghan's shower in '79? A master stroke, perfect timing. And that was after we fucked them over the Ford pay claims. We knew the civil service wouldn't stand for seventeen per cent and would want their own piece of the pie. All we had to do was sit back and watch while everything came crashing down. Margaret is right to hold you in such high regard, you know. I always rated your father as one of the best operators of all time, but I must tell you, Norman, you're in a league of your own. And together, you and I are unbeatable."

"The old firm, eh?" Norman smiled, inordinately pleased about being compared so favourably to his father. "You're right about '79. It all just came together. But I always liked Jim Callaghan. Out of all of our political opponents over the years he, in my view at least, was one of the most decent. I was sorry it was him that we knocked off."

"Don't get sentimental, Norman," Dick cautioned, "that was your father's one downfall. I wouldn't be shedding any tears over Mr Callaghan. I know people say that I've said some stupid things in public over the years, but when old Jimmy got back from sunning himself in the West Indies while the country disappeared under piles of garbage and unburied corpses, and had the nerve to say," Dick's tone now became mocking, "I don't think that other people in the world would share the view that there is mounting chaos... Played right into our hands, the dickhead!"

***

The following day, Conservative Party Headquarters released a statement

From Central Office, Smith Square:

"The Conservative Party Chairman and Chief Government Whip, Sir Dick Billings, unreservedly apologises for any offence that he might have inadvertently caused during an interview recently aired on the City Roundup radio programme. Sir Dick welcomes anyone to this country willing to make a positive contribution, and deeply regrets that general comments made about law and order were taken out of context."

That Friday, Norman Armstrong sat opposite Alf Burton in the City Radio studios atop Padraig Donoghue House, for what would be the new Home Secretary's first extended media interview in nearly a decade.

"Home Secretary, thank you for joining us this afternoon. A very warm welcome to the programme."

"Thank you, Alf, it's nice to be with you."

"Sir Dick Billings's remarks on this very programme last week created a national, in fact an international outcry. Why do you think it took him more than seven days to issue any form of apology, if you could even call it that, or express any regret for the hurt his words caused?"

"Sir Dick was addressing, in a general sense, the lawlessness in many of our communities. Perhaps his choice of words was unfortunate, but he was making a valid point."

"So you're actually in agreement with your Party Chairman, then? You think that people should really be British or bugger off?"

Norman smiled warmly. "As you well know, that is not a phrase I would use under any circumstances. Sir Dick Billings made some comments in the heat of an interview, they were taken out of context, he has since apologised. The matter is closed. The country is moving on. I suggest you do the same."

"So, if you won't endorse his comments, will you come out and strongly denounce them?"

"It's not my place to do either. As far as I'm concerned, the matter is closed."

"With respect, you can't have it both ways, Home Secretary. You either endorse Be British or Bugger Off, or you can go a long way toward reuniting the country right here, this afternoon, by categorically denouncing those comments, and taking a firm stand against institutionalised racism. Which is it to be?"

Norman's smile remained, but his eyes gave a clear warning of impending danger.

"I condemn racialism, like every right-thinking individual. However, I will not condemn Sir Dick Billings for standing up for the rule of law and for British values, which are embraced by people of many backgrounds."

For one brief, euphoric moment, Alf felt an uncontrollable urge to throw away his career, the stifling constraints of his professional life, the necessary sacrifice of many of his deeply held principles, his deal for excusive Number Ten access, defy the Official Secrets Act and even end his friendship with Norman Armstrong. All in one gloriously explosive moment of liberating confrontation.

So, Home Secretary, let's talk in detail about the Donoghue Amendment…We know Sir Dick's Donoghue shares are doing very well. How are yours, by the way? No, I don't really believe that you would be involved in any of that grubby business, that arrogance that makes people on your side of politics feel that they can get away with anything, but you certainly condone it in others. We know what happens when good men stand by and do nothing. I wonder who else has had their snout in the Donoghue trough, and what other favours are going to be done. What are Dick's plans for retirement? A seat on the Donoghue Board? Unlimited free first class travel around the world with Erin Airways? How many pits are you going to close next year? And as for the Irish Revolutionary Brotherhood, a bit hard to tell them apart from your own Special Branch...

"What do you see as the principal challenges facing the Home Office as we move toward 1984?" Alf asked, smiling inwardly. Not this time, bonny lad. I think I'd quite miss you if we weren't marras any more. That time will come. Just not yet.

***

Rick Armstrong pushed through the front doors of the King's Head. He knew that his father sometimes used the old pub for secret plotting and conniving, so it seemed like a reasonable choice of meeting place for his own rather intriguing anticipated encounter. He thought how funny it would be if he saw his father, and was playing over in his mind what could be a comically awkward meeting as they both stammered through a number of implausible excuses for being there, when he felt a light touch on his arm.

"Excuse me, but are you Rick Armstrong? I'm Austin Wells." The two men shook hands, called pints at the bar, then took a seat away from the front doors.

"You don't look much like a senior union official," Rick observed.

"What were you expecting, an overweight northerner in a flat cap calling you Brother Rick?"

"Actually, it's my business partner who is the expert on stereotypes. But, yes, if I'm honest."

"I went straight into the union movement from university, I've never actually worked on a shop floor."

"What union, exactly?"

"I'm currently on secondment to The Amalgamated Fitters and General Shipyard Workers Union. We represent eight and a half thousand employees at the Speers-Donoghue Shipyard on Tyneside."

"I'm not sure how you think I might be able to help you. If you think I might have any influence with the government you'd be totally wrong. I stay well away from my father's political activities. In fact, if getting closer to the government is your objective, any association with me would probably have the opposite effect."

"I understand that. Can I just say, that anything we talk about today must be in the strictest of confidence, regardless of how the meeting turns out? I know you by reputation, my brother is the lead singer with the Forgotten North."

"Freddie Wells. Of course," Rick said, nodding.

"He says you're the only honest man he's met in fifteen years in the music business, and if you can turn a group of revolting unwashed middle-aged punks into genuine mainstream rock and roll royalty, you can do anything. Our own long-suffering parents didn't recognise them when they were on Top of the Pops last weekend. No, sorry, I'm being flippant. I know your work extends well beyond denim-clad guitar players in ripped shirts."

"Go on," Rick encouraged.

"There are rumours — actually I know for a fact — that Speers-Donoghue is going to close. The yard is old, no doubt about it, but there's been little or no investment in new plant for years. It's getting harder to complete with the European yards, as Fincantieri is killing us, one ship at a time."

"Who is this Finn Kartinyeri? Sounds like some sort of mafia hit-man."

"You might not be far wrong. No, Fincantieri, one word. It's the name of an Italian shipyard, modern, efficient and dominant. Years of neglect — and skimming profits, such as they were — has allowed Speers-Donoghue to fall behind. It's hard to compete now, in a year or two, it will be impossible. The problem is, Rick, if we lose the ability to build ships, if we allow ourselves to fall by the wayside in industrial terms, we're out of the game forever. We'll never be an industrial power again. Millions of skilled, proud people callously dumped on the scrapheap along with our industrial heritage. We can't let this happen."

"Look, Austin, I'm no fan of Mrs Thatcher, but is there not some merit in her contention that the workforce is transitioning toward new businesses, new technology, computers, electronics and so forth? Maybe the demise of the shipyard is inevitable, tragic as that might be, but I don't see what this has to do with me."

"We don't believe it is inevitable. Donoghue is going pull the yard down, then redevelop the land. Luxury riverfront flats. I wouldn't be surprised if he's already lined up some government support. The Tories wouldn't shed any tears, because we have the reputation as one of the most militantly unionised yards. One more bullet in the dying corpse of the TUC is the way they'd see it. I don't know for sure, but I think that geriatric racist Billings might have set the wheels in motion before he was shunted out of the Department of Environment. Everyone knows he's in Donoghue's pocket. He's probably been offered the best penthouse in return."

"Look, Austin, I'm sorry that your members are going to lose their jobs, I really am, but I have no stake in politics. I deal mainly in publicity for entertainers and events for corporate clients. And you probably shouldn't say any more, as we've just signed a contract to do all the PR for the Donoghue group. It's likely that we're going to be paid for promoting the merits of this very development. You're placing me in a very awkward position."

"They're going to sack eight and a half thousand people, Rick. How many middle-aged fitters and riveters are going to pick up work programming computers? They're going to bring the northeast crashing to its knees for the last time, just so they can built flats for yuppies with their striped shirts and Filofaxes, and why? To fund Donoghue's new airline, a plaything for Sir Eddie's daughter. Thatcher's Britain at its most brutal. How does that sit with your conscience?"

"I think that's well out of order, Austin." Rick made to stand up. "I think I'd better go."

"Of course I know you've signed with Donoghue," Austin told him. "They can't keep anything secret, I probably knew before you did. But I want you to come and work for us. We need top PR people for our campaign to save the shipyard, and you're the best in the business, Rick, everyone says so. But it goes well beyond just saving the shipyard, the future of the entire Northeast is at stake. This is about saving lives, communities, and a long and proud heritage. And let me tell you this, we're cashed up. We have sources of finance well beyond this country. There are some governments that are very sympathetic to our cause and will support us for as long as it takes. We won't be giving up. You have to make your own decision, but I think you're a nice guy with a lot of personal integrity, so I'll give you a little free advice.

If you stay with Donoghue, make sure you get paid on invoice. Don't let their account blow out, otherwise you'll never see a penny."

"I don't understand," Rick said. "They're worth billions."

"It's all other people's money," Austin replied as he stood up and gathered up his briefcase. "If you don't believe me, ask your father. I'm sure if I know, then he does. They're up to their eyes in debt, loans upon loans upon loans. At some point, maybe next month, next year, or five years from now, it's all going to come crashing down. When that happens, we intend to have a working, profitable shipyard that can be sold as a going concern or, God willing, be nationalised by a new Labour government after the next general election." He handed Rick a business card with his phone numbers.

"Ring me anytime," he said, and left without another word.

***

Just after nine a.m. on a Saturday morning, Rick Armstrong parked his XJS Jaguar a few doors away from his family's Knightsbridge pied-a-terre. As he approached the front door, he was startled to be suddenly confronted by suited man who appeared from nowhere. He produced a badge, then said, "Excuse me Sir, I must ask you to identify yourself. Please keep your hands where I can see them."

"I'm Rick Armstrong, the Home Secretary's son. I take it he's at home then?"

"Yes Sir, he is. Sorry to bother you." He turned and walked away, and Rick noted with some amused confusion that he seemed to have a red ponytail tucked into his collar.

Rick rang the bell, and within a few moments Norman himself answered the door. He couldn't contain his surprise,

"Rick, my boy. It's wonderful to see you." The two men embraced, a little awkwardly, then walked together along the corridor to the downstairs kitchen. In his mind, Rick raised two fingers to the parade of ancestral portraits that he always felt stared down in judgement at his failure to perpetuate the family tradition.

"Coffee?" Norman asked.

"Thanks, Dad," Rick said. "I wasn't sure if you'd be here or at home. I was passing, so I took a chance."

"I'm glad you did," Norman said. "I'm going home tonight, I have a few matters to attend to today. How are Sally and young James?"

"Sally's well, busy as ever. James is the usual handful. We'll be home for next weekend. Will you be there, do you think?"

"I hope so. I have a constituency surgery Saturday morning, but after that I'm all clear. It's been too long since we've spent some proper time together. No doubt James will want to flatten me with his political debating skills."

"Funny how that ability seemed to skip a generation," Rick said.

"So how are things, work wise?"

"Great, great. I'm looking after a rock band, the Forgotten North, they're doing really well all of a sudden, thanks in part to Alf as a matter of fact. Their record is in the charts, they did well on Top of the Pops, and we're advancing a national tour as well."

"Sounds, er, interesting," Norman remarked, and a rather apprehensive, expectant silence ensued.

"Did you know that Erin Donoghue was going to talk to us about doing PR for the Donoghue group?" Rick asked.

"No," Norman replied, "that is, yes, actually. Well, in a way. Yes, and no. Sir Eddie mentioned it to me, but I said that it would have to be a matter between yourselves, and to leave me well out of it. I didn't think you'd appreciate my sticking my nose in."

"It's just that..."

"Just what?"

"This is strictly between us, Dad."

"Of course. I'm quite good at keeping secrets."

"Well, I had a meeting with someone from a ship workers' union, I probably shouldn't mention his name. Anyway, he told me that Speers-Donoghue, the shipyard on Tyneside, is going to be closed, and the site redeveloped, so that Sir Eddie can finance his new international airline, which he, the union guy I mean, described as just a plaything for Sir Eddie's daughter. Apparently more than eight thousand people are going to be put out of work."

Norman did his best to appear nonplussed, but felt the same sense of controlled panic that had gripped him when Alf first revealed he had apparently located the Morris manuscript. Aside from the immediate tragedy of the loss of so many jobs in one already struggling region, the flow-on effects would be crippling, socially and politically. All of the negative representations of the Thatcherite manifesto would be played out — images of smug, well dressed city bankers driving expensive cars and living in luxury flats, against the desolate images of poverty and unemployment in the shadow of a decaying skeleton of a proud industrial past. "Why was he telling you this?" Norman asked

"He was trying to recruit us to do PR for the union, as they fight against the closure."

"That must have been an awkward meeting, given your arrangements with Sir Eddie."

"He also told me that we should demand cash up front for anything we do for Donoghue's because they have no money, well none of their own anyway, and could actually go under at any moment. What do you think?"

Norman thought that this union man, whoever he was, seemed to be remarkably well informed. "I know that they're highly geared, I think that's the expression," Norman replied. "But I don't think it's as bad as all that. City money is quite easy to come by at the moment."

"For some," Rick commented. "There are also rumours that a secret deal has been done with government, overseen by Dick Billings, regarding approval for luxury riverfront flats. He hinted that some government, um, that some money might have changed hands. I mean, there might be some funny business."

"I honestly don't know about that, Rick. But I wouldn't be surprised."

Both men fell silent. Rick wasn't quite sure what to ask next. Instead, he changed tack. "I was accosted by your bodyguard as I came to the door. Was that a ponytail tucked into his suit?"

"Yes, he's just come off some sort of undercover assignment."

"A hippy policeman. There's a plot idea for the next series of *The Young Ones*. Imagine Neil wandering around in a police uniform."

"Neil who?"

"Doesn't matter. Reading between the lines, I got the impression that you were largely responsible for rescuing Alf from the Irish revolutionaries, although you very graciously gave a lot of the credit to that new guy in the Northern Ireland Office. Smee, is it? I'm sorry I didn't ring you during that time, for support, I mean. It must have been quite hard for you, dealing with all of that."

"I always knew you'd be there if I needed you. As I hope you know that I am for you. Look here, would you like to have lunch? We can knock something together here. I'm sure Mrs Sims wouldn't mind if we rummage through her supplies. She must be the most underworked cook-housekeeper in London! Or if you prefer we can go out somewhere. Your choice."

"Sorry, Dad, I can't. I'll be at Donoghue House with the band. A couple of the City Radio DJs are going to pre-record interviews — Alf kindly set it all up for me. Then they're going to do a profile piece for the Sunday Focus."

"Of course, of course."

"Some other time, though."

"Oh yes, yes."

The conversation continued, uneasily at times, until Rick excused himself, embraced his father and then left, leaving both with an almost intangible sense of regret for things unsaid, feelings unexpressed.

As soon as he was alone, Norman's mind turned away from the pitfalls of the father-son relationship and he went straight to work. He phoned Eileen and regretfully told her that he would probably not make it home that night, news that she received with sad acceptance.

His next call was to the Prime Minister at Chequers, then, after a brief but intense conversation, he phoned Sir Dick Billings at home, no longer under surveillance, thanks to Norman's intervention.

"Dick, is it true that Eddie is planning to close his Tyneside shipyard and redevelop the land to fund this new airline of his?"

"Where did you get this from, Norman?"

"Never mind. Actually, I already I know it's true, I just need to know when."

"Early in the New Year. I was working on some legal matters regarding the site redevelopment just before I moved out of Environment. This will be the ultimate test of the Local Government Efficiency Bill. The shipyard is in a Labour council area but we're just going to overrule any of their petty objections."

"The unions know about it, Dick."

"What? My God! How do you know?"

"My source is impeccable. Look here, this closure cannot happen. At least not for another year or two. We can't fight the NUM and deal with this next year. Don't forget, Chatham is closing as well. I've just spoken to Margaret. You're going to have to convince Eddie to delay closure, for the time being at least. In return, we'll see what we can do about some MOD work. That should reassure Eddie's bankers sufficiently to keep things ticking along."

"I don't know if Eddie will be agreeable. He's got his heart set on this new airline and needs the money to fund the final setup. He's done some sort of complicated deal whereby he can leverage more money against projected pre-sales of the flats. I don't really understand it, but the wheels are already in motion. The yard is a millstone around his neck. It would only be a matter of time in any case. Its closure is inevitable. If not next year, then the year after. Its pure economics."

"It may well be inevitable, but it will happen at a time that will better suit us."

"I'm not the chairman of their board, Norman," Sir Dick argued, prompting Norman to think 'not yet'. "I can only suggest, or beg, if it comes to that. But I can't dictate, he's his own man and he'll make a commercial decision. We're not the Labour

Party, since when do we interfere in the inner workings of private companies?"

"Listen Dick, I'm sorry about this, but if you can't convince Eddie, then I will. And you won't like the way I do it."

"You gave your word, Norman, that you'd never let on about Eddie's father."

"This is nothing to do with Eddie's father, I'm saving that one up until we really need it. But I want Eddie to be left in no doubt that if he ever tries to pull a stunt like this again, putting eight thousand people out of work in a depressed area without at least having the common courtesy to consult more widely than your old department, I'll personally fuck him in ways that he could never imagine. I know enough to not only send him broke by scaring off his bankers, but to put him, and a few other people as well, in jail."

It wasn't often that Sir Dick Billings was cowed into submission, but the Home Secretary in full flight was a force of nature. "Norman, you wouldn't," he pleaded. "If Donoghue's went under, the consequences would be, well, it would be disastrous for the country, and for us, politically."

"Of course I wouldn't, Dick," Norman consoled him, "and I'd never do anything to harm our government, to embarrass you, or drag you into this mess, if you get my meaning. But Eddie doesn't need to know that. And our new police commissioner is not averse to allocating significant resources toward the policing of white-collar crime. As you know, he's always taken an extremely dim view of corruption generally."

"I don't really understand what you're saying," Sir Dick said quietly. "Where does this leave us?"

"Exactly where we are. You and I, we're still the old firm. A team. But I won't have Eddie Donoghue thinking he can hold this government to ransom to his own ends. He needs to be brought into line. National interest trumps everything, even friendship, Dick, you said so yourself."

After a brief pause, Sir Dick conceded defeat. The overwhelming sense of terror he felt at the possibility of losing Norman's friendship and support was only just receding in the warmth of Norman's reassurance that they were still rock solid. "You're right, of course, Norman. Hoisted up the flagpole by my own bruised and battered bollocks once again. I'll take care of it."

"I appreciate it, and the Prime Minister does too."

"Thanks, Norman. I mean it. By the way, what did you mean when you said we can't fight the National Union of Mineworkers as well? What's that all about?"

CHAPTER TWELVE

"Rick Armstrong speaking."

"Hi Rick, it's Austin Wells. Have you seen the news?"

"No, I try to avoid it most of the time."

"Well, let me fill you in. Sir Eddie Donoghue himself has come out, on Radio Four no less, to publicly deny that there are any immediate plans to close Speers-Donoghue, and that negotiations are under way with the Ministry of Defence regarding new contracts. It's enough to settle any financing jitters, and has probably bought us a couple of years. It's not a permanent stay of execution, but it's a reprieve."

"Congratulations, Austin. Over eight thousand jobs saved, I'm very happy for you, and your members."

"Unfortunately, given this unexpected turn of events, we have to temporarily withdraw our offer, regarding PR for the union. We won't need you for a year, maybe two if we're lucky. I'm sorry if I've inconvenienced you. I hope there are no hard feelings."

"None at all."

"And thank you, by the way."

"Thank you for what? I haven't done anything."

"Oh, I think you have. And you can drop this façade that you have no interest, or influence, in politics. You're way too modest."

"Modest about what?"

"It's been very nice to meet you, Rick. My brother was right about you, you are a rare man of integrity. *Winter of Discontent* at Number One! Knocked off Culture Club's *Karma Chameleon*! Who would have believed it? There's a nice metaphor, the resurgence of the Forgotten North. Anyway, I have no doubt we'll work together again. Keep in touch. Oh, and pass on my thanks to your father. Alf Burton was right when he wrote that your dad is the friendly face of Thatcherism."

"I don't see what my father has to do with anything, and, incidentally," Rick corrected, "he called him the almost acceptable face of..." But by now Austin had already rung off.

***

In the relentless march of the daily news cycle, even Dick Billings, the new hero of the British nationalist right, disappeared from the front pages as the News of the World exclusively reported on the former police commissioner.

BONKING BOBBY!
FORMER TOP COP'S TRUNCHEON POLISHED BY SOHO STRIPPER

It gave everyone a good chuckle, the story was lurid in its detail, and hinted darkly about the former commissioner's historic links with Soho crime baron Cyril 'Y-Fronts' McCann. The new Commissioner was interviewed, but the damage was minimal and only served to reinforce the government line that a new broom was in place, and policing would be very different under Honest Ron Coburn.

And now another big story was beginning to simmer and, as usual, Alf Burton was particularly well informed about the inner workings of the government. The following Friday's City Roundup once again broke the story.

"My guest this afternoon is the Special Minister of State at the Home Office, Mr Charles Seymour. A very warm welcome to the programme."

"Thank you, Alf, it's nice to be here."

"There are rumours about union disquiet, following a recent appointment within the ranks of government drivers. I'm referring, of course, to a driver recruited directly to the Home Office from outside of the normal career path that a senior government chauffeur might expect. My sources tell me that we're not far away from major industrial action, which may extend way beyond the rarefied world of ministerial chauffeurs and affect the wider government sector."

"We will not be dictated to by militant socialists, intent on doing nothing more than disrupting the government for their own political purposes. If the union leadership take this path, we will fight them with all the resolution we have shown in a number of other battles we've fought over the last few years. Fought and won, I should add."

"But what about their grievance specifically? An untrained driver recruited from outside the normal channels. How do you respond to union concerns that this creates a precedent that not only disadvantages its members, who are poorly paid in any case, but also places senior Ministers at risk by employing untrained, inexperienced drivers."

"Every premise of that question was factually incorrect, with great respect. First, government chauffeurs are not poorly paid at all. Secondly, the individual to whom you're referring was recruited personally by the Home Secretary. He underwent an exhaustive security check and has successfully completed a course of advanced driving with the Metropolitan Police. As well as having been a professional driver for over ten years, he is a decorated Royal Marine with active service dating back to Suez. Can you think of anyone better qualified to drive the Home Secretary?"

"How do you respond to union concerns about drivers' career structure, remuneration and morale?"

"Alf, the Home Office is here to protect Britain. As a result, key people must be chosen on merit, not drawn from a pool of mediocre timeservers intent on earning a lot of money, taxpayers' money I'll remind you, for doing little actual work. This is not the bloated government of Labour, Alf, this is efficiency. Strong, lean and decisive government is what we are about."

"The general tone of your answers seems to imply that you're not open to the union point of view at all. How do you expect to negotiate a satisfactory settlement if you won't even give the other side a fair hearing?"

"I will personally sit down with the union leadership and listen to them until the proverbial cows come home. But not while any threats of industrial action are in the air. This is my message to the union. Give your solemn undertaking that there'll be no strike, call my office this afternoon with that assurance, and we can meet first thing tomorrow. How much fairer can I be, Alf?"

"Special Minister of State at the Home Office, Charles Seymour, thank you very much. After the news, we hear from the

Shadow Home Secretary. We have a big second hour as well: Secretary of State for Northern Ireland, Stanley Smee, joins us live. And in our regular segment in which we get to know members of the government back bench, we're joined by the moderate Lambert Simnel, and I'll be asking him just how difficult it is to be on the damp side of the party with the Dry faction now completely dominating the Tory Agenda."

The following Monday afternoon, Norman was in conference with Sir Godfrey Powell and Commissioner Coburn, discussing the progress toward the establishment of a special police unit for deployment at the Home Secretary's discretion. Roger Davenport was taking minutes, and they all turned toward the door as Janice Best burst in clutching a transistor radio.

"Sorry to barge in," she cried breathlessly, "but you should hear this!"

"Government chauffeurs will stop work at ten p.m. tonight, as a dispute with the Home Office escalates. A union spokesman said today that it is likely that strike action will widen to encompass the entire government sector, if the government continues in its refusal to consider the union demands. Home Office Minister, Mr Charles Seymour, said that the government would not be bullied by rogue unions, and condemned their strike threat..."

"Oh my God," Roger Davenport had turned pale. "All the government drivers. That means local government as well. Bin men, wait a minute, NHS drivers. Ambulances! Oh my God! It'll be the Winter of Discontent all over again!" Roger's mounting panic then slowly dissipated in the face of the general air of serenity surrounding Godfrey, Ron Coburn and the Home Secretary himself. "Hang on, you're all very calm. Why are you so calm? I'm not calm, why are you?"

The telephone extension buzzed, Roger picked it up. After a few seconds he all but threw the handpiece at the Home Secretary, exclaiming in a voice that rose to a comically high pitch, "It's Number Ten!"

Demonstrating enviable reflexes, Norman managed to catch the receiver before it sailed past his ear. "Perry, how are you? Yes, yes, all according to plan. Everything is in place. Yes, he's with us now. I'll do that, and please thank the Prime Minister for her support. Thanks." Norman rang off. "Right, let's move on," he said.

Roger Davenport opened his mouth to speak, then closed it again, considering that blissful ignorance of whatever plan was being hatched would be the best position to hold.

***

That evening, in a rather unexpected development, Austin Wells was admitted into the Home Office at 50, Queen Anne's Gate, where he met with Charles Seymour and the Home Secretary himself.

"Thank you for seeing me," Austin said, after shaking hands with both and taking a seat at the conference table in Charles Seymour's private office. No other staff were present.

"I've been brought in," Austin Wells explained, "as a special negotiator on behalf of the drivers' union. I've been authorised to put forward the following proposal."

"No proposals," Charles immediately said. "You know our terms. Your guarantee of no industrial action, or no further discussion. I agreed in good faith to this meeting, against my better judgement, but you're obviously just wasting our time."

He made to stand up, but Norman placed a restraining hand on his arm.

"It won't do any harm to hear what Mr Wells has to say," he said, and Charles sat down again, glaring across the table at the union negotiator, who met his gaze without flinching. "Go on, Mr Wells," Norman said, smiling.

"We are prepared to allow..."

"'Prepared to allow?'" Charles Seymour's outrage was as convincingly palpable as if he was still Deputy Chief Whip tearing an errant backbencher to pieces. "We're not snivelling factory managers who'll drop their trousers, bend over and let you fuck them in return for industrial harmony. This is the Home Office. You can't come here and use language like 'allow'..."

"Thank you, Mr Seymour, delicately put." Norman soothed. The old double-act was as much fun as ever. "Now Mr Wells, can we cut to the chase? What have you come to say?"

If Austin Wells was offended or unsettled by Charles Seymour's performance, he didn't show it. He put his case calmly. "I'll rephrase. We now understand that the employment of this particular driver is deserving of special consideration. He's clearly unique in terms of his experience and qualifications. The union will make no further representations regarding this case, and will take no action. All we ask in return, and I stress the word ask, is a good-faith assurance that, in future, recruiting and promotions outside of the usual procedures will be subject to consultation."

"That's all?" Norman asked

"That's all," Austin Wells confirmed.

"And no industrial action. Do you have the power to guarantee that?"

"I do, you have my word. Business as usual."

"Agreed." The Home Secretary confirmed

"I won't take up any more of your time. Thank you again for agreeing to the meeting," Austin stood up.

"Thank you, Mr Wells," Norman said, shaking his hand.

"Not at all, Mr Armstrong. One good turn deserves another. And I give you joy of the New Year."

As he departed, Austin turned to the Home Secretary. "Oh yes, I had the great good fortune of meeting your son recently, Mr Armstrong. A fine young man, you must be very proud of him."

After he had left, Norman and Charles reflected on the meeting.

"That was way too easy," Charles observed. "And what a funny way to wish us happy New Year. It's not even Christmas yet!"

"I give you joy," Norman explained thoughtfully, "Was an expression used between military officers around the Napoleonic times. An ancestor of mine was at Waterloo, he wrote about it in his memoir. It was a way of wishing good luck, for instance, 'I give you joy of the day, joy of the battle'. Or congratulations. 'I give you joy of the victory'. Mr Wells wasn't wishing us a happy New Year, Charles, it was his polite way of declaring war."

"Declaring war? If that's the case, why did he cave in on this so easily?"

"Because he's smarter that we thought. This was going to be an ultimately pointless dispute, engineered deliberately by us, over an obscure issue that we were always going to win, and when we did, the union movement, generally, would be just that little bit weaker, and public opinion just that little bit more on our side. All in preparation for the main game next year. But Mr Wells, on this occasion, outsmarted us."

Charles looked puzzled. "What did he mean by one good turn deserves another?"

"He found out about secret plans for the closure of Speers-Donoghue in the New Year."

"My God," Charles exclaimed. "Thousands of jobs! Why didn't we know about this?"

"An unfortunate lapse by our former Environment Secretary. Anyway, it's all academic now, because the closure plans have been shelved, at least for the time being. Mr Wells approached my son — on that occasion he apparently represented the Fitters and Shipyard Workers — to offer Rick's company the PR contract for the union's anti-closure campaign. He also rather cleverly engineered it so that my son would have to come to me to ask questions about Eddie's solvency, and thereby ensure I was aware of the secret closure plans. He probably suspected that members of the government not quite as close to Eddie Donoghue as Dick Billings, might see the wider political damage of the loss of so many jobs on Tyneside. I have a feeling he might have been hoping for my intervention."

"So, he credits you, or at least your influence, for saving the shipyard. One good turn."

"He's going to be a formidable adversary, Charles, we'll need to keep our wits about us."

"Does Eddie really have solvency issues?"

"Not so much now. A couple of defence contracts for the shipyard will settle his bankers, at least for the time being. I gather that, on the basis of this, sufficient additional credit has also been extended to expedite the establishment of his airline. But I wouldn't be relying on a Donoghue share portfolio to fund a comfortable retirement."

"I don't have any Donoghue shares. They were offered, but I told his lackey to bugger off and corrupt somebody else."

"I wish all of our friends and associates had the same level of common sense."

"How did you convince Eddie to keep the yard open?"

"Credit where it's due: Sir Dick can be very persuasive."

"By the way, Norman, what was that about the main game being next year?"

"It's time you knew. The Coal Board is going to embark on a programme to close a large number of unprofitable pits. More than fifty."

"My God, Scargill and the NUM will go mad."

"Exactly, and this time we'll be prepared. No concessions, no backflips, no backing down. And we'll soon have enough coal to last us through next winter and beyond regardless."

"So that's what this new special police unit is for."

"Yes, amongst other things. Had the drivers' dispute escalated, I also intended to use them as relief drivers for the more senior Ministers."

Charles was carefully considering the implications of what he'd just learned. "We're gearing up for the last big fight, the free market versus the socialists," he commented, rubbing his chin. "Winner takes all. The Summer Offensive of 1918 and D-Day all rolled into one. I see why it was so important not to be confronting the closure of Speers-Donoghue at the same time. Very hard to fight and win a war on two fronts."

"I wish I could say that you were overdramatising, but I think your analysis is not too wide of the mark."

"No wonder the lads in the new police squad are calling themselves Armstrong's Army."

The Home Secretary returned to his own office, assembled his red boxes and phoned for Eric to be ready in about fifteen minutes. He stared at his special, secure phone for a moment, weighing up how best to proceed, then made up his mind, lifted the receiver and dialled.

"Archie," Norman said, after a brief pause, "I'm glad I caught you. There's someone apart from Mr Scargill that we need to be keeping an eye on. And I think it's about time we considered getting someone actually inside the NUM."

CHAPTER THIRTEEN

"And this is what we know so far. Two police officers and three members of the public have been killed, and up to ninety others injured, a number critically, after a car bomb exploded in Knightsbridge. Metropolitan Police Commissioner, Ron Coburn, says that investigators believe the IRA planted the bomb near a side entrance to Harrods.

"Mr Coburn confirmed that a coded warning had been received just over thirty minutes before the lunchtime explosion, which, we understand, killed the two of the four police officers who were approaching the suspect car to investigate. The other two officers sustained critical, life-threatening injuries. Christmas shoppers were also caught up in the explosion, which sent thick black smoke, rubble and broken glass into the street.

"A number of Harrods staff and shoppers were treated at the scene, while those suffering more serious injuries were taken to nearby hospitals by ambulances backed up by police and army vehicles. Four hospitals were put on emergency alert to expect serious casualties."

"Next hour, I'll be speaking exclusively to Conservative MP Stuart Farquhar who was nearby when the bomb went off, and was personally involved in providing first aid, assistance and support to those at the scene. Roland Moreland, City Radio news, London."

"Turn it off, please Eric." Norman said.

Eric Baker turned off the car radio. With eyes firmly on the road, he kept perfect distance behind twin police motorcycles, their two-tone sirens echoing and blue emergency lights flashing and reflecting, as they swept a path through the Saturday evening traffic en route to St Mary's hospital, where they would visit some of the injured police and talk to families that had been caught up in the bombing. Seated next to Eric was their detective, ponytail discreetly hidden behind his collar, and in the back seat, with Norman, was PPS Janice Best.

"It sounds like Stuart distinguished himself," Janice observed with a half-smile. "I wonder what Mr Seymour will have to say about that."

"Mr Farquhar is quite a hero, from what I gather," Norman acknowledged. "Perhaps we'd better ask Sir Dick if he can see his way clear to improve Mr Farquhar's office accommodation."

"I thought Roland Moreland was with the BBC, by the way." Janice said.

"He was," Norman replied. "But Alf Burton was so impressed with the number of exclusive interviews Moreland got at the Party Conference he asked Eddie to offer him a contract with Donoghue's. I guess it was an offer he couldn't refuse."

"We're here, Sir," Eric reported as the car came to a smooth stop outside the hospital entrance.

"Speak of the devil," Norman muttered, as he stopped to make a brief statement to the reporters assembled at the hospital entrance. "Good evening, Mr Moreland."

"And to you, Home Secretary. Do you have any comment at this stage?"

Short and to the point, Norman thought approvingly. "Tonight our thoughts and prayers are with those injured, and with the families of those killed. Investigations are of course underway and we'll be providing updates in due course."

"Would the government be considering the proscription of Sinn Fein?" Moreland asked.

"It's far too early to be discussing political implications. Thank you all, and excuse me." The Home Secretary and his small entourage disappeared through the hospital doors.

***

The year was drawing to its close, and Norman was as content as a man with his responsibilities in such troubled times could be, and he found himself in an unusually contemplative mood. He was very happy with this senior staff, and advance planning for the following year's industrial battles was proceeding apace while the new special police unit, now almost officially known as Armstrong's Army, had enthusiastically displayed their military-standard proficiency for the Home Secretary and Commissioner Coburn at a secret training location outside of London.

As Chief Whip in both government and opposition, Norman had been largely out of the public eye for the best part of a decade, but he was now quickly becoming a widely recognisable and respected figure. Someone famously steadfast, upon whom the nation felt it could rely in times of great danger and fear. A further living embodiment of the government's resolute approach. Articles and profiles appeared in newspapers and on television, and even the less friendly factions of the press had to grudgingly concede that having Norman Armstrong once again in the pivotal role of Home Secretary made the country feel just that little bit safer.

Following the Harrods bombing, the Home Secretary's statement to the House of Commons and his responses to MPs' questions had been widely praised. In his regular column, Westminster Watch, Alf Burton wrote:

...For years, Norman Armstrong has been the Conservative government's best kept secret. Rarely commenting in public, his work behind the scenes has played a key role in the recent political success of the Tories, dating back to Margaret Thatcher's ascendancy to the Party leadership in 1975.

But as we are now discovering, he is much more than a backroom political fixer. His conduct as Home Secretary strikes exactly the right balance — the reassuring image of strength and tenacity, yet tempered by well-directed compassion. He is one of the government's best performers in the House, where his calm leadership following the Harrods bombing, clearly taking charge but considering other points of view, represented our democracy at its best.

Those with an eye to the succession must now be considering the Home Secretary as a future Prime Minister, although there's every reason to think that Mr Armstrong may choose a graceful retirement long before our current leader, who shows no signs of running out of steam. It may well be that Norman Armstrong will prove to be the best Prime Minister Britain never had...

It was probably only the seriousness of the times, the subdued, sombre mood of the country, mourning and often fearful, that restrained the Opposition from having a lot of fun at Norman's expense on the back of Alf's references to the leadership. Norman, for his part, was quite embarrassed and annoyed at what he perceived as his friend's deliberate mischief making, but was relieved when the Prime Minister took it all in good humour, telling Norman not to start packing his bags for a move to Number Ten just yet. She also playfully informed him that although he could take some comfort from being the best Prime Minister the country never had, she was in fact the best Prime Minister they ever had.

Several days later, it was Dick Billings's turn, once again, to steal the headlines as the Donoghue broadsheet, the *Daily Focus*, featured the Home Secretary, Denis Thatcher, Sir Dick Billings and Stanley Smee posing in front of the hastily repaired Harrods frontage. Dick cheerfully told the assembled reporters that no damned Fenian was going to stop him from doing his Christmas shopping, prompting the following day's paper to lead with DEFIANT DICK STANDS UP TO BOMBERS.

Sir Eddie Donoghue's commitment to keep Speers-Donoghue open, preventing a devastating loss of jobs on Tyneside, was one less crisis to deal with, in the short term at least. As Norman had predicted, the potential for Ministry of Defence contracts settled the tycoon's bankers in the City and internationally, and it was now more than likely that Erin Airways would be flying a handful of European and Mediterranean routes in time for the summer tourist season, even without funding from the shipyard redevelopment. Norman could not even begin to comprehend the amount of debt that Eddie's various businesses must be accumulating, and suspected that money was being frantically shuffled between various companies within the group, like hammering wedges between the holed timbers of a sinking ship. God help us all when she finally succumbs for the last time, Norman reflected, hoping that Rick had taken Austin Wells's advice and was demanding prompt payment for services rendered.

The government's rigid adherence to its economic policy against persistent attacks from within and without was, Norman could see with satisfaction, now paying dividends, vindicating the Dry approach championed by the right faction, and discrediting the Awkward Squad once and for all. He was full of admiration for Geoffrey Howe and Nigel Lawson, successive Chancellors who had held their nerve and overseen the economic recovery. Although the three million plus unemployed was a constant and painful reminder that all was not necessarily as well as could be, the statistics, in Norman's view, illustrated an overwhelmingly positive outlook, despite what doom and gloom merchants like Alf Burton and Roland Moreland might say. The Chancellor, Nigel Lawson, had confided to Norman following the last Cabinet meeting that economic growth for the year of 1983 was heading toward five percent, while, at 4.6 per cent, inflation was at its lowest since 1966.

It was all enough to prompt Norman to rethink his long-considered plan to retire at the end of the current term. He was also warming to the idea of the Peerage that would inevitably follow if he managed to stick it out until the end of the decade, or just beyond. The conversation in which he informed Eileen that it might be as much as eight more years of perpetual separation — instead of three — was not one that he was looking forward to having.

But more immediately, there was still this nagging anxiety over the so-called Banqueting Club. Harmless old men with a penchant for dressing up, or sinister murderers and political manipulators? Norman was beginning to suspect, with mounting disquiet, that his own family's role in history, a reassuring emotional refuge during tough political times, was perhaps not quite what he had come to know and revere.

As far as everyone knew now, the long feared Morris manuscript was not the destructive expose of Royal and aristocratic misdeeds casting a dark, apocalyptic shadow over the present day, that had been so widely dreaded, but was in fact nothing more than an unpublished Richard Fforbes mystery novel. As a precaution, Sir Archie's department had acquired an advance copy so that they could analyse the text, seeking out any coded or implied revelations, but it appeared that generations of paranoia had been based on little more than rumours borne of a decades-old misunderstanding. At Alf Burton's urging, Donoghue Publishing had pursued and secured joint distribution rights in what was rumoured to have been one of the largest publishing deals in recent history. On pre-orders alone, *A New Beginning* was almost guaranteed to top the Times list of Bestsellers.

So, what of all of these rumours, suspicions and conspiracies? Monarchist vigilantes, murder and manipulation: it seemed all the more ludicrously implausible with the cold sobriety of hindsight. And yet, there were certain nagging facts that were beyond dispute. What of Dorothy Keppel's trip to South Africa following the death of Charlotte Morris? What about the royal doctor who was at the reading of the will? What about the enigmatic Piers Armstrong? Alf obviously had his suspicions. What did it all mean?

And now, there was Sir Godfrey Powell's innocent revelation that his older brother had been a promising detective in the early years of the war, had joined the Special Operations

Executive and was never seen again. A tragic coincidence? Or a vindication of Sir Dick Billings's late night ramblings after all?

In any case, Norman knew that he was hamstrung. If he attempted to make any enquiries of his own, just to satisfy any residual curiosity, it would be inevitable that Sir Archie would become aware in five minutes flat. Although, technically speaking, Prentice had to defer to Norman as Home Secretary or, depending on your interpretation, to the Cabinet Secretary, the intelligence chief was not someone with whom Norman wanted to sow any seeds of distrust. As Ron Coburn had said, Prentice could be a tricky customer. Dick Billings had been more direct, a stark warning. Beware. Even the Cabinet Secretary had advised caution. But why, if all of this was a big load of nothing at all? So many contradictions. But in the end, Norman accepted that the nation's security depended on solid, open relationships between the three most senior security officials: himself, Archie Prentice and the Cabinet Secretary. The 'Winged Mafia' as they had now come to be known, due to their shared RAF history. The national interest trumps everything, Norman reminded himself.

"Sleeping dogs, I think," Norman muttered, as he consciously tried to redirect his attention more closely to some briefing papers detailing security concerns surrounding the ongoing Greenham Common protests. He was also anxious to study in more detail Commissioner Coburn's meticulously compiled report on the exoneration of two Metropolitan Police detectives who had shot an innocent young man in the mistaken belief that he was an escaped prisoner. Reading between the lines, it was apparent to Norman that Coburn had taken issue with the way the judge had seemingly encouraged the jury to acquit, however justice had taken its course, and there was nothing more to be done, other than consider the inevitable claims for compensation. How this would affect the attitudes of communities already suspicious of the police generally, remained to be seen. Norman made a note in the margin to seek the opinion of Janice Best, who continued to be highly attuned to the key issues in her own challenging constituency, and a reliable barometer of attitudes within the inner cities.

But... Norman's attention wandered once again. He removed his glasses and dropped them heavily on his desk, huffing with frustration over his own lack of focus and self-discipline. His mind turned to Sir Godfrey Powell's elderly father, the retired Major who had served in the Natal Rangers and then a South African mounted regiment and who had been a close friend of Fforbes Armstrong. Actually coming face to face with the only living link to the grandfather whom Norman had idolised, but had never met, was enough to tempt him towards a meeting with the old soldier. Godfrey would no doubt be delighted at the prospect, but would any such encounter prove to be just a pleasant, nostalgic sharing of memories over a cup of tea and cake, with a few fascinating stories of the Natal Rangers and the exploits of the legendary Colonel? Or an ill-advised meddling in a Pandora's box, that once opened, could never be closed again?

"Let it go, move on," Norman told himself. He replaced his glasses and returned his attention to his papers, promising himself that he would not look up until he had completed reading them. At that moment, the phone on his desk buzzed, he threw his glasses off again in frustration, pushed the intercom button and barked, "Oh, bloody hell, what is it, for God's sake?"

"Alf Burton on the line, Home Secretary." Roger's voice emerged from the speaker, his tone unaffected by the Home Secretary's palpable anger.

"Thanks, Roger," Norman replied, in a much gentler manner. "Put him straight through, please."

"Comrade Alf!" the Home Secretary cried with genuine pleasure. "Long Live the Revolution!"

***

Dolly Burton looked up from her book, took off her glasses and gazed lovingly at her husband who was contentedly snoring in the chair opposite. The small living room was comfortably warm thanks to the gas fire. While the Christmas decorations, tree ornamented and lit, cards displayed on a string hung above the fireplace, and tinsel wrapped around anything that protruded, all lent a festive air of optimism and joy. Dolly was adamant that this was going to be the best Christmas ever, in celebration of Alf's safe return from his kidnapping ordeal at the hands of those terrible Irishmen. Their Yorkshire terrier, Ernie, equally at blissful ease in the embrace of his little family, was curled up on Alf's lap.

"Alf," Dolly said quietly.

"Aye, pet," he said suddenly, his head jerking upright. "I wasn't asleep!" Alf's sudden and unexpected movement also jolted Ernie wide awake, and he answered with a low growl before settling back down.

"Of course you weren't, my dear. I'm enjoying this new Charlotte Morris, *A New Beginning*. It's a canny read, thank you for letting us see the advance copy. The cover art work is lovely. Did you tell me that Eddie had secured the hardback rights?"

"On my advice, he steamed in and wouldn't take no for an answer. Paid a fortune, but it'll be worth it. This is the literary world's Holy Grail, short of an undiscovered Bronte, Dickens, George Eliot or Jane Austen. Rick and Terry have come up with a huge publicity campaign, they're clever lads. This is going to be the biggest launch for Donoghue Publishing since my triumphant *Decade of Discontent*. I've nearly finished my review for it, by the way, as one of the foremost authorities on Charlotte Morris."

"Your modesty does you credit, pet. But has Eddie already paid out?"

"I don't know. He must have, I suppose. Why?"

"And you're one hundred percent sure it's genuine? It's definitely the work of Charlotte Morris herself?"

"Of course, the writing style is unmistakable. Why do you ask?"

"Ee, it's probably nowt."

"What is?"

"Well, it's just that, as you know, a part of the novel is set during the peace conference in Versailles, just after the war. I don't know as much about these things as you, but those aspects of the story seem to be very well researched, even detailing some of the changing European borders. I've double checked with my encyclopaedia; Charlotte Morris was spot on."

"That's not surprising, pet: she was very well connected politically, and, in any case, it would have been reported widely in the papers at the time. She probably added those factual details into the story to give it a greater sense of immediacy, and realism. Most of the Fforbes stories had at least some basis in real events."

"But when did Charlotte Morris actually die?"

"She caught the influenza in the autumn of 1918, she eventually died in January of the following year, but she'd been bedridden for…"

"Alf, man, are you all right? You've gone white as a sheet!"

"She died in January of 1919!" he cried. "She couldn't have known those details of Versailles!" Alf thought frantically. "Still," he said, thinking aloud, trying not to panic, "she was politically astute, she could very well have predicted…She could have been lucky…Oh God!" Alf slumped back in his chair as Ernie grumbled over the disturbance. "And I was the one who assured Eddie that it had to be the real thing! Over a million pounds down the drain! What have I done?" Alf's distress soon had him reduced to leaning forward in his chair, propelling a disgusted Ernie onto the fireside mat, and hyperventilating into a paper bag while Dolly rubbed his back and softly soothed his breathing back to normal.

"Never mind, pet," she said eventually. Mebbes naebody will notice."

"Having fought resolutely against extravagant government spending, inflation, unemployment, terrorism, foreign military dictatorships, socialists and Tory wets, enemies without and within, the stage was now set for another major struggle. This one would come to define Margaret Thatcher's premiership as a whole, as the Falklands War had come to define her first term. This fight would be violent and bitter, and would entrench hatreds that would still be raw almost a decade later, and will, doubtless, remain for years to come. In 1984, the direct fight would be against Arthur Scargill, Austin Wells and the National Union of Mineworkers, but the collateral implications would reach well beyond."

The concluding paragraph from *Economic Warfare – Thatcher and the End of Consensus*

(Volume 1)

By Alf Burton

© 1992 Donoghue Publishing and Broadcasting.

CHAPTER FOURTEEN
1984

One of the rare periods of pure contented bliss in the life of Sir Dick Billings had been the time surrounding the previous year's general election, when the Conservatives had more than tripled their House of Commons majority. Sir Dick had played a large part in devising the campaign strategy, with then Chief Whip Norman Armstrong, and was still basking in the warm glow of satisfaction. It had also been one of the few times in which he had been almost unanimously celebrated by his own Tory colleagues, many of whom had wrung his hand in emotional gratitude for helping them to increase their own constituency majorities, or in the case of the newcomers, for being elected for the first time. Now, entering his ninth decade, and with half a century in the parliament behind him, the Father of the House could finally take some comfort from the fact that, barring unforeseen disasters, he wouldn't see another change of government in his lifetime. The victory had been sweetened even further by the political demise of his principal nemesis, Labour MP Tony Benn, whom Sir Dick despised with almost as much venom as he had Aneurin Bevan.

So when Mr Benn returned to parliament following the Chesterfield by-election, leaving Dick's own chosen candidate a distant third and trailing Labour by around sixteen thousand votes, the explosion of invective from the Chief Whip's office could be heard the entire length of Downing Street. Sir Dick's transistor radio had also fallen victim to the maelstrom of his frustration, and was now scattered about his office in small pieces. So he proved to be one of the only government members not glued to the radio to hear ominous initial reports of stoppages at a number of pits across the country.

***

"Good afternoon everyone, and welcome to a City Roundup special with me, Alf Burton, on the City Radio network right around Great Britain. We lead this afternoon with the dramatic news that tens of thousands of Britain's miners have stopped work, following the announcement by Coal Board Chairman, Mr Ian McGregor, reported exclusively on this network one week ago, that twenty unprofitable pits would be closed, putting as many as twenty thousand miners out of work. Our coverage begins with the latest from our special correspondent, Roland Moreland, who has compiled this report."

"Around ninety thousand of the nation's one hundred and eighty seven thousand coalminers have stopped work, protesting proposed industry-wide job losses. Miners in Yorkshire and Kent walked out this morning, and have since been joined by colleagues in South Wales and Scotland. Miners at Cortonwood Colliery in South Yorkshire, one of at least twenty earmarked for closure, had already downed tools immediately following the announcement, and National Union of Mineworkers President, Mr Arthur Scargill, has called on members nationwide to join the action, and provide support with flying pickets.

"It appears at this stage, however, that support for the stoppage is far from universal, with some pits in Nottinghamshire, South Wales and Scotland still operating, and there are unconfirmed reports of picket-line violence at the Bilston Glen Colliery. A spokesman for the National Union of Mineworkers, Mr Austin Wells, said that in the coming days, the members still working would see sense and join their striking colleagues in the fight to save their industry. This is what Mr Wells had to say a short time ago."

"The National Union of Mineworkers is fighting for much more than the jobs of miners, upon whose backs the prosperity and prestige of this nation has been built over generations. I can't emphasise enough the domino effect arising from a coal industry brought to its knees. Don't be fooled by the Coal Board's claims that only twenty pits are being targeted for closure, we believe the real figure to be much closer to seventy or eighty. The destructive effect on the railways, steel, engineering, manufacturing and electrical industries will devastate Britain as an industrial power, and lead to poverty and social division on a scale we can barely imagine."

Roland Moreland continued. "It certainly appears that resolve is strong on both sides, with Coal Board Chairman, Mr Ian McGregor, stating that he is more than ready to take on the NUM. Sources have informed us that close to fifty million tons of coal has been stockpiled between the pits and the power stations, in preparation for what both sides anticipate will be a prolonged stoppage. We will, of course, keep you up to date with coverage around the clock on City Radio, and each day in Donoghue newspapers and Independent Television stations right across the country. This has been Roland Moreland, City Radio Network News. And now back to you, Alf."

***

Sir Norman Armstrong listened to the report in his private office at 50, Queen Anne's Gate, in company with Charles Seymour.

"It seems that we were right about our friend Austin Wells," the Home Secretary commented. "It looks like he's going to be in the thick of it."

"Well, then," Charles replied thoughtfully. "To paraphrase Mr Wells himself, I give you joy of the battle, Home Secretary."

"Thank you, Charles. I can't help feeling that joy is going to be in rather short supply in the coming weeks and months." Sir Norman buzzed the intercom on his desk, and asked Roger Davenport to put him through to Ron Coburn.

The Commissioner was on the line in less than a minute, and Charles Seymour smiled as the Home Secretary laid out his instructions. Armstrong's Army was about to mobilise.

***

"We have to stop meeting like this," Austin Wells said, as Rick Armstrong joined him at the crowded bar of the Kings Head.

"Funny, I was going to say the same thing," Rick replied. "What does that say about us, do you think? That we're already middle aged and predictable?"

"Not me, I'm barely past my teenage years, in the sweet bloom of youth."

Rick observed Austin's greying hair and world-weary expression. "You must've have had one hell of a hard life, then," he said.

"Yes, and it's only getting harder."

"You're in for a bit of excitement, by the looks of things. I see you're speaking on behalf of the National Union of Mineworkers now."

"Yep," he chuckled, "the TUC gives me all the easy jobs. They were so impressed by my victory at the Speers-Donoghue shipyard that they think I can achieve anything. But we know the truth of that little operation, don't we? It's not like the credit can be given where it's really due."

"Let's not go down that path again."

"So how's life as Sir Eddie Donoghue's chief propagandist?"

"This is going to be a short meeting if all you're going to do is ask me questions I have no intention of answering."

"I'd like to revisit the offer I made late last year."

"I thought the shipyard was safe. Sir Eddie himself gave a public assurance that the yard would remain operating on the back of new defence contracts."

"Nothing to do with Speers-Donoghue. We want you to work with the NUM. This fight is going to be in the media as much as on the picket lines. We want the country's hearts and minds with us. You're the best in the PR business, Rick. We need you."

"Have you forgotten that my company has just signed a massive contract with the Donoghue Group? I'm not completely naïve, either, Austin. I'm not blind to the fact that recruiting the son of the Home Secretary to fight a very public battle against his government would be a coup in itself. It's not going to happen, under any circumstances. I may not subscribe to my father's politics, but I won't be cynically used, again. This entire discussion is a waste of time."

"What do you mean, cynically used again?"

"Oh, come on. You came to me with that offer to provide PR support for the union fighting the shipyard closure. You cleverly put doubt in my mind over Donoghue's solvency knowing full well I would speak to my father about it. You banked on the fact that he would see the political danger of a closure of that size, and intervene."

"You give me way too much credit, Rick. Conniving and manipulation on that level is way beyond me."

"You once told me I was too modest. I think the same applies to you."

"Eight and a half thousand jobs saved on Tyneside. The result speaks for itself. And was I not right to caution you to keep a close eye on your Donoghue invoices? What did your father have to say about that?"

"Never mind. But I appreciated the advice."

"By the way, we don't want your company, we understand that Armstrong and Cox are committed to Donoghue's. From what I hear, your business partner is particularly committed to Sir Eddie's daughter. We want you, personally. And unlike Sir Eddie, we have reliable funding. You won't be out of pocket."

"The money is not the issue. I have professional commitments which I need to honour, legally and morally. And this battle between the Thatcherites and the miners is not one that I have any desire to join. On either side. Ever."

"All we want is your brain, a little informal consulting that's all. No one need ever know. We can make any payments very discreetly. Offshore account if you like. If you won't take my word for it alone, I can set up a meeting with Mr Scargill himself. We just need a little help in terms of publicity and the promotion of our cause. Nothing sinister. It's not like I'm asking you to defect across the Iron Curtain and sell state secrets."

"Austin, I'm not sure how many different ways I can say no before you understand my position. The answer is no, no and no again."

"Well, perhaps I can talk to you again in the summer. See how you feel then."

"What makes you think I'll feel any different? And the whole thing will be over by then, surely?"

"They said that World War One would be over by Christmas 1914, as well."

"Now you're being ridiculous, there's no comparison."

"Maybe not, but I think you're underestimating what lies ahead of us. Your father's government has been planning for months, even years. Legislating to strip power from the unions, bit by bit, stockpiling coal, training a special police squad to respond to trouble spots. Not your friendly neighbourhood Bobbies either, I'm talking serious riot squad hooligans: the heavy mob, who'll crash through pickets without a second thought, with no quarter given. Actually, here's the comparison to World War One, Rick old son. There you had two groups of powers, each obligated to the other by treaty. Germany and Austria-Hungary, Russia and France, and poor old England, committed to Belgian neutrality. Remember that the Germans gave Austria what they called the blank cheque? However violently they went after the Serbs, Germany would back them. This is exactly what the government has given the Coal Board. A blank cheque to decimate the coal industry and crush the unions. So, here you have the two great powers. The government, the police and the Coal Board on one side, and the entire union movement, and most of working-class Britain, on the other. This is the big one, Rick, we'll be lucky if this is over by the summer after next."

"Even if you're right, and I'm not convinced, it's still not my fight. And I really need to get back to work."

"Belgium wanted to remain neutral, and look what happened there."

The two men shook hands. "I wish you luck, Austin, I really do. You're one of the most persuasive, clever guys I've ever met, you don't need me. I should be offering you a job, not the other way round."

"Depending on how this unfolds, I might be knocking on your door one day."

"No hard feelings, then?"

"None at all. By the way, I see The Forgotten North sold out the Birmingham NEC last week. And their second single is joining their first in the top ten. You're obviously still finding enough time to manage my disreputable brother's musical activities, whilst spruiking the latest Donoghue venture?"

"Oh yes, our staff are very committed to both. Actually, they go hand in hand to a point. The Donoghue radio and television networks, and their papers, have really got behind us. That was Alf Burton's influence, largely, as he played their first single on his show. I slipped him a demo as a matter of fact, he loved it, and got it on to their playlists, and then big profiles in the newspapers."

"Did you say Alf Burton? Do you know him?"

"Yes, he's an old friend of my... he's an old friend of the family. I've known him for as long as I can remember."

"Any chance you could get me an introduction? I might even leave you alone then."

"Anything for the quiet life."

***

When Sir Norman Armstrong returned to his office from the House of Commons he was, as usual, confronted by a long list of messages. But only the most important ones remained for his personal attention, the majority having been referred to Special Minister of State Charles Seymour. On the top of the list of names for the Home Secretary's particular attention, which included Chief Whip Sir Dick Billings and Secretary of State for Northern Ireland, Stanley Smee, was Sir Archie Prentice. Sir Norman phoned him straight away, using his special secure line so that the call would not be minuted by Sir Norman's ever attentive principal private secretary.

"Hello Archie, what's new?" Sir Norman asked.

"Welcome to the club, old boy," Sir Archie replied. "I don't think I've spoken to you since the New Year Honours, have I, Norman? *Sir* Norman, I should say."

"Just Norman is fine, *Sir* Archie."

"Well, congratulations are in order, of course. Not before time, not before time, and thoroughly deserved. I suppose our Young Ronnie will be next."

Norman smiled. Being called 'Young Ronnie' was still one of the few things that could send the ordinarily calm and unflappable police commissioner into paroxysms of spluttering annoyance.

"Now, a little delicate matter," Sir Archie continued. "You've no doubt been receiving our reports on the surveillance of Mr Scargill and Mr Wells?"

"Thank you, Archie, your people are as efficient as ever."

"Good, good. Now, yesterday our friend Mr Wells met up with someone, um, that is to say, I'm not quite sure how to tell you this, but…"

"Go on, Archie," Norman encouraged, puzzled. It was unlike Sir Archie Prentice to be reticent in passing on potentially awkward information. He normally delighted in it.

"Sorry about this, old boy. It was young Rick."

"Are you sure?" Norman asked uneasily.

"No doubt about it, I'm afraid."

"Where was this?"

"The King's Head, a very dubious public house in South London, just off the Lambeth Road. You know it well, Norman, it's where you always used to meet that Burton fellow when you were Chief Whip, when you were trying to stitch someone up, or for a good old fashioned strategic leak."

Norman huffed. Was there no privacy at all in government? Was there nothing that Sir Archie didn't know about? It was a deeply unsettling feeling, Norman had always believed that his carefully planned, discreet meetings with Alf, well away from Westminster gossipers, had been the best kept of his many secrets. But this situation with Rick was the more urgent worry. "Do you know what they were talking about?"

"No, unfortunately we couldn't get the place miked up in time."

"Look Archie, I can't imagine there is anything untoward. Rick is not at all involved in any kind of political activities." Suddenly, to his intense relief, Norman remembered a conversation he had had with his son during their family Christmas. "I know what it would have been about. Austin Wells has a brother, Freddie, he's the lead singer of a scruffy music group called the Forgotten North. My son is their manager and publicist, it must have been some kind of business to do with them. They're very successful apparently."

"Ah, that would explain it then," Sir Archie replied. "We'll say no more about it."

"What about your chap's written report?" Norman asked.

"What report?"

Norman inwardly sighed with relief. "Thanks, Archie."

"We look after our own, Norman, I know you'd do the same for me."

***

As Home Secretary, Sir Norman maintained the same disciplined and often solitary schedule that had underpinned his life as Chief Whip. Each night, Eric Baker delivered him safely home to Knightsbridge and dutifully carried an armful of official red boxes up the stairs to the library, where he invariably touched his chauffeur's cap to the large, imposing portrait of Sir Norman's grandfather.

Once alone, with one measure of scotch poured from old Fforbes Armstrong's own decanter, and seated behind the same desk from which three generations of Armstrongs had plotted and connived their way through the insular political world in which they lived, Norman's first and most important task remained to phone Eileen. Following the usual warm, affectionate discourse about family matters — there was great jubilation over the fact that Rick and Sally were now expecting a brother or sister for thirteen-year-old James — Eileen continued to keep Norman informed about local matters from his constituency office, where she excelled in her role as unofficial, unpaid assistant and was, in Norman's eyes, just as valuable as any PPS or Minister of State.

After a light snack — Norman considered lunch his main meal of the day — he went to work on the briefing papers contained in his red boxes, until the BBC news at nine. Every so often, a spotlight would reflect on the upstairs window of the library as a police patrol passed by. The neighbours were extremely happy about Sir Norman's elevation to Home Secretary. Between his own bodyguards and additional patrols by the metropolitan police area car, their little corner of Knightsbridge was now safest neighbourhood in London.

Although now far less involved in the backroom politics that governed his previous life as Chief Whip, his expertise was still often called upon and his opinion sought on matters well beyond his responsibilities as Home Secretary. Sir Dick Billings — generally speaking still far from popular in the parliamentary party, despite his undoubted talents as a political operator — had got off to a rocky start in his dual responsibilities as Chief Whip and Party Chairman, and there were already dissatisfied mutterings in Cabinet over his handling of the Chesterfield by-election. Now, to compound his problems, the latest opinion polls were showing that the Tories had gone from a sixteen-point lead over Labour to a three-point deficit, in just the past six months.

Sir Dick had vented his frustration in typical fashion during a recent phone call to the Home Secretary, referring to the electorate at large — and many of his own colleagues — as a shower of ungrateful fuckers. Following some calming words from Norman, he was able to take some comfort from their own crushing majority, and the wriggle-room provided by the several years before the next general election fell due. But to the Home Secretary, the message was clear. Mr Kinnock was not a man to be underestimated.

***

Sir Godfrey Powell had been delighted, over the short Christmas respite, to have been able to spend some additional time with his father, now approaching his ninety-third year, and who was a resident at Stonebridge House, an exclusive and very expensive care home in the heart of Sir Norman Armstrong's own safe, affluent constituency.

Albert Powell's private room, overlooking an acreage of deep green lawn and exquisitely maintained gardens, was adorned with a number of photographs and memorabilia from his long and eventful life. The ready access to tangible memories seemed to help him conquer, or at least delay, the inevitability of his slowly failing faculties. Following his retirement from the South African Mounted Rifles, Major Powell had brought his growing family to England and gone to work in the City, a lucrative but forlornly unsatisfying sequel to years of adventure in the colonial armies.

Although his legs let him down more often than not, and he was prone to increasing forgetfulness, on a good day his mind was as sharp as ever and he enjoyed nothing more than discussing and debating current events with his son, who, after the welcome extra time afforded by Christmas, remained a weekly visitor, every Saturday without fail. The elder Powell had been delighted to hear that the new Home Secretary, now several tumultuous months into his tenure, was none other than the grandson of Powell's own commanding officer, Colonel Fforbes Armstrong, a protective mentor when Powell had been a young Captain in the Natal Rangers facing his first action at the Somme.

"I've been saving some of the press clippings about that new Charlotte Morris book," Albert Powell said, as he and Godfrey enjoyed a lunchtime glass of ale, sitting in winged chairs facing the large windows overlooking the gardens. "Came out around

Christmas, I think. There was a big fanfare on the television as well. You probably saw it all. Makes me laugh, some damned fool paid millions to publish it, Irishman named Donoghue. Same cove that publishes that rag." The old Major gestured at a copy of the *Daily Focus* that had been carelessly tossed on to a chair, with some of the broadsheet pages spilling onto the carpet. "Only thing in it worth reading is Westminster Watch, the Alf Burton column. Mind you, he can be a bit too holier-than-thou for his own good. I've been reading his columns for years. I remember he got very worked up over the Harold Wilson resignation — hinted at all kinds of dark conspiracies. It'll be interesting to see how he reports this business with the miners. I think he's a bit of a red deep down. Funny how he was kidnapped by the IRA last year. What was that all about?"

"It wasn't the IRA," Godfrey corrected him. "Some splinter group called the Irish Republican, no Revolutionary Brotherhood. The Irish Revolutionary Brotherhood it was. Not too much has been said about it, but I think Sir Norman was very influential in getting him released unharmed."

"I'm not surprised. If your chap is half the man his grandfather was, he'll prove to be a fine Home Secretary, perhaps even Prime Minister one day, eh? You'd be Cabinet Secretary by then of course. Imagine! What would Reggie have said about that?" The Major turned his gaze to the sideboard, on which a number of framed black and white photographs had pride of place. He focused his eyes on one in particular, a young man, proud and stern in the uniform of the Metropolitan Police.

"I'm fine with Permanent Secretary at the Home Office, Dad. I don't think the current PM, or Sir Peregrine for that matter, have plans to go anywhere in the foreseeable future."

"That's as may be, but Mrs T will need to keep an eye on these opinion polls. This new Labour chap seems a lot more sensible than usual, now what was I talking about before? I've lost the... oh blast, let me think..."

"You were talking about how Donoghue paid millions for the Charlotte Morris book."

"That's right. Of course. Met a few chaps like Donoghue when I worked in the City. I'm sure you've come across them as well. Flash, full of themselves, spent money hand over fist, most of it not their own. A bit like some previous governments we could name, what? Chaps like Donoghue never last." The Major leant forward in his chair. "At some stage he's going to be in for a rather unhappy surprise, Godfrey my boy. That book, if you believe what you read in the papers — mind you, who does, these days, eh? 'The publishing event of the decade.' Hah! Wasn't even written by Charlotte Morris. There's always someone trying to cash in..."

The Major's sudden interest in literary matters was something of a surprise for Godfrey, who'd only ever seen him read newspapers, predominantly the *Financial Times* and the more serious broadsheets, and only the occasional book, political and military histories, most of which he dismissed as rubbish, and made extensive notes in the margins detailing historical inaccuracies.

"How do you know?" Godfrey asked.

"Something I hadn't thought about for years. All this palaver on the news reminded me. I was there when most of it was written. Just after the first war, in Pietermaritzburg."

"Would you like to tell me about it?" Godfrey asked, hiding his scepticism. The old Major still had many, many good days, when his mind displayed the remarkable agility of his younger self. But on occasions Godfrey was reminded that his father was now in his tenth decade, and, as the Major's favourite nurse kindly described his vaguer moments, he was prone, occasionally, to wander off in the fog.

"Not yet," replied the Major. "There's something else I can't quite remember, something I feel is important. I think Colonel Armstrong was mixed up in it somehow. I went to his farm, drove out from Pietermaritzburg, must have been 1919, the war had been over… Yes, it was just as the final communiqué from the peace conference was… It's all a bit jumbled up in my head at the moment, but it'll come back to me. You see if it doesn't! I'll work on it during the week, and hopefully I'll be able to tell you all about it when you visit next weekend."

It was always a sad moment when Godfrey left. Father and son embraced, and from that moment the Major began looking forward to the following weekend. As Godfrey reached the door, the Major called after him. "Godfrey, how do you really get on with Sir Norman? Is he good to work with?"

"Very much so. He's tough, probably the toughest politician I've ever met. But a genuinely nice, decent chap."

Just like his grandfather, Major Powell thought. Tough as nails, but kind. "Do you think it could finally be time?"

Godfrey thought for a moment. "Yes," he replied. "It could very well be. I'll wait for the right moment, then I promise I'll raise the matter. Soon."

As usual, Major Powell waved to his son from the window as Godfrey walked to the car park. He turned, as a knock preceded the opening of the door to his room. It was the duty sister, his favourite, who was also not unlike Colonel Armstrong. Tough as nails, but kind.

"Everything all right, Major?" she asked.

"I'm nearly ninety-two, my legs only work occasionally, some parts of me don't work at all, I can't remember what I said or did five minutes ago and I have to go to the gents' twenty-five times a day. I've been a widower for over forty years and, oh yes, I'm constantly subjected to the ministrations of a nursing sister who would have done well as a sergeant major in my old regiment. Tickety-boo!"

The sister smiled. "Happy days, then," she replied. "Can you do something for me?"

"Anything, my dear, as long as it doesn't involve too much dashing about."

"There's a new arrival, he's not coping well. He was in floods of tears watching his family drive out just now, poor man. If you're feeling up to it, perhaps you could pay him a visit. He's in room twenty-nine. I think you two will get along, he's an old sea captain. Seems very nice."

"The old pins are a bit doddery at the minute, I'll see how I feel a bit later. I normally buck up a bit by the afternoon."

"Thank you. His name's James, by the way, Captain Jim, we call him."

***

Alf and Dolly Burton had, as usual, returned to Jarrow just after Christmas. They always welcomed the annual opportunity to spend time with their extended families, many of whom, after generations of varying fortunes, intimately connected with the local shipyard, now part of the conglomerate controlled by Alf's own employer, Sir Eddie Donoghue, still worked at the traditional shipbuilding trades. In spite of the general state of industry in the Northeast, optimism was high thanks to Sir

Eddie's very strong and public rebuttal of rumours that the shipyard was going to be closed and the site redeveloped. He had also hinted at new contracts from the Ministry of Defence, extending a welcome lifeline to the thousands of shipyard workers, the best Christmas present a struggling community could ever hope for. The planned Nissan factory near Sunderland was another piece of welcome news, a sign that things might be looking up after all.

Alf was a much loved hero in his home town, and couldn't walk more than a few steps along the street before being accosted for autographs, asked for his thoughts on the current state of the country, and questioned about his first-hand recollections of the Jarrow March. His stocks had risen further with the saturation coverage of his kidnapping, elevating the veteran reporter to the status of genuine national treasure. Alf was more than a little grateful for the fact that, thanks to the conveniently applied Official Secrets Act, it was unlikely that the Great British Public would ever find out the truth of that little adventure, certainly not in his lifetime anyroad, ensuring that his hard won reputation for fearlessly confronting politicians of all persuasions, and especially for standing up to even the most strident Thatcherites, the foundations upon which his very lucrative contract with Donoghue Media were based, would remain intact.

Alf was also becoming increasingly uncomfortable about having traded his silence about pit closures as part of his deal for Number Ten access. Now that he could see the menacing reality of the strike, his mind dwelling almost constantly on the potential cost in human and social terms, he found his conscience an unrelenting, gnawing presence, rendering him perpetually agitated and uneasy. Yet, professionally, he was at the top of his game. In addition to his extensive network of secret government informants, 'sources close to the Cabinet', he also had a reliable hotline to the hierarchy of the TUC, and, now, also to the National Union of Mineworkers, in the form of their senior spokesman Austin Wells, thanks to a handy introduction discreetly provided by Rick Armstrong. With his old friend Tony Benn back in the parliament, along with a promising young Labour MP named Jeremy Corbyn, his wide and much envied network was as comprehensive as could be.

Professional status aside, Alf was still deeply traumatised over the embarrassing saga surrounding the publication of the lost Charlotte Morris novel. The fact that Sir Eddie had paid a seven-figure sum to enable Donoghue Publishing to secure worldwide rights for the hardback edition, purely on the back of Alf's assurances beyond any doubt that it was the genuine article, still had him waking up in the middle of the night, shivering and perspiring.

In a strange paradox of fortunes, stellar reputations had been saved only by the fact that, contrary to outrageously bold predictions, a massive publicity campaign and strong pre-orders, the book had almost immediately slipped from the bestseller lists, and had disappeared without trace. Literary critics had not been kind, with one describing the novel, in comparison to Charlotte's other works as 'easily as bad as ever.' As Dolly had hopefully predicted when she uncovered the truth, nobody had, as it turned out, noticed.

Sir Eddie, for his part, had been remarkably magnanimous, and now the paperback rights were to be taken up by the original publisher, who had been enriched beyond their wildest expectations. Once the initial shock had receded, Alf and Dolly made an educated guess that the novel had most probably been completed by Charlotte Morris's editor and secretary. It was the most likely scenario and explained the close adherence to Charlotte's own narrative style. Alf quietly suggested to the rights-holders that, for the sake of historical accuracy, future editions should be credited to Charlotte Morris and Dorothy Keppel.

***

By the following weekend, Albert Powell was no closer to recovering his memories surrounding Colonel Armstrong and the mystery of the Charlotte Morris manuscript, but was delighted to tell Godfrey that he had made a new friend in Captain Jim.

"He's only a young'un," the Major explained, as they enjoyed their regular Saturday lunchtime ale, the new warmth in the air encouraging them to the outside chairs and tables for the first time this season. "Eighty-six last month. At sea all his life. I'm going to be interested to hear all about it. I'll introduce you if we see him."

Godfrey was pleased that his father had found someone to pass the time with, and, as usual, the visit passed pleasantly and all too quickly, the Major as keen as ever to discuss current events. He'd made some notes, having watched the nightly television news throughout the week, and consulted them as he chatted happily away.

"I think your chap might be letting things slip a bit," he commented. "This rabble at Greenham Common seem to be running amok. About time something was done about them, don't you think?"

"The wheels are in motion, as we say, Dad."

"Oh Lord, you're sounding more and more like Humphrey Appleby," the elder Powell told him. "Next you'll be using phrases like 'at the appropriate juncture', and 'in the fullness of time'. Meanwhile those mad fishwives are making your department a laughing stock. About time for a decisive move, put a bit of stick about, what?"

Godfrey smiled, then checked himself before he made a comment about waiting for the right time. "Keep an eye on the news. I don't think you'll be disappointed."

On his way home, Godfrey stopped off at the newsagent and tobacconist, not far from Stonebridge House, to purchase his favourite cigars, a necessary comfort, as, that night, he would be reluctantly accompanying Lady Powell to the West End opening of Starlight Express. Musical theatre was not to Godfrey's taste at all, but, on occasions, dramatic sacrifices had to be made in the interests of domestic harmony. He also bought some chocolates, a gift to try and distract from the lack of enthusiasm he found hard to conceal, and, as he approached the counter, he noticed a display of paperback books. He picked one off the shelf: it was *A New Beginning*. Godfrey noted that the paperback edition, already discounted, had been credited to Charlotte Morris and Dorothy Keppel. His father's apparent connection to the author was intriguing, and he must have been at least partly right about the circumstances in which it had been written. Perhaps he hadn't been wandering off in the fog after all. It was obviously something the Major himself was increasingly anxious to recall, so he added it to his purchases, thinking that it might be just the thing to jog his father's memory.

***

"Excuse me, Home Secretary." Roger Davenport poked his head around the doorway to the Home Secretary's private office.

Working with the door open had been a habit for Norman Armstrong when he was Chief Whip, and was one that he had given up trying to break.

"Yes, Roger?" He looked up from some of the latest surveillance reports from Sir Archie Prentice, relieved that there had been no further mentions of Rick having any contact with Austin Wells, but he noted with interest that Mr Wells had been conversing quite a bit recently with Alf Burton.

"Sorry to disturb you, Home Secretary, but BBC radio is reporting that Gerry Adams has been shot in Belfast, along with three other Sinn Fein members."

"Good God. Is he alive?"

"He's been taken to Royal Victoria Hospital. There's not a great deal of information at this stage. There are also reports that three suspects are in custody. I've already placed a call to the Northern Ireland Office, and asked that Mr Smee update us at his earliest convenience."

"Thank you. I thought Adams was supposed to be in Belfast Magistrates today — obstructing police, wasn't it? Some nonsense over the Irish flag?"

"It was during the court lunch break, apparently. It looks like the other chaps wounded with him were his co-defendants," Roger replied.

"Dear me," Norman replied, and returned his attention to the intelligence reports on the blossoming friendship between Alf Burton and Austin Wells.

By later that afternoon, an outlawed loyalist paramilitary group, the Ulster Freedom Fighters, had claimed responsibility for the shooting, releasing a statement to the effect that, as Mr Adams was to blame for the continuing murder campaign being waged against Ulster Protestants, he was regarded as a legitimate target of war. This was a sentiment with which the Home

Secretary had more than a little sympathy, but the Secretary of State for Northern Ireland, Stanley Smee, came out strongly against the attack, warning against any retaliatory acts and urging both sides to do everything in their power to prevent further violence.

"Whistling in the wind," Norman muttered as he listened to Smee's statement on the BBC's Radio Ulster, but he had, grudgingly, to concede that his old factional enemy was continuing to be a surprisingly accomplished Secretary of State.

***

"I've got something for you," Sir Godfrey Powell told his father the following Saturday morning, and handed him the copy of the book he had bought.

"What's this?" Albert Powell asked as he reached for his glasses, "*A New Beginning*, by Charlotte Morris and Dorothy..."

"Dad. Are you all right?" Godfrey was about to ring for the nurse as his father stared intently and silently at the book's cover for long enough to make his son think that he might be having some kind of attack, a stroke perhaps. "Dad?" Godfrey called, snapping his fingers several times in front of his father's face.

"Will you stop doing that!" Major Powell scolded, and to Godfrey's intense relief firmly pushed his hand away.

"What is it?" Godfrey asked gently.

"I knew her," replied the Major

"Knew who?"

"This Dorothy Keppel. I took her to see Colonel Armstrong, then we... She was staying at the Grand Hotel in Pietermaritzburg, or was it the Royal? We had a dinner there, some old boys from the Queens Own Natal Rifles, the Colonel's old regiment. Something about a duel: I think the old Colonel had killed Charlotte Morris's husband forty odd years before... There was a despatch pouch, QONR insignia, some documents, secrets..."

"Dad, are you all right?" Godfrey asked, thinking regretfully that raking up this ancient history might not have been such a good idea after all. Far from jogging his memory, it seemed to have sent his mind on a journey to nowhere. How much of this had actually even happened?

"Of course I'm all right," Major Powell snapped. "I'm not ready for the knackers' yard yet. Colonel Armstrong, actually Governor Armstrong, was worried about Miss Keppel. He took me aside... we kept her under our protection until she sailed from Durban. My God, in the Lady Georgiana. Damned coffin ship, went down off Spain, Bay of Biscay was it? I think. Poor Miss Keppel, such a charming..."

"Governor Armstrong?"

"Yes, yes!" The Major was becoming increasingly impatient. "The Armstrong Free State of Natal, guarded by his personal militia, old soldiers from the Natal Rangers and the QONR. Mostly wounded, disfigured, shell shock. You had to cross a border post to enter, all very formal, present your compliments to..."

"The Armstrong Free State of Natal? I don't quite understand what you're talking about."

"All such a long time ago. Too many blanks, but I'll remember."

"Perhaps it might be best if I take the book with me. I don't want you to get distressed."

"Stop treating me like I've gone senile! You're not too old for me to kick your patronising backside. You will not take that book, I intend to read it. After all, I helped to write the damn thing."

"You helped to write it?"

"Well, in a way. Miss Keppel wanted to know everything I could tell her about my own experiences at the Somme. I also introduced her to a couple of chaps that fought in East Africa. And then, details of the peace conference, as the news was coming through in our local papers. All part of her research." The Major regarded his son's sceptical expression. "You think I'm making all this up!" he said. "You're thinking that the old fool's finally slipped his moorings, I can see it in your face. Well, you can't ship me off to the jim-jam clinic, I'm already here."

"No, no, I don't think you're making it up, perhaps, just a little confused. It was all such a long time ago..."

"I'm going to get to the bottom of this. Just give me a little time."

Later, as Godfrey left, the Major reminded him of the important matter to be raised with the Home Secretary, then shouted after him, "and bloody well do something about Greenham Common!"

***

As dawn was breaking, and having been waved through police cordons, Eric Baker parked the black ministerial car amongst a number of police sedans, Range Rovers, Transit vans and buses, all assembled within sight of the ramshackle camp outside of the main gateway to the Greenham Common RAF Base. The Home Secretary, having brushed aside protests from Commissioner Coburn, was determined to see the first deployment of Armstrong's Army, his specially trained unit, which was already on hand to support local officers during the eviction of the thousands of peace campers.

Norman was aware that the presiding local authority, Newbury District Council, had previously tried to dismantle the camp, but with little success. Sir Dick Billings, while still Secretary of State for Environment, had facilitated a deal between the Ministry of Defence and the Department of Transport so that the land occupied by the campers was now subject to redevelopment, and construction of a new access road was due to begin as soon as the site was clear. The legal pretext for the eviction was now in place, and the Home Secretary, along with PPS Janice Best, were there to watch.

"I've been meaning to ask, Home Secretary." Janice blew on a steaming foam cup of coffee which Eric had carefully poured from his thermos. "What happened to our favourite, long haired detective? I've just realised I've haven't seen him for weeks."

"He's been reassigned," Norman replied, gingerly sipping his own coffee and inhaling the strong smell with satisfaction. "Back undercover again."

The Home Secretary's new bodyguard, who had been following in a separate car, approached with a senior police officer. "Excuse me, Home Secretary," the detective said. "This is Superintendent Ray Johnson, Thames Valley Police. He's in operational command."

The Home Secretary shook hands with Superintendent Johnson, who advised that they were about to give the protestors one last chance to leave under their own steam, before officers would be ordered to move in. "Carry on, Superintendent, I'm only here as an observer." Johnson had initially been quite flustered by the unexpected appearance of the fourth most senior member of the government at his little operation, but the Home Secretary's friendliness put him quickly at his ease.

When Superintendent Johnson's five-minute deadline had passed with no voluntary movement, around three hundred local officers moved in, supported by a contingent of Armstrong's Army. As the wall of police surged toward the protestors, Norman wondered if his grandfather had stood in similar observance, at dawn, as his soldiers advanced against the enemy. No, Norman thought, the old Colonel would have been right out the front, leading by example, facing Zulus, Boers, and German machine gunners, not a bunch of woolly-hatted...

"Why-aye, bonny lad!" Norman's daydream of heroisms past was interrupted by Alf Burton, who appeared to be in some sort of scuffle with several Thames Valley officers whom Superintendent Johnson had quietly and hastily assigned to beef up the Home Secretary's protection.

"It's all right, let him through," Norman said, and the officers reluctantly stood aside while Alf went through the pretence of indignantly straightening his tie and dusting off his jacket

"Good morning, Home Secretary," he puffed, gratefully accepting the scalding coffee offered by Eric. "Miss Best, Eric, nice to see you all. Any comment?"

"I don't think so," Norman replied. "Just a routine police operation."

"How do you respond to Mr Benn, who has himself already commented on the eviction of the protestors by saying that, and I quote, 'civil liberties in Britain are being removed by order of the government.' Are our civil liberties in danger under your government, Home Secretary?"

"They certainly are not," Norman replied, a little testily. "This area is being cleared in order to make way for a new roadway development. It's a matter of safety."

All eyes abruptly turned to the camp area, from where the audible crackle of flames accompanied rising columns of black smoke, as a number of tents were set on fire. They observed the limp, compliant bodies of protestors being carried away by officers, noting that any resistance seemed to be generally passive. Sensing greater opportunities closer to the action, Alf bade a polite good morning and disappeared toward the fray, his old familiar mac billowing behind him.

***

As Albert Powell shuffled slowly along the corridor behind his Zimmer frame, he noticed Captain Jim heading towards him from the other end. Because of the excruciatingly slow pace at which each of them moved, they had smiled, nodded and waved to each other several times before they finally drew level.

"All right, Bert?"

"Fair to middling, Jim, fair to middling."

"What are you up to?"

"Thought I'd cut along to the lounge and make a start on this book my son brought in for me." Major Powell reached in to his little basket and produced the book. "*A New Beginning*, it's called, by Charlotte Morris and Dorothy Keppel..."

"Sorry, who did you say?" Jim asked, his voice faltering

"Charlotte Morris and Dorothy Keppel. Jim, are you all right?"

"A ghost from the past, that's all," Jim replied, his distressed face belying the composure in his voice.

"Anything you'd like to talk about?"

"Not now. Maybe a little later. I think I'll just go back to my room."

CHAPTER FIFTEEN

It proved to be a busy week for the police squad known as Armstrong's Army. Several days after Greenham Common, they were backing up local police forces in Derbyshire, and Nottinghamshire, as picket line violence between striking and working miners intensified, and confrontations with police escalated.

To his deep disappointment — and to Commissioner Coburn's intense relief — Norman's responsibilities required him to remain in London. He was kept up to date minute by minute thanks to Scotland Yard and the BBC, but less so by the Donoghue network's gun reporting team led by Alf Burton and Roland Moreland, whose frequent updates and news flashes were required listening throughout the government, but which the Home Secretary dismissed as far too sympathetic to the miners' point of view. He was also extremely annoyed that allegations of police heavy handedness and concerns over civil liberties — a term Sir Norman could not abide — had resulted in the scheduling of an emergency debate in the Commons: where the conduct of his own squad would no doubt come under pointless scrutiny from armchair critics, who would do the country a far greater service by minding their own business and letting the government get on with the job it was elected to do. He'd been grateful that the Prime Minister herself had come out strongly in defence of his officers, publicly stating that the police had been marvellous in their support of the rights of miners who wanted to remain working.

The Home Secretary was also receiving strong support from Chief Whip Sir Dick Billings, who was ever vigilant over the resurgence of the Awkward Squad, this being just the type of issue to bring their tattered remnants out of the woodwork. Sir Dick had also warned the Home Secretary to beware of the newly elected Labour member for Chesterfield, predicting that Mr Benn would be sure to bring up any kind of outrageous slur or allegation under parliamentary privilege, by way of announcing his return. In a brief pre-debate, whispered head-to-head in the lobby, Home Secretary and Chief Whip briefly discussed a number of pressing issues.

"Can you talk to Eddie," Sir Norman asked, "see if he can do anything about the Donoghue press coverage of the pickets? I'm not saying they should take our side, necessarily, but a little balance wouldn't be too much to ask, surely."

"You know that Eddie leaves his media division well alone, regardless of his own personal opinions and loyalties," the Chief Whip replied. "God knows we've had it out with him often enough. And besides, I don't really think he's in the mood for doing us too many favours at the moment. In fact, given that he's kept the Speers-Donoghue shipyard open, against any commercial common sense, just to save us from embarrassment over the job losses, he might think that we owe him one this time. Anyway, why are you asking me? You're the one who's supposed to be such good friends with his political editor. Why not remind your *old marra* about how you saved his bacon from the Irish terrorists last year, and that it's high time he showed some gratitude?"

"Yes, well that relationship is a little more complicated, as you know."

"Why not tell him that, unless he does the right thing, all bets are off in terms of the deal that you did for exclusive..." Sir Dick Billings looked around suddenly. "Oh, speak of the devil. Fuck off Burton, you fat pinko twat! This is a private conversation."

"I'll take that as a comment, Chief Whip," Alf said with a smile, and disappeared amongst the throng of MPs and reporters surging toward the Commons.

"And another thing," the Home Secretary continued. "In return for our bulldozing through the Local Government Efficiency Initiative, Eddie promised the Prime Minister a big announcement on jobs about now. He said he had a whole raft of new construction projects planned, thanks to the freedom the legislation afforded, that he was working on the numbers, and, to use his words, we wouldn't be disappointed. A positive announcement of that nature would be quite a handy distraction in the current climate."

"I'll talk to him," Sir Dick promised. "He might consider that he's already done his bit by keeping the shipyard open."

Sir Norman struggled to keep his voice low and measured, and looked around to make sure that they were not being overheard. "The Donoghue Constructions expansion, propped up by our legislative amendment, had nothing to do with the shipyard closure, which, I'll remind you, I found out from another source, not from you. And don't get too misty eyed about his generosity in keeping the yard open for us — the MOD contracts we bribed him with have settled his bankers enough to enable him to borrow enough additional money to finally get this blasted airline of his flying. Of all the hare-brained..."

"All right, all right," Sir Dick soothed. The Chief Whip could bully and intimidate with the best, but he reflected, and not for the first time, that Norman Armstrong in full flight was like a freight train hurtling towards you with no hope of stopping in time, and your feet jammed in the tracks. "Get off your high horse, I'll deal with it. Perhaps in return you might consider accepting his invitation to the launch party for Erin Airways. Young Rick and his people are laying on a big show in their hangar at Birmingham Airport. They're trying to coincide with the opening of the new international terminal there. Eddie would appreciate it, I'm sure. He's still our biggest corporate supporter, don't forget, we owe it to him to make an appearance. Can I ask, are you keeping your distance since you found out about his father's wartime activities? I hope we're able to move past that."

"I told you last year that I wouldn't use that unless we really need to. And another thing, we could use his cable television news station right about now, you know, the one that he promised would be wall-to-wall conservative commentary? What happened to that?"

"I think there are some technical problems with the cabling, I don't really understand it. But there are rumours that the Daily Mirror is up for sale. Maxwell is sniffing around, and I think Eddie wants to position himself for a bid. That might be taking priority."

"We'd better discuss this later," Norman grumbled. He calmed himself down, genially slapped his old friend on the shoulder, and then disappeared into the chamber.

Sir Dick sighed. It was an increasingly intricate challenge to manage the relationship between Sir Eddie Donoghue and the government, like trying to mediate between two feuding castaways — totally reliant on each other but too stubborn to admit it — trapped on the same small desert island, with no chance of escape. Seeking an outlet for his own pent up frustration, he laid eyes on one of the former members of the Awkward Squad, Stuart Farquhar MP, whose recent heroism following the Harrods bombing had done nothing in Sir Dick's eyes to redeem years of troublemaking from the backbench.

"Farquhar, you limp-dick!" the Chief Whip roared. "I want to talk to you…"

***

When Sir Norman Armstrong entered the chamber, he was buoyed by his usual sense of self confidence, comfortable in his own proven ability to handle whatever was thrown at him in the often brutal back-and-forth that defined democracy in the House of Commons. But as the debate intensified, he began to feel that he was just barely holding his own against the onslaught from the Opposition benches, led, as the Chief Whip had astutely predicted, by a sustained tirade from Tony Benn. The Home Secretary had been particularly rattled over questions relating to the tapping of phones — a number of NUM officials were currently on Sir Archie Prentice's radar — as well as the fact that there were undercover police officers infiltrating the pickets, of which the Home Secretary's former bodyguard — their favourite long-haired detective, as Janice Best had described him — was one. To Sir Norman's frustration, Mr Benn had also editorialised very effectively, refusing to give way and hammering his point home time and again.

"When I was in Chesterfield over the weekend," Mr Benn told the House, glaring directly at the Home Secretary. "I checked the figures. There were three thousand, nine hundred applications for supplementary benefit, of which only two thousand, four hundred had been processed. Of those, nine hundred have been refused, and fifteen hundred are awaiting payment. There is a strong suspicion that the government has deliberately slowed down the DHSS arrangements, to put financial pressure upon the miners. I believe that the government have brought the police tactics of Northern Ireland into the heart of Britain. That view is widely shared. In the process they have gravely damaged the relations between the public and the police. When talking privately to the miners, many local police officers have spoken of their dislike of the conduct of police brought in from other areas. The charge that this debate has brought forward is that, above all, the government have denied their responsibility for what has happened and, in a typically cowardly way, have pretended that they have come to the assistance of the police whom they sent in to deal with an industrial dispute for which the government are one hundred per cent responsible. What we have seen in this dispute is part of a much wider attack upon the freedoms of our people. The Prime Minister, supported by her loyal lap-dog, the Tory Chief Whip and Party Chairman Sir Dick Billings, deals with those who dissent in a plain way. They will abolish local authorities that disagree with her, and ban the trade unions that disagree with her."

The Home Secretary noted that the atmosphere had changed markedly since his appearance in the House following the Harrods bombing, where his calm leadership and generous treatment of Opposition questions had been almost universally lauded. Even Northern Ireland Secretary Stanley Smee, in his first major address to the Commons reporting on the Alf Burton kidnapping months before, had commanded the House and had members of all persuasions on their feet yelling their support. In just a few short months, the atmosphere, or the vibe, as Rick might have termed it, had darkened considerably.

The following day Alf Burton's Westminster Watch column predictably celebrated Tony Benn's performance in the House, and then went on to report specifics of the confrontations.

"About one hundred pickets were arrested during violent confrontations with police at working pits in Nottinghamshire and Derbyshire. The National Union of Mineworkers have deployed flying pickets, busloads of striking miners able to respond to areas at short notice, not unlike the Home Secretary's police squad, in actual fact. However, the police at Cresswell Colliery were immediately on the back foot, as up to one thousand pickets descended upon them. Six police officers and at least one miner were injured. In spite of the pickets, almost two thirds of the night shift were able to report for work and the colliery kept operating, but at a reduced capacity. There have been reports of reprisals against working miners, including damage to private cars, and at least one instance of a miner's home having its windows smashed.

Official figures state that forty pits are still operating: out of a national total of one hundred and seventy six. The miners are fighting against the proposed closure of around twenty pits that the Coal Board had assessed as not sufficiently productive or profitable. NUM spokesman, Mr Austin Wells, states that the number of mines earmarked for closure is more like sixty, predicting a nationwide social calamity if the closures are allowed to take place.

Matters were even more fraught at Babbington Colliery, Nottinghamshire, where as many as two thousand pickets fought off police with stones as they made around sixty arrests. Seven officers needed treatment for cuts and bruises while at least one union member was hurt. There have been complaints about the conduct of police, with claims of heavy-handedness, and abuse of power, even of turning away flying pickets as far away as one hundred miles from their destination. There have also been reports that undercover police have infiltrated the pickets. However, Home Office Minister, Mr Charles Seymour, has strongly rejected allegations of police misconduct. "Police are not above the law, and have no wish to be," Mr Seymour said. "They are the servants of the law, and our principal citadel against those who seek to impose their will on their fellow citizens." He has also given an assurance that any complaints against police will be investigated rigorously.

But here is a word of caution to our popular Home Secretary, previously lauded in this column for his strong leadership during fearful times, who is now so closely identified with the police response to the pickets, in the form of a special flying squad created on his own initiative, and nicknamed, by its own members, Armstrong's Army. There is a real danger of the politicising of the police, unleashing a highly trained, aggressive unit upon civilians, on one entire segment of society, as part of a wider ideological battle. It is a dangerous path, a slippery slope, and not what we expect from our great democracy. There are checks and balances, of course, and your columnist has long been an admirer of Honest Ron Coburn, our Metropolitan Police Commissioner and a career-long crusader against corruption and police misdeeds generally. We look to him for common sense and decency in a worsening climate of conflict and division.

CHAPTER FIFTEEN

"Excuse me, Home Secretary, do you have a moment?"

"Of course, Godfrey, sit down."

"Thank you." Godfrey sat down opposite the Home Secretary, and placed a folder on his desk. "Here is the report, including costings, from the West Midlands Chief Constable regarding the recent Wolverhampton riots."

"Damned layabouts," Sir Norman muttered. "If I had my way those scruffy hooligans would be drafted straight into the army. Teach them discipline and respect. This is the inevitable result of the Welfare State which Alf Burton has championed for nearly forty years. Although, in all fairness, I don't think even Attlee's government intended that welfare would evolve from short-term relief for the genuinely unemployed, into a vast basis for generational parasites, living at the tax payers' expense. Lucky Dick Billings isn't Home Secretary. He'd have 'em all in chains in some prison hulk in the Thames Estuary."

"Mind you," Godfrey countered, "it was virtually full employment in those days, wasn't it? I wonder what Mr Attlee and Mr Bevan would have thought of our current rate of unemployment? I guess they had very strong memories of the Depression, people starving and homeless, with no safety net. I understand that Mr Attlee had worked in the East End as a young man, and the experience stayed with him."

"Well now, Godfrey," Sir Norman smiled. "Do I detect a hint of the Burtonian point of view? Don't tell me I have a closet bleeding heart heading up my department?"

"Certainly not, Home Secretary," Godfrey smiled in return. "I have no opinion of my own, I am here to serve the government of the day." And then, with a good dose of mock obsequiousness, "I am here to serve *you*, Home Secretary."

"I have a feeling, Godfrey that it might actually be the other way round. But anyway, what did you want to talk to me about?"

"It's a bit of a personal matter, I'm afraid. I'm trying to do something for my father."

Alarm bells began to ring in Norman's mind. Just when he had put all this distraction to one side, a supreme effort of will was required to keep questioning thoughts from disrupting his concentration every single day. Where was this going to go? His expression gave nothing away. "How can I help?"

"Do you remember that, late last year, at your welcome drinks party, I mentioned my brother? He was a policeman, a young detective, during the war. He went into the SOE, and was killed."

"Yes, of course." In a split second of totally uncharacteristic paranoia, Norman suddenly wondered whether his office was bugged, and whether Archie Prentice was listening in. Stop being ridiculous, he told himself, carefully keeping his expression benign.

"Well," Godfrey continued, "My father, that is, he's never really, I don't quite know how to put this, but..."

"Let's go for a drive," the Home Secretary said suddenly, standing up.

306

"What?" Sir Godfrey said, surprised. "Why?"

"I need some fresh air." He buzzed through to the outer office. "Roger? Ask Eric to bring the car around, straight away please, and let our detective know that we're on the move. Both Sir Godfrey and I will be out for the rest of the day. This is where we can be reached..."

Godfrey was surprised and delighted by the Home Secretary's impulsive decision. Eileen was even more elated when Norman phoned her briefly with the news that he would actually be coming home that very night, and that Sir Godfrey Powell would be their guest at dinner.

***

"Eric, do you know where Stonebridge House is, not far from my home?"

"Yes, Home Secretary," Eric replied, mindful of the presence in the back seat of the Permanent Secretary, and avoiding the easy, and possibly just a little professionally inappropriate, familiarity into which he had fallen after months as Sir Norman's driver.

"Right, there first of all," Norman said, "then to my house. I'll need you to drive Sir Godfrey home later this evening, then come back for me about five in the morning."

'Righto Guv' came out of Eric's disciplined mouth as "Very good, Sir."

***

"Dad. Dad. Wake up, it's Godfrey."

"Stand to!" the Major commanded, then suddenly opened his eyes and sat up straight in his chair. "Good God! Godfrey! What a wonderful surprise! And who is this with you? Is it Sir Norman? I don't believe it!" He tried to raise himself out of his chair, but was clearly struggling.

"Don't get up, Major," Sir Norman said, and extended his hand which the old man took and gripped long and with surprising strength.

"It's an honour to meet you, Sir Norman. You look very much like your Grandfather, I must tell you," Albert Powell said, through the widest smile Godfrey had seen on his often-sad face in as long a time as he could remember.

"The honour is mine, Major Powell. And you must just call me Norman."

"Sit down, sit down, please. Godfrey, in that cupboard there, pour us all a glass. This is a wonderful occasion, finally to be face to face with Fforbes Armstrong's grandson."

Norman had no idea what he could have been thinking. The recklessness of this meeting went against every instinct of his disciplined and rational mind. Seeing the genuine pleasure in the Major's face, and having shaken the very hand that no doubt had shaken the hand of his own grandfather, Norman himself became quite overawed.

"Dad thinks we've been altogether too soft on the women of Greenham Common," Godfrey said as he handed glasses to his father and to Norman.

"I never said any such thing," Albert retorted, then smiled as he said, "but I did notice that they went straight back there after you cleared them out. Forgive me, I'm forgetting my manners. Your very good health, Norman." He raised his glass.

"And yours, Major. And Godfrey." Sir Norman replied, raising his own. "They didn't all go back. We only really needed one area for a new road construction. The Thames Valley Police have it in hand."

"I see you're giving those miners a good going over. Quite right too."

"Well, we have a few challenges at the minute."

"I dare say. I'd be a bit careful of that new Labour chap, Kinnock. Looks like a crafty devil, a lot smarter than the usual leftist hacks."

"I'd rather formed the same view myself."

To see the old Major in delighted, animated discussion over politics and current events, with one of the most senior members of the Cabinet, gave Godfrey more pleasure than he could have imagined, while his opinion of Sir Norman, earnestly engaging in the discussion, listening intently to Major Powell's opinions, rose even higher. As the conversation progressed, the Major also shared a number of memories of Norman's grandfather, including the miraculous discovery of his terribly wounded body just after nightfall following that first disastrous day on the Somme.

"After dark," the Major recalled, "or, as night fell, we were creeping around with the stretcher bearers, trying to find our wounded. There weren't many — almost all were dead. It was like paddling in a sea of corpses, everywhere you trod. And the smell... I overheard a young sapper from another regiment, talking about how they'd seen a body in a red coat in a shell hole, really only a few feet from our own trench. The Colonel had only managed about ten steps before he was hit. I took a couple of my lads and we found him. I thought he was dead, he'd been terribly shot up, then my sergeant said, I'll never forget these words, he said, 'Blimey, Captain — I was still a Captain in those days — Blimey, Captain, the old boy's breathing!'" Norman sat, riveted, as Albert continued. "We managed to get him back to a field hospital. I never thought he would survive, but he was tough as they come. And he wasn't a young man, should have taken a staff job by rights. And the red coat — everyone laughed at the thought that he wore it that day, I guess today we'd call it a Colonel Blimp mentality — well, it saved his life, because if it had not been for that comment by the young lad about having seen a red-coated body, we'd probably never have found him until it was too late. He was half buried as it was, just a small amount of red showing — we'd already missed him once. I remember being at a dinner with some QONR old boys, after the war, they were very…" For some reason, Albert suddenly felt that any discussion about Dorothy Keppel's visit to Colonel Armstrong might not be quite the thing. There were often parts of one's family history better left in the past, and he still didn't have that little interlude straight in his head. He didn't want to give rise to any kind of wrong impression. Perhaps there might be another opportunity later, when he had worked it out a little better, and could consider things, implications, a little more clearly.

Sensing that the Major's account had come to a natural end, Norman, unusually emotional, grasped his hand. "Thank you so much, Major," he said, eyes glistening, "to hear such a first-hand recollection, well, quite, quite overwhelming. Now, I understand there might be something I can do for you."

"Go on, Dad," Godfrey encouraged.

"This is not an easy thing for me to discuss, Norman," Albert said. "I hope you'll bear with me."

"Take your time," Norman reassured.

"My eldest son, Reggie, Godfrey's brother, was killed in the war. SOE."

"Yes, I know, I'm very sorry. Godfrey has told me about it."

"He was a detective. Very promising career before him. I've been so lucky with my son, my sons, Norman. Both fine men and high achievers too."

"I understand your pride. My son is also doing very well."

"I'm glad to hear it. But I've always had my suspicions. You might think these are just the ramblings of an old man..."

"Perhaps I might be able to put your mind at ease. And whatever you confide will go no further."

"Thank you. I knew you might be just the man to help us, that, after all these years, we might be able to get to the truth. Reggie was working on something important. I don't know what it was. We used to talk about his work a lot, he was very enthusiastic. Hated spivs, thought they profited over the bodies of dead sailors with all their black marketeering. He locked them up left, right, and centre." Norman thought how much Alf Burton would have approved, having seen the carnage of the convoy routes at first hand. "He also took a very dim view of those villains who used the raids as a cover for their nefarious activities. Robbery, looting of bombed buildings, stealing from corpses: can you believe it? Assault, and even murder: there was a lot more of that going on than we were ever led to believe. But on this particular occasion he was worried. Whatever he was looking into went way beyond forged ration cards and black market petrol. And he wouldn't tell me anything. Anyway, without warning he was taken off the case, and moved straight to SOE. Excuse me, Norman, but are you, er, are you all right? You look how I feel."

"It's nothing, Major. I'm still a little overwhelmed about what you told me about my grandfather. But I'm listening. Please go on."

For the first time, Godfrey looked at the Home Secretary with a degree of confusion. This was exactly how he had reacted when Godfrey had first raised the issue of his brother during the drinks party, at which time he'd explained away his response by the general grief of losing friends during wartime. But this reaction again, at the mention of Reggie's transfer to SOE. As if he knew something. Godfrey had always dismissed his father's suspicions, but was now not so sure.

"It just seemed a bit convenient to me," Major Powell continued. "He was working on a big case, something that had him genuinely rattled, and I must tell you he wasn't a lad that would worry for no reason, I often envied his presence of mind. Suddenly he's out of the picture, and sent into occupied Holland and that's it."

"I'm told it wasn't unusual for very talented young men to be recruited into these secret organisations," Norman said. "They obviously saw that your son had something to offer."

"You might be right, of course," the Major replied. "But I'd love to know what he was working on. If I knew that, I might be able to get things straight in my head. Norman, it might be presumptuous, but I feel that, thanks to your grandfather, we have a connection, and I know how much my son respects you."

"Rubbish, never said any such thing," Godfrey muttered, smiling.

"I don't have too long to go, but if I could find out what really happened to my son, I'd be at peace."

"You'll outlive all of us," Godfrey contributed.

"It might not be that easy," Norman replied, "Anything to do with SOE is still highly classified, and probably will be for our lifetimes at least."

"I understand, of course," the Major replied. "But I'm really more interested in what happened before he went to SOE. In case there was any, ah, any connection with what..."

"I will certainly do what I can," Norman reassured him, stood up and shook the older man's hand. "It's been a great pleasure to meet you, Major Powell. I hope that we'll have another opportunity to talk again very soon."

The Major beamed. "Thank you, Norman. I can't tell you how much I appreciate your visit."

On their way out, Sir Norman took the opportunity to shake some more hands and do some old-school politicking. His reception amongst the residents was not unlike what their grandchildren might have afforded Wham or Duran Duran. Many had been citizens of the Stonebridge Southeast constituency during his father's time as local MP, at least one even remembered his great-uncle Piers. Norman compared with interest the warm reminiscences of his father, and the more muted toleration of his great uncle. He observed that the reaction from staff to his visit was not quite so enthusiastic, something he put down to their being part of some militant nurses' union, and bound to vote Labour as a result. In any case, they probably lived outside of his constituency, in which non-Conservative voters were, happily, in a tiny minority and barely worth considering at all. As they approached the car, Godfrey turned and found his father waving from his usual place in the window. Both Norman and Godfrey waved back.

"Just give us a minute or two will you, please, Eric," Norman said. Eric nodded and moved out of earshot and over to the security vehicle, happy to resume his conversation with the bodyguard detective, who, he had just discovered, was a fellow former Marine.

"What do you think of your father's suspicions?" Norman asked quietly.

"I had never taken them too seriously," Godfrey replied. "Until today."

"What's changed your mind?"

"Actually, you have, Home Secretary. I feel, and I say this with great respect, that you might know something, and you find this knowledge distressing."

"In all honesty, I don't know anything for certain,"

"But you clearly have your suspicions. Strong suspicions."

After a few brief moments of thoughtful silence, Norman said, "Godfrey, you have my word. If there was anything I could tell you, I would."

"I understand, Home Secretary." Godfrey noted Norman's careful choice of words. He too thought for a moment. He hadn't risen through the ranks of the civil service to become one of the youngest permanent secretaries ever, receive a Knighthood, and be widely tipped as the next Cabinet Secretary, without having a full and realistic understanding — and acceptance — of the lie of the land. "Look, Norman," he said finally. "Let's drop it. After an appropriate interval I'll tell my dad that you've gone into the matter thoroughly, and it all checks out. A perfectly routine recruitment of a very good young detective by SOE, and a tragic end to a dangerous mission. Sleeping dogs."

"I think that's for the best," Norman replied, his relief palpable. He beckoned to Eric, and they were soon on the short drive to Norman's home, their security vehicle hovering a discreet distance behind them.

"I appreciate your, ah, you know…" Norman said as they arrived at his front gate.

"I wasn't born yesterday, Home Secretary," Godfrey replied, admiring the gardens on the verge of their spring glory, as they drove along the short paved driveway to the front door. "Perhaps, one day, you might be able to tell me the truth."

If only I bloody well knew it myself, Norman thought, then smiled as the two family Labradors, Winston and Randolph, came joyfully bounding up to meet them, and he saw the happy smiling face of Eileen framed in the doorway, in his eyes as beautiful and heart-stopping as when they'd first met on a midsummer's day all those years ago.

"I'm very much looking forward to meeting Lady Armstrong again," Godfrey said, as Eric walked briskly around to open the car doors.

"It's our fortieth anniversary this year," Norman replied. "Coincides with the Party Conference. I'm delighted to say that she'll be joining me at Brighton in October."

EPILOGUE

Albert Powell was reclining in his chair, reading *A New Beginning*. Trying to fight his way through the initial chapters, he had found himself so preoccupied chasing his own memories of those few short days in Pietermaritzburg more than sixty years earlier, that he could make neither head nor tail of the complicated plot. He found the main character, Captain Richard Fforbes, colonial officer and amateur sleuth, strongly reminiscent of Colonel Fforbes Armstrong, a connection that Albert found strangely comforting, particularly so since his wonderful afternoon spent in conversation with Sir Norman. In fact, he'd been so buoyed by the visit, and the Home Secretary's assurance that he would do everything he could to get to the truth of his son's death, that he was now scouring the pages with a singular focus, determined to extricate long buried memories, like a prospector digging for a hidden seam in an old, disused mine.

"Permission to enter, Major!" It was a smiling Captain Jim, hovering in the doorway on his frame, looking exhausted from the long walk along the corridor.

Albert looked over his glasses. "Jim," he cried. "Haven't seen you for a while, thought you might have jumped ship, what? Come in, come in. Sit yourself down." Albert gestured to the other winged chair by the window, and in a complicated manoeuvre that he found quite nerve-wracking to watch, Jim unsteadily transferred his grip from his frame to the chair, then lowered himself down, the last several inches a lot faster than he had planned as the seat was unexpectedly low.

"How do you get out of this blasted thing once you're in it?" Jim grumbled as he made himself comfortable.

"I can't, that's why I never sit in it."

The two men passed the time with some small talk, a brief discussion of the miners' strike that was dominating the newspapers and television — a bunch of damned communists in the Captain's opinion, and as for that Scargill — as well as the recent terrible murder of a young WPC on duty near the Libyan Embassy.

"Right here in London," Albert spluttered, outraged. "You know, I don't have much time for that Dick Billings. My son tells me he's suspected of all sorts of shady carryings-on, but I think he had it about right when he was on the radio last year talking about inferior foreign cultures undermining our way of life. I gather that Sir Norman, the Home Secretary, had quite a shouting match with certain members of the Cabinet over what was to become of those murdering swine, something to do with their diplomatic status, or some kind of deal with the Libyan Government. Godfrey and the Cabinet Secretary had to step in to calm things down. You know what I think about that, line 'em up and shoot 'em, I say. I mean those murdering Arabs of course, not the Cabinet."

The discussion on politics and the latest news dwindled away, and, after a few moments of silence, Jim said, "look, old chap, I hope you don't think I've been avoiding you: well, actually I have, but for a reason."

"I think I understand," Albert replied. "I saw your reaction when you read the name on this." He picked up his book and showed the cover to the Captain. "It affected me in much the same way when my son brought it in for me. It would seem that we share a skeleton from our past, no not the right word, a ghost perhaps. A ghost by the name of Dorothy Keppel. I figured you'd tell me about it when you were ready."

"I find it hard, even now, to think about her. How did you know her, if you don't mind me asking?"

"No, not at all. I met her in South Africa, just before she... We had a mutual friend, a retired Colonel named Armstrong. A funny coincidence, my son works with his grandson, Sir Norman, the Home Secretary. I'm finding it hard to remember everything. We visited the old Colonel at his farm. I drove her there in a chum's old car. Nearly got lost in the dark on the way back to Pietermaritzburg! And me, a cavalry major! Would never have heard the end of it. They were both mixed up in something, Miss Keppel and the Colonel, I don't know what, but it related to Charlotte Morris. It was political, I think. Maybe even dangerous."

"That's right," the Captain said thoughtfully. "Miss Keppel had been Charlotte Morris's secretary. She certainly fell on her feet after Mrs Morris's death, didn't she? As well as owning the rights to all of the books, she inherited a large part of Speers Colonial and Speers Shipping. Didn't do her any good in the end though, did it? She was my superior, in a way."

"How so?"

"I worked for the Speers Line all my life. My family, the O'Malleys, had been at sea since before the days of Nelson. An ancestor of mine was Charles Speers's sailing master at

Trafalgar. He went to work for the Speers Line a year or two later. I'll tell you another thing… that is, um..."

"Go on, old chap," Albert encouraged, sensing that Jim was about to confide something of great personal significance.

"I lost her, Bert. She was right there, in front of me, and I lost her. Nothing I could do."

"I don't understand."

"You were at the Somme, weren't you?"

"I was, with the Natal Rangers. Colonel Armstrong was my Commanding Officer. I find something comforting in the familial link with the Armstrongs, especially now that my son works with Sir Norman. Did I mention that? I did, sorry, I tend to repeat myself. Did I tell you that he came to visit? No, I haven't seen you. The Home Secretary himself, came to visit me here! That was my son's doing, he's a good boy. A good son."

"That's nice," Jim commented, then hesitated. "Now where was I?"

"You asked me if I was at the Somme. I answered yes."

"Of course. You lost a great many friends, I shouldn't wonder. From what I've read about that first day, I can't begin to imagine."

"I did. Pretty much all of them, in fact."

"Do you ever wish, deep in your heart, that you had died with them?"

"No, never," Albert replied emphatically, then reconsidered. "Actually, yes, now that you bring it up. I gather it's a common thing. You know, I've never confided this to a living soul. The feeling got a little worse after my son was killed in the last lot, then my wife passed. Pneumonia they said, but I know it was of a broken heart. But I had my younger son Godfrey to set on the right path, so I kept the death-wish well hidden. Why do you ask?"

"I was Third Officer on the Lady Georgiana."

"Good Lord!" Albert Powell stared. "I was at the quay when she sailed from Durban that last time, before she… how did you make it through?"

"I don't rightly know. I was knocked about a bit, in hospital for a month or two. When she went over, she broke up in fact, I ended up popping up from the depths like a cork, so I was later told. I must have been knocked out. When I woke up I was in a lifeboat, half drowned, shivering like mad, still kicking but only just."

"An incredible piece of good fortune," Albert commented.

"Not so sure," Jim replied. "I was the only officer to survive, along with a handful of crew. I can't even think about the number of passengers we lost. Do you know how that feels? How stupid of me, of course you know. You understand my burden exactly."

"What did you mean when you said you'd lost her? Were you talking about Miss Keppel?"

"I'm afraid so. I was overseeing the loading of number three lifeboat, it was pandemonium as you would imagine, but the Captain ordered me away to make sure Miss Keppel was safe. You could feel the ship starting to go down, but I thought I still had a good few minutes. I ran to her stateroom and there she was, cool as a cucumber. It was strange, it didn't look like she was even going to try and save herself, but as soon as she saw me she came towards me. It wasn't easy, the deck was listing, the angle was like a church roof." Jim stopped, lost in his memory, reliving every moment in slow motion, as Albert Powell relived climbing over the parapet at the Somme almost every day.

"Go on, Jim," Albert encouraged.

320

"I yelled at her to take my hand. There was such a list by now that I had to keep hold of the bulkhead with the other hand to keep myself from falling over. I can't describe to you the noise, the structure of the ship groaning, the cries, the desperate yelling and screaming of the passengers, the boilers..."

"Go on."

"The ship went over. Poor Dorothy, Miss Keppel, fell through a gaping great crater that appeared in the deck as the ship broke up."

"You couldn't, that is, she wasn't able to take your hand then?"

"I don't think she even tried. You know, she didn't make a sound, just looked at me calmly, that lovely face, I see it as clearly now. Just as she fell, she thrust an envelope of papers into my outstretched hand. An envelope of papers! That's all I had, and she was gone." Jim went quiet, staring out the window.

"An envelope, you say?" Major Powell asked, if only to keep the flow of conversation.

"Yes. I don't mean like a letter, it was bigger, like it held documents of some kind. There may have even been some kind of official seal, I can't really remember it in that much detail. In the circumstances..."

"Of course, of course," the major replied

"It might have contained company papers, for all I know."

There was so much Major Powell wanted to remember, but in his disordered mind there were just fragments, like dust particles in the air, visible in a certain light then when you reached for them they disappeared. So many unanswered questions. "What happened to the envelope?" he asked.

"I don't know," Jim replied. "I remember tucking it into my coat, then we went over, the next thing I remember is waking up in the lifeboat. I never really gave it another thought, it must have been lost when I went into the drink. Wait, I was asked about it…"

"Asked about it?"

"I haven't thought about this for years. I think I'd consciously blocked out anything to do with the Georgiana. There was a board of enquiry, I had to give evidence of course. One of the board members was an MP, he'd once been First Lord of the Admiralty, years before, I can't think of his name. He seemed ancient, just sat quietly for most of the proceedings. It was all straightforward, loose mine from the North Sea barrage, although there were a few questions about why the Calcutta Queen had been withdrawn and about the general condition of the Georgiana… let me think… I explained how I'd tried to save Miss Keppel but… I must have mentioned the envelope, because suddenly he was very interested. I remember thinking at the time that it might have been nice if he'd shown the same level of concern when the names of the dead passengers and crew had been read out. Maybe there was something important in those papers after all, but I guess we'll never know. And what does it matter now? It was all so very long ago."

Major Powell was coming to the opinion that it did matter. That it mattered a great deal, even though he couldn't quite grasp the reason why. An old soldier's instinct, sensing the presence of a hidden enemy? Perhaps. "Remember I mentioned earlier that I'd taken Miss Keppel to meet my old Colonel, Fforbes Armstrong…"

"That's who it was!" Jim exclaimed, snapping his arthritic fingers. "That MP on the board of enquiry. Piers Armstrong. Cold fish, sinister I would say."

The Major thought for a moment. "How would you like to embark on a little adventure?" he asked.

"An adventure?" Jim's eyes lit up and he sat up straight. "Not too much chance of that in this place, but it's a wonderful thought."

"I think it's time we both laid some demons to rest. Time for some investigations of our own."

"Couldn't agree more, but how?"

Major Powell leaned forward and tapped the side of his nose with his finger. "It just so happens that I'm very well connected at the Home Office."

HISTORICAL NOTE

Although a number of true-life public figures make appearances throughout the story, the principal characters are wholly fictitious and should not be taken to represent the individuals that really held senior government positions at that time. Likewise, our major corporate players, the Donoghue Group and its owner, Sir Eddie Donoghue, and Speers Colonial, are entirely fictional and not intended to represent any real people or entities.

On occasions our characters assume their roles following the departure, in disgrace, of unnamed officials. For instance, Norman Armstrong's incompetent predecessor as Home Secretary is not in any way representative of the real office holder at that time, nor is the tainted police commissioner who exits to allow our own man to assume the role.

Our characters are key players in the course of many true events, however a degree of dramatic licence has been applied. Their actions, and their racial and political attitudes, are drawn from the author's own take on the general overriding politics of the times, and are not intended to reflect any definitive historical record of the real thing, nor of the real protagonists. Any misdeeds perpetrated by our own characters, particularly our corrupt Environment Secretary, then Tory Party Chairman, Sir Dick Billings, are not intended as any representation of the behaviour of those who really held comparable positions, or of the government as a whole, at that time.

Much of the background research, including comments attributed to real people, and some adapted for use by our own characters, has been sourced from a wide variety of books and television documentaries, websites official and unofficial, media reports of the day, Colliers Weekly, Hansard, and transcripts of political speeches. The BBC Podcast website, an incredibly generous resource, has also provided important background from key participants in the real events. Those of particular value have been *Desert Island Discs, UK Confidential, Witness, Great Lives, the New Elizabethans, Stories in Sound, Report*, and many others from Radio Four, World Service, Radio 5 Live, and Radio Ulster.

Roland Moreland's reporting of the Harrods' bombing, and early accounts of the Miner's Strike by both Moreland and Alf Burton, were inspired principally by BBC News reporting.

The Story Continues in *Armstrong's Army*
Coming soon

The summer of 1984 is eventful, to say the least, in British politics. Riots, bombings and the murder of a police officer have all occurred. Besides, the miners' strike is in progress, policed (or aggravated) by the special unit dubbed 'Armstrong's Army'.

The strike affects the whole nation. The murder of a taxi driver and an undercover Special Branch agent; police informants infiltrating the miners' pickets. Numerous claims are being made of police corruption and crime.

Home Secretary Sir Norman Armstrong and his old friend; outspoken, left wing commentator Alf Burton, find themselves entrenched on opposite sides of this increasingly bitter and deadly fight. Can their decades-old friendship survive?

Meanwhile, what of the papers lost years ago, with the sinking of the *Lady Georgiana?* Alf Burton uncovers increasingly disturbing links to the current day, and finds Sir Norman's own family heavily implicated. What was the secret they concealed?

Y Wiwer Ddireidus

Y Wiwer Ddireidus

Stori Siân Lewis
yn seiliedig ar sgript wreiddiol Meinir Lynch

Lluniau Cynyrchiadau Siriol

CYMDEITHAS LYFRAU CEREDIGION Gyf

'Jac Do!' galwodd Sali Mali. 'Dwi am bicio i'r siop. Cofia ofalu am y tŷ imi.'

'Crawc–crawc!' meddai Jac Do.

'O! A chofia gau ffenest y gegin,' meddai Sali Mali. 'Mae'r gwynt yn oer.'

Teimlai Jac Do'n bwysig gan ei fod yn cael gofalu am y tŷ i Sali Mali, ac aeth ar ei union i'r gegin.

'CRAWC!' gwaeddodd nerth ei big. Roedd gwiwer lwyd newydd ddringo drwy'r ffenest agored.

'Crawc crrrawc crawwwc!' dwrdiodd Jac Do. Dychrynodd y wiwer a tharo yn erbyn hoff blatiau Sali Mali wrth neidio o'r ddresel.

CRATSH! CRASH! CRENSH!

Cwympodd y platiau a malu'n deilchion ar y llawr.

'O, crooowc!' ochneidiodd Jac Do.

Cododd Jac Do'r platiau a gwneud ei orau i'w trwsio, ond aeth darn o blât yn sownd yn ei big.

'Crrrawc!' meddai, gan ysgwyd ei ben a thaflu'r darn i'r llawr.

'Beth ydy hwn, Jac Do?' holodd Sali Mali. Roedd hi wedi dod yn ôl o'r siop. Cododd y darn o blât ac edrych yn flin ar Jac Do.

'Wyt ti wedi torri fy mhlatiau gorau i?' gofynnodd. 'O, Jac Do, dyna aderyn drwg wyt ti!'

'Creeewc?' meddai Jac Do yn syn. Roedd yn cael bai ar gam. 'Crawc crawc!' meddai, gan bwyntio at y wiwer, ond doedd Sali Mali ddim yn edrych nac yn gwrando.

'Paid ti â disgwyl imi chwarae efo ti, Jac Do,' meddai'n ddig. 'Dwi'n mynd i eistedd yn dawel a gwau.'

Tra oedd Sali Mali'n nôl ei gwlân, sbonciodd y wiwer drwy'r ffenest a thynnu pecyn cnau o'r fasged siopa.

'CRAWC!' gwaeddodd Jac Do. Cydiodd yn dynn ym mhen arall y pecyn a thynnu yn erbyn y wiwer lwyd.

RHHHIC! Rhwygodd y pecyn cnau a syrthiodd Jac Do ar ei gefn ar lawr. 'O, crooowc!' llefodd.

Clywodd Sali Mali'r holl sŵn a rhedodd i'r gegin. 'Jac Do!' meddai. 'Mi dorraist y platiau a rŵan rwyt ti wedi bwyta pecyn o gnau. Dyna aderyn drwg wyt ti heddiw!'

'Creeewc!' meddai Jac Do. Roedd yn cael bai ar gam eto.

'Well i mi daflu'r pecyn gwag 'ma i'r bin,' meddai Sali Mali'n flin.

Ond cyn gynted ag y trodd Sali Mali ei chefn, sleifiodd y wiwer ddireidus drwy'r ffenest a chipio'r gwau.

'Crr-hei-c!' gwaeddodd Jac Do, a hedfanodd ar ei hôl.

Ar y glaswellt o dan y ffenest gwelodd lwybr o gnau. Dilynodd Jac Do'r llwybr nes iddo ddod at goeden a thwll ynddi.

'Cr-o-ho-wc!' meddai, gan hedfan yn ôl at Sali Mali ar ras.

Yn y gegin roedd Sali Mali'n chwilio am ei gwau.

'Jac Do!' meddai'n gwta. 'Ble mae 'ngwau i?'

'Crawc crawc!' llefodd Jac Do gan bwyntio at y ffenest.

'Hmmm,' meddai Sali Mali. 'Mi ddo i i'r ardd, ond gobeithio nad un o dy driciau dwl di ydy hwn.'

Aeth Jac Do at y goeden a dangos y twll i Sali Mali.

'O!' meddai Sali Mali'n ddistaw bach gan sbecian i'r twll. 'Mae gwiwer yn cysgu yn y goeden. Ac mi wela i gnau a gwau – a thamaid bach bach o blât yn ei blew.'

'Crawc!' meddai Jac Do yn wên i gyd.

'O, Jac Do bach,' meddai Sali Mali.
'Mae'n ddrwg gen i. Mi gest ti fai ar gam.
Y wiwer wnaeth yr holl ddrygau.'
    'Cro-o-awc,' meddai Jac Do'n hapus.
A neidiodd i freichiau Sali Mali.

'Well i ni adael y wiwer,' meddai Sali Mali. 'Mae hi wedi mynd i gysgu dros y gaeaf. Bydd y gwau yn ei chadw'n gynnes ac, os deffrith hi, bydd ganddi gnau i'w bwyta.' 'Creee-wc?' meddai Jac Do.

'Paid â phoeni, Jac Do,' meddai Sali Mali.
'Does dim rhaid i ti gysgu dros y gaeaf! Mi gei
di godi'n gynnar bore fory i chwarae efo fi.'
'Crawc crawc,' meddai Jac Do.
'Nos da,' meddai Sali Mali.

Cyhoeddwyd gan Gymdeithas Lyfrau Ceredigion Gyf.,
Ystafell B5, Y Coleg Diwinyddol Unedig, Stryd y Brenin,
Aberystwyth, Ceredigion SY23 2LT.
Argraffiad cyntaf: Awst 2001
Ail argraffiad: Ebrill 2003
Hawlfraint y cyhoeddiad © Cymdeithas Lyfrau Ceredigion Gyf. 2001

Stori gan Siân Lewis
yn seiliedig ar sgript wreiddiol Meinir Lynch
a ysgrifennwyd ar gyfer Cynyrchiadau Siriol ac S4C.
Cymeriad a grëwyd gan
Mary Vaughan Jones yw Sali Mali.

ISBN 1-902416-52-X

Diolch i adrannau Cyngor Llyfrau Cymru am bob cymorth.
Dyluniad gan Gary Evans.
Argraffwyd gan Wasg Gomer, Llandysul SA44 4QL.